Praise for *New York Times* bestselling author RaeAnne Thayne

"RaeAnne Thayne gets better with every book."
—Robyn Carr, #1 *New York Times* bestselling author

"RaeAnne Thayne is quickly becoming one of my favorite authors…. Once you start reading, you aren't going to be able to stop."
—*Fresh Fiction*

"This issue of the Cape Sanctuary series draws the reader in from the first page to the gratifying conclusion."
—*New York Journal of Books* on *The Sea Glass Cottage*

Praise for author Darby Baham

"The plot highlights the union between friends, family values and how love always wins over fear… This is my first book by this author, and it won't be the last. The clever way Ms. Baham shows Raegan's emotional journey was unique."
—*Harlequin Junkie* on *The Shoe Diaries*

"A thoughtful and sweet book about figuring out what you really want from life…. It was a wonderful warm hug, and I'll definitely be picking up the first book in this series!"
—*Llama Reads Books* on *Bloom Where You're Planted*

"A really sweet, heartfelt, and insightful book."
—*Courtney Reads Romance* on *Bloom Where You're Planted*

D0951176

NEW YORK TIMES BESTSELLING AUTHOR

RaeAnne Thayne

A BRAMBLEBERRY SUMMER

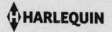

If you purchased this book without a cover you should be aware that this book is stolen property. It was reported as "unsold and destroyed" to the publisher, and neither the author nor the publisher has received any payment for this "stripped book."

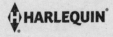 HARLEQUIN®

ISBN-13: 978-1-335-66250-7

Recycling programs for this product may not exist in your area.

A Brambleberry Summer
First published in 2021.
This edition published in 2023.
Copyright © 2021 by RaeAnne Thayne LLC

The Shoe Diaries
First published in 2022.
This edition published in 2023.
Copyright © 2022 by Darby Baham

All rights reserved. No part of this book may be used or reproduced in any manner whatsoever without written permission except in the case of brief quotations embodied in critical articles and reviews.

This is a work of fiction. Names, characters, places and incidents are either the product of the author's imagination or are used fictitiously. Any resemblance to actual persons, living or dead, businesses, companies, events or locales is entirely coincidental.

For questions and comments about the quality of this book, please contact us at CustomerService@Harlequin.com.

Harlequin Enterprises ULC
22 Adelaide St. West, 41st Floor
Toronto, Ontario M5H 4E3, Canada
www.Harlequin.com

Printed in U.S.A.

CONTENTS

RaeAnne Thayne finds inspiration in the beautiful northern Utah mountains, where the *New York Times* and *USA TODAY* bestselling author lives with her husband and three children. Her books have won numerous honors, including RITA® Award nominations from Romance Writers of America and a Career Achievement Award from *RT Book Reviews*. RaeAnne loves to hear from readers and can be contacted through her website, raeannethayne.com.

Books by RaeAnne Thayne

The Cliff House
The Sea Glass Cottage
Christmas at Holiday House
The Path to Sunshine Cove
Sleigh Bells Ring

Haven Point

Snow Angel Cove
Redemption Bay
Evergreen Springs
Riverbend Road
Snowfall on Haven Point
Serenity Harbor
Sugar Pine Trail
The Cottages on Silver Beach
Season of Wonder
Coming Home for Christmas
Summer at Lake Haven

Visit the Author Profile page
at Harlequin.com for more titles.

A BRAMBLEBERRY SUMMER

RaeAnne Thayne

To all the readers who have asked me
to write Rosa's story over the years.

Chapter 1

Summer Saturdays in a busy tourist town like Cannon Beach, Oregon, were not for the faint of heart.

As always, the sidewalk outside Rosa Galvez's gift shop, By-The-Wind, was packed with tourists. Kids in swimming suits. Parents with sunburned noses, their arms loaded with buckets and towels and umbrellas. And, her favorite, older people arm in arm, enjoying an afternoon of browsing through the local stores.

The long, wide stretch of beach that gave the town its name was only a half block from her store, which meant she had a nonstop view of the action, both in front of her store and farther down the beach.

One could never grow bored watching the kites, the recumbent bicycles, the children building sandcastles.

Some hardy souls were even swimming in the shallows, though Rosa always considered it entirely too cold. Maybe her childhood in Honduras had left her too warm-blooded.

Instead, she was busy working the cash register at her gift shop while her newest employee and dear friend, Jen Ryan, rearranged a display of tiny hand-carved lighthouses an artist in Lincoln City had crafted for her.

Nearby, Jen's six-year-old daughter, Addie, giggled at something in the small children's area Rosa had created, complete with a miniature kitchen and dollhouse. The children's area worked beautifully to keep little hands away from the more breakable items in the store while their parents browsed.

While she finished ringing up a cute handmade teapot for her customer, she kept a watchful eye on Jen. This was only her second day working in the store, though she and Addie had been in town for a few weeks. She still seemed anxious, and was constantly looking toward the door as if she expected something horrible to burst through at any moment.

Rosa hoped that with time her friend would lose that skittish air, the impression she gave off that at the slightest provocation, she would grab her child and bolt out the door of the shop.

How could Rosa blame her, after everything Jen had been through? It was a wonder she could even go out in public. All things considered, she was doing remarkably well and seemed to be settling into life here in Cannon Beach. Having her living at Brambleberry House was a joy.

She finished carefully wrapping the customer's teapot in bubble wrap so it would be safe in whatever corner of luggage it was stuffed into.

"There you are," Rosa said, handing over the bag. "Thank you for shopping at By-The-Wind."

"Thank *you*. This is such an adorable shop. We've been to every store in town and you have the best merchandise. Authentic and charming souvenirs. I'll definitely be back before we leave town."

"I am very glad to hear this." She smiled and waved the woman and her husband on their way. She was replenishing her supply of bubble wrap under the counter when the front-door chimes rang out again.

She happened to be looking in Jen's direction and didn't miss the way her friend's features tensed with fear and then visibly relaxed when a woman came in, trailed by a young teenager.

Rosa's day, already good, immediately brightened even further, as if the sun had just come out from behind the clouds.

"Look who it is," she exclaimed. "Two of my favorite people!"

"*Hola*, Rosa," the girl said, beaming brightly at her with a mouth full of braces.

"Hello, my dear." Her friend Carrie Abbott brushed her cheek against Rosa's.

"What a wonderful surprise. How may I help you? Are you looking for a gift for someone? I have some gorgeous new purses in and also some fantastic jewelry from an artisan in Yachats you might like."

"Where's the jewelry?" Like a little magpie, Bella was instantly drawn to anything shiny.

Rosa showed her the new display and they spent a moment looking over the hand-beaded pieces.

"Ooh. Those turquoise starburst earrings are gorgeous! How much are they?"

She named an amount that had the girl's shoulders slumping. "I better not. I'm saving for an electric scooter."

"You know, that's the markup amount. I can probably drop the price by ten dollars."

Bella looked tempted. "I'm babysitting this weekend. If they're still for sale, I'll come back and get them."

"I'll set them aside until you can get back in," Rosa promised, which earned her another braces-filled smile.

"You're too tempting!" Carrie said, shaking her head. "I could blow my entire mad-money budget in here. Believe it or not, we didn't come in to buy earrings, no matter how lovely they are."

"Is there something else I can help you find? You should try the new soaps from Astrid Larsen."

Carrie laughed. "Stop. We're not supposed to be shopping! I came in because I need to talk to you."

Against her will, Rosa's gaze shifted to Bella and then back to the girl's mother. "Oh?" she said, hoping her voice sounded casual.

Carrie leaned against the counter. "Yes. How are you, first of all? I haven't talked to you in forever."

Carrie did not usually drop in just to chat. What was this about? She looked back toward Bella, who was holding the turquoise earrings up to her ears and looking in the mirror of the display.

"I have been good." She smiled. "Summer is always such a busy time here but I am glad for the tourists. Otherwise, I would not be able to keep the store open. And how are you?"

"Good. Busy, too. Bella is going in a hundred different directions, between babysitting and softball and her music lessons."

Such a normal, happy childhood. It warmed her heart. "Oh, that is nice."

"Did I tell you, we have tickets to the theater in Portland next month?" Bella said. "It's a traveling Broadway production of *Hamilton*. And then we're driving down the coast to San Francisco. I cannot *wait*!"

Rosa hid a smile. Bella had only mentioned the upcoming trip about a hundred times since spring, when she and her parents had first started talking about it. "That will be wonderful for you."

"Other than that, everything is pretty good," Carrie said. "Well, okay. I do have one small problem I was hoping you might be able to help us out with."

"Of course. What can I do?"

"Don't answer so quickly. It's a huge favor."

Carrie had to know Rosa would do anything for her. Theirs was that kind of friendship.

"I was wondering if you've found a tenant to sublease your empty apartment until fall, when your renters come back."

Rosa lived on the top floor of a sprawling old Victorian, Brambleberry House. She managed the property for her aunt and her aunt's friend, Sage Benedetto Spencer.

Right now, Jen lived in the second-floor apartment, but the older couple who had been renting the furnished ground-floor apartment for the past year had moved to Texas temporarily to help with an ill family member.

"It is still empty for now."

She didn't have the energy to go the vacation-rental route, with new people constantly coming in and out.

Carrie's features brightened. "Oh, yay! Would you consider renting it for the next month or so?"

Rosa frowned. "Why would you need a place to rent? Are you doing something to your house?"

Carrie and her husband lived in a very nice cottage about a mile from Brambleberry House. She had recently remodeled the kitchen but perhaps she was thinking about doing the bathrooms.

"Not for me," Carrie assured her. "For Wyatt and Logan."

Rosa tensed at the mention of Carrie's brother and his young son. While the boy was adorable, seven years old and cheerful as could be, his father was another matter.

Wyatt Townsend was a detective for the Cannon Beach Police Department and always seemed to look at her as if she was up to something illegal.

That was surely her imagination. She had done nothing to make him suspicious of her.

"I thought he was staying with you while his home is being repaired."

"He is. And I would be fine with him living with us until the work is done, but everything is taking so much longer than he expected. It has been a nightmare of wrangling with the insurance and trying to find subcontractors to do the work."

Wyatt's small bungalow had been damaged in a fire about a month earlier, believed to have been caused by faulty wiring. It had been a small miracle that neither he nor his son had been home at the time and that a neighbor had smelled the smoke and called the fire department before widespread damage.

Rosa knew from Carrie that the fire damage still meant he had to renovate several rooms and had been living with his sister and her husband while the work was being completed.

"That must be hard for Wyatt."

"I know. And after everything they have both been through the past three years, they didn't need one more thing. But he's doing his best to rebuild."

Rosa certainly knew what it mean to rebuild a life.

"The work will take at least another month."

"That long?"

"Yes. And to be honest, I think Wyatt is a little tired of sleeping on the sofa in my family room with his leg hanging over the edge. Since the insurance company will cover rent for the next few months, he said last night he was thinking about looking around for somewhere to stay temporarily. He even brought up the idea of renting a camp trailer and parking it in his driveway until the repairs are done. I immediately thought of your empty apartment and thought that would be so much better for him and Logan, if it's still available."

The apartment was available. But did she really want Wyatt Townsend there? Rosa glanced over at Jen, who was talking to Addie in a low voice.

She could not forget about Jen. In the other woman's situation, how would she feel about having a police detective moving downstairs?

"I know it's a huge ask. You probably have a waiting list as long as my arm for an apartment in that great location."

Rosa shook her head. "I have not really put it on the market, to be honest. I have been too busy and also I know the Smiths want to move back if they can at the end of the summer, after June's mother heals from her broken hip."

That still did not mean she wanted to rent it to Wyatt

and his son. She could not even say she had a compelling reason not to, other than her own unease.

The man made her so nervous. It did not help that
he was extraordinarily good-looking.

He always seemed to be looking at her as if he knew
she had secrets and wouldn't rest until he figured them
out.

That wouldn't bother her, as she did not usually have
much to do with him. Except she *did* have secrets. So
many secrets. And he was the last man in town she
wanted to figure them out.

She should just say no. She could tell Carrie she had
decided to paint it while it was empty or put in new
flooring or something.

That wasn't completely a lie. She had talked to Anna
and Sage about making a few cosmetic improvements to
the apartment over the summer, but had not made any
solid plans. Even if she had, none of them was urgent.

The apartment was in good condition and would be
an ideal solution for Wyatt and his son while repairs
continued on their house.

She had to let him stay there. How could she possibly
say no to Carrie? She owed her so very much.

What would Jen think? Maybe she would find comfort in knowing a big, strong police detective lived
downstairs. Their own built-in security.

"Yes. Okay. He can stay there, if he wants to."

"He will," Carrie assured her, looking thrilled. "I
should mention that he has a dog. He's the cutest little
thing and no trouble at all."

Rosa was not so sure about that. She had seen Wyatt
and Logan walking the dog on the beach a few times
when she had been walking her own dog, Fiona. Their

beagle mix, while adorable, seemed as energetic as Logan.

"It should be fine. The Smiths had a little dog, too. The ground-floor apartment has a dog door out to the fenced area of the lawn. Fiona will enjoy the company."

"Oh, how perfect. It's even better than I thought. I can't thank you enough!"

"He probably will want to take a look at it before he makes any decisions. And we need to talk about rent."

She told her what the Smiths had been paying per month and Carrie's eyes widened.

"Are you kidding? That's totally a bargain around here, especially in the summer. I know the insurance company was going to pay much more than that. I'm sure it will be fantastic. You are the best."

Carrie and Bella left the store a few moments later, with Bella promising to come back so she could pay for the earrings.

As soon as the door closed behind them, Rosa slumped against the jewelry counter. What had she done?

She did *not* want Wyatt Townsend living anywhere close to her. The man looked too deeply, saw too much.

Ah, well. She would simply work a little harder to hide her secrets. She had plenty of practice.

"Sorry. Run that by me again. You did what?"

Wyatt gazed at his sister in shock. She lifted her chin, somehow managing to look embarrassed and defiant at the same time. "You heard me. I talked to Rosa Galvez about you moving into her empty apartment at Brambleberry House."

He adored his older sister and owed her more than

he could ever repay for the help she had given him the last three years, since Tori had died. But she had a bad habit of trying to run his life for him.

It was his own fault. He knew what Carrie was like, how she jumped on a single comment and ran with it. He should never have mentioned to her that he was thinking about renting an apartment until the fire renovations were done. He should have simply found one and told her about it later.

"When I mentioned I was thinking about moving out, I didn't mean for you to go apartment hunting right away for me."

"I know. When you said that, I remembered Rosa had an empty apartment. As far as I'm concerned, you can stay on my family-room couch forever, but I thought a three-bedroom apartment would be better than a little camp trailer for a grown man and an active seven-year-old."

Wyatt could not disagree. In truth, he had made a few inquiries himself that day, and had discovered most of the available rental homes were unavailable all summer and those that were left were out of his price range.

What else did he expect? Cannon Beach was a popular tourist destination. Some of the short-term rentals had been booked out years in advance.

He did not mind living with his sister, brother-in-law and niece. He loved Carrie's family and Logan did, as well. But as the battle with his insurance company dragged on about doing repairs to his bungalow, he had been feeling increasingly intrusive in their lives.

Carrie was already helping him with his son. She didn't need to have them taking up every available inch of her living space with their stuff.

"The apartment at Brambleberry House is perfect! You can move in right now, it's fully furnished and available all summer."

"Why? I would have thought Rosa would want to rent it out on a longer lease."

"The couple who have been living there are supposed to be coming back in a few months. I don't think Rosa is very thrilled about having vacation renters in and out all summer."

"What makes you think having Logan and me downstairs would be better for her?"

"She knows you two. You're friends."

He was not sure he would go that far. Rosa hardly talked to him whenever they were at any kind of social event around town. He almost thought she went out of her way to avoid him, though he was not sure what he might have done to offend her.

"She said it was fine and that you can move in anytime. Today, if you want to. Isn't that wonderful?"

Again, Wyatt wasn't sure *wonderful* was the word he would use. This would only be a temporary resting place until the repairs were completed on their house.

On the other hand, it would be better for Logan than Wyatt's crazy camp-trailer idea. He couldn't deny that.

Poor kid. His world had been nothing but upheaval the past three years, though Wyatt had tried to do his best to give him a stable home life after Tori died.

Wyatt had been working as a police officer in Seattle when his wife went into cardiac arrest from a congenital heart condition none of them had known about. Logan had been four.

Numb with shock at losing his thirty-year-old, athletic, otherwise healthy wife, he had come home to Cannon Beach, where his sister lived, and taken a job with the local police department.

He hadn't known what else to do. His parents had wanted to help but both were busy professionals with demanding careers and little free time to devote to a grieving boy. Carrie had love and time in abundance, and she had urged him to move here, with a slower pace and fewer major crimes than the big city.

The move had been good for both of them. Wyatt liked his job as a detective on the Cannon Beach police force. He was busy enough that he was never bored but he was also not totally overwhelmed.

He worked on a couple of drug task forces and the SWAT team, which had only been called out a handful of times during his tenure here, all for domestic situations.

The move had been even better for Logan. He loved spending time with his aunt, uncle and older cousin, Bella. He had a wide circle of friends and a budding interest in marine biology.

Wyatt loved seeing his son thrive and knew Carrie and her family were a huge part of that. Logan spent as much time at her house as he did their own.

During the past month, both of them had spent more than enough time with Carrie and her family, since they were living there.

Another month and they could move back to his house, he hoped.

Wyatt counted his blessings that his bungalow hadn't been a complete loss. Fire crews had responded quickly and had been able to save most of the house except the kitchen, where the fire had started, probably from old, faulty wiring. The main living area had also been burned. Even so, all the rooms had suffered water and smoke damage.

Dealing with the renovations was a tedious job, filled with paperwork, phone calls and aggravation, but Wyatt could definitely see the light at the end of the tunnel.

"What do you think?" Carrie looked apprehensive but excited. "Don't you think it's a fabulous idea? Brambleberry House is so close, you can easily drop off Logan when you need me to watch him."

Location definitely was a plus. Carrie's house and Rosa's were only a few blocks apart. Brambleberry House was also positioned about halfway between his house and his sister's, which would be convenient when he was overseeing the repairs.

Wyatt knew there were many advantages to moving into an apartment at Brambleberry House. Wouldn't it be good to have their own space again? Somewhere he could walk around in his underwear once in a while if he needed to grab a pair of jeans out of the dryer, without having to worry about his sister or his niece walking in on him?

"It could work," he said, not quite willing to jump a hundred percent behind the idea. "Are you sure Rosa is okay with it?"

"Totally great." Carrie gave a bright smile that somehow had a tinge of falseness to it. What wasn't she telling him? Did Rosa Galvez really want to rent the apartment or had Carrie somehow manipulated her into doing it?

He wouldn't put it past his sister. She had a way of persuading people to her way of thinking.

Wyatt's cop instincts told him there was more to

Rosa Galvez than one could see on the surface. She had secrets, but then most people did.

The bottom line was, he was not interested in digging into her secrets. She could keep them.

As long as she obeyed the law, he was not going to pry into her business. Rosa could have all the secrets she wanted. It was nothing to him.

So why, then, was he so apprehensive about moving into Brambleberry House?

He did not have a rational reason to say no. It really did make sense to have their own place. It would be better for Logan, which was the only thing that mattered, really.

It was only a month, maybe two at the most. Wyatt would survive his unease around her.

"Are you sure the apartment is affordable?"

"Absolutely. She told me how much she's charging and you won't find anything else nearly as nice in that price range. It's well within your budget. And I forgot to mention, the apartment already has a dog door for Hank and a fenced area in the yard."

That would be another plus. Logan's beagle mix was gregarious, energetic and usually adorable, but Carrie's two ragdoll cats were not fans of the dog. They would be more than glad to have Hank out of their territory.

"It sounds ideal," he said, finally surrendering to the inevitable. "Thanks for looking into it for us."

"As I said, the apartment is ready immediately. You can stay there tonight, if you want."

He blinked. How had things progressed so quickly from him merely mentioning the night before that he was thinking about moving out to his sister handling all the details and basically shoving him out the door today?

He could think of no good reason to wait and forced a smile. "Great. I'll start packing everything up and we can head over as soon as Logan gets home from day camp."

Carrie's face lit up. "You can at least wait for dinner. I imagine Rosa is probably working until six or seven, anyway."

"Right."

"I think you're going to love it. Rosa is so nice and she has a new tenant, Jen Ryan, who has a little girl who is a bit younger than Logan. Rosa has a wonderful dog, Fiona, who is more human than dog, if you ask me. I'm sure Hank will love her."

At the sound of his name, Wyatt's beagle mix jumped up from the floor, grabbed a ball and plopped it at Wyatt's feet. He picked it up and tossed it down the hall. Hank scrambled after it, much to the disdain of one of the ragdolls, who was sprawled out in a patch of sunlight.

He had seen Rosa on the beach, walking a gorgeous Irish setter. They were hard to miss, the lovely woman and her elegant dog.

Rosa was hard to miss anywhere. She was the sort of woman who drew attention, only in part because of her beautiful features and warm dark eyes.

She exuded warmth and friendliness, at least with everyone else in town. With Wyatt, she seemed watchful and reserved.

That didn't matter, he supposed. She was kind enough to let him live in her apartment for the next month. He didn't need her to be his best friend.

Chapter 2

Now that the deed was done, Rosa was having second, third and fourth thoughts about Wyatt Townsend moving in downstairs.

Why had she ever thought this would work?

That evening as she pulled weeds in the backyard after leaving the store, she had to fight all her instincts that were urging her to call up Carrie right now and tell her she had made a mistake. The apartment was no longer available.

"There is no law against changing your mind, is there?" she asked out loud to Fiona, who was lying in the grass nearby, watching butterflies dance amid the climbing roses.

The dog gave her a curious look then turned back to her business, leaving Rosa to sigh. She yanked harder

at a stubborn weed that had driven deep roots into the
ground.

She would do nothing. She had given her word and
could not back out now. Integrity, keeping her word,
was important. She had learned that first from her own
mother and then from her adopted parents.

Lauren and Daniel Galvez were two of the most honorable people she knew. They would never think of re-
neging on a promise and she couldn't, either.

Yes, Wyatt made her extremely nervous. She did not
want him moving in downstairs. But she had given her
word to his sister. End of story.

Because of that, she would be gracious and welcoming to him and to his sweet son.

Thinking about Logan left her feeling a little bit better about the decision. He was a very adorable boy, with
good manners and a ready smile.

It was not the boy's fault that Wyatt made her so
nervous.

She had almost talked herself into at least accepting the new status quo, when an SUV pulled up to the
house a half hour later.

Fiona lifted her head to sniff the air, then rose and
hurried over to the vehicle to greet the newcomers.

Rosa climbed to her feet a little more slowly, pulled
off her gloves and swiped at her hair before she headed
for the vehicle. She might be accepting of her new tenants, but summoning the same kind of enthusiasm her
dog showed so readily would be a stretch.

When Rosa reached the vehicle, Logan was opening the back door and jumping to the ground, his little
dog close behind.

Fiona barked a greeting, then leaned in to sniff the

newcomer, tail wagging. The Townsends' dog sniffed back, and a moment later, the two were circling each other with joy.

At least Fiona was happy to have them here.

"Hello, Logan," Rosa said.

"Hi." The boy beamed at her, showing off a gap in his teeth that she found adorable.

"Guess what?" he said. "We're moving into your house! Dad says we can stay here until our house is done and I'll have my own bedroom and won't have to sleep in Aunt Carrie's sewing room anymore."

"This is so wonderful, no?" She smiled down at him, trying not to pay any attention to his father walking around the vehicle, looking big and serious and intimidating.

"What is the name of your dog?"

"This is Hank. Don't worry. He's nice."

"I never doubted it for a minute," she assured him. "Hello, Hank."

She reached down to pet the dog, who responded by rolling over to have his belly scratched. Rosa loved him immediately.

"This is Fiona. She is also very nice."

Logan grinned and petted Fiona's long red coat.

Wouldn't it be lovely if she only had to deal with the boy and the dog? Unfortunately, the boy had a father. She had to say something to Wyatt, at least. Bracing herself, she lifted her attention from the two dogs and the boy, and faced the man who always looked as if he could see through her skin and bones into her heart, and was not convinced he liked what he saw.

She drew in a deep breath and forced a smile. "Hello. Welcome to Brambleberry House."

He nodded, always so serious. "Thank you for allowing us to stay here until our house is repaired. It's very kind of you."

She shrugged. "The apartment was empty. Houses are meant to be lived in. Brambleberry House in particular seems a little sad without people, especially children."

She immediately regretted her words, especially when Wyatt raised a skeptical eyebrow.

"Your house seems sad."

Logan giggled. "Houses can't be sad. They're just houses."

She shrugged. "This is no ordinary house. I think you will find that after you have been here a few nights. Come. I will show you your apartment."

She did not wait for a response, but simply walked up the front steps and into the entryway.

"There are three levels of the house with three apartments, one taking up each level. We share the foyer. We try to keep the outside door locked for the security of our residents. I will give you the code, as well as the key."

She was even more vigilant about that right now for Jen's sake.

Wyatt nodded. "Makes sense."

"Your apartment has a separate key. It is on the ground floor. I live on the top floor. If you have any questions or problems, you can find me there or at the store."

"My sister told me you have another new tenant on the second floor."

Rosa's protective instincts flared. "This is true. Her

name is Jen Ryan. She lives there with her daughter, Addie, who is six."

"I don't believe I know her."

It was one thing for Wyatt to look at *her* with suspicion. She could not let him turn his police detective's scrutiny toward Jen.

"Jen and Addie only moved here a short time ago from Utah. She is a friend of mine from university."

"Ah. That must be why her name doesn't ring a bell. What brought her to Cannon Beach?"

Rosa's hackles rose. Jen did not need all these questions. It would not do for Wyatt to become too curious. "She works for me. She was looking for a change and I needed someone to help me at the gift store."

He nodded. "Guess I haven't been in for a while or I might have met her already."

He hadn't been in ever, as far as she could remember. But then, Wyatt Townsend was not the sort to buy shell wind chimes or lighthouse-shaped knickknacks.

"I can introduce you after I show you your apartment, if you would like."

"Sure."

Better to get their introduction out of the way. With luck, Wyatt could then forget about Jen.

She would have to send a text to Jen to warn her before showing up at her door with a police detective.

She had already told the other woman about the new tenant moving in. As she had expected, Jen had been both apprehensive and relieved, for a complex mix of reasons.

"This house is big," Logan exclaimed, looking up at the grand entry stairway, one of Rosa's favorite parts of Brambleberry House.

She smiled, in full agreement. "Yes. Each apartment has at least two bedrooms and two bathrooms. And each has a lovely view of the ocean."

She unlocked the first-floor apartment and swung open the door. Immediately, the sweet scent of freesia drifted through the air.

It wasn't unusual to smell flowers at random places in the house. She knew her aunt Anna and Sage Spencer believed the ghost of the previous owner still walked the halls.

Abigail Dandridge had died a decade ago and left the house jointly to Anna and Sage. She had been dear friends to them and also had left Anna By-The-Wind, the gift shop in town that Rosa was a part owner of and now running.

All the old-timers in town still remembered Abigail with fondness. Hardly a week went by when someone did not come into the shop with a memory of Abigail.

Rosa wished she could have known her. She also wanted to be the sort of person whom people remembered with such fondness.

She wasn't sure she believed the stories that Abigail still lingered in the home she had loved and she was also quite certain a no-nonsense police officer like Wyatt Townsend would never believe a benevolent spirit drifted through the place.

She couldn't deny that scent of freesia, though, which had no logical explanation.

Ignoring it for now, she let them inside the apartment.

"This apartment is the largest in the house. It has three bedrooms and a very nice sunroom. The master bedroom and the kitchen face the ocean. The other two bedrooms each have a view of the garden."

"Oh, I like this place." Logan ran into the sunroom, which had an entire wall made of glass.

"That looks like a great place to read a book on a stormy afternoon."

"Yeah. Maybe you can read me more of *The Hobbit*," Logan said.

"Sure thing."

Wyatt smiled down at his son with a softness Rosa had not seen before. Instead of looking stern and foreboding, he looked younger and far more handsome.

A little shiver of awareness blossomed in her stomach. She swallowed, taken completely off guard.

No. No, no, *no*. She did not want to be attracted to this man. It was nothing personal against Wyatt Townsend. She wasn't interested in romance at all. Okay, it was a *little* personal. She especially didn't want to suddenly find herself attracted to a police detective who was trained to be suspicious of people.

She let out a slow breath. This was ridiculous. He was her tenant and her friend's brother. That was all. She was not attracted to him. She would simply not allow it.

She had too much to worry about right now, keeping Jen safe. She did not have time to be distracted by a gruff detective, no matter how sweetly he smiled at his adorable son.

"The laundry room is off the kitchen there. You can control the temperature of your apartment independently of the other two units in the house. The control is in the hallway. The garbage trucks, they come on Monday. This apartment has a dog door so that Hank can go out into the fenced area of the yard during the day if he needs."

"That will be handy."

"The garden is for all the guests to use at any time. We have a swing in the tree that Logan might enjoy. I know that Addie does. We also have direct access to the beach, but I ask that you keep the gate locked for security reasons. It is the same code as the front door, which I have written on the paper for you, and your key will also open it."

"Got it."

"Do you have any questions?"

"I have a question," Logan said. "Can Hank and me play with your dog sometime?"

She smiled. "Of course. Anytime. She comes to the store with me most of the time during the day, but when we are home, she would love to play with you."

She looked up to find Wyatt watching her with an expression she could not read. It still made her nervous.

"If you think of any other questions, my phone number is there on the desk."

"Got it. Thank you again. We'll try not to be any trouble for you."

His features were stern once more, making her wish suddenly that he would smile at her as he smiled at his son.

"Yes. We don't like trouble here at Brambleberry House. I would hate to have to call the *policia* on you."

Logan's eyes went big. "My dad is the *policia*!"

She smiled at him. "I know. I was only teasing. Do you have things I could help you carry in?"

"Not much. A couple of suitcases. Logan and I can get them."

"Only that?"

"We're traveling pretty light these days. A lot of our

things were damaged in the fire by the smoke and by the water from the fire hoses."

She needed the reminder that they had been through difficult things the past few months. It was a small sacrifice to offer a home to them, which she could easily do.

She could also be kind and gracious to them, despite her personal misgivings about having Wyatt in her space.

"I am sorry for that. If there is anything else you need, please let me know."

"Carrie said you have dishes and pots and pans and things."

"Yes. The apartment is fully furnished."

"That will be handy. Thanks."

His poor little boy. First, he lost his mother, then he lost his house to a fire. She wanted to cuddle him close and make everything all better.

"What about food? You will need to get groceries."

"Carrie sent along some meals I only have to thaw and heat for the first few days. We'll head to the grocery store this evening to pick up some staples after we unload our things. Most of the time, we eat pretty simply, don't we, Logan?"

The boy nodded. "Except Aunt Carrie says we go out to eat too much and I need more vegetables." He gave Rosa a conspiratorial look. "I don't really like vegetables."

"Yes, but you must eat them, anyway, if you want to be strong and healthy when you grow up. My mother used to tell me 'Rosa, if you eat enough vegetables, soon they will taste like candy.' They never did, but I still like vegetables."

He laughed, as she'd hoped, and Rosa felt a little pang. She loved children but didn't expect she would ever have any of her own, for a wide variety of reasons.

"Your mother sounds funny."

"She was. She always tried to make me laugh, even when things sometimes felt very dark."

She missed her mother deeply. The older she got, the more Rosa realized how many sacrifices Maria Elena made on her behalf. She had never been hungry, even though she knew her mother barely made a living cleaning homes for some of the more well-off people in their village. Her mother had always insisted she work hard at school so she could have a brighter future.

She pushed away the memories of her childhood. Her first fifteen years sometimes seemed a lifetime ago, as if they had happened to someone else.

"Oh," she said, suddenly remembering. "I wanted you to meet Jen and Addie, who live upstairs from you."

"All right."

"Let me check if she can meet you."

She quickly sent a text to her friend. After a longer-than-usual pause, Jen replied that she and Addie would come down to the foyer.

"She said she would meet us outside your door," she explained to Wyatt.

"Okay."

"You will like Addie, Logan. Maybe you will make a new friend."

"Maybe."

Life could be filled with so much pain sometimes, Rosa thought as they walked out into the hall to wait for Jen. Each of the inhabitants of Brambleberry House had walked a hard road.

At least for now, they had a safe place to rest, a beautiful home set on the seashore surrounded by flowers, one that might contain a friendly spirit who could not seem to leave.

As Wyatt waited for his upstairs neighbor to come down to meet him and Logan, he couldn't shake the feeling that this was too good to be true.

The apartment was perfect for their needs, with a good-size bedroom for Logan and a very nice en suite for him, as well as an extra room he could use for an office if he needed.

It was actually bigger than their little house and certainly had a bigger yard for Logan to play in.

Brambleberry House would be an ideal temporary home for them while the construction crew repaired the fire damage at his place.

He still had misgivings but Rosa had been welcoming enough. She was certainly kind to Logan, if still distant toward Wyatt.

He followed her into the foyer, with its sweeping staircase and elegant chandelier, to find a woman walking down with a young girl's hand clutched tightly in hers.

She had brown hair pulled back into a tight ponytail and quite striking blue eyes with shadows under them.

"Jen, here are the new tenants I was telling you about," Rosa said in her melodious, accented voice. "This is Wyatt Townsend and his son, Logan. Wyatt is a police officer in Cannon Beach and Logan is seven years old, starting second grade when the summer is over."

"Hello."

She was soft-spoken and didn't meet his gaze directly.

Just what he needed. Another woman here who had secrets.

"Pleasure to meet you." He purposely kept his voice calm, neutral, as he did when he walked into a situation where a witness or a suspect might be prone to bolt.

He didn't miss the way Rosa placed her body slightly in front of her friend's, as if to protect her. He had a feeling Jen didn't miss it, either.

From him? Did Rosa really think he posed a threat to either of them?

The little girl seemed to have none of her mother's skittishness. She stepped forward with a big smile. "Hi. My name is Addie and I'm six years old."

"Hi, Addie." Wyatt was happy to see she seemed well-adjusted and friendly. Whatever was going on with her mother hadn't impacted her yet.

"Hi," she said to Logan, who hadn't said anything yet. "My name is Addie."

"I know. I heard you before."

"What's your name?"

"Logan. I'm seven." His son spoke with a tinge of superiority over his advanced age that made Wyatt hide a smile.

He caught Rosa's gaze and didn't miss her surprised look. What? Did she think he never smiled?

Addie pointed behind them. "Is that your dog?"

Wyatt turned to find Hank plopped in the doorway as if he owned the place.

"Yep," Logan answered. "His name is Hank."

"Will he bite?"

"Only if you bite him first," Logan said, which made Addie giggle.

"I'm not going to bite a dog! That would be gross."

"You can pet him, if you want."

She plopped onto the ground and Hank, predictably, rolled over to have his belly scratched. The dog was shameless for affection.

"I don't have a dog, I have a cat. Her name is Lucy. She's old," Addie explained. "Sometimes I pretend that Fi is my dog."

"Who is Fi?" Logan looked confused.

"Fiona," Rosa explained. "My dog, remember? Sometimes we call her Fi. And you can pretend all you want, darling."

"I will," the girl said cheerfully.

"How are you enjoying Cannon Beach so far?" Wyatt asked Jen Ryan.

She focused her attention somewhere over his shoulder, still not meeting his gaze.

"I like it here. The people are friendly, for the most part, and the scenery is amazing."

"Rosa said you came from Utah. I've got friends there. What part?"

He wasn't surprised when his innocent-seeming question made both Rosa and Jen tense. As he suspected, she was in some kind of trouble. Was she running from an abusive relationship or a custody problem? Or something else?

The two women looked at each other for a moment then Jen gave a smile that looked forced. "A small town in Utah, near the Idaho border. No one has ever heard of it."

She answered in such an offhand manner, he knew she was being deliberately evasive.

He wanted to ask her what town in Utah, but suspected she would shut down fast if he asked.

He also didn't want to raise the wrath of Rosa Galvez. Not when she was doing him a big favor by letting him stay here.

Anyway, Jen Ryan was only a neighbor. Not a suspect.

She probably had very legit reasons to be cautious of strangers.

Sometimes he needed to remind himself to separate the detective from the man. They would be sharing this house for the next month, but likely would not see much of each other, anyway. Did he really need to know the poor woman's life story?

"Rosa says you are a police detective."

"Yes."

"I see."

She didn't sound thrilled at the confirmation. He couldn't help feeling a little defensive. He was passionate about his job, protecting and serving, and tried to do it with compassion and dedication toward all.

"It was nice to meet you," she said, though he suspected she was lying. "I hope you're comfortable here."

"Thank you."

"Come on, Addie."

The girl protested a little but still took her mother's hand and the two of them went back up the stairs again. Addie sent a smile over her shoulder all the way up the stairs at Logan and Hank and her pretend dog, Fiona.

That one would be a little heartbreaker when she

grew up. He could tell she already knew how to charm people.

He turned back to Rosa in time to see her watching Jen with a worried expression. When she felt his gaze, she quickly wiped it away.

"There. Now everyone knows everyone else living in the house."

"Yes." One big not-so-happy family. "We'll just grab our things and settle in."

She nodded. "Be sure to contact me if you have any questions."

"Thank you."

"Good night, then. Come on, Fiona. We have tools to put away."

She walked outside in the fading sunlight and he and Logan followed her to grab their suitcases and the few boxes of belongings he had brought from his sister's house.

When they returned from the last trip outside, Logan collapsed onto the comfortable-looking couch. "I like this place. It feels nice."

Logan was the reason he was here. Wyatt was grateful for the reminder. He and his son needed their own place until the house was ready. It was only a short time, and then they could get back to their real life.

Yes, he might be uncomfortably attracted to Rosa Galvez, but he wasn't about to make the mistake of acting on that attraction.

No matter how tempting.

Chapter 3

The busy summer season and her responsibilities at By-The-Wind, combined with her volunteer activities, meant Rosa only saw her new tenants in passing for several days after they moved in.

Even when she didn't actively see them, she was aware of them. Knowing that Wyatt was living two floors below her, she couldn't seem to stop imagining him walking around the house at night. Taking a shower, sprawling out on the big king-size bed wearing next to nothing...

Her entirely too vivid imagination annoyed her severely. When she would catch her mind dwelling on him, she would quickly jerk away her attention and make herself think about something boring, like taking inventory or meeting with her tax accountant. Anything to keep her mind off the attractive man who lived downstairs.

She wasn't sure how she would make it through an entire month or more of this.

Rosa was trying hard to remember that Wyatt and Logan were guests in the house. A month wasn't long, especially during the busy tourist season, when the store was so busy she didn't have much free time, anyway.

She could endure having them there, even if their stay dragged into two months, especially as it was one small way she could work on repaying her vast debt to his sister.

Nearly a week after Wyatt and Logan moved in, Rosa sat in her spare bedroom at the desk she had pulled beneath the window overlooking the Pacific, wishing for rain. For the last few days, the weather seemed as unsettled as she felt. The days had been overcast, brooding like a petulant teenager.

Outside, the ocean seethed and churned, restless in the random moonbeams that found their way through the gathering clouds.

Perhaps a storm would blow through and wash away the unseasonable heat that seemed to have settled over the area.

Brambleberry House did not have air conditioning, as summers here along the coast were mild. The nights usually turned cooler, but until the sun went down, her apartment on the third floor of the old house could be stultifying.

Rosa spent most of her evenings working in the garden. She missed Sonia Davis, the woman who had lived on the second floor until two Christmases earlier, when her estranged husband had come to fetch her, and Rosa had learned her tenant had been living under an assumed name.

Rosa's thumb wasn't nearly as green as Sonia's, and her friend now lived happily with her husband in Haven Point, Idaho. The gardens didn't look as good as they had under Sonia's care, but Rosa did her best.

To her delight, Jen and Addie joined her most evenings. She enjoyed both the company and the help, and was thrilled to see Jen becoming more at ease here in Cannon Beach.

Her friend was settling in. She seemed more comfortable at the gift shop, as well, no longer looking as if she wanted to escape every time a man walked in.

Rosa felt good about her progress. She had wondered if encouraging Jen and her daughter to leave behind their life in Utah was the best decision. Seeing her friend begin to relax into her new life gave her hope that she had been right.

Rain suddenly clicked against the window and she looked up from her laptop. Finally! Perhaps a storm would at last blow away the heat.

Unable to resist, she opened the window more and leaned down to watch the storm roll in.

Lightning arced across the sky, followed closely by a low rumble of thunder. In the blast of light, she could see the sea, dark and tumultuous.

Rosa loved a good storm. They probably should frighten her, especially after some of the intense storms she had experienced in Honduras, but she always found them invigorating. Refreshing in their own way.

She gave up work and decided to relax with a book. The only thing better than a storm was curling up with a good book while she enjoyed it from a safe shelter.

Books had saved her when she first came to the United States. She had always loved to read, but the book selection had been limited in their village.

Once she had moved in with Daniel and Lauren, she had free rein at the town library in Moose Springs and at the school library. Books helped her learn English. Like most other girls her age, she had fallen in love with Harry Potter. Lauren had been wise enough to buy her both the Spanish and the English versions. Rosa would read both at the same time, comparing the words and the sentences to help with her word fluency and her grammar construction.

She still reread the books often. Once in a while she would read the Spanish version so that she didn't lose touch with the language of her heart, but mostly she read in English.

She was currently reading a cozy mystery by one of her favorite authors. She settled into her favorite reading spot, a wide armchair in the corner of her bedroom, and was deep into the story when she was distracted by a sudden banging from outside.

The sound stopped as abruptly as it started. She sank back down and picked up her book again, then she heard it once more.

With a sigh, she set aside the book. If only she had a landlord she could call. Unfortunately, things that banged in the night were *her* responsibility.

She had a feeling she knew what the trouble was. The door on the garden shed wasn't latching tightly. She had noticed it the last time she had mowed the lawn.

If she wasn't mistaken, that was the door to the shed blowing open, then banging shut.

Lightning flashed again, and in that burst of light,

she could see she was right. The garden shed door was wide open.

As much as she didn't want to go out into the rain, she couldn't let the banging continue all night, for her tenants' sake, as well as to protect the contents of the shed.

Rosa threw on her rain boots and coat and found a flashlight, then hurried down the stairs.

When she reached the bottom step, the door to the ground-floor apartment swung open suddenly. Startled, she almost stumbled but caught herself just in time.

Wyatt stood there, silhouetted by the light coming from inside the apartment. He looked rumbled and gorgeous, his hair messy as if he had been dozing.

He was wearing jeans and a T-shirt, and was barefoot. Through the open doorway, she could see a television on inside with a baseball game playing.

Logan was nowhere in sight, which led her to believe he must be sleeping.

Her mouth felt dry suddenly and Rosa had to grip the railing of the stairs to keep her balance.

Ridiculous. What was *wrong* with her?

"Sounds like trouble out there."

She nodded. "Nothing major. I believe it is the door to the garden shed. It is not latching the way it should."

"You're not going out in that, are you? Some of those lightning strikes seem close. That's nothing to mess around with."

"I know. But I cannot let it bang all night to disturb everyone."

He gave her a long look, then nodded. "Give me a moment to throw on some shoes, then I'll come with you."

"That is not necessary," she protested. "I can wedge it closed with a rock if I can't fix it."

"Wait. I'll only be a minute."

She really could handle it by herself, but didn't want to be rude so she waited. A few moments later, he returned wearing tennis shoes and a raincoat with a Cannon Beach Police Department logo.

Together they walked out of the house. The temperature had cooled down considerably. Rosa shivered a little at the wet wind that blew through the porch.

Her eagle-eyed neighbor didn't miss her reaction. "I can handle this, if you want to stay here on the porch, where it's dry."

She shook her head. "*You* should stay here where it's dry. Taking care of the house is my responsibility."

"Fine. We'll both go."

She pulled up her hood and hurried down the steps toward the garden shed.

When they reached it, she was grateful for his help. The door was heavy and the wind made it hard to move. She wasn't sure she could have wrestled it on her own.

"I don't think you're going to be able to fix the latch tonight. Where's the rock you were talking about so we can keep it closed until the weather is a little better?"

"I will have to find something."

Lightning flashed again, followed almost immediately by thunder. It was one thing to enjoy the storm from the comfort of her easy chair. It was something else to be out in the middle of it, with the wind whipping raindrops hard at her face.

She fumbled to turn on the light inside the shed. Wyatt joined her in the small space and she was instantly aware of him. He smelled delicious, some sort of masculine scent that reminded her of the mountains around Moose Gulch, covered in sagebrush and pine.

His gaze landed on a heavy concrete block. "That should do it for now."

He reached down to pick it up and brushed against her. Rosa quickly took a step back, though there wasn't much room to escape.

He didn't appear to notice, much to her relief.

He left the shed again. She took a moment to draw a steadying breath, then turned to follow him. As she reached to turn the light off, her hand caught on something sharp inside.

Pain sliced through her and she couldn't help her gasp.

"What is it?"

"Nothing," she said. "Only a scratch. I am fine."

In another lightning flash, she saw he looked doubtful but he didn't argue with her.

He muscled the door shut, then wedged the concrete block in front of it.

"That should do it, barring a hurricane tonight." He raised his voice to be heard over the storm.

"Let us hope we do not have a hurricane. I had enough of those when I was a girl."

He gave her an interested look but didn't ask questions. Another lightning bolt lit up the sky, followed by the loudest thunder yet, a rumble that seemed to shake the little garden shed.

"That one was too close." Wyatt frowned. "We need to get to shelter. We're too exposed here."

He led the way to the closest entry to the house, the door to his sunroom.

This was one of her favorite parts about Brambleberry House. If she was ever tempted to leave her third-floor sanctuary, it would be to move to this floor so that she could have the sunroom, with the glorious view of the ocean.

Rosa could spend all day every day here. She would probably put in a bed so she could sleep here on long summer nights with the sound of the sea and the breeze blowing through.

She liked the idea of it but the reality probably would not be as appealing. She would feel too exposed here. Anyone could walk up from the beach, climb over the beach gate and break a window to get in.

She would have no defenses.

That was the reason she had not given this apartment to Jen, though both had come vacant at the same time and this apartment was larger. Jen needed to feel safe, above all else.

Security wasn't an issue for Wyatt. Something told Rosa the man could take care of himself in all situations.

"Now," he said when they were inside, "let's take a look at your hand."

Rosa tensed, suddenly aware of how cozy this sunroom was in the middle of a storm.

She should not have come in here with him. Not when she was fighting this unwanted attraction.

"It is fine. I only need to put a bandage on it. I can take care of it upstairs."

Wyatt frowned. "It's your right hand, which is always harder to bandage for someone who is right-handed. Let me take a look."

How had he noticed she was right-handed? Something told her Wyatt was a man who did not miss much.

He flipped on the light inside the sunroom and

held out his hand. Unless she wanted to run through the apartment and up two flights of stairs in her awkward rain boots, she had no choice but to show him the wound.

The cut on her palm was about two inches long, shallow but bloody.

Rosa felt her knees go weak at the sight of those streaks of red. To her great embarrassment, the sight of blood always left her feeling as if she would faint.

Her mother used to be a healer of sorts and people would come to their small house for care. Maria Elena had even delivered a few babies.

Rosa had never liked seeing blood or having to help her mother clean it up. It was a weakness she despised in herself, but one she couldn't seem to help.

"Sit down and I'll go grab my first-aid kit. Normally, I keep one in the kitchen but it burned up in the fire. Lucky for you, I've got another one out in my vehicle."

Was she lucky? Rosa would have liked to argue but she was trying too hard not to look at the blood dripping off her hand.

After he left, she tried to focus instead on the storm still rumbling around them.

He and Logan had already left a mark on this room. It was obviously well-used. A couple of children's chapter books were stacked on the table and she could see some small trucks on the floor.

Wyatt returned a moment later with a red case. "Come into the kitchen, where we can wash off the blood. I should have had you do that while I was getting the first-aid kit. Sorry. I wasn't thinking."

She followed him, trying to come up with the words

to tell him again that she could take care of her very minor injury on her own.

No words would come to her other than the truth—that she was afraid to let him touch her.

Since she couldn't tell him that, of course, she followed him into the kitchen.

Here, again, he and Logan had made the space their own. A couple of art-class projects had been stuck with magnets to the refrigerator and homework was spread out on the table.

Hank, his cute little dog, wandered into the room and stretched in a dog-yoga pose as Wyatt pulled a few paper towels off the roll.

"Come over here by the sink."

Keeping her gaze fixed away from the cut, she followed him. He turned on the sink and ran his hand under it for a few moments to gauge the temperature, then carefully gripped her hand and guided it under.

Rosa held her breath. Why did he have to smell so good?

He turned her hand this way and that to rinse off the blood. "I don't think you need stitches. It's fairly shallow."

"That is what I thought also."

"We can clean it off pretty well and I think I have a bandage big enough to cover it."

She didn't see any point in arguing with him when he was trying to help her. "Thank you."

Why did her voice sound so breathy and soft? She had to hope he did not notice.

Lightning flashed again outside, followed almost immediately by a loud clap of thunder. She managed to swallow her instinctive gasp.

"How does Logan sleep through such a noise?"

He smiled softly and she felt those nerves sizzle inside her again.

"He can sleep through just about anything. It's a talent I wish I shared."

"I, as well." She was unable to resist smiling back. He seemed a different person when talking about his son, much more open and approachable.

He looked at her for a moment, then seemed to jerk his attention back to her hand.

He patted it dry with a bit of gauze from the first-aid kit. "I didn't see what you scratched your hand on out there."

"A nail, I think. I am not sure. I will have to look more closely in the daylight."

He nodded. "Any idea when your last tetanus shot was? If it was a nail, it might be rusty. This is the coast, after all. Everything rusts."

"I had the shot only a few years ago after I stepped on a rock at the beach and needed a few stitches."

It was a good thing she had been with friends that time. Her foot had bled so much, she probably would have been too light-headed to walk to her car.

"Good news, then. You shouldn't need a second shot. I'm just going to put a little first-aid cream on it. If it doesn't start to heal in a few days, you will probably want to see your doctor."

"Yes. I will do that."

She missed having Melissa Fielding living in this apartment. Melissa was a nurse and was great at patching up scrapes and cuts. Now she was happily married to Eli Sanderson, who was a doctor in town. Eli was a wonderful stepfather to Melissa's daughter, Skye, and they had a new baby of their own, Thomas.

Wyatt squeezed out the antibiotic cream on the bandage before sticking it onto her skin.

"That is smart."

"A little trick my mother taught me."

"She sounds like a very wise woman."

He smiled a little and she again had to order her nerves to behave. "She is. She's a judge in Portland. That's where Carrie and I grew up."

"I thought your mother was friends with Abigail." She frowned a little, trying to make the connection.

"She was, sort of. It was really our grandmother who was best friends with Abigail. My mother grew up here, in a house not far from Brambleberry House. Her parents lived there until they died several years ago. I can remember visiting Abigail a few times, back in the days when the house was all one unit, with no apartments."

The curtains suddenly fluttered and Hank, who had just settled down on the kitchen rug, rose again to sniff at the air. Rosa could swear she suddenly smelled freesia.

"Do you smell that?"

He sniffed. "What?"

"Flowers."

He raised an eyebrow. "I smell vanilla and berries. It's making me hungry."

She could feel herself flush and was grateful he probably could not tell with her brown skin. That was her shampoo, probably.

"I thought I smelled freesia. That was Abigail's signature scent."

"Why would it still smell like her?"

"My aunt and her friend who own the house think Abigail still wanders through the house. Do not worry. If she is here, she is a kind spirit, I think."

"Do you buy that?"

"Not really. Sometimes I must wonder, though."

He seemed to take the news of a ghost in stride. "I suppose I'm a big skeptic. I haven't noticed anything in the time we've been living here."

"Did you not see Hank standing in the corner, looking at nothing? Fiona sometimes does that. She makes me wonder what she can see that I cannot."

"I hadn't really noticed."

She studied him. "Would you mind if Abigail were still hanging about?"

"Not really. I remember her as being very kind when I was a boy. She always gave me butterscotch candy."

He smiled a little at the memory.

"As long as she doesn't watch me while I sleep, we should get along fine."

Rosa had a hard enough time not thinking about him sleeping a few floors below her. She didn't need another reason to picture it.

"I do not know if you can tell a ghost she is not welcome in your bedroom."

He smiled. It wasn't a huge smile and certainly not anything as overt as laughter. She still found it enormously appealing.

She wanted to stare at his mouth, will his lips to lift again into a smile as heat soaked through her.

After an awkward moment, she forced herself to look away. She slid her hand back and pressed it into her stomach against the silly butterflies dancing there.

"I should go," she said. "Thank you for your help with the door and with this."

She raised her hand and, as if she had waved a magic wand, another bolt of lightning lit up the kitchen and an instant later the lights flickered and went out.

"Oh, dear," she exclaimed. "I was afraid of this happening."

"It would not be a storm along the coast without some kind of power outage."

He went to the window of the living area that faced out to the street. "I don't see any lights on in the whole neighborhood. It looks like the power is out everywhere."

Rosa knew that was not unusual. Electricity often went out during big storms in the area.

She knew there was nothing to fear. Still, she could feel herself begin to panic. Full darkness always did that to her. It reminded her too much of hiding in the back of a pickup truck, afraid she would not see another day.

"Where is my flashlight? Did I leave it in your sunroom?" She looked around the dark kitchen, as if she could summon it with her will, and tried not to panic.

He must have sensed some of her unease. Wyatt reached out a comforting hand and rested it briefly on her arm. Heat radiated from where he touched her and she wanted to lean into his warmth and solid strength.

"I'll find it. Stay here. I don't want you to hurt yourself again."

She leaned against the kitchen sink, breathing deeply and ordering herself to be calm.

A moment later, he returned with her flashlight on, pointed to the ground so he didn't shine it in her eyes.

"Here you are."

"Thank you."

She felt silly at her overreaction, wishing for a different past that wasn't filled with moments of fear and pain.

"Thank you again for your help. Good night."

She turned to leave and somehow wasn't surprised when he followed closely behind her.

"I'll walk you up the stairs to your place."

She shook her head slightly. "That is really not necessary. I can find my way. I am up and down these stairs all the time."

"Maybe so. But not in the dark. I would hate for you to fall on my watch."

She didn't want to argue with him. Not when he was being so helpful. She gave an inward sigh as she headed for the apartment door and out to the main foyer.

Wyatt followed her up one flight of stairs. When she saw Jen's door, Rosa immediately felt guilty. She had been so busy trying not to become stupid over Wyatt Townsend, she had not given a thought to her friend and how nervous Jen and Addie might be in the dark.

She was a terrible friend. The worst.

She paused outside the door and turned to face him. "I should probably check on Jen and Addie."

"They might be asleep."

"I do not believe so. I saw lights on inside earlier, when we were out by the shed. She might be nervous with the power outage."

"Good idea."

She knocked softly on the door. "Jen? This is Rosa. Are you all right?"

A moment later the door opened. Jen held a candle in one hand and a flashlight in the other.

Rosa couldn't see her face well, but her blue eyes seemed huge in the dim light.

"Everything is fine here," Jen said. "Thank you for checking." She suddenly noticed Wyatt and seemed to freeze. "Oh. I thought you were alone."

Rosa shook her head. "Wyatt helped me fix the banging door on the garden shed and now he seems to think I need his help or I will fall down the stairs."

"How nice of him to help you." Jen smiled a little, though her anxiety still seemed palpable. "Quite a storm, isn't it?"

"Yes. But do not worry. The power should be back on soon. I see you have a flashlight. Do you need anything else?"

"Only for the power to come back on." Jen's gaze shifted down the stairs behind them, as if she expected someone else to come racing up any moment.

Oh, the poor thing. She had been through so very much. Rosa's heart broke all over again for her.

She knew very well what it felt like to be so afraid of what might be lurking around every dark corner. Rosa had seen plenty of real boogeymen in her life and knew that reality could be worse than any horror movie.

That was a long time ago, she reminded herself. A world away from this beautiful house, which might or might not contain a friendly spirit who smelled like flowers.

She tried to give Jen a reassuring smile. "It should not be long," she repeated. "But if you need anything at all—even company—you know where to find me. In fact, if you would like, you and Addie could sleep in my guestroom."

Jen looked up the stairs as if tempted by the idea,

then shook her head. "We should be all right. It's only a storm. But thank you."

Impulsively, Rosa reached out and hugged the other woman, sensing Jen needed reassurance as much as Rosa did.

"Good night, my friend. Everything will be better in the morning. That is what my mother always told me."

"I might have to hold you to that."

Jen waved at them both then closed the door. Rosa could hear the sound of the dead bolt locking. Good. Jen could not be too careful.

She and Wyatt continued up the final flight of stairs. She had not locked her door when she'd left in such a hurry. Behind it, she could hear Fiona whining.

She hurried to open it and was met with a warm, worried dog, who came bounding out to lick her hand.

"I'm here. Safe and sound, darling. Were you worried about me? I am so sorry I left you."

She rubbed her dog until Fi settled down enough to go over to investigate Wyatt.

He reached an absent hand down to pet her. Here on her apartment landing in the dim light of the flashlight, a quiet intimacy seemed to swirl between them.

She wanted to kiss him.

The urge came over her, fiercely undeniable.

She *had* to deny it. She should get that crazy thought out of her head immediately. Wyatt wasn't the man for her and he never would be.

It was hard to remember that now, here in this cozy nook with the rain pounding against the glass and his scent swirling around her.

"What is your neighbor downstairs running from?"

Rosa tensed, all thought of kissing him gone in her instant defensiveness over Jen.

"What makes you say that?"

"I've been in law enforcement for a long time. I can tell when someone is scared of something. Jen is frightened, isn't she?"

She could not betray her friend's confidence. If Jen wanted Wyatt to know what had happened to her over the past year, she would have to be the one to tell him.

"I cannot tell you this."

"Can't? Or won't?"

"What is the difference? She is my friend. Her business is her business."

"Just like your secrets are your own?"

What did he know about her secrets? Rosa felt panic flare. Carrie would not have told him what she knew, would she?

No. She could not believe that. Carrie had agreed never to tell anyone the things she knew about Rosa's past and she trusted her friend completely.

"Everyone has secrets, do they not? Some they share with those they trust, some they prefer to keep to themselves."

He was quiet for a long moment. "I hope you know that if you ever want to share yours, you can trust me."

She trusted very few people. And she certainly wasn't going to trust Wyatt, who was only a temporary tenant.

"If I had any secrets, I might do that. But I don't. I'm a completely open book."

She tried for a breezy smile but could tell he wasn't at all convinced. In fact, he looked slightly disappointed.

She tried to ignore her guilt and opted to change the

subject instead. "The lightning seems to have stopped for now. I am sure the power will be back on soon."

"No doubt."

"Thank you again for coming to my rescue. Good night. Be careful going back down the stairs."

"I will do that. Good night."

He studied her, his features unreadable in the dim light of her flashlight. He looked as if he wanted to say something else. Instead, he shook his head slightly.

"Good night."

As he turned to go back down the stairs, the masculine scent of him swirled toward her. She felt that sudden wild urge to kiss him again but ignored it. Instead, she went into her darkened apartment, her dog at her heels, and firmly closed the door behind her, wishing she could close the door to her thoughts as easily.

Chapter 4

He didn't want this.

As Wyatt returned down the stairs at Brambleberry House, his own flashlight illuminating the way ahead of him, his thoughts were tangled and dark.

He didn't want to be attracted to Rosa but couldn't seem to shake her image. The high cheekbones, the warm, dark eyes, the mouth that looked soft and delicious.

He had wanted to taste that mouth, with a hunger he hadn't known for a long time.

He didn't want it. He wasn't ready. He didn't know if he ever would be.

Tori had been the love of his life. His childhood sweetheart. He had loved her fiercely and wholeheartedly.

She had been funny and smart, a little acerbic sometimes but kind. A dedicated school guidance counselor, she had loved her students, their home, their family.

He had fully expected they would have a lifetime together. Her death, especially coming out of nowhere, had shattered Wyatt's entire world. For the last three years, he had done his best to glue back together the pieces, for Logan's sake.

He thought he had done a pretty good job for his son. He knew Logan missed his mother. How could he not? Tori left a huge hole to fill. But by moving to Cannon Beach, Wyatt had made sure Logan had his aunt Carrie to fill in some of those gaps. She was there with hugs at the end of the school day, she baked him cookies and she helped him with his homework.

His son was happy. That was the most important thing.

As for Wyatt, he knew he couldn't stay in this odd limbo forever.

For the first two years, he had been in a daze just trying to survive with work and being a single father. About six months ago, he had started dating a little here and there, mostly going out to lunch or coffee while Logan was in school.

Those experiences had been such a bust that he had decided he wasn't ready to move on.

Maybe he would never be ready.

He would be okay with that, though he knew Tori wouldn't have wanted him to be alone forever.

He kept recalling a conversation between them when they were driving home from some event or other, just a month before her death. Almost as if she'd had some instinctive premonition, Tori had brought up what should happen if one of them died.

He worked in law enforcement, was at much higher risk for a premature death, so he had assumed she had been thinking about what she would do if *he* died.

They both said they wanted the other one to move on and find happiness again. She had been insistent about it, actually, saying she would hate thinking about him being lonely and would haunt him forever if he didn't find another woman.

Maybe she and Abigail were in cahoots. The thought made him smile a little, imagining a couple of ghostly matchmakers, scheming in the background.

Now that the raw pain of losing Tori had faded to a quiet, steady ache, Wyatt knew he should probably start thinking about the rest of his life.

He wasn't ready, though. The past three years had been so hard, he didn't know if he could ever risk his heart again—and there was no point in even thinking about it in connection to someone like Rosa Galvez, who didn't seem to like him very much.

Rosa had secrets. He had known that for some time. She always seemed evasive and tense whenever he was around, especially on the rare occasions he was wearing his badge.

Maybe she didn't like the police. He knew there were plenty of people in that camp, for some very justifiable reasons.

She could keep her secrets. They were none of his business. He was living in her house for only a short time and then he and Logan would be back in their own home, away from a woman who smelled like vanilla and berries and made him ache for things he wasn't ready to want again.

* * *

A major fraud investigation kept him busy over the next week and Wyatt didn't see much of his lovely land-lady or his intriguing, skittish neighbor on the second floor. He was grateful, he told himself. At least about the former. He didn't need any more temptation in the form of Rosa Galvez.

He had decided it was easier all around to pretend his attraction to her was only a figment of his imagination.

By the Friday of the week after the storm, Fourth of July weekend, he was looking forward to extended time with Logan. He had the weekend off and he and his son had a whole list of fun things to do before he had to go back to work on Monday—fishing, going for a bike ride and picking out new furniture for Logan's room in their house.

Right now, his focus was dinner. Wyatt hadn't given any thought to what to fix and Hank was run-ning around in circles after spending all day cooped up.

He decided to solve both problems at the same time. "Why don't we take him for a walk down the beach and grab some dinner at the taco truck?"

"Tacos!" Logan exclaimed joyfully, setting down the controller of his device.

After Wyatt changed out of his shirt and tie and into casual weekend attire, they hooked up Hank's leash—a tricky undertaking while the dog jumped around with excitement.

Neither Rosa nor Jen and her daughter were out in the large yard of Brambleberry House as he and Logan walked through the garden toward the beach gate at the back of the property.

The early evening was beautiful, the air scented with the flowers blooming all around them.

Though it was still a few hours from sunset, the sun had begun to slide toward the water, coloring the clouds orange as it went.

The beach was crowded with weekend visitors. Everybody seemed in a good mood, which was one of the benefits of working in a town frequented by tourists.

"What did you do at camp today?" he asked Logan as they walked across the sand. With Carrie's help, Wyatt had been lucky enough to find a place for his son in one of the most popular science day camps in town.

"Tons of stuff. We went tide pooling and I saw about a zillion starfish and a cool purple anemone. And when we had free time, I played on the slide with my friend Carlos, mostly."

"Do I know Carlos?"

"He just moved here and he's my age. He likes *Star Wars*, just like me."

Logan went on to enumerate the many wonderful qualities of his new friend as they walked a few blocks along the packed sand toward the parking lot just above the beach, where their favorite taco truck usually parked.

"And after lunch and free time, we did another art project, the one I showed you. And then you came to get me to go home."

"Sounds like a fun-packed day."

"Yeah," Logan said cheerfully just as they turned up toward the taco truck.

"There it is. Yay. I'm starving!"

Seven-year-old boys always seemed to be starving.

"Are you going to get the usual? A soft chicken taco and a churro?"

"Yes!"

The taco truck was busy, as usual. The food here was fresh and invariably delicious. He and Logan joined the queue and were talking about some of the things they planned to do that weekend when Logan's face suddenly brightened.

"Look who's here! Hi, Rosa. Hi, Fiona. Hank, look. It's your friend Fiona!"

Hank sidled up to greet Fiona with enthusiastic sniffing, as if they hadn't seen each other for months, while Wyatt tried to calm the ridiculous acceleration of his heartbeat.

He had not been able to stop thinking about Rosa since the night of the storm.

She beamed at his son but avoided meeting his gaze. Was it deliberate or accidental?

"¡Buenas, Logan! ¿Cómo estás?"

"I don't know what that means."

"It means 'good evening. How are you?'"

"How do I say I'm good?"

"You can say *soy bueno* or just *bueno.*"

"Bueno," Logan said, parroting her. *"¿Cómo estás?"*

She smiled. *"Soy buena."*

Wyatt had to again fight the urge to kiss her, right there in front of everyone in line.

"This is our favorite taco truck," Logan told her. "Do you like tacos, too? Oh, yeah. You probably do because you speak Spanish."

He winced at his son's cultural misassumption but Rosa didn't seem offended. "Except I am from a country called Honduras and these are tacos from Mexico. I like them very much, though. The owner is also my friend."

They reached the order window at that moment and the owner in question, Jose Herrera, ignored Wyatt for a moment to greet Rosa in Spanish.

Wyatt had taken high-school Spanish and had tried to work on his language skills over the years. Unfortunately, he still understood best when Spanish speakers spoke slowly, which didn't happen often in general conversation.

He had no idea what the guy said. Whatever it was, it made Rosa laugh. She answered him in rapid-fire Spanish, which sparked a belly laugh in Herrera.

"Go ahead and order," Wyatt said to her.

"You were here first."

"We're still trying to decide," he lied.

She gave her order then stepped aside for him and Logan to do the same.

"Don't forget my churro," Logan instructed.

"How could I?" Wyatt smiled at his son.

When he finished, the three of them moved together to one of the open picnic tables set around the truck that overlooked the beach.

"And how are you, Señor Logan?" Rosa asked.

"Señor means 'mister.' We learned that in school."

"You are correct."

"I am fine. I like living in your house. It's friendly."

She smiled with warm delight. "I am so happy you think so. Some houses, they are cold. Brambleberry House is not that way. When you step inside, you feel like you are home."

"And it always smells good, too. Like flowers," Logan said.

Rosa met Wyatt's gaze with an expressive eyebrow, as if to say *See? I told you.*

"Aren't we lucky to live in such a nice place with beautiful flower gardens that smell so good?" Wyatt replied blandly.

"How is your house coming along?"

Was she in a hurry to get rid of them? No. Rosa had been nothing but accommodating.

"We're making progress. They're painting soon, then we need to do the finish carpentry."

"That *is* progress. You will be home before you know it, back in your own bedroom. Your dog will like that, yes?"

He loved listening to her talk, completely entranced by her slight accent and unique phrasing. Okay, the truth was, he was completely entranced by *her*. She could read a lawn-mower instruction manual and he would find her fascinating.

"I think so far he's having fun being friends with Fiona," Logan said.

The two dogs did seem pretty enamored of each other. Hank hadn't been around a lot of other dogs and it was good to see him getting along well with the Irish setter.

Rosa smiled at his son. "Fiona can be a charmer. She is quite hard to resist."

That made two of them. Wyatt sighed. This had to stop. He didn't want this attraction. Even after a short time, he still hadn't come to terms with his growing interest in his landlady.

Seeing her again here in the July sunshine, bright and vibrant and lovely, only intensified the ache that had been growing since the night of the storm.

He pursed his lips, determined not to think about that. "How is Jen settling in, living in Cannon Beach?"

He had only seen the second-floor tenant in passing a few times. She still seemed as anxious and uncomfortable around him as before.

"Good, as far as I know. She and Addie seem content for now."

Something told him that was a new state of affairs. He didn't know what the woman was going through but was glad at least that she was finding peace here.

"We bumped into Addie and Jen at the grocery store the other night. Jen seems a little uncomfortable around me."

If he hoped Rosa might take the bait and tell him what was going on with Jen, he was doomed to disappointment. She quickly changed the subject away from her friend.

"I'm sure I don't know why. Logan, did I see you walking past my store window today with a bucket?"

"I don't know. Maybe. My day camp went tide-pooling."

"Oh, I love doing that at low tide. What did you see?"

"About a zillion sea stars and some anemone and a sea cucumber. Only it's not the kind you can eat."

"How wonderful. Is it not fun to see what can be found beneath the water?"

"Yeah. It's like another whole world," Logan said. He started regaling Rosa with a few stories of interesting things he had seen during previous tide-pooling trips.

"My teacher said you can sometimes go snorkeling and be right in the water looking at some different habitats. That would be fun, don't you think?"

"Yes. Very fun. Maybe your father should take you to Hawaii. Or to my country, Honduras."

Logan's face lit up. "Can we go, Dad? And can Rosa come with us?"

Wyatt cleared his throat, his mind suddenly full of images of warm tropical nights and soft, flower-scented breezes.

"That would be fun. But Rosa has a busy job here. She probably wouldn't have time."

Logan seemed unconcerned. "Maybe we could go with Aunt Carrie, Uncle Joe and Bella. That would be fun, too."

Not as fun as Hawaii or Honduras with Rosa, but, of course, Wyatt couldn't say that. To his relief, a moment later Logan's attention was diverted from snorkeling and travel when he saw another friend from school ride up to the taco truck along with her parents on bikes.

"There's my friend Sadie," he announced. "I need to tell her something."

He handed the leash to Wyatt and hurried over to talk to his friend. Wyatt realized that left him alone at the table to make conversation with Rosa.

"What part of Honduras are you from?"

He didn't miss the way she tensed a little, then seemed to force herself to relax. "A small fishing village near the coast. I left when I was a teenager."

"How did you go from a small village in Honduras to living at Brambleberry House and running a gift shop on the Oregon coast?"

She shrugged. "A long story. The short version is that *mi Tia* Anna is part owner of the house, along with her friend Sage. Anna and her husband live in Portland while Sage and her family spend most of their time in

California. Anna needed someone to run the gift shop for her. I have a retail marketing degree and was working a job I didn't enjoy that much in Park City."

"Utah?"

"Yes. Have you been there?"

"No. I'm not much of a skier. My parents used to take us to Mount Hood when I was a kid. I never really enjoyed it."

She smiled a little. "I do not ski, either. It seems a silly pastime to me."

"I guess some people like the thrill. You're not an adrenaline junkie?"

"No. Not me. I have had enough adventure for a lifetime, thank you."

He wanted to pursue that line of questioning but didn't have a chance as Logan and their food arrived at the picnic table at the same time.

They had never really made a conscious decision to eat together, but it somehow felt natural, especially as their dogs were nestled together and had become fast friends.

What happened to Hank's restlessness? Wyatt wondered. Right now, the dog did not look like he wanted to move.

The food was as good as always, the chicken flavorful and the salsa spicy.

He spent a moment helping Logan get situated, then turned his attention back to Rosa. "So you were saying you lived in Utah but you don't like to ski. And that you have had enough adventure and aren't an adrenaline junkie."

She took a drink of the *horchata* she had ordered. "Utah is beautiful year-round. In the summertime, I do like to hike in the mountains and mountain-bike with my parents and *primos.* Cousins," she explained at Logan's quizzical look."

"I have one *primo.* Cousin. Her name is Bella."

Rosa smiled at him. "I know your cousin very well."

"You sound like you are close to your family," Wyatt said.

"Oh, yes. Very. My family is wonderful. My parents, Daniel and Lauren Galvez, are the most kind people you will ever meet. Daniel is in law enforcement, as well. He is the sheriff of our county."

"Is that right?" He found the information rather disheartening. If she had law-enforcement members in her own family, his occupation wasn't likely to be the reason she was so distrustful of Wyatt.

"Yes. Everyone loves him in Moose Springs and the towns nearby. And my mother, she is the doctor in town."

"The only one?"

"It is not a very big town. Some people go to Park City when they need specialists, but Lauren is the best doctor in the whole world."

She spoke of her parents by their first names, which made him wonder at the relationship.

"Is she also from Honduras?"

He wasn't surprised when her jaw tensed at the question. "No. She is from Moose Springs. Daniel, as well. They adopted me when I came to this country."

He wanted to pursue that line of questioning but reminded himself this was a casual encounter over tacos, not an interrogation. She had the right to her privacy. This was obviously a touchy subject for her and he didn't want to make her uncomfortable.

"So. What do you think of your taco?" she asked Logan.

"Muy delicioso," he said with a grin. "That means 'very delicious.' I learned that from my friend Carlos. That's what he says every day at lunch."

"That is the perfect thing to say about the tacos here. They are definitely *muy delicioso.*"

She and Logan spent a few more minutes comparing ways to gush about their meals, leaving Wyatt to wonder what made Rosa so uncomfortable when she talked about her past.

What was she hiding? She did not like to talk about herself, which he found unusual. In his line of work, he had learned that most law-abiding people loved talking about themselves and their lives. With a few well-aimed questions, Wyatt usually could find out anything he wanted to know.

People who had things to hide, however, learned techniques to evade those kinds of questions.

Her secrets were not his business, he reminded himself. She was a private person and there was certainly no law against that.

He would be smart to remember that her history was her own. He wasn't entitled to know, especially when their only relationship was that of landlady and tenant.

Chapter 5

The man was entirely too curious.

It didn't help that she couldn't seem to keep her usual defensive techniques in place when he looked at her out of those blue eyes. She forgot about protecting herself, about concealing the parts of her life she preferred to forget. She forgot everything, lost in the totally ridiculous urge to lean across the picnic table and press her mouth against his. Anything to stop his questions.

Wouldn't that go over well? She could just imagine how he would react. It almost made her wish she had the nerve to try it.

To her relief, he seemed to give up his interrogation as they finished dinner. He sat back and let her and Logan chatter about Logan's friends, his day camp and the very cool dinosaur bones he saw at a museum in Portland with his aunt Carrie.

He was really an adorable boy, filled with life and energy. He loved *Star Wars*, Legos, his dog and his father, not necessarily in that order.

She enjoyed their company immensely, especially once Wyatt stopped digging into her life.

"Good choice on dinner, kiddo," he said with a warm smile to his son.

Seeing him with Logan was like glimpsing a different person. He was more lighthearted, and certainly more approachable. He had smiled more during dinner than she had seen in all the time she had known him.

The Townsend men were both extremely hard to resist.

"That was so yummy," Logan said as he balled up the wrapper of his taco and returned it to the tray. "Thanks, Dad."

"I didn't do much except pay for it, but you're welcome. You should tell Jose how much you enjoyed it."

At that moment, the taco-truck owner was delivering another tray to a nearby table so Logan jumped up and hurried over to him.

"*Gracias* for the taco. It was *muy delicioso*."

Jose, bald head gleaming in the fading sunlight, beamed down at the boy with delight. "You are welcome. You come back anytime."

He fist-bumped Logan, who skipped as he hurried back to their table.

"That was very nice of you," Rosa said. "People like to feel appreciated."

"My dad taught me we should always tell people thank you for things they do. Sometimes we might be the only ones all day who say it to them."

Rosa had to smile at that. Her gaze met Wyatt's and

she found him watching her out of those unreadable blue eyes again.

"That is probably true. Then I must say thank you for sharing dinner with me. I enjoyed it very much."

"So did I," Logan said.

"As did I," Wyatt said to her surprise.

He rose and took her trash and his to the garbage can and dumped it, then returned to the table. "Are you walking back to Brambleberry House?"

"Yes."

"We're headed that way, too. We can walk together, if you want."

Did she? A smart woman would tell him she only just remembered an errand she needed to run at one of the little shops close to the taco truck. Spending more time with Wyatt and Logan was definitely dangerous to her peace of mind.

She couldn't think of anything she needed at any of the touristy places in this area of town, anyway.

"Sure. It makes sense as we are going the same place."

Fiona jumped up from her spot beside Hank, almost as if she had been following the conversation and knew it was time to go.

Sometimes Rosa thought the dog had to be the smartest animal in the world.

As if on cue, Hank jumped up as well, then sat on his haunches and looked pointedly at his owner, as if to tell him he was ready to leave, too.

"I'll take Hank," Logan said and picked up the leash. He led the way, still chattering, as they headed along the sand toward Brambleberry House.

"Looks like it's going to be another gorgeous sunset."

Wyatt looked out across the water at the clouds fanning out across the sky in shades of apricot and plum.

"Lovely."

It was the sort of beautiful, vibrant summer evening meant to be spent with a special someone.

Too bad she didn't have a special someone.

Rosa sighed. She hadn't dated anyone seriously since she moved to Cannon Beach four years earlier.

She really should go out on a date or two. All of her friends were constantly trying to set her up, but lately it all seemed like so much bother. Maybe that would distract her from this unwanted and inconvenient attraction to Wyatt.

Rosa was not a nun or anything. She dated, when she found someone worthy of her time, though it was rather depressing to realize she hadn't dated anyone seriously in a long time. Not since college, really?

For two years, she had been very close to a fellow business major whose parents had emigrated from Peru. She and Santos had talked about returning to South America to open a string of restaurants.

As far as she knew, he might have even done that. They had lost track of each other after graduation and she rarely thought of him anymore.

Santos and the few other serious relationships she'd had had taught her that sex could be beautiful and meaningful with someone she cared about.

She was happy with her life. She was running a successful business, she lived in a beautiful home and she loved the surroundings in Cannon Beach. She had good friends here and back in Utah and loved her volunteer work for the local women's shelter.

Okay, maybe she was sometimes lonely at night.

Maybe she sometimes wished she could have someone to cuddle with, to talk to at the end of the day, to share her hopes and dreams.

Fiona was lovely but talking to her had its limitations since she couldn't respond.

At the same time, she was not sure she was ready for the inherent risks of trusting her heart to someone.

She had told no one else about the things that had happened to her. Not even Santos or the few other men she had dated seriously had known the entire truth. She had told them bits and pieces, but not everything.

Maybe that was why those relationships had withered and died without progressing to the next level, because she had never completely trusted them to know.

She certainly wasn't about to spill her life story to Wyatt, as much as she enjoyed the company of him and his son.

The walk back to the house passed quickly, mostly because Logan dominated the conversation. He pointed out a kite he liked, told her about riding a bike along the hard-packed sand near the water, went into a long story about the time he and his dad took a charter out to see whales up near Astoria.

"Sorry about Logan," Wyatt said in a low voice when the boy was distracted by something he saw on the sand and ran ahead with Hank to investigate. "He's in a chatty mood tonight. Some days I wish I could find a pause button for a minute."

She smiled. "I do not mind. I love listening to him. Your son is terrific."

"Agreed," he said gruffly. "He's the best seven-year-old I know, even if he does tend to show off a little in front of pretty women."

Rosa felt flustered and didn't know how to answer that. Fortunately, they had reached the beach gate at Brambleberry House.

She punched in the code and the door swung open. As they walked through the back garden, she suddenly saw a strange car in the driveway, a small late-model bright red SUV she didn't recognize.

Rosa tensed, worrying instantly for Jen. She was reaching for her phone to check in with the woman when two females hurried around the side of the house. She recognized them instantly—Carrie and Bella—and shoved her phone back into her pocket.

She smiled and waved, happy at the unexpected visit even as she could feel the usual mix of joy and tension settle over her.

"Hi!" Bella called out to all of them, waving vigorously.

"Hi, Bella," Logan shouted, then beamed toward Rosa. "That's my cousin, Bella, and her mom."

"It is good to see them," Rosa said.

As they moved toward each other, she thought she saw Carrie look between her and Wyatt with a surprised sort of look, as if she wouldn't have expected to see them walking up from the beach together.

"There you are! We rang both your doorbells but nobody answered."

"We bumped into each other while we were grabbing dinner and walked back together," Rosa said quickly, so that his sister didn't get the wrong idea about the two of them.

"We got tacos at the food truck."

"Oh, I love that place," Bella gushed. "My friends and I like to stop there after school. I love their churros."

"Me, too," Logan declared, as if the cinnamon and sugar still dusting his clothes wasn't enough of a give-away.

Rosa had to smile. She thought she saw Carrie give her a speculative sort of look but couldn't be certain.

"I came by to show off my new wheels," her friend said. "What do you think?"

"Let's take a look," Wyatt said.

They moved toward the driveway and the small red SUV.

"Nice," Wyatt said, walking around the vehicle to check it out.

"I like your new car," Logan said. "It's pretty."

"Thank you, dear." Carrie beamed at him.

"And guess what?" Bella's voice vibrated with excitement. "We're keeping Mom's old car and when I start learning how to drive, I get to practice in that one."

Driving. Bella would be driving in only a few more years. How was it possible that she had grown so much?

"There's plenty of time for that," Wyatt said, looking alarmed.

"Not really. In less than two years, I'll be old enough to get my learner's permit. I'll be driving around town before you know it."

"Good luck with that," Wyatt said to his sister.

"I know. I remember Dad teaching me how to drive. It was a nightmare. And I believe you wrecked a car or two in your day."

"You wrecked cars, Uncle Wyatt?" Bella looked at him wide-eyed and so did his son.

Wyatt gave his sister a rueful look. "One. And it wasn't my fault. A guy T-boned me in an intersection. He got the citation."

"In that case, I'm sorry I impugned your driving credentials," Carrie said.

He shrugged. "I will confess that in the past, I might have had a propensity to drive too fast. Good thing I can do that legally now, with lights and sirens going."

He tapped Bella lightly on the head. "But remember, I'm a highly trained officer of the law. You should always stay within the legal speed limit."

Bella giggled. "What about you, Rosa. Where did you learn to drive? Here or in Honduras?"

She always felt strange talking about her childhood life with Bella and Carrie. "Here. My father taught me when I was in high school. He and my mother were tired of driving me to after-school activities all the time. We had many ranch roads in Utah, where they live, so we practiced for hours until I could feel comfortable behind the wheel."

That was one more gift Lauren and Daniel had given her. Independence. They had wanted her to have all the skills she would need to make a success of her life. She knew they were proud of what she had done and how far she had come. At the same time, she knew Lauren especially worried about her love life.

What would Lauren think about Wyatt? Rosa could guess. She would probably adore him—first because he was in law enforcement like Daniel and second because he was a good man who loved his child.

She would be over the moon if she had any idea how Rosa couldn't seem to stop thinking about him.

She didn't plan to tell either of them about her new tenant. Her parents and siblings were coming to town just before Labor Day, but Logan and Wyatt would be back in their own home by then. She would have to tell them nothing.

Oddly, the thought of the Townsends moving out left her feeling slightly depressed.

"When I get my learner's permit," Bella said, "I'm going to need a lot of practice time. Rosa, maybe you and Uncle Wyatt can help and give my mom and dad a break so they don't always have to ride with me."

Rosa couldn't find words for a few seconds, she was so honored that Bella would even consider allowing her to help her learn how to drive.

"I would enjoy that," she said, her voice a little ragged.

"It's a deal," Wyatt said. "It will be good practice for when I have to teach this kiddo how to drive."

Would she be here when Bella was learning how to drive? Rosa wasn't sure. She had never intended to stay in Cannon Beach for long, but once she had moved here, it had been hard to drag herself away. Now that she was a part owner of the gift store, it became even more difficult.

She didn't like thinking about leaving all the friends she had made here, but perhaps she would one day find it inevitable.

"Showing off my car wasn't the only reason we dropped by. I know you have the weekend off. Joe and I were thinking of grilling steaks and then watching the fireworks on Sunday. We would love to have you. Rosa, you're invited as well. And your friend Jen, if she would like to come."

Rosa wasn't sure if she was ready to have another social outing with the irresistible Townsend men. On the other hand, how could she refuse an invitation from Carrie?

At her hesitation, Carrie made a face. "I know it's rude to just drop in with an invitation two days beforehand. I should have planned better. Please don't worry if you already have plans. But if you can come, we will eat at about seven thirty."

"I do not have plans," she said. In truth, she had been so busy at work, she had not given the holiday weekend much thought.

She could handle a few hours in Wyatt's company. She would simply spend the evening talking with Carrie and Bella.

"Dinner would be nice. What should I bring?"

"Yourself. That's the main thing. But if you want to bring a salad or a fruit plate, that's always good."

She nodded. "Yes. I can do that."

"Oh, lovely. We will see you Sunday, then. Now we're off to take this beauty for a drive down the coast. With me behind the wheel, of course," she assured them, which made Bella moan in mock disappointment.

A moment later, she stood beside Wyatt and watched the little red SUV back out of the driveway.

"Your sister. She is wonderful."

Rosa could not even put into words her deep gratitude toward Carrie.

"She is pretty terrific. Our mom had breast cancer when I was in high school and Carrie basically stepped in to take care of all of us while Mom was having treatment. She was a young bride herself but that didn't stop her."

"That is wonderful. My mother died of breast cancer when I was fourteen."

She wasn't sure why she told him that. It was another part of her past she didn't usually share.

He gave her a sympathetic look. "I'm sorry. That's a hard loss for a teenager."

She had been so frightened after her mother died. She had no one to her pain except a few of her mother's friends.

They had been as poor as Rosa and her mother and couldn't help her survive when they were barely subsisting. She had known she was on her own from the moment her mother had died.

That cold truth had led her to making some terrible decisions, with consequences she could never have imagined.

"Hey, Dad, can I show Rosa what I built out of Legos this week?"

Wyatt shook his head. "We've taken up her whole evening. I'm sure she has things to do."

Rosa did have things to do, always. Most small-business owners never really stopped working, even if it was only the constantly turning wheels of their subconscious.

But at the disappointed look on Logan's face, she smiled at the boy. "I do have things to do tonight but I would love to see your creation first."

She could tell Wyatt wasn't particularly pleased at her answer. Why not? Was he in a hurry to get rid of her? Too bad. He could survive a few more moments of her company, for his son's sake.

Wyatt unlocked the front door. As she stood in the entryway waiting for him to open his apartment, Rosa smelled the distinctive scent of flowers that had no logical reason to be there.

Hank sniffed the air and so did Fiona. They both went to the bottom of the stairs, wagging their tails.

Apparently, Abigail was active tonight. Rosa rolled her eyes at her own imagination. She did not believe in ghosts, benevolent or otherwise. If she did, she would never be able to sleep for all the ghosts haunting her.

The dogs followed them as they went into the ground-floor apartment.

"My room is back here," Logan said. He grabbed Rosa's hand and tugged her in the direction of his space.

A *Star Wars* blanket covered the bed and toys were scattered around the room. It made her happy to see the signs a child lived there, and somehow she had the feeling it would have made Abigail happy, too.

"It's over here. This was the biggest set I've ever made. It had over two hundred pieces! I wasn't sure I could do it but my dad helped me."

He showed her a complicated-looking brick master-piece, which she recognized as a spacecraft from one of the *Star Wars* movies, though she couldn't have said for sure which one.

It warmed her heart to think about the boy and his father working together on the project.

"How wonderful. It must have taken you a long time."

"Not really. It's not that hard if you follow the picture directions. My friend Carlos got one, too, and he was able to put it together and Carlos can't even read in English very much."

"Can't he?"

"He's getting better." Logan looked as if he didn't want to disrespect his friend. "Anyway, he hasn't been here very long, only a few months. He told me he speaks

Spanish at home all the time. I want to learn Spanish so I can talk to him better but I don't know very many words."

His eyes suddenly grew wide. "Hey. You speak Spanish *and* English. You could teach me."

"Me?" Rosa was so shocked at the suggestion that she didn't quite know how to respond.

"Rosa is very busy with her store," Wyatt said from the doorway. "We don't need to bother her. You and I can keep reading the books and practicing with the language app on my phone."

How could she be anything but charmed at the idea of Wyatt and his son trying to learn Spanish together so Logan could talk to his friend?

"I would not mind practicing with you when I can," she said quickly. "I should tell you that I have been speaking mostly English almost as long as I spoke only Spanish, so some of my vocabulary might be a little rusty."

"Oh, yay! Thanks, Rosa. *Gracias.*"

"*De nada.* I am usually home after six most nights. You can come knock on my door and if I'm home, we can practice a little in the evening."

"Cool! Thanks!"

To her shock, her gave her a quick, impulsive hug. Her arms went around him and she closed her eyes for a moment, grateful for this tender mercy.

When she opened her eyes, she found Wyatt watching her with a strange look in his eyes.

"Okay. Bath time. Tell Rosa good-night, then go find your pajamas and underwear. The clean ones are still in the dryer."

"How do I say 'good night' again?"

"*Buenas noches.* Or sometimes just *buenas.*"

He repeated the words, then hurried off to find his pajamas.

"Thanks for your patience with us," Wyatt said in a low voice after the boy had left.

"I do not mind. He is a sweet boy. I enjoy his company."

And yours, she wanted to add. *Even when I know I should not.*

"If you don't really have time to practice Spanish with him, don't worry about it. He'll probably forget by tomorrow morning."

She frowned. "I will not forget. I promised to help him and I would not make a promise I did not intend to keep."

He looked down at her, that odd light in his eyes again. "An admirable quality in a person."

She was not admirable. At all. If he knew her better, he would know that.

"I meant what I said. I will be happy to help him. Send him up any evening he is free or even outside when I am working in the yard. I do not know if I would be a good teacher, but I will do my best."

"I'm sure you will be great," he said. "I just don't want my son to bother you."

"He is never a bother. I will enjoy it."

"Thank you, then. He will probably learn faster from a native speaker than any app could teach him."

"I will do my best," she said again. "Now if you will excuse me, I must go."

She really needed to leave soon, before she did something foolish like throw herself into his arms.

"Good night," she said, edging toward the door.

"Buenas noches," he replied, with a credible pronunciation. "I guess I'll see you on Sunday at Carrie's house."

Oh. Right. She had almost forgotten the invitation. "Yes. I guess so."

"We could always walk over together."

What would Carrie think if the two of them came together to her dinner party? Rosa suspected his sister was already getting the wrong idea about them after seeing them together tonight.

Still, it made sense. It would be silly to drive when the house was so close. "All right. Come, Fiona," she called.

Her dog rose from the rug, where she was cuddled with Hank, and gave the little dog a sorrowful look, then followed Rosa up the stairs to her apartment.

Something seemed to have shifted between her and Wyatt during this evening spent together, but she couldn't have said exactly what.

He was attracted to her.

She wasn't sure how she knew that but she did. Maybe that look in his eyes as he had watched his son hug her... Touched, surprised...hungry.

She was imagining things. Wyatt Townsend was certainly not hungry for her.

If he was, it was only because he didn't know the truth. All the secrets of her past, which she had pushed into the deep corners of herself, where no one else could see.

Chapter 6

Summer evenings along the Oregon coast could be magical, especially when they were clear, with no sign of coastal fog.

As they walked the short distance between Brambleberry House and his sister's place on Sunday, the air smelled of the sea, mingled with pine and cedar and the flowers that seemed to grow in abundance this time of year, spilling out of flower baskets and brightening gardens.

Independence Day turned out to be perfect. He and Logan had spent the morning fishing in their favorite spot along the nearby river. Even though the fishing was a bust and they didn't catch anything big enough to keep, Logan still had a great time.

Afterward, they had gone on a hike at one of their

favorite trails in Ecola State Park and then had spent the afternoon playing in the sand.

He wouldn't be surprised if Logan fell asleep early.

Of course, he wasn't anywhere close to sleeping now. He was having too much fun quizzing Rosa about the Spanish word for everything they passed.

"How do you say *mailbox*?" Logan asked, pointing to a row of them across the road.

"Buzón."

"And *house* is *casa*, right?"

"Yes. Very good. And we are walking. *Estamos caminando.*"

"Yes. To my aunt Carrie's *casa.*"

She smiled down at him, looking bright and lovely in the golden evening light. To himself, Wyatt could admit that the main reason the evening seemed particularly beautiful had to do with the woman he was walking beside.

"Excellent," she said. "You and Carlos will be jabbering up a storm in Spanish before you know it."

"I think his English will always be better than my Spanish."

"But you are trying to learn for your friend. That is the important thing. It was very hard for me when I came to this country and could not always find the words I wanted. I am grateful I had very patient family and friends to help me."

He had to wonder again at her story. She had said her mother died when she was fourteen, which meant she had probably come here by herself. But what were the circumstances that had led to her being adopted by a family in Utah?

None of his business, he reminded himself. She was

his landlady, nothing more, though it was hard to remember that on an evening like this, especially when his son slipped his hand in hers, as if it was the most natural thing in the world.

Rosa looked down at Logan and their joined hands with an expression of astonishment, and then one of wonder, that touched Wyatt deeply.

"How do you say *whale*?" Logan asked when they passed a house that had a little whale-shaped bench out front.

"Ballena."

"What about *tree*?"

"Arborio."

"How about *library*?"

"Biblioteca."

Rosa never seemed to lose her patience with the constant barrage of questions. He could only guess how relieved she must have been when they reached Carrie and Joe's house a short time later.

"Now you tell me. What was *door* again?" she asked him as they approached the porch.

"Puerta."

"No. *Puerto. Puerta* means *port*."

"It's so confusing!"

"English is far more confusing," she said with a laugh. "Try figuring out the difference between *there*, *they're* and *their*."

"I guess."

"You are doing great. We will keep practicing."

His son was already enamored with Rosa. They had practiced together the night before while Rosa was working in the small vegetable garden at the house. Wyatt had come out ahead in the arrangement, as she had sent Logan back to their apartment with a bowl of fresh green beans and another of raspberries, his favorite.

He always felt a little weird just walking into his sister's house, even though he had been living there only a few weeks earlier. He usually preferred to ring the doorbell, but this time he didn't have to. Bella opened the door before they could and grinned at them. "I saw you all walking up. *Hola.*"

"Hola." Rosa's features softened. "That's a very cute shirt. Is it new?"

Bella twirled around to show off her patriotic red, white and blue polka-dotted T-shirt. "Yeah. I picked it up this afternoon on clearance. It was super cheap."

"I like it very much," Rosa said.

"I'm going with some friends to watch the fireworks in Manzanita."

He thought he saw disappointment flash in Rosa's dark eyes before she quickly concealed it. "Oh. That will be fun for you."

"I'm going to go play on the swings," Logan announced, then headed out to the elaborate play area in the backyard.

"I'll take these into the kitchen," Wyatt said, lifting the woven bag that contained the bowl of Rosa's salad, the one he had insisted on taking from her when they met up outside Brambleberry House for the walk here.

He found his sister in the kitchen slicing tomatoes. He kissed her cheek and she smiled. "You're here. Oh, and Rosa's here, too. You came together."

"Yes," Rosa said. "It was such a beautiful evening for a walk. I made a fruit salad with strawberries from my garden."

"Oh, yum. How is your garden this year? I've had so much trouble with my flowers. I think I have some kind of bug."

"They are good," Rosa replied. "Not as lovely as when Sonia was here to take care of them but I do my best with it."

"I miss Sonia," Carrie said. "I guess we should call her Elizabeth now."

Rosa nodded. "I will always think of her as Sonia, I am afraid."

Wyatt knew the story of Rosa's previous tenant. For several years, she had lived in Cannon Beach as Sonia Davis but a year earlier, she had admitted her real name was Elizabeth Hamilton. For many complicated reasons, she had been living under a different name during her time here, until her husband showed up out of the blue one day to take her back to their hometown. It had been the talk of Cannon Beach for weeks.

Rosa had been good friends with her tenant and Carrie had told him how astonished she had been at the revelation that the woman she thought she knew had so many secrets.

"How is Sonia Elizabeth?" Carrie asked, the name some of the woman's friends had taken to calling her. "Do you ever talk to her?"

"Oh, yes. We speak often," Rosa said. "I texted her the other day to ask her a question about a plant I didn't recognize and we did a video call so she could take a better look at it. She seemed happy. Her children are happy. She said she isn't having seizures much anymore and she and her husband are even talking about taking in a foster child with the idea of adopting."

Carrie looked thrilled at the news. "Oh, that's lovely.

Do you know, I was thinking about Sonia the other day. I bumped into Melissa and Eli and Skye at the grocery store. Do you see them much?"

Melissa Fielding Sanderson had been another tenant of Brambleberry House. She had married a doctor, Eli Sanderson, whom Wyatt had known when he used to visit his grandmother here during his childhood.

"Oh, yes," Rosa answered. "We still meet for lunch or dinner about once a month. She's very busy with the new baby."

"Thomas is such a sweetheart," Bella said. "I watched him last week when Melissa had a test."

Melissa, a registered nurse, was studying to be a nurse practitioner and juggled school with being a mother and working at the clinic with her husband and father-in-law. Somehow she made it all work.

"What time is Jaycee's mom picking you up?" Carrie asked her daughter.

"Not until eight."

"Then you probably have time to eat with us. Why don't you and Rosa start carrying things out to the patio? We thought it would be nice to eat outside and take advantage of the gorgeous weather. Bell, you can take the plates and silverware and Rosa can take these salads."

Rosa looked delighted, which Wyatt thought was odd. Maybe she was just happy to have a task.

"Yes. That is a wonderful idea. I am happy to help."

She picked up the fruit salad she had brought and the green salad Carrie had just finished preparing, then carried them through the back door to the patio. Bella joined her, arms laden with plates and the little basket full of silverware Carrie used for outdoor entertaining.

As they opened the door, Wyatt caught the delicious scent of sizzling steak.

"What can I do?"

"I think that is it for now." Carrie paused, then gave him a meaningful look. "Rosa is lovely, isn't she?"

Oh, no. He knew where this was going. Carrie seemed to think it was her job now to find him dates. She was always trying to set him up with women she knew, despite his repeated attempts to convince her he was perfectly happy and not interested in dating right now.

He gave her a stern look, though he feared it would do no good. Carrie wasn't great at taking hints.

"Yes. She's lovely."

"Inside and out," his sister said, then gave a careful look to make sure she and Bella were busy setting the patio table.

"You know, so many people could have let what she has been through turn them bitter and angry. Not Rosa. I think it's only made her stronger and more empathetic to everyone."

Wyatt frowned. "What has she been through?"

Carrie gave him a vague look. "Oh, you know. Life in general. Coming here when she was young. Losing her mother when she was just a girl."

What else did she know about Rosa's background? He wanted to push, but then had to remind himself that he was already becoming too entangled in her world. The more he learned about her, the harder it was becoming to fight off this attraction.

Bella came back into the kitchen as he was wrestling against his curiosity to know everything he could about the intriguing Rosa Galvez.

"What else can we take out?" she asked. "Also, Dad is asking for a platter for the steaks."

Carrie pulled one out of the cabinet above the refrigerator and handed it to Bella, who immediately headed back outside with it.

"I only meant to say that Rosa is a lovely woman," she said when they were alone again. "When you're ready to start thinking about dating again, she would be an excellent choice."

Wyatt shifted, vowing to do his best that evening to keep his sister from figuring out that he was already fiercely drawn to Rosa. Once she realized that, Carrie would never give up trying to push them together.

"What if I'm never ready?"

"Oh, don't say that." His sister looked anguished. "You are a young, healthy man. You can't spend the rest of your life alone, for your sake or for Logan's. You know Tori would never have wanted that."

Yes. He knew. That conversation with her had been running through his head more and more often. But a hypothetical discussion with his wife when he still thought they would have the rest of their lives together was one thing. The reality of letting someone else into his heart was something else entirely.

He was tired of being alone, though. Maybe there had been a few nights lately when he had thought it might be lovely to have someone in his life again. Someone to make him laugh, to help him not take himself so seriously, to remind him that life was a beautiful, complex mix of joy and hardship.

Even if he was ready to move on, he sensed that Rosa wasn't that person. She was wonderful with Logan but it was clear she didn't trust *him*.

Just as well. Since he *wasn't* ready, there was no point in dwelling on the issue, especially on a sweet summer night.

Rosa always loved spending time with the Abbotts. Joe and Carrie were deeply in love, even after being married more than twenty years. They held hands often, they touched all the time and they kissed at random moments.

And Bella. Being around the girl was a unique experience, like constantly walking a razor wire between joy and pain.

At dinner, Bella wanted to tell Rosa all about a boy she liked named Charlie, who might or might not be going to the same place in the nearby town to watch the fireworks.

"I really like him but I'm not allowed to date until I'm sixteen. That's not fair, is it?"

Rosa looked over to where Carrie was talking to Joe and Wyatt. She did *not* want to interject herself into a dispute between Bella and her parents over rules.

"I think that your parents have your best interests at heart. You should listen to them."

Bella clearly did not welcome that answer. "It's not like we're going to go somewhere and make out. We're watching fireworks with about a billion other people."

Rosa did not want to come across as a boring old woman but she also felt compelled to offer some advice. Bella looked on her as an older sister of sorts, just the person who *should* be giving counsel.

"You should stay with your friend and her parents, especially since they are giving you a ride."

"I know. I would never ditch my friends over a boy, no matter how cute he is."

"What cute boy are you talking about?" Carrie asked, overhearing her daughter's words.

Bella looked as if she didn't want to answer her mother but she finally sighed. "Charlie. He texted me to tell me he might be going to the fireworks."

Carrie looked vaguely alarmed. "You didn't tell me that."

"Because I knew you would blow everything out of proportion. We're not going together. I might not even see him there."

She gave Rosa an annoyed look, as if it was *her* fault Carrie had overheard their conversation.

"I don't even know if I like him that much," Bella said. "You don't have to make a big deal about it."

"I just want you to be careful. You have plenty of time for boyfriends," her mother said.

"I know. I told you he's not my boyfriend. I like him a little but that's all. I need to go find my portable phone charger. Jaycee's going to be here any minute."

"Don't forget to take a hoodie. It's going to be much colder once the sun goes all the way down."

"I know." Bella hurried off to her room and Rosa had to fight the urge to go after her and warn her again not to leave her friends.

"I hope I can make it through these teenage years," Carrie said, shaking her head.

"You can."

"All this talk of boys and learning to drive. She's growing up, isn't she?"

Rosa nodded, that bittersweet joy a heavy weight in her heart.

Chapter 7

The barbecue was one of the most delightful evenings Wyatt had experienced in a while. He always enjoyed hanging out with his sister and considered his brother-in-law one of his closest friends. But having Rosa there, listening to her laugh with Carrie and Bella, tease Joe and trade corny jokes with Logan, somehow turned the night magical.

He tried to tell himself he was simply savoring the delight of good food and family. That didn't explain how the stars seemed to sparkle more brightly and the air smelled more sweet.

"Everything was delicious," he said to Carrie. "That cherry pie was divine. Did you try a new recipe?"

She shook her head. "No. I'm using the same one Grandma always made. She got it from Abigail Dandridge, actually. The cherries are just extra delicious this year, I think."

"That must be it."

"Looks like somebody is out for the count," Joe said, gesturing to their outdoor sofa, where Logan had curled up a little while ago.

Wyatt followed his gaze and found his son sound asleep under the blanket Carrie had brought out for him earlier, after the sun had gone down and the evening had turned chilly.

He wasn't completely surprised. Their day had been filled with activity and fun.

Love for his son washed over him. Logan was the greatest gift.

"Good thing he can sleep anywhere."

"He is very lucky," Rosa said. "Some nights, I cannot even sleep in my comfortable bed with cool sheets and soft music playing."

What was keeping her up at night? Did she also ache for something she didn't have?

"We're watching Logan for you tomorrow and you said you're going into work early, right?" Carrie asked.

He made a face. "Yeah. Sorry about that."

"You know it's no problem at all. But I've got a great idea. Why don't you just let Logan stay over here for the night? He can sleep in and so can we, since tomorrow is the official holiday and we don't have a single thing planned."

That did make sense, though Wyatt didn't like spending even a night away from his son.

"Are you sure?"

"Yes. If you want the truth, I would rather sleep in

tomorrow, since I imagine we will be up late worrying until Bella gets home safely."

Rosa looked concerned. "I am sure she will be fine. Bella is a smart girl and she is with her friend Jaycee and Jaycee's parents. They will make sure she does not get into any trouble."

"Parents always worry. It's what we do." Carrie shrugged. "Intellectually, I know Bella will be fine. I'll still probably stay up, which means I'll be doubly glad not to have to get up at six a.m., when you come to drop off Logan."

"I didn't bring any clothes for him."

"He has as many clothes here as he probably does at Brambleberry House. We have everything he should need. Swimsuits, shorts and sweatshirts. Even extra socks. It will be great."

Seriously, what would he have done without his sister and her family over the last three years, when they had stepped in after Tori died to help him raise his son?

"That does seem like a good solution, then. I'll carry him into the guest room."

"Afraid we're going to leave him out here on the patio to sleep?" Joe teased.

Wyatt smiled. "He probably wouldn't care. The thing is, Logan would never even notice if it started raining."

Only after he and Rosa had helped clean up and he had carried a still-sleeping Logan and tucked him into the sewing room daybed did Wyatt realize one significant issue he had overlooked.

If his son stayed here, that meant he and Rosa would be walking home alone together.

He frowned, suddenly suspicious. Carrie had been awfully quick to suggest that Logan stay the night, hadn't she? Were her reasons really about convenience and sleeping in the next day, or was she trying to do some behind-the-scenes matchmaking again?

He gave his sister a swift look, remembering that conversation in the kitchen.

Her reasons didn't matter. The deed was done. He and Rosa were walking back to Brambleberry House together and he could do nothing about it.

A short time later, they left the house, with Rosa carrying the bag with the bowl she had brought, now empty and washed.

Why had he thought it was a good idea to walk here earlier? If he had driven, they could have been home in two minutes.

The walk wasn't far, only a few blocks, but there was an intimacy to walking alone with Rosa that left him uncomfortable.

He hadn't noticed it at all on the walk to Carrie's house, probably because Logan had kept up a constant chatter. His son had provided a much-needed buffer.

"The night turned a little cooler, didn't it? That came on suddenly."

She had brought a sweater, which she had put on earlier. Even so, she shivered a little.

"Yes. And it looks as if the fog they've been talking about is finally moving in."

Tendrils of coastal fog stretched up from the beach, winding through the houses. It added to the strange, restless mood stealing over him like the fog creeping up the street.

He put it down to leaving his son back at his sister's house. Surely that's what it was, not anything to do with his growing feelings for Rosa.

"You were right—Logan can sleep through anything. I would not have believed it but he did not even open his eyes when you carried him to bed. Will he wake up confused in a strange place?"

"I don't think so. He's spent the better part of the past two months sleeping there, except for the few weeks we've been at Brambleberry House. He's probably as comfortable there as he is in his own bed. I, on the other hand, probably won't sleep at all."

She gave him a sideways look. "Why is that?"

He shrugged, wishing he hadn't said anything. "When I don't have Logan nearby, I feel like part of me is missing."

She looked touched. "He is a very sweet boy."

"You've been very kind to help him learn Spanish for his friend. I know you're busy. Please let me know if it becomes too much of a burden."

"Impossible," she declared. "I am always happy to speak Spanish with someone. Sometimes I worry I will forget the language of my birth."

He suddenly remembered the conversation he'd had with his sister about her. What had she been through, the reasons Carrie said she deserved to be happy?

"That fog is growing more thick. I hope it goes out again in the morning so the weather stays good for the rest of the holiday weekend. It is a busy time for my store."

"Don't you have better business if it starts to rain? I would have thought fewer people would want to sit at the beach when it's raining, so they're more inclined to go shopping instead."

"Sometimes. Or sometimes they decide since it's raining to take a drive down the coast to Lincoln City, or even farther down to some of the other lighthouses like Heceta Head."

"The police department is busy whether it's raining or not. It seems like holiday weekends always bring out the worst in people."

"Do you like your job as a detective?" she asked as they turned onto the Brambleberry House road.

The question took him by surprise. Not many people asked him that. He pondered for a moment before answering, wanting to be as honest as possible.

"I like when I have the chance to help people. That doesn't always happen. The past few years have made me question my job choices. I've seen a lot of injustice and been frustrated by it. Attitudes are changing, I think. It's just taking longer than it should. At the end of the day, I hope I can say I've worked for victims and for justice."

She said nothing for several long moments. When she spoke, her voice was low. "I will always be grateful for the *policia*. My father is the sheriff and he saved my life and the lives of my friends."

She turned onto the walk of Brambleberry House as if her words hadn't landed between them like an errant firework.

After his first moment of shock, he quickly caught up with her. "How did he do that?"

In the moonlight, she looked as if she regretted saying anything at all. "It is a long story, and not a very nice one. I do not like to talk about it."

Wyatt wanted to point out that she had been the one to bring it up. He had the odd feeling Rosa wanted to tell him about her past, but was afraid of his reaction.

"Well, if you ever decide you're willing to share your story with me, I like to think I'm a pretty good listener."

"I have noticed this. That is probably a help in your line of work, when you are fighting crime."

"I hope so."

He knew he had to get up early for his shift the next morning, yet he didn't want the evening to end.

To his vast relief, she didn't seem in a hurry to go to inside, either. She stood looking at the big, graceful old house in the moonlight. It was mostly in darkness except for a light in the shared entry and two lights glowing on the second floor.

In the wispy coastal fog, it looked mysterious, intriguing, though not nearly as interesting as the people who lived inside.

"Looks like our neighbor is home."

Wyatt didn't miss the way Rosa looked protectively toward the second floor, where a shadow moved across the closed curtain.

"Yes. I think she and Addie planned a quiet evening."

"She doesn't go out much, I've noticed."

"Have you?"

As he expected, she didn't take the bait, so he came right out and asked the question he had been wondering since he moved in.

"What is Jen's story? You can tell me, you know."

In the moonlight, he saw Rosa's features tighten. "I don't know what you mean."

She did. She knew perfectly well. "Why does she seem so nervous around me?"

"Nervous?"

"Yeah. She has allowed her little girl to play with Logan a few times, but Jen herself clearly goes out of her way to avoid me. I'm not sure she's ever looked me in the eye."

Rosa looked away herself. "Maybe she does not like policemen."

"Is she in some kind of trouble? Do you know?"

"Why would you ask that?" Her innocent-sounding question didn't fool him at all. She knew exactly what was going on with Jen.

"I can't help her if nobody will tell me what's going on," he pointed out mildly. He didn't want to intrude, but he was an officer of the law and his job was to protect and serve. That included those who shared the same house with him.

"She has work at the store and she has a safe place to live. That is good for now." She paused. "But thank you for being concerned for her."

"I'm here to help, if you or she ever want to tell me what's going on."

She nodded slowly. "I will tell her this."

"You know I'm one of the good guys, right? At least I try to be."

She gave him a long look in the moonlight. "Yes. I know. I would not have let you move in if I did not think that."

Her words made him feel as if he had passed some kind of test he had no idea he'd been taking.

He was suddenly glad that Carrie had encouraged him to take this apartment for the month, grateful for summer nights and lovely women.

Again, he felt an overwhelming urge to kiss her, this woman with secrets who was filled with so much compassion for those around her.

She didn't trust him. He looked at the house, hat-ing the idea of his empty apartment and his empty bed and the loneliness that had been such a part of his life since Tori died.

"I should probably go in."

"Yes. You are working early tomorrow."

He nodded. "Thank you for the lovely evening. I enjoyed the walk home. I think maybe I've forgotten how much I enjoy talking with a woman."

She gazed at him, eyes wide. In the dim light of the moon, he saw her swallow and her gaze seemed to slide to his mouth.

The scent of her, sweet and feminine, with hints of vanilla and berries, drifted to him. He wanted to close his eyes and inhale her inside him.

"I am glad I could remind you of this," she finally said.

He knew he should walk away, turn around and go into the house, to that empty apartment and the even emptier bed. He couldn't seem to make his muscles cooperate. The pull of her was too strong and he had no tools to withstand this slow, aching desire churning through his blood.

"I would like to kiss you right now."

As soon as he heard the words, he wanted to call them back, but it was far too late. They danced between them like petals on the breeze.

He thought she would turn and walk away since he couldn't seem to do it. Instead, she only gazed up at him out of those soft brown eyes he wanted to sink into.

"Would you?" she finally asked, her voice soft and her accent more pronounced than usual.

"Yes. Would you mind?"

After a brief hesitation, as if she was debating with herself, she shook her head slightly.

That was all the encouragement he needed. He lowered his mouth to hers, his heart beating so loudly in his ears it almost drowned out the ever-present sound of the ocean.

If he had forgotten how much peace he could find talking with a woman, he had *really* forgotten how much he loved to kiss a woman in the moonlight.

Her mouth tasted of strawberries and cream, and her lips trembled slightly. She must have set down the bag she had been carrying because one hand grasped his shirtfront and the other slid around his neck.

It was the perfect moment, the perfect kiss. He had no other way to describe it. A light breeze stirred the air around them, the ocean murmured nearby and the moonlight played on her features.

He wanted to stay right here, with his heart pounding and her mouth soft and sweet and generously responding to his kiss.

Here, he could focus only on the perfection of this moment. Not on the pain of the past or the mysteries that surrounded her or all the reasons they could never have anything but this kiss.

Chapter 8

In her secret dreams, Rosa had wondered before what it would be like to kiss Wyatt. Having him live downstairs from her these last few weeks had only increased her attraction to the man, so, of course, she would wonder.

She had suspected kissing him would be an unforgettable experience.

She had not expected it to knock her legs out from under her.

Rosa closed her eyes, her heart pounding as his mouth explored hers.

Now, as he kissed her, she could admit that she had been attracted to him for a long time. Long before he had moved to Brambleberry House, she had been nervous around him. She had told herself it was because of his position with the police department. Now she could admit it was because of the man himself.

His kiss staggered her.

Why? She had kissed other men, of course. Not counting the awful time in her youth that she didn't like to think about, she had had boyfriends.

She wanted to think she had a healthy relationship now with men, with sex, especially after the counseling her parents had insisted on.

She didn't blame all men for what had happened to her.

Even so, Rosa was fully aware that she usually gravitated toward a different sort of man. Someone who was not as masculine as Wyatt.

Those kind of men were the safer bet, she realized now. They didn't threaten her. She always had held most of the control in every other situation.

Not with Wyatt. Kissing him felt like being caught in a riptide, as if she were whirling and spinning from forces beyond her control.

Sometimes when she saw the intensity between Lauren and Daniel, or her aunt Anna and Harry, Rosa wondered if she had something fundamental broken inside her.

She had assumed that the scars she bore so deeply inside made it impossible for her to feel that kind of passion.

Kissing Wyatt in this moment made her question every single one of those foolish assumptions.

She could want, with a searing intensity that left her breathless.

She wanted to drag him to the dewy grass and kiss him for hours. And more. She wanted more with him.

And then what?

Cold, hard reality seemed to push through the dreamy haze that surrounded her.

After this kiss, then what? Try as she might, she couldn't envision a scenario where she and Wyatt could have anything but a few wild kisses. Where they could live happily ever after.

He was a police detective and she was…herself. A product of what had happened to her and the choices that had led her here to this moment.

They could never be together, so what was the point in setting herself up for more pain?

She drew in a breath, willing her hunger to subside. When she thought she had herself under control enough that she could think straight again, she slid her mouth away, cooled by the night air that swirled around them. After another inhalation, she made herself take a slight step back.

She couldn't see him clearly, but she could tell he had been as caught up in the kiss as she was.

He gazed down at her, his eyes slightly unfocused and his hair messy from her fingers. He looked so delicious, she had a hard time not stepping straight back into his arms.

She had to say something, but all the words seemed tangled up inside her like fishing line discarded on the beach, a jumble of Spanish and English that made no sense, even to her.

She finally swallowed hard and forced a smile.

"That was a surprise."

He continued to look down at her, his face so close she could see each distinct long eyelash and the fine network of lines etched into the corners of his eyes.

He released a long breath. "Yes. It was."

"I thought you meant a little good-night kiss like a friend would give a friend."

"That was substantially more, wasn't it?"

She could feel the imprint of his mouth on hers, could still taste him on her tongue—the wine and mint, the strawberries and cream from the dessert his sister had made. She shivered a little, wishing she could lean in for another kiss.

"Indeed." She hated this awkwardness between them, especially after the closeness they had shared on the walk from his sister's house. She shook her head. "I'm sorry if I turned the kiss into more than you wanted."

"You didn't. That is the problem. I want, though I know I should not."

He gave a slightly raw-sounding laugh, as if startled by her honesty. "Same. I want. And I know I should not. What are we going to do about that?"

Rosa spent a delicious moment imagining what she would like to do. She wanted to drag him up two flights of stairs to her cozy bedroom under the eaves and spend the entire night exploring all his muscles and hard edges.

That was impossible, for a hundred reasons. The biggest one was right now at the house they had come from.

"I don't know what you will do, but I will go inside, take a soak in the tub and try to focus on something else."

A muscle worked along his jawline as if he was trying to keep himself from responding. He finally nodded. "I suppose that's for the best."

Rosa managed a smile, trying to pretend she wasn't fighting with everything inside her to keep from doing what she longed to do—tug him back into her arms and kiss him again until they both forgot all the shoulds and should nots.

"Good night to you, Wyatt. I enjoyed the evening… and the kiss."

"Rosa…" he began, but she didn't wait to hear what he said. She hurried up the steps, unlocked the front door with hands that trembled and rushed up to her apartment.

As she took the stairs quickly, she thought she felt an odd cold spot on the stairs and had the strangest feeling that the house or its inhabitants were disappointed in her.

She and Wyatt had decided not to take the dogs with them because of Carrie's spoiled and rather unfriendly cats. Inside the apartment, Fiona rose to greet her, giving her an unblinking stare, as if she knew exactly what Rosa had just been doing in the moonlight with their downstairs neighbor.

"Not you, too."

Fi snorted as if she had plenty to say but only regretted that she did not have the words.

"What do you want me to do?" she said aloud to her dog. "You know I cannot invite the man up. He is a police officer. He would not be interested in me, if he knew the truth."

Fiona whined. She needed to go out, but Rosa wasn't eager to go down the stairs again and risk meeting up with Wyatt. Her dog's needs came first, though.

"Don't be like that," she said as she hooked up Fi's leash. "You know it is true. I have too many secrets I cannot tell him."

The dog didn't look convinced.

"I cannot," Rosa insisted. "You know I cannot. They are not only my secrets. I cannot tell him."

Wyatt was a good man, A decent, honorable man, she thought as she walked down the stairs again and outside into the moonlight. To her relief, she didn't see any sign of him.

He reminded her so much of Daniel, who would always be her hero for rescuing her in her darkest moment.

She loved her adopted father dearly so she supposed it was only natural that she would be so fiercely drawn to a man who had all of Daniel's best qualities.

"It doesn't matter," she said. She didn't feel foolish carrying on this conversation with her dog. Fiona was the best possible confidante, who listened to all her inner thoughts and only judged a little.

She didn't tell the dog that she suspected she might be falling for Wyatt, though she knew he would never feel the same. Not if he knew the truth.

She knew he was still grieving for his wife. Even if the two of them shared a few kisses, she knew Wyatt wasn't in a good place for anything more.

She wanted things to be different. If only they were both free of their pasts and had met under other circumstances. But she knew she wouldn't have been the same person without all that had happened to her and she thought the same of Wyatt.

She would not kiss him again. What would be the point? Nothing could come of it and she would only end up with more pain.

With the Oregon coast in full tourist season, Rosa didn't have time to think about that kiss more than about two or three dozen times a day at random moments.

Over the next week, she made several day trips out of town to the central coast and to Portland to pick up inventory from some of their vendors.

Today she was busy revamping her window display a week after Independence Day, adding in the new products she had collected to feature, while Jen worked the cash register and assisted customers.

Rosa was thrilled at the change in her friend. Jen had come so far over the past few weeks. She was far more relaxed with the customers. She smiled and chatted easily and seemed to have lost that haunted look she used to wear at random moments.

"Thank you. Come back again. We have new inventory all the time," she told the final customer at her register. A few other browsers were looking at their selection of T-shirts, but they didn't seem in any hurry so Rosa left the window to walk over to Jen and check on her.

"How are things going?" she asked.

"Great. Really good." Jen smiled, looking far more like the woman Rosa remembered from their college days together. "It's hard to be in a bad mood when the weather is so glorious, isn't it?"

They really had been blessed with unusually sunny weather. It was good now, but made her worry about forest fires later in the season.

"You seem to be more comfortable with the customers."

"I am enjoying the work, but to tell you the truth, I'm starting to miss teaching. This is the time of year when I would usually start thinking about my classroom decorations for the next school year and working on lesson plans."

Jen had been a third-grade teacher in Utah and had loved her career. That was one of the things that angered Rosa the most, that her friend had been forced to leave all that she loved in order to escape.

"I can understand that."

"I was actually wondering if I could take a day off tomorrow. I know it's short notice."

"Of course," Rosa said immediately. "I can rearrange the schedule. If I cannot find anyone to cover for you, I will work myself. That should not be a problem, especially now that the holiday weekend is over."

"Thank you. You won't believe this but I already have a job interview lined up!"

"Oh, that's wonderful!"

Rosa knew Jen had recently finished the process to certify her Utah teaching license in Oregon and that she had started applying in the area.

"The first school I contacted called me today and want to talk to me tomorrow. It's at Addie's school, which would be ideal."

"Oh, that is so exciting. Of course, you can have the day off. Or more than that, if you need it."

"To be honest, I'm not sure if I should apply. If I found a job, I would have to quit working here before the tourist season is over in September."

Rosa waved a hand. "Don't worry about that for a moment. I have temporary seasonal workers who have asked for more hours, so I can give them your shifts if you get a new teaching contract. I'm just happy that you like it enough here in Oregon to think about staying for a while."

Jen hugged her and Rosa was happy to note that she

had started to gain weight again and seemed to have lost that frail, hunted look.

"It's all because of you," Jen said. "I can't thank you enough for all you've done since I moved here. Giving me this job, a place to live. You have been amazing."

Rosa was only happy she had been in a position to offer help.

"I have been grateful to have you and Addie here. You would have a job here at the store as long as you want, but it would be wonderful for you to return to teaching. You were made to be a teacher."

The T-shirt customers came over to ask a question, distracting them from further conversation. The door opened and more customers entered, so Rosa moved to help them.

A constant flow of traffic moved in and out of the store over the next few hours and she was too busy to have another chance to talk to her friend about her interview.

Finally, things seemed to slow near the end of Jen's shift. One of the other seasonal workers, Carol Hardesty, came in a little early for her own shift and Rosa was about to tell Jen to take off for the day when she suddenly heard a loud crash.

Rosa jerked up her head, instantly alert, to find Jen staring out the window, the shards of a broken coaster scattered at her feet.

Fortunately, it was a fairly inexpensive one in a design that hadn't been particularly attractive, anyway.

"Is everything okay?" she asked, when Jen continued to stare out the window.

Her words seemed to jolt the woman back to her

senses. Jen looked down at the mess, a dawning look of horror on her features.

"Oh, no. I'm so sorry."

Rosa moved quickly to her. "You look frightened. Are you all right? Has something happened?"

"Yes. No. I don't know. I just… I thought I saw…"

"A ghost?" Carol hurried up with a broom and dustpan and started sweeping in her no-nonsense way. "We get those here in Cannon Beach. Once, I swear I saw a man all wrapped up in bandages walking around the side of Highway 101. When I slowed down to see if he needed help, he was completely gone. Spooky!"

"Yes. It must have been…something like that."

Jen looked like a ghost herself with her suddenly pale features.

"And the really creepy part is," Carol went on, "when I mentioned it to a few people, I found out Bandage Man is kind of a legend around here. There was even a stretch of the old highway called Bandage Man Road. Weird, right?"

Jen hardly seemed to hear her, still staring out the window.

"You need to sit down for a minute."

"Yes," Carol urged. "I've got this mess and I'll handle any customers. Don't worry about a thing."

Rosa guided a numb Jen to the back room she used as an office, which was also where most of the employees took their breaks. Jen sagged into a chair and Rosa crouched beside her, holding her hand.

"Who did you see? Was it the man you fear?"

Jen shook her head. "Not him. But maybe a friend of his. I can't be sure. I only caught a glimpse of him through the window, but I think he was looking at me as if he knew me."

Her panic was only too familiar to Rosa. She knew just how it felt to be hunted. The memories crowded into her mind but she pushed him away.

This was not about her. This was about Jen and her fear and the man who had made her life hell for months.

Rosa did not offer platitudes because she knew how useless they could be.

"What do you need? Do you want me to call the police? You know you can trust Wyatt. Detective Townsend. He is a good man."

For a moment, Jen looked as if she would consider doing just that, then she shook her head. "What would I say? That I think I might have seen a man who might be friends with a man who scares me but who has never actually touched me? He will think I'm crazy."

"He will not think you are crazy." Rosa did not know how she knew this so completely, but she had no doubt that Wyatt would take Jen's concerns seriously. "Stalking is against the law in Oregon, just as it was in Utah. I believe Wyatt will help you. He will want to know what you think you saw."

Again, Jen looked tempted. Rosa even pulled out her phone, but her friend finally shook her head firmly. "I'm imagining things. I'm sure of it. It was only a man who looked like someone from our town. I don't want to bring Wyatt in."

"You know he will help."

"Yes. If there was anything he could do, but there's not. I cannot run from shadows for the rest of my life. Aaron would have no reason to know I'm here. He doesn't know one of my dearest friends lives here. I never mentioned you to him. And if it was his friend, he couldn't possibly recognize me. I don't look the same. I've lost thirty pounds, my hair is shorter and a different color. I have contacts now instead of glasses. He would have no reason to even connect Jen Ryan with the woman he knew as Jenna Haynes."

Rosa was still not convinced. She had heard the fear, the sheer terror in Jenna's voice when Rosa had called her. She thought it would just be a regular phone call to wish her a happy birthday. Instead, Jenna had spewed out such a story of horror that Rosa had been physically sick to her stomach.

"You must come here," she had told her college friend firmly in that phone call. "I have an empty apartment right now. Just bring Addie and come tonight."

"I can't drag you into this," Jen had replied through her tears. "You've been through enough."

"That is why I have to help you. You are my friend. I cannot let you live in fear if you do not have to. Come to Oregon, where this man does not know anyone. You will be safe here."

Jen had been desperate enough to escape her situation that she had finally agreed, leaving in the middle of the night with only their clothes.

She was finally beginning to relax and enjoy her life again. Rosa hated to think of her living in fear again.

"Please. Consider talking to Wyatt," she said now. "He knows something is wrong. He asked me about it the other night. You know he is a good man. He will do what he can to keep you safe."

"I'll think about it," Jen finally said. Color had returned and she seemed to be breathing more easily, Rosa was glad to see.

"Give me a moment and I will give you a ride home."

Worried that the man stalking her had put a trace on her vehicle, Jen had traded her car in the Boise area for an older model sedan that had seen better days. It was currently in the shop, where it had been for several days.

Jen shook her head. "No. Thank you, though. I would rather walk."

"Are you sure?"

"It's less than a mile and I can pick up Addie on the way. The walk will clear my head."

"Are you sure?"

Jen nodded. Her features grew soft. "I meant what I said earlier. I cannot thank you enough for all you've done for me. You've given me hope that someday soon I will stop looking over my shoulder. I wish there was some way I could repay you."

"You have, a hundred times. I love seeing you take back your life. You and Addie deserve everything wonderful I know is in store for you."

Jen smiled, though traces of panic still lingered in her eyes. As soon as she left, Rosa almost picked up her phone and called Wyatt herself, but she decided against it. Jenna's story was her own. She had her reasons for keeping it to herself.

Rosa, who had plenty of secrets of her own, could not fault her for that, even though she knew Wyatt was the kind of man who would do everything he could to keep Jenna and Addie safe.

Chapter 9

After leaving Carol and another of her part-time workers to close the store, Rosa returned to Brambleberry House tired, but in a strange, restless mood. She needed to bake something. The urge did not hit her very often, but when it did, she tried to go with it.

Baking reminded her of her mother. Maria Elena had been an amazing baker who used to make delicious delicacies she would sometimes sell in the market. Anything to make a few lempiras.

Rosa still liked making the treats of her childhood, but today she was feeling more like good old-fashioned chocolate-chip cookies, a treat she had come to love as a teenager.

She was just taking the first batch out of the oven when her phone rang. For a moment, she thought about ignoring it. Hardly anyone ever reached out to her with a phone call anymore, unless there was some kind of trouble. It might be Lauren, though, who still liked to have long chats on the phone since they couldn't connect as often in person.

Without looking at the caller ID, she tapped her earbud to answer the call as she slid the tray of cookies onto the cooling rack and put the next tray into the oven.

"Buenas," she said, distracted.

"Hello?" a male voice replied. "Is this Rosa Galvez?"

Her heartbeat accelerated as she recognized Wyatt.

Oh, this was so stupid. They had shared one kiss. Granted, it had been earthshaking for her, but that did not explain why she became weak in the knees, simply knowing he was on the other end of a telephone call.

She was tempted for a moment to tell him "no, wrong number," and disconnect the call. That would be childish, though. What was the point of hiding from the reality that she was falling for a completely inappropriate man?

"Si. Yes. This is Rosa."

"Hola, Rosa. This is Wyatt Townsend. From downstairs."

As if she knew any other Wyatt Townsends who could make her head spin. "Yes. I know. Is everything all right?"

He sighed. "Not really. I have a little problem and was wondering if I could ask for your help."

The word shocked her. Wyatt was not the sort of man who could ask for help easily. "Of course. What do you need?"

"I just got called to cover an emergency and Carrie, Joe and Bella have gone to Portland. They're leaving for San Francisco from there. I'm in a bind and need someone to watch Logan for a few hours."

"Of course," she said instantly. "Fiona and I would be glad to help you. I can be down in ten minutes, as soon as I take some cookies out of the oven."

"You don't have to come down. I can bring him upstairs to you. He's used to sleeping on the couch."

"Don't be silly. He would be more comfortable in his own bed. We will be there in ten minutes."

She had more dough, but decided she could put it in the refrigerator for now and later freeze it for another day.

"Thank you. I appreciate that. Hopefully I won't be gone past midnight."

"Even if you are, I won't mind," she assured him. "I'll be down soon."

While she waited for the timer, she gathered her laptop and a small knitting project she had been working on. She also waited for the first batch of cookies to cool enough before transferring them to a plate to take downstairs with her. As soon as the timer went off, she turned off her oven, pulled out the cookie tray and transferred the cookies to another cooling rack, then headed down the stairs with Fiona following close behind her.

Wyatt opened the door before she could knock, as if he had been watching for her.

"I'm really sorry about this."

"Please do not apologize. I'm happy to do it."

"Logan is already in bed. He'll be sorry he missed you."

She was disappointed that she wouldn't have a chance to hang out with the sweet boy and teach him more Spanish words. She would have enjoyed reading him a story and tucking him in.

"Too bad. I brought him some cookies. Ah, well. He can have one when he wakes up."

"If I don't eat them all first. They look delicious."

He smiled and she had to remind herself she was here to watch his child, not to moon over the boy's father.

She did her best to ignore how fiercely she wanted to kiss him again. It helped to focus on the gleaming badge he was wearing over the pocket of his sports coat, which reminded her of all the differences between them.

"Anything special I need to know or do?"

"Not really. Since the fire, Logan does have the occasional nightmare. If he has one, you only have to stay close and help talk him through it until he falls back asleep."

"Oh, *pobrecito*," she exclaimed.

His eyes seemed to soften. "Yeah. He's been through a few things. The nightmares are not as frequent as they were right after the fire. He probably won't even wake up but I wanted to warn you, just in case."

"Got it."

"Thank you again."

"Do not worry about things here. Go take care of what you have to do. I will be here. And take a cookie with you."

He grabbed one with a smile that left her feeling slightly light-headed. She told herself it was because she had only eaten a warm cookie for dinner.

After he left, she was again struck by how Wyatt and Logan had settled into the space. A video-game controller sat on the coffee table, along with a trio of plastic dinosaurs and several early-reader chapter books.

The house smelled like Wyatt, that combination of scents she couldn't pinpoint. She only knew it reminded her of walking through a forest after a rainstorm.

A light was on next to the easy chair in the sunroom. She wandered in and found a mystery novel with a bookmark halfway through on the side table. A small bowl of popcorn sat next to it.

Rosa's own limited detective skills told her he must have been reading and enjoying a snack when he got the call from work. She liked thinking about him here, enjoying the sound of the ocean in the night through the screens.

While Fiona found a comfortable spot on the rug next to Hank, Rosa continued on her tour. She briefly went to the room she knew Logan used and opened the door a crack to check on him.

The boy was sleeping soundly, sprawled across the bed with a shoebox that looked like it contained treasures tucked nearby.

She fought the urge to go to him, to smooth away the hair falling into his eyes.

The night of the storm, Wyatt had said Logan was a sound sleeper, but she still didn't want to run the risk of waking him and having him be confused at finding her here and not his father.

She did, however, take a moment to adjust the blanket more solidly over his shoulders.

Oh, he was dear boy. Just looking at him made her smile. He looked a great deal like his father, but his lighter coloring and the shape of his nose must have come from his mother's side.

Rosa had to wonder about the woman. She had seen

a picture of them all together at Carrie and Joe's house. She had been pretty, blonde, delicate-looking.

Carrie had told her Tori Townsend had been a talented artist and writer, in addition to a school guidance counselor. Though she had been a runner who regularly worked out, she had tragically died of a previously undiagnosed heart condition at a shockingly young age.

Logan must grieve for her terribly, she thought. *Both of them must.* It made her heart ache, thinking of this sweet boy growing up without his mother.

At least he had a father who doted on him and an aunt, uncle and cousin who showered love and affection on him, as well.

After she had assured herself Logan was sleeping comfortably, she returned to the living area. It felt strange to be here in Wyatt's space without him. She wasn't quite sure what to do with herself.

She finally turned on the audiobook she was listening to through her ear pods and picked up her knitting. While the dogs slept tangled together at her feet, she worked and listened to the audiobook above the sound of the wind in the trees and the ever-present song of the ocean.

The chair was comfortable and her day had been long. Soon she gave in to the inevitable and closed her eyes, thinking she would only doze for a moment.

She had a dream she was running. It was cold, bitterly cold, and she was barefoot. She was so afraid, not only for herself. She had nowhere to go and the winter snow blew past her and through her. So cold. Always so cold. She had been used to sunshine and heat and could never seem to warm up here.

Everything hurt. Her face, her arms, her stomach where she had been kicked and beaten. She needed help but didn't know where to go.

And then she saw him. A police officer. She thought at first it was Daniel but as he came closer she saw it was Wyatt, looking down at her with concern.

"What happened? Why are you running?"

She shook her head, too afraid to tell him. What would he think if he knew? He would never look at her the same way.

"It does not matter," she told the dream Wyatt. "I must keep running. If I don't, they will find me."

"Who?"

"The ghosts," she told him. Tears were running down her face. She could feel them dripping down her cheeks and reached to brush one away but it dried before she could touch it.

"I will protect you. I'm with the *policia*. Just like Daniel. Trust me, Rosa. Trust me. Trust me."

As she watched, the fear still coursing through her with every heartbeat, his image grew more and more faint until he completely disappeared, leaving her alone again.

She awoke with gritty eyes, a dry mouth and the unsettling sensation that she was not alone.

Rosa blinked for a moment in the darkness, not sure exactly where she was. Not her bedroom in Brambleberry House. She would remember that. Not her room at her parents' home in Utah, either.

A man was there, she suddenly realized. She could see the outline of him in the darkness. She struggled up, tangled in yarn, as instinctive fear and dark memories crowded through her, leaving little room for rational thought.

She had to escape. Run. Hide.

A hand was suddenly on her arm. "Easy. It's okay. It's me."

The voice, calm and measured, seemed to pierce her sudden panic. She knew that voice. Wyatt Townsend.

Was this still part of her nightmare?

Not a nightmare. She blinked a little more as the room came into focus and her consciousness seemed to calibrate again. Right. She had been watching his son for him while he went out to a crime scene and she must have fallen asleep.

Rosa drew in a deep, shuddering breath, embarrassed that she had given in to unreasonable panic for a moment. She thought she had come too far for that.

"You startled me."

"I'm sorry. I didn't mean to. I was just debating if you would be more annoyed with me for waking you or for letting you sleep here until the morning."

"I am not annoyed with you," she assured him. "I was having a bad dream. I am glad you woke me from it."

"Do you mind if I turn on the lamp?"

She probably looked horrible, with her hair tangled and her eyes shadowed. She carefully reached a hand up to her cheek and was relieved when she didn't feel any moisture. The tears must have only been in her dream.

"It's fine. Go ahead."

He did, and that's when she saw the fatigue in his eyes. This was more than physical, she realized instinctively. Something was very wrong. She wasn't sure how she knew but there was an energy that seemed to be seething around him. Something dark and sad.

"What is it?" She could not resist asking, though she wasn't sure she wanted to know the answer. "What has happened?"

He released a sigh that sounded heavy and tired. "It was a long, difficult night. That's all."

Whatever he had been dealing with seemed to have impacted him deeply.

She had seen that look before on her adopted father's face when he would return from a bad crime scene or accident. He would walk in the door and go immediately to Lauren, wherever she was, and would hold her tightly, as if she was his only safe haven in a terrible storm. She would hold him, comfort him, help him put the pieces of his soul back together before she sent him out again to help someone else.

She could not do that for Wyatt and it made her sad, suddenly. She was no one's safe haven.

"How can I help? Can I make you some tea?"

As soon as she made the offer, she thought it was silly to have even suggested it, but for some reason she thought something warm and comforting might be exactly what he needed to ease the turmoil.

He gave a ragged sound that wasn't quite a laugh. "I don't have any tea. And before you say you've got some upstairs and it will only take you a moment to run and get it, I'll tell you thank you but no. I probably need sleep more than anything. And maybe one of your cookies, but I might save those for breakfast."

"Are you certain? I don't mind going to get tea."

He shook his head. "No. You have done more than enough. I'm sorry I kept you so late."

"What time is it?"

"Nearly two. I thought I would be back long before now but the case was…more complicated than I expected."

"I do not mind. I was glad to help."

"I'm deeply grateful to you for staying with Logan. Let's get you back home so you can at least spend a few hours in your own bed."

She rose, again fighting the urge to go to him, wrap her arms around his waist and let him lean on her for a moment.

"Did everything go okay with Logan?" he asked. "No nightmares?"

She'd had one but hadn't heard a peep out of the boy. "Yes. Just fine. I checked on him when I first arrived and he was sleeping soundly. He doesn't keep the blanket on, though, does he?"

"Not usually. Sometimes I go in three or four times a night to fix it. He rolls around like he's doing gymnastics in his sleep. Once when we went camping, I actually woke up with bruises on my rib cage from him kicking me in his sleep."

He was a good father who adored his child. She could picture him checking on the boy and making sure he was warm in the night. It touched her heart.

"I cannot think you enough for coming down at the last minute and helping out. None of our usual babysitters were available. With Carrie and Joe out of town, I didn't know what else to do."

"I really did not mind. I was honored that you would ask. Please do not hesitate to ask me again."

"If I do, I'll try not to keep you up until the early hours of the morning."

She shrugged and slung her bag over her shoulder. "I slept more soundly here than I probably would have at home. Please do not worry."

He smiled a little at that, but she could tell his eyes were still hollowed. What had happened?

"Do you have everything? Can I carry something?"

She wanted to roll her eyes when she realized he really did intend to walk her upstairs. "I have told you before, it is only two flights of stairs. I think I will be fine by myself. Get some rest."

"I need to move a little bit after tonight."

She nodded, understanding that sentiment. After that terrible time, she had needed to take long walks with Lauren, finding peace and comfort and a sort of meditation in the rhythm and the movement.

"Do you...want to talk about what happened tonight?" she finally asked.

"You don't want to hear. It was ugly."

She couldn't help it. She rested a hand on his arm. "I am sorry, whatever it was," she said quietly. "I can tell you are upset. If you were not, if you did not care and did not let the ugly touch you, then you would not be the good man you are."

He gazed down at her hand, his features tortured. After a moment, he made a sound of distress, then he folded her into his arms and held on tight.

"Why are people so horrible to each other?" he said, his voice sounding raw and strained.

She had no answer. What could she say? It was the question that had haunted her for fifteen years. One she was quite certain she would never be able to answer.

She only held him tightly, as she had seen Lauren do for Daniel, and tried to give him a little of her strength.

She wanted to whisper that she would not let him go, no matter what, but, of course, she could not say that. How foolish to think that she, Rosa Vallejo Galvez, could protect anyone from the storm.

"Sometimes they are horrible," she agreed finally. "I do not know why. I wish I did. But more often people are good. They try to help where they can. I try to focus on the helpers instead."

They stood in the front room of his apartment, holding each other as emotions seemed to pour out of him. He didn't make a sound, but every once in a while, she could feel his shoulders shake as if it was taking everything inside him to keep from breaking down.

"Most of the time, I'm fine," he finally said, his voice still strained. "I like to think I can handle just about anything. But this one was hard. So hard."

"Tell me," she murmured.

"It was a murder-suicide. A domestic. A father who had lost a custody fight because of drug use and mental illness. Instead of accepting the court ruling or trying to fix his problems so he could have visitation, he decided that if he couldn't have his son, the mother wouldn't, either. He shot the boy and then shot himself. The kid was only five. A kindergartener. Younger than Logan."

At the despair in his voice, her heart cracked apart. She could only imagine how excruciating it must have been for Wyatt, who did everything possible to make his son's world better, to witness this kind of a crime scene.

Aching for him, she could do nothing but tighten her arms around him. "I'm so very, very sorry," she murmured.

He clung to her for a long time, there in the apartment, and she felt invisible threads between them tighten. Finally, he eased away, looking embarrassed.

"I'm sorry. I didn't mean to lose it like that. I'm... not sure why I did."

She suspected he had no one to share this kind of pain with since his wife died, which made her heart ache all over again.

"You hold too much inside," she said softly. "It cannot be easy, what you deal with every day."

"Yeah. Sometimes." He studied her, his expression intense. "This helped. More than I can ever tell you."

"I am glad. So glad. If you have another bad night, you know where to find me. Everyone needs someone to hold them when the world seems dark and hard."

"Thank you."

"You are welcome, Wyatt."

Something flashed in his gaze, something hungry and fierce. "I love the way you say my name."

All of the breath seemed to leave her in a whoosh. She swallowed as an answering heat prickled across her skin. "I do not say it in any way that is special."

"It is. It's unlike the way anyone else says it. Don't get me wrong. You speak beautiful, fluent English. I wish I could speak Spanish as well as you speak English. But sometimes your native language comes through on certain words."

The heat seemed to spread across her chest and down her arms. "I am sorry."

"No. Don't ever apologize. I like it."

He looked embarrassed that he had said anything, even as the first hint of a smile lifted the edges of his mouth.

He liked the way she said his name. She couldn't

hear anything different in her pronunciation, but she wasn't going to argue.

"Wyatt," she repeated with a smile. "If it makes some of the sadness leave from your eyes a little, I will say it again. Wyatt. Wyatt. Wyatt."

His smile widened, becoming almost full-fledged for a brief moment, and Rosa could feel those invisible threads go taut.

After a moment, his smile faded. "What am I going to do about you?" he murmured.

She swallowed again. A smart woman would leave this apartment right now, would turn and hurry up the stairs to the safety of her own place. "There is nothing to do. We are friends. Friends help each other. They lean on each other when they need help."

He gazed down at her, his expression one of both hunger and need. "Do friends think about kissing each other all the damn time?"

Chapter 10

Wyatt knew he shouldn't have said the words.

As soon as they were out, he wanted a do-over. Not because they weren't true. God knows, they were. He thought about Rosa Galvez constantly. Since the last time they had kissed, thoughts of her seemed to pop into his head all the time. She was like a bright, beautiful flower bringing happiness to everyone around her.

He was no exception. Thinking about her made him smile. Since he was thinking about her all the time, he was also smiling more than he had done in years. He knew it was becoming a problem when even other police officers had remarked on it.

Not that he really had anything to smile about. He and Rosa could not be together. Yeah, they had shared a brief, intense embrace. But that was the end of it.

If he could only get his brain to get with the program,

he would be fine. But every single time he thought about her, he thought about kissing her. And every time he thought about kissing her, he tried to remind himself of all the reasons why it was not a good idea for him to kiss her again.

None of that stopped him from yearning. He wanted Rosa Galvez in his arms, in his bed, in his life.

In some ways, Wyatt felt as if he had been living in a state of suspended animation for the past three years, as if he had been frozen, like some glitch on one of Logan's video games, while the world went on around him.

It wasn't a good place, but it wasn't really terrible, either. He could still enjoy time with his son, with his sister and her family, with his friends.

He handled his day-to-day responsibilities, cared for Logan, managed to do a good job of clearing his caseload. But whenever he thought about what the future might hold for him, all he could see was a vast, empty void.

Nothing had been able to yank him out of that emptiness. Even when his house caught fire, he hadn't really been devastated, only annoyed at the inconvenience.

His own reaction had begun to trouble him. People had told him that a house fire was one of the most traumatic things that could happen to a person, but Wyatt had merely shrugged and moved into problem-solving mode. Where they would live, what he might change about the house as he was having crews work on the renovations.

Even something as dramatic as being displaced hadn't really bothered him.

He could see now that his reaction had been a self-protective mechanism. After Tori's shocking death and the vast grief that had consumed him, he had slipped into some kind of place where he did not let anything touch him deeply.

Now he felt as if kissing Rosa had somehow kicked him in the gut, jolting him off his axis—that safe, bland existence—and into a world where everything seemed more intense.

A few months ago, he would have felt sad about the crime scene he had dealt with earlier, but it wouldn't have left him feeling shattered.

He was beginning to feel things more deeply and wasn't at all sure he liked it. A big part of him wanted to go back to the safety of his inertia.

If kissing her once could jerk him into this weird place, maybe kissing her a second time would help set things back the way they were before.

Even as he thought it, he knew kissing her again was a stupid idea. That did not stop him from reaching for her, pulling her into his arms again and lowering his mouth to hers.

She made a small, surprised sound, but didn't pull away. If she had, he would have stopped instantly. Instead, her arms went around his neck again and she pressed against him. She kissed him back, her mouth soft, sweet, delicious.

As she parted her lips and touched him tentatively with her tongue, he went a little crazy, all the raw emotions of the evening consolidating into one, his wild need for Rosa Galvez.

He deepened the kiss, his mouth firm and demanding on hers. He had to be closer to her. To touch her, to feel her against him.

She said his name again with that sweet little accented pronunciation, this time in a voice that was throaty and aroused.

He wanted to absorb it inside him.

He wanted to lose himself inside *her.*

His body ached with it, suddenly, the need he had shoved down for so long. He wanted to make love to Rosa Galvez right here in his living room. To capture her gasps and sighs with his mouth, to see her shatter apart in his arms.

Her breasts were pressed against him and he wanted more. He wanted to see her, to taste her. He reached beneath the hem of her shirt, to the warm, sweet-smelling skin beneath.

She shivered. The movement rippled over his fingers and brought him to his senses.

What the hell was wrong with him?

This woman had just spent hours sleeping in his easy chair to help him with his son and he repaid her by groping her in his front room?

He couldn't seem to catch his breath, but he did his best as he dropped his arms from around her.

She was breathing hard, too, her hair loose from the messy bun she had been wearing. She gazed at him out of eyes that looked huge and impossibly dark.

She had been so sweet to him, so comforting and warm when he needed it most. He had been at the lowest point he could remember in a long time and she had held him and lifted him out of it. In return, he had let his hunger for her overwhelm all his common sense.

"I'm sorry," he said, his voice ragged. "I don't know what happened there."

"Do not apologize." Her voice wobbled a little bit.

"Are you…okay? I didn't hurt you, did I?"

Her gaze narrowed, as if he had offended her somehow. "You only kissed me. I am not like some glass figure in my store falling off the shelf. I cannot be broken by a kiss, Wyatt."

There was his name again. It seemed to slide under his skin, burrowing somewhere in his chest.

What was he going to do about her?

Nothing, he told himself again. He just had to suck it up and forget about the way her kisses made him feel alive for the first time in years.

"I'll walk you upstairs."

She didn't argue, much to his relief. She only turned away, gathered her things and called to Fiona, then she and her dog hurried up the stairs.

Wyatt caught up with them on the second landing. The dog seemed to give him a baleful look, but he thought maybe that was just a trick of the low lighting out here in the stairway.

At her apartment, Rosa unlocked the door and opened it. "Good night."

Before he could thank her again for helping him out with Logan, she slipped inside and closed the door firmly behind her.

Wyatt stood for a moment, staring at the beautiful woodwork on the door, a match to his own two floors below.

That was as clear a dismissal as he could imagine. She had literally shut the door in his face.

He couldn't blame her. It was now nearly three and he knew she had to open the store early the next day, just as he had another shift.

He turned and headed down the stairs. He gripped

the railing and told himself the shakiness in his legs was only exhaustion.

Something told him it was more than that. That kiss had just about knocked his legs right out from under him.

He was falling for her.

The reality of it seemed to hit him out of nowhere and he nearly stumbled down the last few steps as if the fabled ghost of Brambleberry House had given him a hard shove.

No. He couldn't be falling for Rosa. Or for anyone else, for that matter.

He didn't *want* to fall in love again. He had been through that with Tori. Once was enough, thanks all the same. These feelings growing inside him were only attraction, not love. Big difference.

Yes, he liked her. She was sweet, compassionate, kind. And, okay, he thought about her all the time. That wasn't love. Infatuation, maybe.

He wouldn't let it be love.

The next day, Rosa was deadheading flowers in one of the gardens when Jen drove up in her rickety car, now running but not exactly smoothly. It shimmied a little as it idled, then she turned off the engine.

Rosa waved and Jen and Addie walked over.

"Hello, there," Rosa said. "How did the interviews go?"

"Good. Great, actually. The school offered me a job on the spot."

"Oh, that's terrific! We should celebrate. Have you eaten?"

"Yes. Sorry. Addie wanted a Happy Meal today."

"No problem. Maybe we can celebrate later. I have a bottle I've been saving for something special."

"It's a deal, as long as it goes with your famous chocolate-chip cookies."

Rosa had to smile. She had taken a plate down before she headed to the store and left them outside Jen's front door.

"Can we help you with the gardening?"

"Yes. Of course. That would be great. Thank you."

Addie frowned. "Why are you pulling all the flowers, Rosa? That's naughty. My mommy says I can't pick the flowers or they die."

She smiled, charmed by the girl even as she felt a little ache in her heart. "I am not picking *all* the flowers. Only the ones that have finished blooming and have started to die. This way the flower plant has more energy to make new blossoms. You can help, if you want to. You just pop off the flower if it's brown or the petals have come off and put it in the bucket there."

"I can do that!"

Addie began the task, humming a little as she worked, which made Rosa smile.

"I have a confession," Jen said after a few moments. "After my interview, I probably could have come in and worked this afternoon. Instead, I picked up Addie from day care early and we played hooky for most of the afternoon."

"Good for you," Rosa said, feeling a twinge of envy. "Did you do something fun?"

"Yes. It was wonderful. We made a huge sandcastle and then played in the water a bit, then took a hike around the state park near Arch Cape."

"Oh, I love that area. It is so beautiful and green, like walking through a movie, with all the ferns and moss."

"Yes. Addie thought it looked like a fairy land."

Oh, Addie was cute. She had such an innocent sweetness about her. Rosa hoped she could keep it forever.

"So," Jen said after a moment. "You and Detective Gorgeous. Is that a thing now?"

Rosa, yanking out a nasty weed that had dug its roots in deep, almost lost her balance.

She could feel her face grow hot. "Why would you say such a thing?"

"I *might* have heard two people going up the stairs together in the early hours of the morning."

Rosa could only be grateful they had kissed in his apartment and not in the stairway for her friend to overhear.

"So are you two…dating or something?"

She had a sudden fervent wish that she could say yes. The idea of doing something as ordinary and sweet as dating Wyatt seemed wonderful but completely out of reach.

"No. We are not dating. Only friends." *Who kiss each other as if we can't get enough*, she wanted to add, but, of course, she couldn't say that to Jen.

"He needed someone to watch his son last night while he went out on an emergency police call. His sister is out of town and he did not have anyone else to ask. It was an easy thing for me to help him."

Jen made a face. "Too bad. I was thinking how cute you two would be together. And it's obvious his son likes you."

Rosa could feel herself flush. She was coming to adore both Townsend males, entirely too much. "I am not interested in dating anyone right now." *No matter how gorgeous.*

Jen nodded and carefully plucked away at a rose that had bloomed past its prime. "I totally understand that and feel the same way. I'm not sure I'll ever date again."

Her emphatic tone made Rosa sad. Jen had so much love inside her to give. It was a shame that one bad experience had soured her so much on men.

"Your husband, he was a good man, yes?" Jen and her husband had met after college and Rosa had only met him at their wedding, and the few times they had socialized afterward, before she moved to Oregon.

"Oh, yes," Jen said softly. "Ryan was wonderful. After he died, I never thought I would find anyone again."

She plucked harder at the rose bush. "I wish I hadn't ever entertained the idea of dating again. I obviously don't pick well."

Rosa frowned. "You did well with your husband. Nothing else that happened to you is your fault. I wish I could help you see that. You had no way of knowing things would turn out like they have."

"That's what I tell myself," Jen said quietly. "Most of the time I believe it. In the middle of the night when I think about everything, it's harder to convince myself."

"You did nothing wrong," Rosa repeated in a low voice so that Addie didn't overhear. "You went on three dates with this man then tried to stop dating him when you began to see warning signs. You had no way of knowing he would become obsessive."

Jen sighed. "I still wish I could go back and do everything over again. I wish I had said no the very first time he asked me out."

"I know. I am sorry."

Rosa became angry all over again every time she thought about how one man's arrogance and refusal to accept rejection had forced Jen to flee her life and live in fear.

She was so glad her friend seemed to be trying to put the past behind her and make plans for the future.

"And while I don't think I am the best judge of character right now and don't seem to pick well for myself, I do like Detective Townsend. He seems very kind and he is a wonderful father."

Rosa could not disagree. She felt a little ache in her heart at the reminder that she and Wyatt could not be together. Soon, he and his son would be moving out of Brambleberry House.

"He is a good man and, I think, cares very much about helping people."

She paused, compelled to press the situation. "He would help you, you know. You should tell him what is going on."

"I don't know about that."

"I do. Wyatt is a man you can trust. While he is living here, he can look around for anything unusual. Like having security on site."

"I suppose it is a little like that."

Rosa nodded. "That is one of the reasons I agreed to let him move in. I was worried about you and thought it might make you more comfortable to know he is only downstairs."

Jen gave her a sidelong look. "You mean it wasn't because of those beautiful blue eyes?" she teased.

Rosa flushed and tried to pretend she was inordinately fascinated with clipping back a climbing vine. "Does he have blue eyes? I do not believe I had noticed."

Jen snorted a little, which made Rosa smile. She was happy to be a subject of teasing if it could bring a smile to Jen's face.

"You said you're not interested in dating. Why is that?"

"I date," Rosa protested. "I went out three weeks ago to a concert down in Lincoln City."

"With a seventy-five-year-old widower who had an extra ticket."

"Mr. Harris is very sweet. And also lonely, since he lost his wife."

"You know you don't have to take care of everyone else in town. You should save a little of your energy for going after what you want."

If only it could be that easy. She knew what she wanted. She also knew she could not have it.

She didn't have a chance to answer before a vehicle pulled into the driveway. She stood up, suddenly breathless when she recognized Wyatt's SUV. She had not seen him since that emotional, passionate kiss the night before and wasn't sure how to act around him.

He climbed out, and a moment later opened the back door for his son, who hopped out and raced over to them.

"Logan! Hi, Logan!" Addie made a beeline for the boy, who waved at her.

"Hi, Addie. Your hands are muddy."

"I'm picking flowers. Rosa said I could, to help the other flowers grow better."

"Remember, you should only pick the flowers when a grown-up tells you it's okay," Jen said.

She looked momentarily worried, as if afraid Addie would wander through the entire beautiful gardens of the house pulling up the flowers willy-nilly.

"I want to help pick flowers. Can I?" Logan asked Rosa.

"You will have to ask your father if he does not mind."

The father in question drew nearer and she felt tension and awareness stretch between them. He gave her a wary smile, as if he didn't quite know how to act this evening, either. Seeing his unease helped her relax a little.

Yes, they had shared an intense, emotional kiss. That didn't mean things had to be awkward between them.

"Can I pick flowers?" Logan asked Wyatt. "Rosa said it's okay."

"We are taking away the dead and dying flowers to make room for new growth," she told him.

"I want to help, too," Logan said.

"Fine with me. As long as you do what Rosa says."

"Not a bad philosophy for life in general," Jen said, which made Rosa roll her eyes. She wasn't handling her own life so perfectly right now. Not when she was in danger of making a fool of herself over Wyatt.

"Is there something I can do to help?" Wyatt asked. "Were you trying to hang this bird feeder?"

She followed his gaze to the feeder she had left near the sidewalk.

"Yes. It fell down during the wind we had the other night. I was going to get the ladder and hang it back up."

"That would be a good job for Logan and me. Let me put our groceries away and I'll be right back out to do that for you."

"I'm sure you have enough to do at your house. You don't need to help me with my chores."

"Hanging a birdhouse is the least I can do after you pinch-hit for me last night with Logan."

To Rosa's dismay, she felt her face heat again. Oh, she was grateful her blushes were not very noticeable. She felt as red as those roses.

She couldn't seem to help it, especially when all she could think about was being in his arms the night before, his mouth on hers, and the way he had clung to her.

Something seemed to have shifted between them, as if they had crossed some sort of emotional line.

She, Jen and the children continued clearing out the flower garden and moved to another one outside the bay window of Logan's room.

A few moments later, Wyatt came out of the house. He had changed out of his work slacks, jacket and tie into jeans and a T-shirt that seemed to highlight his strong chest and broad shoulders.

"Is the ladder in the shed?" he asked.

"Yes. It should be open."

"Come help me, Logan. You, too, Addie. This might be a job for three of us."

She watched them go to the shed and a moment later Wyatt emerged carrying the ladder mostly by himself, with each of the children holding tightly to it as if they were actually bearing some of the weight, which she knew they were not.

"He's really great with kids," Jen murmured.

Maybe so. That didn't make him great for *Rosa*.

It did not take him long to rehang the birdhouse in the tree she pointed out. While she would have liked to hang it higher up on the tree, on a more stable branch, she knew she would not be able to refill the feeder easily without pulling out a ladder each time.

After Wyatt and his little crew returned the ladder to the shed, they came back out and she set them to work helping her clear out the rest of the weeds and dead blossoms in the garden.

Her back was beginning to ache from the repetitive motion, but Rosa would not have traded this moment for anything. There was something so peaceful in working together on a summer evening with the air sweet from the scent of flowers and the sun beginning to slide into the ocean.

"So how did you two meet?" Wyatt asked them.

"College," Jen replied promptly. "We were assigned as roommates our very first day and became best friends after that."

Both of them had been apprehensive first-year college students. Rosa had been quite certain she was in over her head. She had only been speaking English for three years. She hadn't known how she would make it through college classes. But Jen had instantly taken her under her wing with kindness and support.

She owed her a huge debt that she knew she could never repay.

"Here you are, living as roommates again, of a sort," Wyatt said casually.

"Yes," Jen answered. "Isn't it funny how life works sometimes? I was looking for a change and Rosa had an empty apartment. It worked out for both of us."

Wyatt looked at the children, now playing happily on the tree swing. "What about Addie's father? Is he in the picture?"

Jen gazed down at the flowers, grief washing across

her features. "Unfortunately, no. He died two years ago of cancer. Melanoma."

"I'm sorry," Wyatt said gently.

He knew what it was to lose someone, too, Rosa thought. In fact, the two of them would be perfect for each other. So why did the idea of them together make her heart hurt?

Jen sighed and rose to face him. "I might as well tell you, Jen Ryan is not really my name."

Rosa held her breath, shocked that her friend had blurted the truth out of nowhere like that. She could tell Wyatt was shocked, as well, though he did his best to hide it.

"Isn't it?"

"Well, it's not wholly a lie. My name is Jenna Michelle Haynes. Ryan was my late husband's name."

He studied her. "Are you using his name for your surname now as some kind of homage?"

"No." She looked at Rosa as if asking for help, then straightened her shoulders and faced Wyatt. Rosa could see her hands clenching and unclenching with nerves. "Actually, if you want the truth, I'm hiding from a man."

Chapter 11

Wyatt stared, shocked that she had told him, though not really by what she said.

He had suspected as much, judging by her nervous behavior and the way Rosa was so protective of her. He just didn't know the details.

He suddenly felt as protective of her as Rosa did. Who would want to hurt this fragile woman and her darling little girl?

He immediately went into police mode. "Who is he? Can you tell me? And what did he do to make you so afraid?"

She sighed and looked at the children, who were laughing in the fading sunshine as Logan pushed Addie on the swings. The scene seemed innocent and sweet, completely incongruous to anything ugly and terrifying.

She swallowed hard and couldn't seem to find the

words until Rosa moved closer, placing a supportive arm through hers. Jen gave her a look of gratitude before facing him again.

"His name is Aaron Barker. He's also a police officer in the small Utah town where I was living after my husband died. He… We went out three times. Three dates. That's all."

Rosa squeezed her arm and Jen gripped her hand. One of the hardest parts of his job was making people relive their worst moments. It never seemed to get easier. He didn't want to make her rehash all the details, but he couldn't help her if he didn't know what had happened.

She seemed to sense that because after a moment, she went on. "Aaron was very nice at first. Showering me with affection, gifts, food. Sending flowers to the school where I taught. I was flattered. I was lonely and—and I liked him. But then he started pushing me too hard, already talking about marriage. After three dates."

She shook her head. "I finally had to tell him he was moving too fast for me and that I didn't think I was ready to start dating again."

Her voice seemed to trail off and she shivered a little, though the evening was warm. He didn't like the direction this story was taking. It had to be grim to send her fleeing from her home to Oregon.

"What happened?"

"He wouldn't take no for an answer. He kept asking me out, kept bringing me gifts. I finally had to be firm and tell him we weren't a good match and I wasn't going to change my mind. I thought he understood, but then he started driving past in his squad car at all hours of the day and night. He kept calling and texting, sometimes dozens of times a day. I had to turn my phone off. I went out to dinner one day with another teacher, a coworker and friend who happens to be a man. Nothing romantic, just friends, but that night Aaron sent me a long, vitriolic email, calling me a whore, saying if he couldn't have me, no one could, and all kinds of other terrifying things. I knew he must have been watching me."

"Why didn't you report him to the police?"

"I tried but this was a small town. The police chief was his uncle, who wouldn't listen to me. He wouldn't even take my complaint. I tried to go to the county sheriff's department but they said it was a personnel issue for our town's police department. I think they just didn't want to bother and didn't want to upset Aaron's uncle."

Again, Wyatt had to fight down his anger. He knew how insular small-town police departments and their surrounding jurisdictions sometimes could be. Often, police officers for one agency didn't want to get other agency police officers in trouble.

He had also been involved in stalking investigations and knew just how difficult the perpetrators could be to prosecute. Most laws were weak and ineffective, leaving the victim virtually powerless to stop what could be years of torture.

"This went on for months," Jen said. "I can't explain how emotionally draining it was to be always afraid."

Rosa made a small sound, her features distressed. He sensed she was upset for her friend but had to wonder if there was something else behind her reaction. Why wouldn't she tell him her secrets, like Jen was finally doing?

"I understand," Wyatt said quietly. "I have worked

these kinds of cases before. I know how tough they can be on the victims."

"Aaron was relentless. Completely relentless. I changed my number, my email, closed down my social-media accounts, but he would find a new way to reach me. He…started making threats. Veiled at first and then more overt. When he mentioned Addie in one of his messages, I quit my teaching job and moved closer to my sister, about an hour away, but the night after I moved, my tires were slashed. Somehow he found me anyway."

So things had taken an even uglier turn. Wyatt wasn't surprised.

"How did you end up here?"

"Rosa happened to reach out to me out of the blue, right in the middle of everything. We hadn't talked in a while and she was just checking up on me. Calling to wish me a happy birthday. I didn't want to tell her, but everything just gushed out and I finally told her everything that had been going on."

She squeezed Rosa's arm. "I don't know what I would have done without her. I was telling her that tonight. She invited me to come stay with her here for a while. She offered me a job and an apartment. It seemed perfect, and honestly, I didn't know what else to do."

"I only wish I had known earlier what was happening to you," Rosa said, looking guilty. "I should have called you sooner."

"Don't ever think that. You reached out right when I was at my lowest point and offered me a chance to escape."

Jen turned back to Wyatt. "I packed up what we had and drove as far as Boise. Maybe I watch too much

Dateline, but I traded my car on the spot at a used-car lot, in case Aaron had put some kind of tracker on my vehicle, then I drove here."

"That was smart."

"I don't know about that. I had a nice little late-model SUV with four-wheel drive that was great for the Utah winters. Now I've got a junker. It was probably the best swap the dealer ever made. But it got us here to Brambleberry House, where I have felt safe for the first time in months."

"I am so glad," Rosa said.

"I can't tell you how nice it has been not to constantly look over my shoulder."

"Do you think he's given up?" Wyatt hated to ask but didn't have a choice.

Her expression twisted with distress. "I want to think so. I hope so. But I don't know. I don't know how to find out without possibly revealing my new location."

"He was obsessed," Rosa said, placing a protective arm around her friend. "Jenna is only telling you a small portion of the things this man has done to her."

Wyatt hoped the man had given up, though he worried that by fleeing, she had only stoked his unhealthy obsession.

Moving several states away might not be enough to escape a determined stalker, especially not one with law-enforcement experience.

"Thank you for telling me this. I know it wasn't easy, but you've done the right thing. I'll do what I can to help you. You said his name is Aaron Barker?"

"That's right."

"Do you have a picture or description?"

"Yes. I can email you a picture and also link you to his social media."

"Texting me is better. He might have hacked into your email."

"He's done that before but I changed my account and password."

That might not be the deterrent she hoped. Someone determined enough could find ways around just about anything.

"Once you get me a picture of him and a description, I'll pass it around to other officers in the local PD and sheriff's department so we can be on the lookout. You're in Cannon Beach now and we take care of our own."

"Thank you." Jen looked overwhelmed to have someone else on her side. He understood. Victims of stalking could feel so isolated and alone, certain no one else would understand or even believe them and that their ordeal would never end.

"You're welcome."

He glanced at Rosa and found her looking at him with such warmth and approval that he couldn't seem to look away.

Addie came running over, with Logan close behind.

"Mommy," she said, tugging on Jen's shirt, "I have to go to the bathroom."

Jen gave her a distracted look then seemed to sharpen her focus on her child. "Right. The door is locked. I'll get it for you."

She turned back to Wyatt. "Thank you," she said again. "I'll get you that picture."

"That's the best thing you can do right now."

"I'm glad I told you. Rosa was right."

She gave Rosa a look he couldn't quite interpret, but

one that left him feeling as if he had missed something significant, and then Jen grabbed her daughter's hand and hurried for the house.

After she left, Wyatt turned to Rosa and found her looking at him with that same expression of warmth and approval.

"What were you right about?" he asked.

She shrugged. "I told her she could trust you. That you would help her if you could."

If she believed that, why wouldn't she trust him herself?

He could not ask. "I don't know how much I can do. I hope she's right, that he has lost interest."

"But you do not think so."

He couldn't lie. "If the man was willing to break the law to hack into her emails and completely disrupt her life to that extent, I can't see him giving up easily. I think he will keep searching until he finds her."

"What can we do?"

"Not a great deal unless he does something overt. I'm sorry."

"I feel so helpless."

"I know. It's a terrible feeling. I'll do a little internet sleuthing and see what I can dig up on the guy without coming right out and contacting his department. I don't want to run the risk of him getting wind that a detective in Oregon is looking into him, or that will certainly clue him in that she's here. Meanwhile, I'll circulate the picture around here when she gives me one and we will keep our eyes open."

It didn't sound like much, even to Wyatt. He hated that he couldn't do more. If this Aaron Barker was obsessed enough about Jenna and Addie, he would figure out a way to find them.

"Why can't some men take no for an answer?" she asked quietly.

He gave her a searching look but she quickly shifted her gaze away.

"It usually has to do with power and control. And some men just can't accept rejection."

"She has already been through so much, losing the man she loved with all her heart. It is not fair."

"No. It's not. I hate when any man hurts or threatens a woman, but I especially hate when he's in law enforcement."

"Thank you for believing her. That was the most important thing. Everyone else she told thought she was making it up to get attention or to get this man in trouble."

"You believed her."

"I know fear when I see it," Rosa said simply. "She is afraid or she would not have taken her daughter away from her family and her friends."

Something told him Rosa knew plenty about fear, as well. He wanted to press her to tell him but held his tongue.

"Have you had dinner?" he asked instead. "We were about to order takeout from the Thai place in town. Buying you dinner is the least I can do for your help last night."

She looked shocked by the invitation. For a moment, he thought she was about to say yes. She looked at Logan, who was now digging in the dirt nearby, with a softness in her eyes that touched him deeply.

After a moment, she looked back at Wyatt, her expression shielded again.

"No, thank you."

He wasn't expecting the outright rejection and didn't know what to say for a few seconds. "If you don't like Thai food, there's a good Indian place with fabulous curry that just opened on the other side of town. I've heard they deliver, too. Or we can hit up the trusty taco truck down the beach."

"I like Thai food," she said, her voice low.

He gazed at her, confused. Was it *him* she didn't like? "Have you already eaten, then?"

She shook her head. "No. I'm not really hungry and I have much work to do tonight."

"We can help you after we grab dinner," he suggested.

After a moment, she sighed, looking distressed again. "I...think it is best if we do not spend a great deal of time together."

"Why not?" He was either being particularly dense or she was being obtuse. "I thought we were friends. That's what you said last night."

"Yes. And then you kissed me and I forgot about being friends and...wanted more."

He felt his face heat up. He could be such an idiot sometimes. Did he really think they could go back to a casual friendship after he had basically had a breakdown in her arms the night before, and then kissed her with all the pent-up loneliness and need inside him?

"Neither of us is looking for romance right now," Rosa went on, deliberately looking away from him. "I know this. But when you kiss me, I forget."

He did, too. When he kissed her, when he felt her

arms around him and her soft mouth under his and the curves he longed to explore, Wyatt wanted to forget everything and get lost in the wonder and magic of holding her.

Rosa was right. Neither of them was looking for romance. The more time they spent together, the harder it was becoming for him to remember that.

It would be better to keep their distance until his house was fixed, when he and Logan would move out. Once things were back to normal and he didn't run the risk of bumping into her every time he came home, they would be able to go back to their regular lives.

No more moonlit kisses on the stairway, no more quiet talks on the front porch of Brambleberry House.

Just him and his son and his work.

The future seemed to stretch out ahead of him, gray as a January day.

What if he was beginning to want more?

Chapter 12

A week later, he stood at his sister's kitchen sink, helping Carrie thread vegetables onto skewers for the grill.

"Thanks for having us for dinner. I've been so busy, I haven't had much time to cook and I think Logan is getting a little tired of the taco truck for dinner."

Carrie laughed. "Surely not. Who could be tired of that?"

He impaled a yellow squash on the metal skewer, followed by a mushroom and then a slice of onion. "I feel like I haven't seen you since the Fourth. Tell me all about your trip."

After taking Bella to the concert in Portland a week earlier, Joe and Carrie had driven down to San Francisco for a few days with her.

"It was fun. We did all the touristy things. Alcatraz, riding a cable car, going to Fisherman's Wharf. And, of course, shopping. You can't visit San Francisco without spending too much money. We bought some cute school clothes for the new year."

He needed to start thinking about the new school year. Logan would be starting second grade. Wyatt still had a hard time believing he was that old.

He was finishing the last of the skewers while Carrie did some shrimp and some chicken when the doorbell rang.

"Are you expecting someone else?"

His sister somehow managed to look coy. "Sounds like Bella is getting it. That will be Rosa."

He nearly impaled his finger instead of a mushroom. "Rosa is coming to dinner, as well?"

He had been trying to stay away from her the past week, at her request. How the hell was he supposed to do that when his sister invited them both over for dinner?

"Yes. I happened to drop into her store today and mentioned Joe was going to grill tonight, and we had plenty. She seemed a little down and I thought it might cheer her up a bit. I hope you don't mind."

Why was she down? He wanted to rush out and ask if she was all right but made himself stay put.

"And you didn't think to tell me until now that she was coming?"

"Does it matter?"

Yes. Most certainly. He would have refused Carrie's last-minute invitation if he had known the dinner party included a woman who had specifically told him they should avoid spending more time together.

"I just wish you had told me."

Carrie made a face. "I'm sorry. I just thought one more person for dinner wouldn't make a difference."

He frowned. This was the second time in only a few weeks that Carrie had invited them both over for a meal at the same time. That couldn't be a coincidence, could it? She had already mentioned she thought he should think about dating her friend.

Did his sister suspect he was beginning to have feelings for Rosa?

If Carrie had any idea about the attraction that simmered between them, Wyatt knew she wouldn't hesitate to do whatever she could to push them together as much as possible. She wouldn't be subtle about it, either.

He wanted to say something but before he could, Rosa and Bella came into the kitchen, Bella chattering a mile a minute about their trip.

Rosa didn't seem to notice him at first. She was listening intently to Bella's story about the ghost tour they went on, and smiling at the girl's animation.

The two of them shared similar coloring. The same dark hair and dark eyes. With their heads together like that, they looked as if they could be sisters, catching up after a long time away.

He frowned suddenly as a crazy thought flitted across his brain. No. Impossible. He pushed it away just as Rosa lifted her head and caught sight of him.

Her eyes widened with shock. "Oh. Wyatt. Hello. I did not know you would be here."

If she had known, he had a feeling she would have refused his sister's invitation. Well, they were both here. Might as well make the best of it.

"Hi," he answered, just as Logan came in from the

family room, where he had been playing a video game with Joe.

He, at least, looked thrilled about the other dinner guest.

"Rosa! Hi, Rosa!" he exclaimed. He rushed to her and wrapped his arms around her waist as if he hadn't seen her for months.

It had only been a few nights ago when he had gone up to her apartment for another Spanish lesson and had come back down naming every single kind of fruit they had in their house in Spanish.

"Buenas," she said to him. "How are you tonight?"

"I'm good. Guess what? We're having *piña* and *fresas* tonight."

"Delicious. Pineapple and strawberries. My favorite."

"I didn't know strawberries were *fresas*. I don't think I learned that in Spanish class last year. How did you know?" Bella asked.

"Rosa's teaching me Spanish so I can talk better to my friend Carlos."

Carrie beamed at them and gave Wyatt a significant look. Yeah. She was definitely matchmaking, despite the way he had basically told her to stand down the last time.

He was going to have to do whatever he could to deflect any of Carrie's efforts in that department.

To his relief, his sister was not overtly obvious over dinner, though she did suggest he and Rosa take a look at how her climbing roses were growing, something they both managed to avoid by changing the subject.

Having his sister and her family there, along with Logan, helped make things a little less awkward between them, but he still couldn't help remembering his hurt when she had told him they should avoid being together.

The food was good, at least. Carrie had a great marinade he always enjoyed and Joe was a whiz at the grill. Really, any time Wyatt didn't have to cook, he was happy.

Rosa was too busy talking to Bella and Logan to seem bothered by his presence.

After they ate, Rosa was the first to stand up. "Thank you for dinner, but things were so chaotic as I was leaving work that I am afraid I was not thinking. I just remembered I left some invoices I need to pay tonight on my desk. I would not want to leave them there overnight. Will you excuse me?"

Carrie made a face. "You're not staying for dessert? It's homemade vanilla ice cream that Bella helped me make this afternoon."

Rosa gave a vague smile. "It sounds very good but I really do need to go. Thank you, though."

She hugged both females and Logan, then waved to Wyatt and Joe before hurrying away.

After she left, some of the sparkle seemed to go out of the evening. Wyatt knew he wasn't the only one who felt it.

She was definitely trying to avoid him. He could only hope that everyone else didn't guess that her reasons for leaving so abruptly had anything to do with him.

"I'll have ice cream," Logan said.

"Same here," Bella said. "It's delicious."

He had to agree. It *was* delicious. But all that frozen, creamy sweetness still couldn't remove the sour taste in his mouth.

"Dinner was great," he said after everyone had finished dessert. "Logan, let's help with dishes."

His son groaned a little but stood up to help clear away plates and carry them back inside the house.

When the dishwasher was loaded, Bella asked if she and Logan could take Hank for a walk before Wyatt left with the dog for home. He almost said no but was in no hurry to return to the tension of Brambleberry House.

"Sure. I can wait a little longer."

Logan was staying the night again with his aunt and uncle because Wyatt had an early meeting.

Joe got a phone call from his parents, who lived in Arizona, and excused himself to talk to them for a few moments, leaving Wyatt alone with Carrie.

"How's the house coming?" Carrie asked after her husband left the room.

"Almost there, I'm happy to report. We should be able to move back in another few weeks."

"That seems fast. But living at Brambleberry House worked out well, didn't it?"

A week ago, he would have said yes. "It's been fine. Logan has enjoyed having his own room again. It's a lovely old house and our apartment is roomier than our actual house."

"I'm glad. And your neighbors are nice, both of them. I like Jen and Rosa."

That was another area of frustration. He hadn't been able to make much progress in Jen's situation, other than to alert the department and do a little online sleuthing. Aaron Barker seemed to be a good cop, from what he could find out. He had no black marks on his reputation that Wyatt could find after a cursory search.

At least nothing suspicious seemed to have happened

since Jen had told him about her stalker. He had been extra vigilant but hadn't learned anything new.

"Rosa is lovely, isn't she?" Carrie said in a casual voice that did not fool him for an instant.

He finally voiced the suspicion that had been nagging at him since he discovered Rosa had also been invited to dinner.

"I don't suppose there's any chance you're trying to push Rosa and me together, even after I told you not to, is there?"

"Me? Would I do that? Don't be silly." She gave him a shocked sort of look but he knew his sister well enough to see past it easily. She would do that kind of thing in a heartbeat, if she thought he might have the slightest interest in Rosa.

"Are you sure? This is the second time you've invited us both to dinner. Come to think of it, you seemed pretty determined that I move into her empty apartment at Brambleberry House."

"Only because it was the perfect solution when you yourself talked about moving out! I was only trying to help. As for dinner, it just so happens she is my dear friend and you are my brother. I like spending time visiting with each of you. I can't help it if sometimes those visits overlap."

"Can't you?"

"I didn't realize it would be a problem," she said rather stiffly. "I thought you and Rosa were friends. Logan is always talking about how she's teaching him Spanish and how much he loves her dog and how you go out for tacos together."

He frowned. "That was one time, when we bumped into each other at the taco stand. Rosa and I are friends.

That's all. Neither one of us is in the market for a relationship right now. I told you that."

"But you two are perfect for each other!"

Wyatt felt that little tug on his heart again, remembering how Rosa had held him during his moment of despair over the ugly crime scene he had just left, generously offering him a comfort and peace he had desperately needed.

He was beginning to think Carrie was right, at least on one side of the equation. Rosa was perfect for him. Smart, sweet, kind. He loved how warm she was with Logan and how compassionate and protective she was for her friend.

None of that mattered. Not when she had made it clear she wanted nothing to do with him except friendship.

"It's not going to happen. Get it out of your head, please. I would hate for you to make things awkward between us."

Carrie looked deeply disappointed. "It's just that I love her, you know? I want her to be happy. I want *you* to be happy. Why shouldn't you be happy together? I guess I just thought…after everything she's been through, she deserved a wonderful guy like you."

He frowned. "That's the second time you've made reference to something in her past. What do you know? What has she been through?"

Carrie immediately looked away, but not before he saw guilt flash in her eyes. "Life can be hard for people trying to make it in a new country. She came here with nothing. She didn't even speak the language well. How fortunate she was to find her adoptive family, Anna Galvez's brother and his wife."

There was something else here. Something he couldn't quite put his finger on. A suspicion had begun to take root but it was one he didn't even dare ask his sister.

What if he was wrong?

Meantime, he had to do what he could to divert Carrie's attention and prevent her from meddling further between the two of them.

"Rosa is an extraordinary woman. I agree. But I'm not looking for anybody, no matter how extraordinary. Got that?"

She looked as if she wanted to argue, but to his relief, she finally sighed. "Fine. I won't invite you both to dinner, unless it's a party that includes a bunch of other people."

Would he be able to handle even that much? Right now, he wasn't sure. At least he would be moving away from Brambleberry House within the next few weeks. When he wasn't living downstairs from her, perhaps he could stop dreaming about her and wishing he could hold her again.

Chapter 13

It was fully dark when Rosa returned to Brambleberry House after stopping at By-The-Wind and running the bills to the post-office drop box.

She hadn't been lying about the invoices. She really had forgotten them, though mailing them certainly could have waited until the next day. That had been sheer fiction, an excuse to escape the tension between her and Wyatt.

She always loved spending time with the Abbotts. Carrie was invariably warm and kind and Joe treated her like a beloved younger sister.

And then there was Bella, full of energy and fun and enthusiasm for life. Her mood always seemed to rub off on Rosa, leaving her happier than when she had arrived.

This time, though, Rosa couldn't shake a deep sense of melancholy.

She knew the reason. Because Wyatt and Logan had been there. Spending time with them was beginning to make her ache deep inside.

She knew she was setting herself up for heartbreak. She could sense it hovering, just out of sight.

She was falling for them. Both of them.

Logan was impossible to resist. His sweet personality and eagerness to learn touched something deep inside of her. She would be so sad when he was no longer a regular part of her life.

And Wyatt. She brushed a lock of hair from her eyes. It was very possible that Wyatt was the most wonderful man she had ever met. She wanted to wrap her arms around him and not let go.

She could not, though. Rosa knew she could not have what she wanted.

She knew people who spent their entire lives wanting something other than what they had. Rosa tried not to be that person.

As a girl growing up with little in the way of material things, she had become used to that feeling of lack. Mostly, she had learned to ignore it, instead finding happiness with what she *did* have.

She was part owner in a business she loved running, she lived in a beautiful house at the seaside, she had cherished friends and a loving family. Most of the time, those things were enough.

Once in a while, though, like on moonlit summer nights, she caught glimpses of the future she might have had if not for a few foolish choices, and it made her heart ache.

Rosa sighed, a sad sound that seemed to echo in the emptiness of her apartment. Fiona nudged at her leg, resting her chin on Rosa's knee and gazing at her out of eyes that seemed filled with empathy.

Sometimes the dog seemed to sense her emotions keenly and offered exactly the right thing to lift her mood.

"You want to go for a walk, don't you?"

Fiona wagged her tail wildly in agreement. Rosa sighed again. She had let her dog out when she first came home a short time earlier, but apparently that was not enough for her, especially when the work day had been so hectic and she hadn't had time to take her on a walk.

Rosa was tired and not really in the mood for a nighttime walk. Part of being a responsible pet owner, though, was doing what she didn't always feel like doing when it was in the best interest of her beloved Fi.

"Okay. Let's find your leash."

Fiona scampered to the hook by the door of the apartment, where Rosa kept all the tools necessary for a walk. A hoodie, Fi's leash, a flashlight, treats and waste bags.

A few moments later, she headed down the steps. They had just reached the bottom when the door to Wyatt's apartment suddenly opened.

She gave a little gasp of surprise when he and Hank came out, the cute little dog all but straining on the leash.

"Oh," Rosa exclaimed. "You startled me."

Wyatt made a face. "Sorry. Hank was in a mood and nothing seemed to be settling him down. I was just going to take him on a quick walk. Are you coming or going?"

"Going. Fiona was in the same mood as Hank."

"Maybe they're talking to each other through the pipes."

Despite her lingering melancholy, Rosa had to smile a little at that idea. Fiona was smart enough that she could probably figure out a way to communicate to other dogs inside the house.

She looked behind him. "Where is Logan?"

"He's sleeping over at Carrie's again. I've got an early meeting tomorrow so they offered to keep him after dinner so I don't have to drag him out of bed so early."

"That is nice of them. Your sister is very kind."

"Truth. She is the best. I would have been lost without her after Tori died. Totally lost. She and Joe have been amazing, basically stepping in to help me parent Logan."

The dogs seemed delighted to see each other, sniffing like crazy with their tails wagging a hundred miles an hour.

She knew it was impossible, but Rosa still could not shake the suspicion that somehow her dog had manipulated events exactly this way, so that she and Wyatt would meet in the entryway of the house.

He opened the door and they both walked out into the evening, lit by a full moon that made her flashlight superfluous.

"Want to walk together?" he asked after a moment.

His suggestion surprised her so much that she did not know how to answer for a moment. Intellectually, she knew she was supposed to be maintaining a careful distance between them. She did not want to fall any harder for him.

How could she say no, though? Especially when she knew her time with him was so fleeting?

"That makes sense, doesn't it?"

"Which direction were you going? To the beach?"

Usually she liked to stick to the paths with streetlights and some traffic when she was walking late at night. Since Wyatt was with her, that wasn't necessary.

"Yes. Let's walk on the beach. The water always calls me."

They walked through the gardens, the air sweet with the scent of flowers and herbs. He opened the gate for her and she and Fiona went first down the path to the sand.

The moon was bright and full, casting a pearly blue light on everything. She certainly did not need her flashlight.

They walked mostly in silence for the first few moments, content to let the sounds of the waves fill the void. Despite everything between them, it was a comfortable silence.

She was the first to break it. "You said at dinner that your house is almost finished. Is everything going the way you like?"

"Yes. We had a few issues early on. It's an old house with electrical issues, which is what started the fire in the first place. I want to make sure everything is exactly right. I think I have been getting on the electrician's nerves a little, but we're getting there."

He gave her a sidelong look. "I'm sure you'll be glad when everything is finished so we can get out of your way."

"You are not in my way," she protested. It wasn't exactly the truth. He was very much in the way of her thoughts constantly. "You know you can stay as long as you need."

"I know. Thank you for that."

"I am sure you are more than ready to be back in your house."

He shrugged. "I suppose."

"You do not sound convinced."

"It's just a house, you know? I bought it after Tori died, when I knew I needed help and the best thing would be to move near Carrie and Joe. That one was available and it was close but it's never really felt like a home."

She had not been to his house and couldn't offer an opinion, but she had to wonder if the house needed a woman's touch.

She did not want to think about any other woman going in and decorating his house with warm, comfortable touches. She wanted to be the one turning his house into a home.

She pushed away the thought.

"You had many changes in a short time. That can be hard for anyone."

"I guess."

They walked in silence for a few more moments, stopping only when Hank lifted his leg against a tuft of grass.

"Carrie said something tonight that made me curious." He spoke slowly, as if choosing his words with care.

"Oh?"

"Something about you. She implied you had a tough time after you came to the United States. It made me wonder again how you came to be adopted after you arrived. That seems unusual. You were a teenager, right?"

Rosa tensed, remembering that horrible time in her life, full of fear and darkness and things she did not like to think about.

"Yes. Fifteen."

"And you didn't have family here or back in Honduras who could have helped you?"

Her heart seemed to squeeze at the memory of her dear mother, who had tried so hard to give Rosa a better life. She gripped Fiona's leash. The dog, who had been cavorting with Hank, suddenly returned to her side as if sensing Rosa's distress.

"No."

"How did you get here?"

That was a long and twisted story.

"I told you my mother died. I had no money and no family. A friend of my mother's told me I could find work at a factory in the city. She helped me find a place to live with some other girls and gave me a little money."

"That's nice."

"Yes. But then some men came to the factory telling us they knew of many jobs we could do across the border. I was afraid and didn't want to, but other girls, my friends, said yes. Then I…had some trouble with my boss at the factory and he fired me."

She thought of how innocent she had been in those days. Her mother had tried to shelter her when she was alive. As a result, Rosa knew little about the world or how to protect herself from men who wanted to take advantage of her. First her boss, then those offering riches and jobs in a new world. She had been monumentally naive, had thought maybe she would be working in another factory in the United States, one that paid better.

She had been so very wrong.

She was not going to tell any of that to Wyatt.

"What did you do then?"

"I came here and shortly after, I met Daniel and Lauren and they took me in and helped me go to school and then become a citizen," she said quickly.

He gave her a searching look through the darkness, as if he knew full well there had to be more to her story. She lifted her chin and continued walking, pretending that Fiona had led her a little ahead of him and Hank.

She didn't want him to press her about this. If he did, she would have to turn around and go back to the house without him. To her relief, he seemed to know she had told him all she was going to about that time.

"They must be very kind people."

She seized gratefully on his words. "The best. I told you Daniel is a sheriff in Utah and Lauren is a doctor. I was very lucky they found me."

She knew it was more than luck. It was a miracle. She had prayed to the Virgin and to her own mother that someone would help her, that she could find some light in the darkness. And then, literally, a light had found her hiding in the back of a pickup truck in the middle of a January storm. She had been beaten and bloodied, and had been semiconscious when Daniel and Lauren had found her. They had pulled her from that pickup truck and had saved her. An answer to her prayers.

They had stood by her then as she had spoken out against those who had hurt her. And they had stood by her later when she had to make the most difficult decision of her life.

"Carrie talked about how much courage it must have taken you to make your way in a new country."

Rosa loved her country and her people. People from Honduras called themselves and each other *Catrachos*, a name that had come to mean resilience and solidarity.

She would always consider herself part *Catracha* but this was her home now.

If her mother had not died, she might have stayed and built a happy life there. She probably would have married young and would have had several children by now.

After Daniel and Lauren rescued her, she had been able to get an education that would have been completely out of reach to her in that small, poor village.

"Courage? No. I had nothing there after my mother died. And here I had a family. People who loved me and wanted the best for me. That was everything to me. It still is."

Wyatt could not doubt the quiet sincerity in her voice. She loved the people who had taken her in.

He was suddenly deeply grateful for them, too. He would have loved the chance to have met them in person to tell them so.

They walked in silence for a few more moments, heading back toward Brambleberry House, which stood like a beacon above the beach a short distance away.

He could tell Rosa did not like talking about this. Her body language conveyed tension. He should let it go now. Her secrets were none of his business, but since she had told him this much, perhaps she would trust him and tell him the rest of it.

"You said you were fifteen when you came here?"

"Yes," she said, her voice clipped.

How had she even made it across several borders? And what about the men who had promised her work in the United States?

He wasn't stupid. He could guess what kind of work they wanted from her and it made him sick to his stomach. Sex trafficking was a huge problem, especially among young girls smuggled in from other countries.

Was that what Daniel and Lauren had rescued her from?

He couldn't seem to find the words to ask. Or to ask her how she had escaped. He was quite sure he would not like the answer.

How was it possible? She was the most loving and giving person he knew, kind to everyone. How could she have emerged from something so ugly to become the person he was falling for?

Maybe he was wrong. He truly hoped he was wrong.

"You could have found yourself in all kinds of danger at that young age."

"Yes."

She said nothing more, only looked ahead at her dog and at the house, now only a hundred feet away.

He thought again of his suspicions earlier that evening at dinner. He was beginning to think they might not be far-fetched, after all.

"I think my sister is right," he said quietly when they reached the beach gate to the house. "You are a remarkable person, Rosa Galvez."

Her face was a blur in the moonlight as she gazed at him, her eyes dark shadows. She shook her head. "I am not. Lauren and Daniel, who reached out to me when I was afraid and vulnerable, they are the remarkable ones."

Tenderness swirled through him. She was amazing and he was falling hard for her. Learning more details about what she had endured and overcome, including the things she hadn't yet shared with him, only intensified his growing feelings.

"We will have to agree to disagree on that one," he finally said. "Every time I'm with you, I find something else to admire."

"Don't," she said sharply. "You don't know."

"I know I think about you all the time. I can't seem to stop."

"You shouldn't."

"I know that. Believe me, I know. But you're in my head now."

And in my heart, he thought, but wasn't quite ready to share that with her yet.

"May I kiss you again?"

Because of what he suspected had happened to her, it became more important than ever to ask permission first and not just take what he wanted.

He thought she would refuse at first, that she would turn into the house. After a long moment, she lifted her face to his.

"Yes," she murmured, almost as if she couldn't help herself.

This kiss was tender, gentle, a mere brush of his mouth against hers.

All the feelings he had been fighting seemed to shimmer to the surface. He could tell himself all he wanted that he was not ready to care for someone again.

He could tell everyone else the same story. That did not make it true.

He had already fallen. Somehow Rosa Galvez, with her kindness and her empathy and her determination to do the right thing, had reached into the bleak darkness where he had been existing and ripped away the heavy curtains to let sunshine flood in again.

He was not sure yet how he felt about that. Some part of him wanted to stay frozen in his sadness. He had loved Tori with all his heart. Their marriage had not been perfect—he wasn't sure any healthy marriage could be completely without differences—but she had been a great mother and a wonderful wife.

Wyatt wasn't sure he was ready to risk his heart again.

But maybe he didn't have a choice. Maybe he had already fallen.

He wrapped his arms around her tightly, wanting to protect her from all the darkness in the world. She made a small sound and nestled against him, as if searching for warmth and safety.

"I lied to my sister," he said, long moments later.

He felt her smile against his mouth. "For shame, Detective Townsend. How did you lie to Carrie?"

He brushed a strand of hair away from her face. "She admitted after you left that she invited us both to dinner because she has some wild idea of matchmaking."

Instead of continuing to smile, as he thought she would, Rosa suddenly looked distressed.

Her eyes widened and her hands slipped away from around his neck. "Oh, no."

He nodded. "I told her to get that idea out of her

head. I told her we were only friends and would never be anything more than that."

She stepped away. "You told her the truth. That is not a lie. We *are* friends."

"But we're more than that, aren't we?"

She folded her hands together, her mouth trembling a little. "No. What you said to her is the truth. We are friends. Only that."

"You can really say that after that kiss?"

"Sharing a few kisses does not make us lovers, Wyatt. Surely you see this."

He wasn't sure why she was so upset but she was all but wringing her hands.

"This thing between us is not exactly your average friendship, either. You have to admit that. I have lots of friends and I don't stay up nights thinking about kissing them."

She made a small, upset sound and reached for her dog's leash.

"We cannot do this anymore, Wyatt. You must see that. I was wrong to let you kiss me. To—to kiss you back. I should have stopped you."

She started moving toward the house. He gazed after her, hurt at her abrupt dismissal of what had felt like an emotional, beautiful moment between them.

He knew she had felt it, as well. Rosa was not the sort of woman who would kiss someone with so much sweetness and eagerness without at least some feeling behind it.

He quickly caught up with her just as she pushed open the beach gate and walked into the Brambleberry House gardens.

"Why are you so determined to push me away? What aren't you telling me?"

"Nothing. I told you before—I am not looking for this in my life right now."

"I wasn't, either, but I think it's found us. I care about you, Rosa. Very much. For the first time since Tori died, I want to spend time with a woman. And I might be crazy but I suspect you wouldn't kiss me if you didn't have similar feelings for me. Am I wrong?"

She was silent for a moment. When she faced him, her chin was up again and her eyes seemed without expression.

"Yes. You are wrong," she said, her voice muted. "I do not have feelings for you. It is impossible. You are the brother of my friend and you are my tenant who will be leaving soon. That is all you are to me, Wyatt. I… You must not kiss me again. Ever. Do you understand this? No matter what, you must not."

She turned and hurried for the house, leaving him staring after her, hurt and confusion and rejection tumbling through him.

She sounded so very certain that he could not question her conviction. Apparently he had misunderstood everything. All this time, he had been falling for her, but the feeling apparently was not mutual.

She had told him they should stay away from each other. Why had he not listened?

He knew the answer to that. His feelings were growing so strong that he couldn't believe they could possibly be one-sided.

Lord, he was an idiot. No different than Jenna's cop, who couldn't accept rejection even after it slapped him in the face.

He should have kept his mouth shut. She had told him over and over that she was not interested in a relationship with him, but he'd been too stubborn to listen.

Now he just had to figure out how he was going to go on without her.

Rosa sat in her darkened apartment a short time later, window open to the ocean and Fiona at her feet. Usually she found solace in the sound of the waves but not now.

This night, it seemed to echo through Brambleberry House, accentuating how very alone she felt.

What had she done? With all her heart, she wished she could go downstairs, knock on his door and tell Wyatt *she* was the one lying now.

I do not have feelings for you. It is impossible. You are the brother of my friend and you are my tenant who will be leaving soon. That is all you are to me, Wyatt.

None of those words were true, of course. Or at least not the whole truth. She cared about Wyatt, more than any man she had ever known. She was falling in love with him. Here in the quiet solitude of her apartment, she could admit the truth.

She realized now that she had started to fall for him the first time she met Carrie's brother with the sad eyes and the adorable little boy.

How could she not love him? He was everything good and kind she admired in a man. He was a loving father, a loyal brother, a dedicated detective. An honorable man.

That was the very reason she had no choice but to push him away. Wyatt deserved a woman with no demons. Someone courageous and good.

If he knew the truth about her and her choices, he would quickly see how wrong he was about her.

The walls of the house did not embrace her with comfort, as they usually did.

Somehow, it felt cold and even sad. For some ridiculous reason, Rosa felt as if she had faced some sort of test and she had failed spectacularly.

It was a silly feeling, she knew. Houses could not be sad.

Fiona lifted her head suddenly and gazed off at nothing, then whimpered for no reason. Rosa frowned. There was no such thing as ghosts, either. And absolutely no reason for her to feel guilty, as if she had failed Abigail somehow.

"I had to push him away," she said aloud, though she wasn't sure just who she was trying to convince. Fiona, Abigail or herself. "Someday he will see that I was right. He will be glad I at least could see that we cannot be together."

Fiona huffed out a breath while Abigail said nothing, of course.

As for Rosa, her heart felt as if it was going to crack apart. She knew it would not. She had been through hard things before—she would figure out a way to survive this.

In a short time, he and his son would be moving out of Brambleberry House and back to their own home. As before, she would only see them occasionally. Maybe on the street, maybe at some town celebration. Maybe even at a party with Joe and Carrie. She could be polite and even friendly.

Wyatt did not ever need to know about these cracks

in her heart, or how hard she found it to think about moving forward with her life without him, and without Logan.

Chapter 14

Somehow, she wasn't sure exactly how, Rosa made it through most of the next week without seeing either Logan or Wyatt.

They seemed to leave early in the morning and come back late at night. She could only guess they were hard at work on the part of renovations Wyatt was handling on their house and getting it ready for their move back.

This guess was confirmed when she came home for lunch one day and found a note tucked into her door.

Repairs to the house are done, the note said in bold, scrawling handwriting. *We will be moving out tomorrow. Wyatt.*

Rosa had to catch her breath as pain sliced through her at the brusque, clipped note and at the message it contained.

Tomorrow. A week earlier than he had planned. He

must have spent every available moment trying to finish things in his eagerness to get out of her house and her life.

She returned to the store with a heavy heart but a sense of relief, as well. She could not begin to put back together the pieces of her life when he was living two floors below her.

Even when she did not see him or Logan, she was still constantly aware they were both so close and yet completely out of her reach.

When she walked into the store, she found Jen laughing at something with a customer. The change in her friend was remarkable. She looked bright and pretty and happy, a far cry from the withdrawn, frightened woman she had been when she first came to Cannon Beach.

Jen finished ringing up the customer with a genuine smile Rosa once had feared she would not see again.

"You are in a good mood," she said.

"Yes. I heard from the online graduate program I've been in touch with. I've been accepted for fall semester and they're offering a financial-aid package that will cover almost the whole tuition."

"That's terrific! Oh, Jen. I'm so happy for you. How will you juggle teaching, graduate school and Addie at the same time?"

"It's going to be tricky but I think I can handle it, especially now that she's starting first grade. I can do the coursework at night after she's in bed. It will take me a few years, but when I'm done, it will open up other career doors for me."

"Oh, I am so happy for you."

Jen beamed at her. "It's all because of you. I never

would have had the courage to even apply if you hadn't been in my corner, pushing me out of my comfort zone."

Rosa might not have a happily-ever-after with the man she was falling in love with. But she had good friends and wanted to think she was making a difference in their lives, a little bit at a time.

"We should celebrate tonight," Rosa said.

"You don't have a hot date?"

She made a face. "Not me. I have no date, hot or otherwise."

"What about our sexy neighbor?" Jen teased.

That terse note of his flashed through her mind again and her chest gave a sharp spasm.

"He will not be our neighbor long. Wyatt and Logan are moving out in the morning."

Jen's smile slid away. "Oh, no! Addie will miss having them around. She has really enjoyed playing with Logan in the evenings. I thought they wouldn't be moving for a few more weeks."

"Apparently, their house is finished. Wyatt left me a note on the door when I went home for lunch and to bring back Fiona."

Jen gave her a sharp look that Rosa pretended not to see.

"My evening is totally free," she said, "and I would love nothing more than to celebrate with you. Do you want to go somewhere?"

Jen gazed out the window. "It looks like it's going to be another beautiful night. I would be just as happy taking Fiona for a walk on the beach and then grabbing dinner at the taco truck. I think Addie would be all over that, too."

Rosa was not sure she would ever be able to eat at the

taco truck without remembering that delightful evening with Logan and Wyatt, but for the sake of her friend, she would do her best.

"Done."

The store was busy with customers the rest of the afternoon. Rosa preferred it that way. Having something to do gave her less time to think.

Jen's shift was supposed to end at five, but during a lull in the hectic pace about a half hour before that, Rosa pulled her aside. "Your shift is almost over and Paula and Juan will be here soon for the evening shift. Why don't you go pick up Addie from her day care and I will meet you at home?"

"Sounds great."

Jen took off her apron, then hung it on the hook in the back room and quickly left.

Rosa was going to miss having her around when school started, not just because she was a good worker, but Rosa enjoyed her company. They made a good team.

She finished ringing up two more customers, then spent a few more moments talking to the married older couple who helped her out a few nights a week during busy summer months.

Finally, she and Fiona walked out into a lovely July evening. The dog was eager for a walk and Rosa was, too. She was looking forward to the evening with Addie and Jen. Tacos and good friends. What was not to enjoy?

When she neared the house, she didn't see Wyatt's SUV. Rosa told herself she was glad.

Perhaps she wouldn't have to see him at all before he moved out the next day.

Fiona went immediately to the backyard. When Rosa followed her, she found Jen and Addie on the tree swing.

Addie's legs were stretched out as she tried to pump and she looked so filled with joy, Rosa had to smile.

"Look at me!" Addie called. "I'm flying!"

"You are doing so well at swinging," Rosa exclaimed.

"I know. I never went so high before."

She almost told her to be careful but caught herself. She wanted all little girls to soar as high as they dared.

"We got home about a half hour ago and haven't even been inside yet," Jen said with a laugh. "Addie insisted she had to swing first."

"It is very fun," Rosa agreed. Addie's excitement and Jen's good mood went a long way to cheering her up.

She might not have everything she wanted but her life could still be rich and beautiful. She had to remember that.

"I noticed the handsome detective isn't home yet. I was going to see if he wanted to come with us to the taco truck."

Jen spoke so casually that Rosa almost missed the mischievous look in her eyes.

Rosa avoided her gaze. "He is probably at his house making sure things are ready for him and Logan to return home tomorrow."

"I'll miss them."

Rosa wasn't sure she liked that pensive note in her friend's voice. Was Jen interested in Wyatt, as well?

Why wouldn't she be? He was a wonderful man and Jen was exactly the sort of woman who could make him happy. The two of them would be very good together, even though the idea of it made Rosa's chest hurt.

"When you are ready to date again, maybe you should think about dating Wyatt. You both have a lot in common."

Jen gave her a shocked, rather appalled look that Rosa thought was out of proportion to her mild suggestion. "Besides being single parents, I don't think so."

"He's a widower, you're a widow," she pointed out.

"True. And that's the only thing we have in common. Don't get me wrong. I like Wyatt a lot. He seems very nice. But I don't think he would be interested in me. His interests appear to lie…elsewhere."

Jen gave her such a significant look that Rosa could feel her face heat.

I care about you, Rosa. Very much. For the first time since Tori died, I want to spend time with a woman. And I might be crazy but I suspect you wouldn't kiss me if you didn't have similar feelings for me.

Wyatt would soon forget her and any wild idea he had that he might have feelings for her.

Before she could answer, she heard a noise and saw someone walk around the side of the house to where they were.

For a moment, with the setting sun shining on his face, she thought it might be Wyatt. Her heart skipped a beat and she felt foolish, hoping he hadn't heard their conversation.

Jen suddenly gasped, her features going instantly pale, and Rosa realized her mistake.

This was not Wyatt. It was a man she didn't recognize.

This man was big, solid, with wide shoulders and a rather thick neck. He had close-cropped brown hair and blue eyes that should have been attractive but were somehow cold.

Fiona, at her feet, instantly rose and growled a little, moving protectively in front of the two of them. That didn't seem to stop the man, who continued walking until he was only a few feet away.

"Jenna," he said, gazing at her friend with an odd, intense, almost possessive look. "Here you are. It is you. It took me forever to track you down."

Rosa knew instantly who this was. Who else could it be? Aaron Barker, the police officer who was stalking Jen and had driven her from her Utah home to Cannon Beach. She should have realized it the moment the color leached away from Jen's features.

Jenna stood frozen for a moment as if she couldn't remember how to move, then she quickly moved to the side and stopped the swing, pulling Addie off and into her arms.

"Hey!" the girl exclaimed. "I'm not done swinging."

Addie started to complain but something of her mother's tension seemed to trickle to the girl. She fell silent, eying the adults around her with sudden wariness.

"What do you want?" Jen asked. Her voice shook slightly.

"I've missed you so much, baby. Aren't you happy to see me?" He took another step forward as if to embrace her. Jen quickly stepped back.

Rosa didn't know what to do. They were on the side of the house without an entrance. The only way to get inside to safety was through the front door. To get there, they would have to go around this man.

Aaron Barker was dangerous. She recognized the fierce, violent look in his eyes. She had seen that before…

Old, long-suppressed panic started to bubble up inside her, those demons she thought she had vanquished long ago.

Rosa drew in a harsh breath and then another, suddenly desperate to escape.

No. She had to protect her friend. She wouldn't let her be hurt again.

"What do you want?" Jen asked again. She took a sideways step, Addie in her arms, and Rosa realized she was edging closer to the front door.

"Just to talk. That's all."

Jenna shuffled to the side another step and Rosa moved, as well, hoping he hadn't noticed.

"I don't want to talk to you. I tried that before and you wouldn't listen. Please. Just leave me alone."

He moved as if to come closer but Fiona growled. She wasn't particularly fierce-looking with her long, soft fur and her sweet eyes, but she did have sharp teeth.

The dog's show of courage gave Rosa strength to draw upon her own.

"You heard her."

Jen took another sideways step and Rosa did, too. The front porch was still so very far away.

"This is private property," she went on. "You are trespassing. Please leave."

"I'm not leaving without talking to Jenna." When he spoke, she caught a definite whiff of alcohol on his breath. He had been drinking and he already had to be unstable to put Jenna through long months of torture. Rosa knew this was not a good combination.

"She clearly does not want to talk to you."

"She has to."

"No. She does not." Hoping to distract him further from realizing she and Jenna had maneuvered so that they were now closer to the door than he was, Rosa reached into her pocket for her cell phone. "I must ask you again to leave or I will have to call nine-one-one."

"You think that worries me? I'm a police officer."

"Not here," she said firmly. "The police here do not stand by while someone hurts a woman, even if he is also a police officer."

She had to hope that was true of all officers in the Cannon Beach Police Department and not only Wyatt.

"Now. I am asking you for the final time to leave or I will call the police."

Now Jenna was backing toward the door and Rosa did the same, with Fiona still standing protectively in front of them.

He frowned. "I'm not leaving without Jenna. We love each other."

He took another step closer and from behind Rosa, Jen made a small sound of panic.

"Jenna. Go inside. Call nine-one-one."

She must have made a move toward the house because several things happened at once. Aaron Barker growled out a sound of frustration and lunged for her. Fiona jumped into protective mode and latched on to his leg and he kicked out at the dog, who whimpered and fell to the ground.

"No! Fi!" Rosa cried out. The coward pulled his leg back as if to kick again and Rosa instantly dropped to the ground, her body over the dog's.

Seconds later, she felt crushing pain in her back and realized he had kicked *her* instead of the dog.

This was the first time in fifteen years someone had struck out at her in anger. Instantly, she was transported to another time, another place. The past broke free of the prison where she kept it, the memories pouring over her like acid.

Other boots. Other fists. Again and again until she was in agony as vicious words in Spanish called her horrible names and told her she was going to die.

Something whimpered beneath her and the past suddenly receded—she was back in the present with her back throbbing and her dog wriggling beneath her.

Fiona was alive, and was just winded like Rosa. Thank God.

She could not just lie here trying to catch her breath. She had to protect her friend. Already, the man was making his way past Rosa and the dog toward the porch, where Jenna was desperately trying to punch in the code to unlock the door.

"I'm sorry, baby," Rosa said to Fi, then rose shakily to her feet. Her amazing dog was right behind her and she realized Fi had been whimpering for her to get up so they could both keep fighting.

Rosa ignored her pain as she limped after him.

"Stop. Right now," she said. He had almost reached the porch and Rosa did the only thing she could think of to slow him down. Though her back groaned with pain, she jumped on him, her arms around his neck as she had been taught in the self-defense classes Daniel had insisted she take.

He cried out in frustration and swung his elbows back, trying to get her off. One elbow caught her mouth and she tasted blood but still she clung tightly.

"Stupid dog!" he cried out again and she realized Fiona must have bitten him again to protect them.

She was so busy hanging on for dear life, she almost missed the sound of the door opening as Jenna finally managed to unlock it. She could see the other woman looked undecided whether to go inside to safety or come to Rosa's aid.

"Go," she yelled to Jenna. "Call nine-one-one."

An instant later, she heard the sound of the dead bolt. She was so relieved, she relaxed her hold slightly, but it was enough for him to shake her off as Fiona would with a sand fly.

She fell to the grass, barely missing the walkway, and rolled out of the way of his kicking boots. Fiona was still growling but had retreated also, and now came to stand in front of her.

"You bitch," he growled. "You stupid bitch. This is none of your damn business."

She could hardly breathe, but she managed to squeeze out a few words. "My friend. My house. My business."

He started for the door and she grabbed the closest weapon she could find, a rock from the flower garden. Rosa stood up and held it tightly.

"I will not let you hurt her," she gasped out.

He appeared genuinely shocked by that. "I would never hurt Jenna. Never. I love her and she loves me."

He ran a hand through his hair. The man was definitely unhinged, whether from his obsession or from alcohol, she did not know. What did it matter? She only knew there was no point in arguing with him. She longed for the safety of the house, but didn't know how she could get inside without him following her and having access to Jenna.

"How can you say you love her? She ran away from you."

"I've been out of my head, worried about her. She

disappeared in the middle of the night and no one would tell me where she went."

He sounded so plaintive that she would have felt sorry for him if she didn't know the torture he had put Jenna through these past few months.

"How did you…find her?" She was so afraid and in pain, she could barely breathe enough to get the question out, but had some wild thought that if she could keep him talking, perhaps the police would arrive before he killed her.

"Luck," he growled. "Sheer luck. A friend who knew how broke up I was about her leaving said he thought he saw someone who looked like her working in a gift shop when he was here on vacation with his family."

Rosa closed her eyes, remembering that day Jen had thought she saw someone she recognized. She had been right. Completely right.

"How did you know it was Jenna?"

He shrugged. "I'm a cop. I've got connections. I traced her Social Security number and found an employment record here at some shop in town. I figured they wouldn't tell me where she lived so I asked at the shop next door."

All their efforts to protect her hadn't been enough. Rosa had never thought of putting their neighboring stores on alert. She felt stupid for not thinking of it.

"As soon as I heard she might be here, I had to see if it was her." His face darkened. "I have to talk to her. Make sure she's okay."

"You have seen her. Jenna is fine. She wants you now to leave her alone."

"I'm not going to do that. We love each other. She's just being stubborn."

Rosa stood in front of him on the porch, Fiona growling at her side. "You cannot see her now."

She could see his talkative mood shift to anger again.

"Get out of my way," he said slowly and deliberately, and moved a step closer.

"No," she said, gripping the rock more tightly.

"You think I'm going to let some stupid little bitch keep me away from the woman I love after I've come all this way?"

Always, it was about him. Not about the woman or the child he had displaced from their home, forced to flee his unwanted obsession.

Rosa was shaking and she realized it was a combination of fear, pain and anger.

"Get out of my way. If you think I'm leaving, you don't know a damn thing about me."

Rosa lifted her chin. "I know all I need to know about you, Aaron Barker. I know you are a coward, a bully, a despicable human being. You have terrorized Jenna, one of the kindest women I know, who has already been through enough, because you refuse to believe a woman is not interested in you."

"Shut up. Jenna loves me."

"Then why did she move eight hundred miles to get away from you?"

His face turned red with anger. "Move. Last warning."

"I am not going anywhere."

He reached to shove her aside and Fiona lunged again. He kicked out at the dog, but she would not let her sweet canine protector be hurt again.

Rosa lifted the rock with both hands and, with every ounce of strength she had left, she slammed it into the side of his head. He stared at her in shock, dazed, then staggered backward, stumbling off the porch.

Rosa stared at him for only a second before she rushed to the door. She was fumbling to punch in the code when she heard sirens and a door slam, then a voice yelled out, "Don't move!"

Wyatt!

He had come.

Vast relief poured over her and Rosa, shaking violently now, sagged to the ground, her back pressed against the door and her arms wrapped around her brave, wonderful dog.

Chapter 15

Wyatt restrained the son of a bitch, who seemed groggy and incoherent, and was mumbling about how much he loved Jen and how she had to talk to him.

It took every ounce of control he had not to bash the man's head against the porch steps, especially when he saw blood trickling out of Rosa's mouth.

This man had hurt Rosa. And not just physically. She looked...shattered. He wanted to go to her, but he needed to secure the scene first before he could comfort her.

"Where are Jen and Addie?" he asked. He had been at his sister's house when Jen had called, her voice frantic. He hadn't been able to understand her at first, but had quickly surmised through her distress that her stalker was there and he was hurting Rosa and Fiona.

She had hung up before he could ask any questions

and he had assumed she was calling 911 as he heard the call go out of an assault while he was en route, screaming through town with lights and sirens blazing.

The door opened. "I'm here," Jenna said. "I sent Addie into our apartment. Oh, Rosa. You saved us."

She wrapped her arms around her friend and Wyatt didn't miss the way Rosa winced. She had more aches and pains than just the bloody lip he could see.

The bastard was bleeding, too, from what looked like a nasty contusion. Wyatt looked around and found a large rock with blood on it. Had Rosa hit him with that? Good for her.

He finished handcuffing Barker and read him his rights, all while the man kept babbling about being a police officer and how this was all a big mistake.

"Tell them, Jenna. Tell them you love me."

The woman looked down at the man who had so tormented her, driving her away from her home with his obsession.

"I despise you," she said clearly. "I hope you rot in hell."

Barker made a move toward her but Wyatt yanked the restraint.

"We can straighten everything out down at the station," Wyatt said, just as backup officers arrived to help him secure the scene.

Only after they had taken custody of the man and another officer started taking Jenna's statement about the incident and the months of torment preceding it could Wyatt finally go to Rosa, who was now sitting on the porch steps.

She forced a smile when he approached and he saw her lip was cracked and swollen.

"He hurt you." He reached a hand out and tenderly caressed her face.

She let out a little sob and sagged into his arms. He held her, burying his face in her hair as he tried not to think about what might have happened to her.

How would he have endured it? He had already lost one woman he loved. He couldn't stand the idea of losing another.

"I am all right," she murmured. "Jenna is safe. That is the important thing. But I have to take Fiona to the vet. That man kicked her. She was so brave."

They both were incredibly brave. He looked over her shoulder, where Fiona's tail was wagging. She almost looked like she was smiling as the two of them embraced. "She seems okay to me."

Rosa drew away a little and he instantly wanted to pull her back into his arms.

"I would still like to have her checked out. The veterinarian is my friend. I will call her."

An ambulance pulled up, followed by a fire truck. The whole town was coming to her rescue, which was only proof about how well-regarded Rosa was in town.

Right behind them, a couple he recognized came racing up the driveway.

"Rosa!" Melissa Sanderson exclaimed. "What happened? We saw all the police racing past and hurried right over."

"I am fine," Rosa said. "A man came to hurt Jen but she and Addie were able to get to safety."

"Because of you," Jenna said as she approached with her daughter in her arms. "You saved us."

She hugged her friend again and Wyatt could see Rosa was trying not to wince.

"You look like you've gone a few rounds with a heavyweight champion." Melissa's husband, Eli, a physician in town, looked concerned. "You should let me have a look."

Rosa, his battered warrior, glowered at them all. "This is all too much fuss for a sore lip."

"He kicked her in the back, too," Jenna said. "At least once. Maybe more. I don't know. I was so scared."

"You need to go to the ER," Wyatt said.

She shook her head. "Not until Fiona sees the veterinarian."

"You can at least let Eli and the paramedics check you out while I call the veterinarian," Wyatt said.

She gave him a grateful look. "Yes. I will do that. Thank you."

Chapter 16

To his deep regret, that was the last chance he had to talk to her for the next few hours. He didn't want to leave, but as the on-scene arresting officer, he had paperwork and an investigation to deal with.

He had tried to interrogate Barker but the man was sleeping off what appeared to be a large quantity of alcohol, as well as a concussion delivered by Rosa and her trusty rock and several dog bites from Fiona.

By the time he left the station, the sun was beginning to set.

He knew from the other officers on scene that Rosa had refused transport to the hospital, though she had allowed Eli to clean and bandage her cuts.

Stubborn woman.

Only now, as he walked up the front steps to the

house hours later, did Wyatt feel his own adrenaline crash.

He had never been so scared as the moment when Jenna had called him, her voice thready with panic. All he had registered were her words that Rosa was being hurt.

It seemed odd to be here without either Hank or Logan, but Carrie had offered to keep both of them overnight.

"You do what you need to for Jen and Rosa," she had told him when he called from the station. She had been half out of her mind with worry for her friend and only his repeated assurances that Rosa's injuries appeared to be minor had kept Carrie from rushing to the house herself.

He half expected to find Rosa in the flower gardens around Brambleberry House, seeking peace and solace amid the blossoms and the birds, as she so often did. But from what he could see, the gardens were empty except for a few hummingbirds at the bright red feeder. They immediately flitted away.

The big house also seemed quiet when he let himself inside. He walked to the third floor and knocked, but Rosa didn't answer. He couldn't hear Fiona inside, either.

He frowned, not sure what to do.

As he headed back down the stairs, the door on the second-floor landing opened. Jenna peeked out. "I thought I heard you come in."

"Yeah. How are you?"

"I've had better days."

"It has to help to know that Barker is in custody, doesn't it?"

She shrugged and he could see she wasn't entirely convinced her nightmare was over. He couldn't blame her for the doubt after the way the system had already treated her, but Wyatt was quick to reassure her.

"You should know that Barker won't be going anywhere for a long time. He's facing extensive state and federal charges. And we haven't even started on the stalking charges. That will only add to his sentence. He won't bother you again."

"I hope not."

He knew it would probably take time for that reality to sink in.

"Is Rosa with you?"

"No. I heard her take Fiona out about a half hour ago."

She paused. "I never wanted her to get hurt. I hope you know that. I thought we would be safe here. If I had for a moment dreamed he would find me and would come here and hurt Rosa and Fiona, I never would have come."

"I know that and I'm sure Rosa doesn't blame you for a second."

Jenna didn't look convinced about this, either. "She was amazing. I wish you could have seen her. She was so fierce. Aaron was twice as big, but that didn't stop her. She's an incredible woman."

"Agreed," he said, his voice gruff.

"She risked her life to protect me and Addie." Jenna's voice took on an edge and she gave him a hard stare. "For the record, I will do the same for her. Anybody who hurts her in any possible way will live to regret it."

Was that a threat? It certainly sounded like one. He couldn't decide whether to be offended that she could ever think he would hurt Rosa, or touched at her loyalty to her friend. He settled on the latter.

"You and I are the same in that sentiment, then," he said quietly.

She studied his features for a moment, then nodded. "I saw her from my window as I was putting Addie to bed. She and Fiona appeared to be heading for the beach."

He smiled and on impulse reached out and hugged her. After a surprised moment, Jenna hugged him back.

He headed for the beach gate, his heart pounding. As he went, he carried on a fierce debate with himself.

Rosa had basically ordered him to keep his distance and told him she wasn't interested in a relationship. He had tried his best. For a week, he had worked long hours at his house so that he and Logan could move out as soon as possible. The whole time, he had done his best to push her out of his head and his heart.

It hadn't worked.

The moment Jenna had called him in a panic, the moment he knew they were in danger, Wyatt had realized nothing had changed. He was in love with Rosa and would move heaven and earth to keep her safe.

He pushed open the beach gate and found her there, just beyond the house. She was sitting on a blanket on the sand, her arm around Fiona and her back to him as she watched the sun slipping down into the water in a blaze of color.

She didn't hear him come out at first. Fiona did. The dog turned to look at him, but apparently decided he was no threat because she nestled closer to her human.

He moved across the sand, still not sure what he

would say to her, only knowing he had to be close to her, too.

He saw the moment she registered his presence. Her spine stiffened and she turned her head. He couldn't see her expression behind her sunglasses.

"Oh. Hello."

"Here you are. I was worried about you."

"Yes. We are here. The sunset seems especially beautiful tonight."

He had to agree. Streaks of pink and purple and orange spilled out in glorious Technicolor. "May I join you?"

She hesitated. He could see her jaw flex, as if she wanted to say no, but she finally gestured to the empty spot on the blanket, which happened to be on the other side of her dog.

He would have liked to be next to Rosa, but this would do, he supposed.

"Where are Logan and Hank?"

"They were both with Carrie when Jenna called me. After Carrie heard what happened to you and found out I was part of the investigation, she insisted they stay the night with her."

"Ah."

He reached out and rubbed her brave, amazing dog behind the ear. His hand brushed against Rosa's and it hurt a little when she pulled her hand away.

"How's Fiona?"

"Fine. Dr. Williams said she might be a little bruised, but nothing appears to be broken. I am to watch her appetite and her energy over the next few days and tell her if I see anything unusual."

"You're a good, brave girl, aren't you?" He scratched Fi under the chin and the dog rested her head on his leg.

All the emotions he had put away in the heat of the moment as he did his duty and stood for justice seemed to come rushing over him again, all at once.

"What you did—protecting your friend. It was incredibly brave."

She gave a short laugh. "I think you mean to say stupid."

"I would never say that. Never. You were amazing."

He reached for her hand, unable to help himself. He thought she would pull away again, but she didn't. Her fingers were cool and seemed to be trembling a little, but he couldn't say whether that was from the cool coastal air or from the trauma of earlier.

She drew in a breath that sounded ragged, and before he quite realized it, she let out a sob and then another.

Oh, Rosa.

His poor, fierce Rosa.

Fiona, blessed Fiona, moved out of the way so that Wyatt could pull Rosa into his arms. He held her while she cried silently against his chest, not making a sound except the occasional whimper.

His heart ached for her, both for the fear she must have felt and for everything else she had endured.

"I am sorry," she finally said, sounding mortified. "I think I have been holding that in all afternoon."

"Or longer."

She shifted her face to meet his gaze. Somehow, she had lost her sunglasses and he could see her now, her eyes dark and shadowed in her lovely face. Instead of answering his unspoken question, she focused on the events of the day.

"I was so frightened. I thought this man, he was going to kill me, then get to Jenna and Addie. I could not let him."

"He won't get to Jenna now. He is in custody and will be charged with assault, trespassing, drunk driving, driving across state lines with the intent to commit a felony and a whole host of other charges related to whatever stalking charges we can prove. He's not going to get out for a long time."

"I hope that is the case."

"It is," he promised. He would do whatever necessary to make sure of it.

"I suppose I should be relieved I did not kill him with that rock."

"You were pretty fierce."

"I could not help it. I could only think about protecting Jenna and Addie from someone who wanted to hurt them. Something seemed to take over me. Maybe some part of my brain that was fifteen years old again, focused only on surviving another day."

As soon as she said the words, she looked as if she wished she hadn't. She closed her eyes. He thought she would pull away from him but she didn't. She continued to nestle against him as if he was providing safe shelter in a sandstorm.

With his thumb, he brushed away a tear that trickled down her cheek, his heart a heavy ache. "Tell me what happened when you were fifteen."

"I have already told you too much. I don't talk about that time in my life, Wyatt. It is the past and has nothing to do with who I am now."

"You don't have to tell me. I understand if you prefer to keep it to yourself. But I hope you know you can trust me, if you ever change your mind."

She eased away from him and sat once more on the blanket beside him. Fiona moved to her other side and plopped next to her. Rosa wrapped her arms around her knees and gazed out at the water, a pale blue in the twilight.

She was silent for a long time, so long that he thought she wasn't going to answer. But then she looked at him out of the corner of her gaze and he fell in love with her all over again.

"Sometimes it feels like it all happened to someone else. Something I read about in a terribly tragic novel."

He did not want to hear what was coming next, but somehow Wyatt sensed it was important to both of them that she tell him. This was the reason she had pushed him away. He was suddenly certain of it.

That moment when he had rushed onto the porch earlier, he had seen raw emotion in her expression. That was the image he couldn't get out of his head. She had looked at him with relief, with gratitude and with something else, too.

She thought her past was a barrier between them. If he could show her it wasn't, that together they could face whatever demons she fought, perhaps she would stop pushing him away.

"I told you about the men who offered me a job in this country and who…brought me here."

"Yes."

"It was not a factory job they were bringing me to, as I thought. I was so stupid."

"I didn't think it was."

She closed her eyes. "You are a detective. I am sure you can guess what happened next."

"I've imagined a few possible scenarios since the night you told me."

"Pick the worst one and you might be close enough."

He gripped her hand tightly, not wanting to ever let go. "Human trafficking."

She made a small sound. "Yes. That is a polite phrase for it. I was brought here to work in the sex trade. Me, an innocent girl from a small town who had never even kissed a boy. I barely knew what sex was."

Everything inside him went cold as he thought about what she must have endured. "Oh, sweetheart. I'm so sorry."

"I refused at first. The men who brought me here, they did not care whether I was willing or not."

How was it possible for his heart to break again and again?

"You were raped."

She looked at him, stark pain in her eyes. "Now you know why I don't like thinking about the past. Yes. I was raped. At first by the men who wanted to use me to make money for them. Then by some of their customers. I did not cooperate. Not one single time. They threatened me, hurt me, tried to make me take drugs like the other girls, so I would be quiet and do what they said. I would not. I only cried. All the time."

"That couldn't have been good for business."

She gave a short, humorless laugh. "No. Not at all. Finally, they left me alone. I still do not know why they did not kill me. It would have been easy for them. But then one of the girls died of too much drugs. She was…not well, so they had let her do all the cooking and cleaning for the other girls. They let me take her place. At least I no longer had to let strangers touch me."

He squeezed her fingers. How had she possibly emerged from that hell still able to smile and laugh and find joy in the world, with a gentle spirit and a kind heart? Most people would have curled up and withered away in the midst of so much trauma.

"This went on for a few months and then I made a mistake. I knew I had to do something to change my situation. I could not stay. I tried to escape but they... caught me. They would have killed me that night. They knew I could tell the police who they were. I expected to die. I thought I would. But somehow, I did not. I do not know why. I only knew I had to do all I could to survive. Mine was not the only life at risk that night."

"One of your friends?"

She gave a tiny shake of her head and gazed out at the undulating waves. He waited for her to explain. When she did not, suddenly all his suspicions came together and he knew. He didn't know how. He just did.

"You were pregnant."

She met his gaze, her expression filled with sadness and pain. "No one else knew. I did not even know myself until I was too far along to—to do anything. I told you I was innocent."

"How did you get away?"

She shrugged. "A miracle from God. That is the only thing it could have been."

He had never heard her being particularly religious but the conviction in her voice seemed unswerving. He would take her word for it, since he hadn't been there.

"We were kept above a restaurant in a tourist town in Utah. They left me to die in a room there, but I did not. I had only pretended. After they left, I saw they had not locked the door, like usual. They thought I was dead. Why should they?"

How badly had she been hurt? Wyatt didn't even want to contemplate. And she'd only been a child. Not much older than his niece. How had she endured it?

"Somehow, I found strength to stand and managed to go out, stumbling down the back stairs. I still cannot believe they did not hear me. Once I was out, I did not know what to do. Where to go. I knew no one. I was certain I only had moments before they found me and finished what they had started, so I… I somehow climbed into the back of a truck."

"With a stranger?"

He thought of all the things that could have happened to her by putting her trust in someone she did not know. On the other hand, she was escaping certain death so she probably thought anything was better than the place she was leaving.

"I was lucky. There was a blanket there for the horses and I was able to pull it over me so I did not freeze. The man was a rancher. He did not spot me until we were away from town, when he had a flat tire and found me sleeping."

"What did he do?" Wyatt was again almost afraid to ask.

"He called the police and a kind sheriff and a doctor came to my rescue. Daniel and Lauren. My parents."

Chapter 17

Rosa could feel herself trembling, though the night was pleasant. She knew it was probably a delayed reaction from the attack earlier and from the emotional trauma of reliving the darkest time in her life.

When Wyatt wrapped his arm around her and pulled her close to his heat, she wanted to sink into him. He was big, safe and comforting, and offered immeasurable strength.

She could not tell by his expression what he thought about what she had told him. She thought maybe that wasn't such a bad thing. Did she want to know what he was thinking about her?

"They took you in."

"They were not married at the time. Not even together. I like to think I helped them find each other. But, yes. Lauren took me home with her. I was still in danger. I had information about the men who took me. I knew who they were, where they were, so I—I stayed with Lauren until all the men were caught."

"All of them?" Wyatt's voice had a hard note she had not heard before, as if he wanted to go to Utah right now and find justice for her.

Oh, he was a dear man. A little more warmth seeped into her heart. How was she supposed to resist him?

"Yes. Some were deported. Others are still in jail here in this country. Daniel made sure all the girls were rescued and the men were punished."

"I would like to meet Sheriff Galvez," he said gruffly.

"You two are similar. I think you would be friends. That is one reason why I…" Her voice trailed off and she felt her face heat, as she was unable to complete the sentence. *Why I fell in love with you.*

"Why you what?"

"Nothing," she said quickly. "I only wanted to tell you, after Daniel and Lauren married, they gave me a home and then legally adopted me."

"They sound wonderful."

"The best. Though they can be too protective of me."

"That's understandable, don't you think?"

She nodded. "Yes. I do understand but this is one reason I think I had to move somewhere else. Somewhere I would not be poor Rosa Galvez."

"What about your baby?" he asked.

Ah. Here was the most difficult part. The other things that had happened—the abuse, the beatings. Even the rapes. Those scars had healed. She hardly thought of them anymore.

Her child. That was a wound that would never close completely.

She chose her words carefully, wishing she did not have to tell him this part. "I had a baby girl ten weeks later and...she was adopted."

There. The words still burned her throat.

He was quiet for a long time. Was he recoiling now from her? She could not blame him. It had been a terrible choice for someone who had been little more than a child to have to make.

"It's Bella, isn't it? Your daughter?"

That was the last thing she expected him to say. In horror, she jerked away and scrambled to her feet. Fiona immediately moved to her side, as if sensing more danger.

"No! Bella? How ridiculous! Do not say this. You are crazy."

He rose, as well, gazing at her across the sand. The rising moon lit up one side of his face, leaving the other in shadow. "I'm not crazy though, am I?" he said quietly. "I'm right."

She didn't know what to say. How could she convince him he had made a terrible mistake? She had no words to undo this.

"No. This is not true," she said, but even she could hear her words lacked conviction. "I do not know how... Why did you think of this?"

"The time frame lines up. Bella is the right age and she was adopted through your aunt Anna. You're her birth mother." If her own words lacked conviction, his did not. He spoke with a growing confidence she had no way to combat.

"I don't know why I didn't see the resemblance before. Maybe I didn't want to see it. Does she know?"

Rosa stared at him, not sure what to say. All of her

instincts were shouting at her to go inside the safety of the house, but she couldn't leave. She had started this by telling him her history. It was her fault. He was a police detective. How could she blame him for connecting all the pieces of the jigsaw and coming up with the correct picture?

This was the part of the story she did not want him to know. The part she had been trying to protect him from. What must he think of her now? She had abandoned his niece, a girl he loved. She had given birth and handed her over to another woman to be her mother, then went on with her life. Learning English. Finishing school. Dating boys. Going to college.

Why did he not seem angry? Why was he looking at her like that, with a tender light in his eyes? Did he not understand what she had done?

She could not think about that now. For this moment, she had to focus on controlling the damage she had done. She should not have told him anything. Since she had, now she had to make sure he did not ruin all the care she had taken during the years she had lived in Cannon Beach, so close to her daughter but still far enough away.

"No. She does not know," she finally said. "And you cannot tell her. Oh, please. Do not tell her."

"I would never, if you don't want me to."

"You must promise me. Swear it."

He seemed to blink at her vehemence, but then nodded. "I swear. I won't tell her. This is not my secret to tell, Rosa. Again, please trust me enough to know I would never betray you."

Oh, she wanted to trust him. The urge to step back into his arms was so overpowering, she had to wrap her own arms around herself to keep from doing it. "I thank you. She might have come from an ugly time in my life but none of that was her fault. She is the most beautiful, precious girl. From the moment I felt her move inside me, I loved her. I wanted so much to keep her but it was… It was impossible."

"You were only a child yourself."

"Yes. What would I do with a baby? I had no way to take care of her myself, though I wanted to."

"It's obvious you love her. Whether she knows the truth or not, there is a bond between you."

"How could anyone not love her? Bella is wonderful. Smart and pretty, always kind. She reminds me of my mother."

"That's funny. She reminds me of *her* mother, now that I know who she is."

She blushed at the intensity in her voice. "Carrie is her mother. She has loved her and cared for her far better than I ever could."

"Do Joe and Carrie know?"

"Yes. Of course. I would not have come here without telling them. When Anna asked me to come to help her with the store, I knew I must tell Carrie and Joe first. I called them to see how they might feel if I moved to town. I did not want to cause them any tension or discomfort."

"What did they say?"

"They welcomed me. They have always been so kind to me. Always. From the day we met in the hospital. They never once made me feel as if I had…done something wrong."

"Because you hadn't!"

She sighed. It was easy for others to say that. They

had not lived her journey. "I know that most of the time but sometimes I do wonder. I made foolish choices. Dangerous choices. And because of that, an innocent child was born."

He reached for her hands again and curled his fingers around hers. To Rosa's shock, he lifted her hands and pressed first one hand to his mouth and then the other.

"You did nothing wrong, Rosa. *Nothing.* You were an innocent child yourself, looking for a brighter future. You couldn't have known what would happen to you."

Tears spilled out again at his words and the healing balm they offered. He was not disgusted by her story. She did not know why. It seemed the second miracle of her life.

He pulled her back into his arms. She knew she should try to be strong but she couldn't. Not right now. She would try to find the strength later to restore distance between them but right now she needed the heat and comfort of him. She wrapped her arms around his waist and rested her head against his chest again, wishing she could stay here forever.

"If Carrie and Joe know the truth, why doesn't Bella?"

Thinking about it made her stomach hurt. This was her greatest fear. Every day, she worried Bella would learn the truth and would come to hate her.

"They wanted to tell her but I—I begged them not to. I thought it would be better for her if I could be in her life only as a friend. Maybe like a sort of…older sister or cousin."

"Why would that be better?"

She shrugged against him. "How do I tell her that

she was created through an act of violence at a time in my life I wish I could forget?"

"You wouldn't have to tell her that part."

"What do I say when she asks me about her father? I did not know how I could answer that. I still do not know. How can I tell her I do not even know his name? No. It is better that she not know the truth."

His silence told her he didn't agree.

"When I came here, I did not want to intrude in her life," she said. "Carrie and Joe are her parents in every way that matters and they have been wonderful to her. I only wanted to…see her. Make sure she was happy. Healthy. I thought I would only be here a short time but then I came to love her and to love Cannon Beach and Brambleberry House. Anna offered me a partnership in the store and it became harder to think about leaving."

"I am glad you stayed. So glad," he said. And before she realized what he intended, he lowered his mouth and kissed her with a sweetness and gentleness that took her breath.

Her mouth still burned where she had been hit, but she ignored it, lost in the peace and wonder of kissing the man she loved on a moonswept beach.

He still wanted to kiss her, after everything she told him. All this time, she had been so afraid for him to learn the truth. He now knew the ugliest part of her past and yet he kissed her anyway with a tenderness that made her feel…cherished.

"Thank you for coming to my rescue." She realized in that moment she had not really told him that yet. And while she was speaking about earlier, with Aaron Barker, her words held layers of meaning.

He smiled against her mouth. "I don't think you

needed help from me. You were doing just fine. You're pretty ferocious, Rosita."

The endearment—Little Rosa—made her smile, too. Her mother had always called her that and Daniel still did.

"Ow. Smiling still hurts."

"Oh. I forgot about your mouth. I shouldn't have kissed you. I'm sorry."

"I am glad you did." To prove it, she pressed her mouth, sore lip and all, to his.

All of the emotions she could not say were contained in that kiss. All the love and yearning she had been fighting for so long.

When he lifted his head, Wyatt was breathing hard and Rosa realized they were once more on the sand, sitting on the blanket she had brought.

"I have to tell you something," Wyatt said after a long moment. He gripped her hands again, and even through the darkness, she could see the intense light in his eyes.

"I was scared to death when Jenna called me and said you were in trouble. I made all kinds of deals with God on my way to Brambleberry House, begging Him to keep you safe until I could get here."

"You...did?" She didn't know what to say, shaken to her core by the emotion in his voice. Her heart, already beating hard from the kiss, seemed to race even faster.

"Yes. Though I suppose I should have known you could take care of yourself," he said with a little smile. "You're amazing, Rosa. One of the most amazing women I have ever met."

She could not seem to wrap her mind around this man speaking such tender, wonderful words.

"I do not understand," she finally asked. "How can

you say that after—after everything I have told you about my past? About what I had to do? About…about giving my baby to someone else?"

"All of those things only make me love you more."

She thought she must have misheard him.

"Love me. You cannot love me." She stared through the darkness, wishing she could see him better. She wanted to drag him back to the house so she could look at him in the light to read the truth.

"Yet I do," he said, his voice ringing with so much truth she had to believe him. "What you did was remarkable. Even more so because of what you have been through. You were scared to death but you still risked your life to protect your friend. You make me ashamed of myself."

"Ashamed? Why? You came as soon as you heard we were in danger."

"I don't have your kind of courage. I have been fighting falling in love with you for a long time. I think long before I moved to Brambleberry House."

"Why?" She was still not sure she could believe it but she wanted to. Oh, she wanted to.

"I loved my wife," he said simply. "When she died, I thought I had nothing else to give. I did not want to love someone else. Love brought too much pain and sadness and it was easier, safer, to keep my heart locked away."

He kissed her gently, on the side of her mouth that had not been hurt. "I am not brave like a certain woman I know who has endured horrible things but still manages to be kind and cheerful and loving."

His words soaked through her, more comforting than she could ever tell him.

"This woman. She sounds very annoying. Too good to be true."

He laughed. "She isn't. She's amazing. Did I tell you that she also reaches out to those in need and is willing to protect them with every fierce ounce of her being?"

She was not the perfect woman he was describing. But hearing how he saw her made her want to be.

Wasn't that what love should be? A window that allowed you to discover the best in yourself because someone else saw you that way?

She didn't know. She only knew she loved Wyatt with all her heart and wanted a future with him, as she had never wanted anything in her life.

"I know something about this woman that you might not," she said.

"What's that?"

The words seemed to catch in her throat as those demons of self-doubt whispered in her ear. No. She would not listen to them. This was too important.

"This woman. She very much loves a certain police detective. She has loved him for a long time, too. Probably since he moved to town with his sad eyes and his beautiful little boy."

He gazed down at her, those eyes no longer sad but blazing with light, joy and wonder. "Well. That works out then, doesn't it?"

He kissed her again, his arms wrapped tightly around her. Her entire journey had been leading her to this moment, she realized. This moment and this man who knew all her secrets and loved her despite them. Or maybe a little because of them.

She loved Wyatt. She wanted a future with him and

with Logan. Thinking about that boy who already held such a big part of her heart only added to her happiness.

She could clearly picture that future together, filled with laughter and joy. Kisses and Spanish lessons and walks along the beach with their dogs.

She had no doubt that it would be rich and beautiful, full and joyous and rewarding. The scent of freesia drifted across the sand and Rosa smiled, happy to know that Abigail approved.

Epilogue

One year later

What a glorious day for a wedding.

Rosa woke just as the sun was beginning to creep over the horizon in her third-floor apartment of Brambleberry House.

She stayed in bed for a moment, anticipation shivering through her. For a few disoriented moments, she wasn't sure why, then she caught sight of Fiona's head on the bed, the dog watching her intently, and she remembered.

Today was the day. This day, she was marrying Wyatt and becoming Logan's stepmother.

In a few short hours, they would stand in the gardens of Brambleberry House and exchange their vows.

Everyone was in town. Her parents, Anna and Harry, Sonia Elizabeth and her husband, Luke.

Fiona made the little sound she did when she wanted to go for a walk and Rosa had to smile.

"I am not even out of bed yet. You really want a walk now?"

The dog continued to give her a steady look she could not ignore.

With a sigh, she slipped out of bed, threw on sweats and a baseball cap and then put on Fiona's leash. A moment later, they headed down the stairs of Brambleberry House.

This was her last morning in this apartment and her last morning as Rosa Vallejo Galvez. Tonight she would be Rosa Vallejo Galvez Townsend.

A wife and a mother.

After their honeymoon, she and Wyatt would be returning to the ground-floor apartment of Brambleberry House. They had decided to stay here for now.

He was going to rent out his small bungalow and they would move to the larger apartment, with its sunroom and extra bedroom. It was larger than his house, plus had extensive grounds where Logan could play, as well as his best friend, Addie, living upstairs.

She knew it wouldn't last. At some point, they would probably want to find a house of their own. For now, she was glad she did not have to leave the house completely.

She knew it was silly but Rosa felt like Brambleberry House was excited about the upcoming wedding and all the coming changes. She seemed to smell flowers all the time and wondered if Abigail was flitting through the house, watching all the preparations.

The summer morning was beautiful, with wisps of

sea mist curling up through the trees. It was cool now but she knew the afternoon would be perfect for a garden wedding overlooking the sea.

The decorations were already in place and she admired them as she walked through with Fi toward the beach gate.

Fiona, usually well-behaved, was tugging on the leash as Rosa walked onto the sand. She lunged toward a few other early-morning beach walkers, which was completely not like her.

It looked like a man and a child walking a little dog, but they were too far away for her to see them clearly. Suddenly Fiona broke free of Rosa's hold and raced toward them, dragging her leash behind her.

The boy, who Rosa was now close enough to recognize as a nearly eight-year-old boy with a blond cowlick and his father's blue eyes, caught Fiona's leash and came hurrying toward Rosa.

"Rosa! *Buenos*, Rosa!"

"Buenos, mijo." When he reached her, he hugged her hard and Rosa's simmering joy seemed to bubble over.

A few more hours and they would be a family.

A year ago, she never could have imagined this day for herself. She expected she would be content going to other people's weddings. She would dance, laugh, enjoy the refreshments and then go home trying to ignore the pang of loneliness.

Destined to be alone. That is what she had always thought.

She could not have been happier to be so very wrong.

"I don't think I'm supposed to see you today. Isn't it bad luck?" Wyatt's voice was gruff but his eyes blazed with so much tenderness and love, she felt tears of happiness gather in hers. He always made her feel so cherished.

"I think you are not supposed to see me in the wedding dress. I do not think the superstition means you cannot see me in my old sweatpants, when I have barely combed my hair and look terrible. Anyway, I do not care about such things. We make our own luck, right?"

He laughed and reached for her. "Yes. I guess we do. To be safe, I won't tell Carrie and Bella we bumped in to you on our walk. They *do* care about that kind of thing."

Rosa smiled and her heart seemed to sigh when he kissed her, his mouth warm and firm against the morning chill.

"You do not have to tell me. I have heard every superstition about weddings from them since the day we became engaged."

"I don't know how it's possible, but I think Bella is even more excited about this wedding than we are."

Rosa smiled, adding even more happiness to her overflowing cup when she thought of his niece. Her niece, after today.

And her daughter.

After talking with Joe and Carrie several months earlier, she had decided she must tell Bella the truth.

They had all sat down together and, gathering her courage and without giving all the grim details, Rosa had told Bella she was her birth mother.

To her shock, Bella had simply shrugged. "And?" she had said. "I've only known that, like, forever."

"You have not!" Rosa had said, shocked nearly speechless. "How?"

"It wasn't exactly hard to figure out. You just have

to look at a selfie of us together. We look enough alike to be sisters."

"Why didn't you say anything?" Carrie had looked and sounded as shocked as Rosa.

"I figured you all would say something eventually when you wanted me to know. What's the big deal? You're like one of my best friends, anyway."

Rosa had burst into tears at that and so had Carrie.

Nothing seemed to have changed between them. Bella still confided in her about boys she liked, and Rosa still tried to be like a wise older sister.

In that time, Bella had never asked about her father. Maybe some day, when she was older, Rosa would figure out a way to tell her something. For now, she was grateful every day for the bright, beautiful daughter who seemed happy to let her into her life.

"She has done a great job of helping me plan the wedding. I would have been lost without her," she said now to Wyatt.

Bella was one of her bridesmaids and could not have been more excited to help her work out every detail of the wedding, from the cake to the dresses to the food at the reception. In fact, Rosa thought she might have a good future as a wedding planner, if she wanted.

"I'm sure she's done a great job," he said. "It's going to be a beautiful day. But not nearly as gorgeous as you."

She smiled as he kissed her again. A loud sigh finally distracted them both. "Can we be done kissing now? You guys are gross."

"Sorry, kid." Wyatt smiled down at his son but made no move to release her. "We both kind of like it."

That was an understatement. They were magic together. She loved his kiss, his touch, and could not wait until she could wake up each morning in his arms.

"Fiona and Hank want to take a walk," Logan informed them. "So do I."

Wyatt kissed Rosa firmly one more time then drew away. "Fine," he said. "But you'd better get used to the kissing, kid."

He reached for Rosa's hand and the three of them and their dogs walked down the beach while gulls cried and the waves washed against the shore.

The perfect day and the perfect life seemed to stretch out ahead of them and Rosa knew she had everything she could ever need, right here.

* * * * *

Darby Baham (she/her) is a proud New Yorker of six years who has had personal blog posts appear in the *Washington Post's* relationship vertical, plus Blavity, *FEMI Magazine* and more. She's also worked in the communications industry for more than two decades. Originally from New Orleans, LA, Darby lived in the Washington, DC, area for fifteen years, where she cultivated a beautiful, sprawling shoe closet and met some of the best people in her orbit. Her debut novel, *The Shoe Diaries*, was released January 2022. The follow-up, *Bloom Where You're Planted*, was released May 2022.

Books by Darby Baham

Harlequin Special Edition

The Friendship Chronicles

The Shoe Diaries
Bloom Where You're Planted

Visit the Author Profile page
at Harlequin.com for more titles.

THE SHOE DIARIES

Darby Baham

To all the little Black girls, like me,
who devoured the rare romance stories
they read about women who looked like them.
I hope you know that love for you isn't rare at all.
It's actually quite beautiful in its commonness.

Part 1: Life is a Journey Made Better with Great Shoes

"A journey of a thousand miles begins with a single step (and a great pair of shoes!)."

—paraphrased from Lao-tzu

Prologue

February 13, 2016

"With this ring, I thee wed, and with it, I bestow upon thee the treasures of my mind, heart and hands…"

Staring at my friends from my seat, I noticed more than just their words as they recited their vows. I saw their hands clasped together throughout the ceremony, and the smiles they wore even through their tears; the way they focused on each other like no one else was present even while a hundred and fifty of us stared at them with glee. But most important, I saw the love that was undeniable between the two of them. Strange, but I was all at once happy and sad, amazed and hurt. In them I saw hope for a future. Here were two people who'd found love and decided that nothing else was more important than their union. Yet, standing less than two feet away from them, I also saw the man I'd hoped would be my future—and it hurt me to my core to know that we would never have this same moment.

Every few minutes I caught myself peeking over at him during the ceremony, hoping he would turn to me, and we would have some kind of knowing thought between us. That we would have a brief second where no words were necessary, and through our eyes, we'd say, "I know it didn't work for us, but I still love you." I craved that moment more than anything I'd ever wanted before, wishing with all my might he would just look over. Just glance at me…and smile.

That look never happened.

I knew from the moment my friends announced their engagement that their wedding would be special. They were *those* kinds of people. The ones who managed to turn something very simple into the most extraordinary event you would attend, so it was pretty much a guarantee that their wedding was going to be *a show*. And Candice and Lance did not disappoint. Their ceremony, cocktail hour and reception were all held at the famed Loews Philadelphia Hotel—platinum-style decor and black-tie attire requested. I just hoped I could get past my feelings of seeing my ex-boyfriend, Jake, on the big day, and that I could experience the love all around me without disappointment in my heart.

For months I'd known he was going to be there. Well, that wasn't true. For months I'd known he was going to be in the wedding party, which is an entirely different thing to handle. And yet, I'd managed not to make a big deal about it. I attended the engagement party with no problems. I broke bread with his sister at the bridal shower like nothing was wrong. I shopped for my dress for the wedding, packed the last few days before the wedding, made my way to Philly, spent time with friends the night before and still hadn't quite let myself think about the fact that I would see the man I'd wanted to marry stand up in support of our friends who were planning to spend the rest of their lives together.

That was until I stepped off the elevator and into the lobby of the floor where the ceremony was being held. Then suddenly, I felt my heart thud in my chest and my feet go numb. *What am I doing?* I questioned. How was I going to make it through tonight?

I was two seconds away from having a complete meltdown—hyperventilating, ugly tears, the whole nine—when I peered down at my shoes, and they somehow helped me will myself into gaining control of my emotions. I took one slow, deep breath, then another, eyed my friends who'd joined me that weekend to see if they noticed my momentary freak-out, and quietly composed myself before taking another step forward. Thankfully, Robin and Jennifer were far too busy scoping out the crowd to notice my meltdown, but they eventually realized I was no longer in step with them and turned around to see me stuck in place next to the elevator. I was nearly twenty steps behind them by then.

"Are you all right?" mouthed Jennifer, concern on her face.

I nodded, then changed my mind and shook my head, then after one more breath, nodded again.

As I began walking toward them, I focused my mind on my girls, who were impeccably dressed, smiles ablaze with anticipation for the evening, and reminded myself of one important thing: this night was not about me. I refused to let them know all the thoughts running through my head, and I refused to be that person who takes over someone else's moment with their drama.

Instead, I straightened out my floor-length, sky blue gown, swept the bottom of the dress to my left side and gathered it in my hand while the three of us walked into the ceremony hall. Confidently. Our curves swaying with power. My crystal-sequined shoes glistening underneath and helping to center my five-foot-three frame as we made our way to our seats.

"Reagan, you sure you're all right?" Robin whispered in my ear as we sat down.

"I'm sure."

"Because, I mean, we would all understand if you weren't."

"No, seriously, I'm fine. Just had a moment, but everything is good now."

"Okay," she replied with just a slight twinge of disbelief and a quick tap of her hand on my thigh.

We'd barely had time to settle in our seats when a hush came over the crowd as the pastor and Lance walked to the front of the room. Lance was beaming. His outfit was sharp—crisp black bow tie, suit tailored to perfection, cuff links just slightly peeking out—but the real standout was the smile he couldn't get rid of throughout his entire walk up to the front. Once the men arrived at their positions, the music started up, and two by two, each bridesmaid entered the aisle with a groomsman on her arm. They walked slowly but with purpose, their eyes focused solely on their destination.

When it was Jake's turn, my heart skipped a beat as soon as he entered the room. I watched him as he offered his arm for his bridesmaid to hold and walked her down the long, silver-carpeted aisle. I yearned for him as his lips creased slightly upward, dimple peeking out ever so slyly as he attempted to steady his breathing. I could tell he was nervous but working hard not to show it; his head held high and body facing straight to the altar. It was almost as if he was worried that he might be distracted if he looked anywhere to his left or right.

By the time the rest of the wedding party walked down the aisle, most of the crowd was standing, turned toward the door and waiting for the bride to enter. But I lingered just a bit longer toward the altar, first at Jake, and then on the groom to see if he was as nervous as everyone else seemed to be. There he stood, running his hands down his tuxedo to straighten it out—and maybe dry off his hands, too—as he prepared to see his bride in her dress for the first time. He definitely was nervous, but his smile had yet to disappear. And within a minute, the Bridal Chorus began playing, and there was Candice, walking down the aisle with her dad, her maid of honor trailing behind to make sure the train on her dress didn't tangle. We could barely keep our eyes off her, but she was gracefully and beautifully only looking at her husband-to-be.

When Candice finally walked up to Lance, her stunning sequined mermaid gown sparkling under the lights, not a dry eye was found in the room.

You could see how clear it was they were meant to be husband and wife. And that? That clarity was something Jake and I never had. We always had the passion and chemistry, but never the certainty. It was what we lacked and what Candice and Lance had in absolute abundance.

I turned to glance at Jake once more and thought I

briefly caught him staring back at me. I wasn't quite sure, but with Jake, that was par for the course. He'd say he was in love with me one minute and afraid to commit the next. Instead of dwelling on what might be, I decided to concentrate on what I knew for sure; that he never wanted it to be us standing in front of our friends and family, which meant I needed to move on.

Looking back at the bride and groom, I noticed him hold her trembling hand as they began their vows. "With this ring, I thee wed, and with it, I bestow upon you the treasures of my mind, heart and hands," she said.

I wondered if I'd one day have the same courage as Candice, standing there pledging her heart and body to one man. For the rest of her life. Vowing that her "I" was now permanently a "we" and that she would love this man until the end of her days. Right then, it seemed highly unlikely.

After they exchanged their vows and the wedding party had proceeded out of the room, we walked over to the cocktail reception, the women at the wedding gingerly stepping along so as not to trip in their stilettos or get their heels caught in their dresses. In between laughs and drinking, we struck sly poses to show off what we were wearing. We shifted in our shoes, stuck out our legs and placed hands on our hips, all just to get someone to ask that blessed question: "Where did you get that dress?" What I really wanted to do was place bets on how long each woman would be able to keep her shoes on that night.

I already knew my responses to both, of course. Neiman Marcus for the dress, and one hour, tops, on the shoes. Made of crystal sequins and gold-plated, five-inch heels, they made an impression throughout the room, but they were also *killing* my feet. Unfortunately, I'd committed the cardinal shoe sin of wearing a pair of heels at an event before breaking them in, and I was paying for it. The only upsides were that I knew I had some foldable flats in my purse for later, and, since I was so concentrated on my shoes, they were inadvertently keeping me calm under pressure. So calm, in fact, that I didn't see Jake when he approached a group of us. I was standing around gabbing with some of the girls about the rest of our plans for the weekend when I suddenly heard his voice call my name from behind.

"Rae," he said, using the nickname my parents gave me that most of my close friends had co-opted over time.

I turned around slowly, dreading what was to come next, and there he was, giving me the attention that I'd been waiting for in the ceremony. Jake stood squarely in his black tuxedo and bow tie, with a Tiffany-blue pocket square peeking out, his shoulders just out of reach unless I stood on my tippy toes. His hair was closely shaved down in a low-cut Caesar fade; his five-foot-eleven frame matched only by the smile he had on his face that quite literally lit up the room. *Damn, he looks good.*

"Hey, Reagan." He gave himself just enough time to take my outfit all in as he spoke, but the tension between us was evident from the beginning.

"Hi, Jake," I replied, desperately trying not to focus on him directly.

"You look very beautiful tonight."

"Th-thank you," I stammered. "You look…really nice as well."

"And those shoes. Phew! I see some things never change. You're still rocking the most fire shoes in the whole room."

"Oh, yeah? You like?" I asked, jokingly turning around in a circle to show him the full outfit, but also giving myself a chance to try to remain calm. He was half-right. My *feet* were surely on fire in my shoes, but I didn't plan on letting him or anyone else know that. As I made my turn, I noticed that the women I'd been speaking to had long abandoned me for another conversation, and I couldn't rely on them to get me out of my situation. I had to do it on my own.

"I do, very much." His response, so bold and fast, jolted me out of my thoughts.

By the time I made it back around to him from my circle, he was staring directly into me with an intense glare that snapped away my smile instantly. Jake had a way of doing that, a way that made many of our friends feel uncomfortable when they were around us, like they'd gotten stuck in our bedroom on accident. This time I was just as shocked by the way he could still conjure up such a look for me.

I cleared my throat to keep from buckling under the weight of his eyes on me. "Well, it's good to see you."

Jake said no words in response but reached out his hand to push back the one dark brown curl daring to fall from my loose chignon onto my face, drawing his body even closer to mine. I knew there was only so much longer I could stand in front of him without breaking down and asking all the thoughts that had been running through my head since I saw him walk down that aisle. Things like, "Why not us? Did you ever love me? Do we still have a chance?" I also remembered that he knew me better than anyone, and he could tell my façade was seconds away from giving. The last thing I wanted was for that to happen. Not after he'd made the choice to move and not fight for us.

I stepped back to gain some more space between us. "You, too," he finally said.

Jake watched me as goose bumps formed on my arms, knowing the exact effect he was having. He stepped back into my space, leaned in and kissed me so softly he barely grazed my skin. His lips landed just off to the side of mine, touching me ever so slightly, but enough to incite chills down my spine. In those few seconds I had time to breathe in his cologne and feel the gentle tickle of the stubble left after shaving his beard. He lingered just long enough to remind me of our first kiss and send signals to my body to go running for the door, get away from everyone and cry. Instead, I closed my eyes and swallowed my tears. When I opened them, I saw him standing in front of me, a slight smirk on his face like he'd won a long-fought battle.

"You know what?" I started before realizing whatever I said wasn't going to be worth it.

"Never mind." I turned around on my crystal heels and left him standing there without as much as a goodbye.

"Wow, this is a real, legit platinum wedding!"

"I know! It's just…wow."

Robin, Jennifer and I overheard a few people commenting on the look of the reception, and we giggled to ourselves. That was the exact reaction we knew our friends wanted when they planned everything. The excited women behind us were right, though, of course.

Surrounding us were crystals and sparkles, Tiffany-blue accents and silver trappings. It could almost have been mistaken for an event designed by famed celebrity event planner David Tutera, it was so extravagant.

The place was decadent, but in a good way. Blue-and-silver balloons hung from the ceiling, and each table was adorned with a centerpiece that could have been a chandelier in another lifetime. The decor of the room was only matched by the music and the drinks that were flowing. In fact, the only thing really missing from the wedding was the fourth to our quartet since college, Christine, who was recovering from gall bladder surgery and couldn't make it to Philly. She would have loved every drop of the decadence in the room, and I made a note in my head to remember to take photos so she could see.

For the next hour Jenn, Robin and I took turns dancing to the likes of Stevie Wonder and Bruno Mars, watching Candice and Lance spin around the room to the melodies of their first song, and joining them on the dance floor for Earth, Wind & Fire's "September," the epic ode to love and dancing the night away that had long become a staple at many weddings and Bar Mitzvahs. It was in the midst of all that joy that my feet finally caved to the pain from my Cinderella-style shoes.

I knew it. I knew they wouldn't last more than an hour at this reception.

Luckily, Jenn and Robin seemed to be in the same predicament. After one more quick trot around the dance floor, we looked at each other with knowing glances, and took off in the direction of our table so we could try to seamlessly change into our new shoes for the rest of the evening.

It was like we were in a race. And maybe we were, but only to see who could get relief the fastest. Robin, with her long legs, easily beat me and Jennifer, quickly striding to our table with what seemed like fewer than ten steps. By the time we both sat down to pull our flats out of our purses, she was already remarking how amazing she felt after removing her ankle-strapped, four-inch stilettos.

"Oh, my God, I'm so glad we had the foresight to put our flats in our purses," she sighed, just as Jenn and I plopped down in our seats.

"Are you kidding me? No way we would have made it without them," Jennifer said. She slid off her right shoe, waving it in the air to us both, before continuing her point: "These things here are pure death traps. Why do we wear them again?"

"Because they look good and we look good in them," I chimed in.

"Oh, right, ha ha, that," Jennifer agreed, laughing. "I guess that does help."

"Mmm-hmm, especially when you want the ex you haven't seen since college to drool over you." Robin cleared her throat as she paused and nodded in my direction, making it very clear her joke was aimed at me.

"Whoop! I think that's you," Jennifer said, slapping me on my thigh as they both cracked themselves up.

"Whatever," I said, rolling my eyes. I wasn't exactly interested in getting into the Jake conversation as we changed into our flats at a dinner table full of people.

"Nah, nah, not whatever. We saw you guys over there being all flirty with each other," Robin said.

"I think anyone with eyes could see that," Jennifer added. She stood up from her seat after sliding on both her shoes, her slender five-foot-six frame suddenly appearing pretty small without the benefit of four-inch heels.

"What you saw was me caught off guard for a second, but nothing more than that. Don't worry."

"So you don't want to see him again tonight?" Jennifer asked.

"I mean... I don't..." I hesitated, trying to find the words to what I'd been feeling for the past few hours without giving them more ammunition for a serious conversation. "Look, all I know is it's been four years since we broke up, and we haven't talked since then. It's a little...hard to see him, that's all."

"You think it's because you still love him?" Jennifer asked.

"I do," Robin jumped in.

"Honestly? I think it's because I'm still hurt that he chose to move after college and didn't fight for us."

"I get that. I do." Jennifer, ever the compassionate foil to Robin's snark, was trying to make me feel better, probably after sensing the conversation was getting a bit too real for our circumstances. "But that doesn't mean you don't want to see him."

"Mmm-hmm, exactly," Robin said, chiming in again. "In fact, I think you better decide quickly if you do because from what I can tell, he's walking up to us in three, two, one..."

Robin stood up as Jake neared our table, her face giving way to any excitement she'd been trying to hold in. Just like earlier in the evening, I looked up and there he was, standing in front of me as I slid my foot into my second flat shoe.

"Rae."

"Jake, we have to stop meeting like this," I said, standing up.

"Ha ha. I guess somehow I do keep sneaking up on you."

"And suddenly, everyone leaves when you come by as well," I said, motioning my hands to show how once again my friends had left me with him.

Jake stepped one foot closer to me.

"I see you took your shoes off," he said, casually changing the conversation.

"Yeah, it was time, but now that I have on my ballet flats, I can properly tear up the dance floor."

I kicked out a leg from underneath my dress to try to break up some of the tension between us, thinking that showing off my flat shoes might lighten the mood.

"Nice," he laughed. "I kinda wish I'd gotten a chance to dance with you in the heels, though."

"Dance with me?" I gave him a quizzical look.

"Yeah, you're not going to save a dance for me?" He smiled like he always did when he was, well, being him. Kind of like the real-life version of a cartoon character who was so charming, a star glistened in one eye when he winked at you.

"Um, sure." I hesitated, realizing I was caught between Jake and the table and couldn't back away. "But why would you need me to have on heels for that?"

"Oh, I don't. I just figured it would've been easier with you a little taller. Now I might end up stepping all on your dress."

"Ohhhh, you think you're funny. Okay, jerk. I got you." I chuckled and began moving to his side so I could walk away again but was stopped when he grabbed my hand.

"All jokes aside. Reagan Doucet, can I have this dance?"

"Oh, you meant, like, now?"

"Yeah. Now."

He spoke slowly and deliberately, staring daggers into my eyes and melting my resistance under his spell. As soon as our eyes connected, it was like he could read the pages to my inner thoughts with just one look. And once again, he knew it.

"Okay," I breathlessly mouthed before he took my hand in his and walked me to the dance floor, John Legend's "For the First Time" playing in the background.

Walking with one hand in his, I was keenly aware of Robin's and Jenn's eyes on us and also the gentle but firm way he held me, cupping one of my hands in his and his other hand guiding me by the small of my back.

"Do you know how much I've missed you?" he asked as we reached our spot on the dance floor, our eyes once again connecting while I lifted my arms to place them on his shoulders.

"I missed you, too, Jake, but we can't just act like everything's okay between us—"

"I know it's not, Rae, but let's not *but* this evening away, okay?" he said, interrupting me with a statement that also sort of felt like a plea. "Don't you miss how good our skin feels together?" His hand began dragging circles in my palm as he moved one of my arms from his shoulder to his side. "How our bodies fit perfectly?" With his other hand still on my lower back, he pulled me closer to him. "How our breaths match?"

"I remember," I said, taking in my own deep breath.

"Then can we just stay in that for now?" Once again,

his eyes poured into mine, cajoling me to do whatever it was he wanted.

I nodded my head and with a sigh, lowered it and placed it on his chest as we began dancing to the music together.

In that moment everything was a blur. I smelled his cologne and began hearing the smooth sounds of Luther Vandross and Cheryl Lynn's "If This World Were Mine." I mouthed the beginning of the song as if I were part of the duo. It was everything I also wanted Jake to say so I closed my eyes and pretended he was.

Right before leaving the wedding, a few of us gathered around Lance and Candice for one last shot to celebrate them. With our purses and shoes in one hand, we raised our glasses in the other, ready to clank them together to mark the occasion.

"To the McCoys!" screamed out the best man.

"To the McCoys!"

I instantly felt hair grow on my chest after downing my shot of whiskey and slammed the glass on the table to try to mask the fact I felt like my insides were burning.

I covered my mouth, coughing, but hoping to still disguise it when I felt a man's hands and arms wrapping around my waist from behind me. I knew it was Jake without even needing to turn around.

"Um, what are you doing?"

"Oh, my bad, is this not allowed?"

"No, it's not allowed," I replied, joking and twisting myself away from his grasp.

"Hmm, just in public or like, period?"

"What are you talking about?" I was genuinely confused about where he was going with the conversation. *Is he drunk?* I wondered. Or maybe taking our moment on the dance floor a bit too far?

"Don't worry about it," he said, changing the conversation and gently pulling me off to the side so we could speak privately. "Can you believe Candice and Lance are married? This stuff's still pretty wild to me."

"I know. It's like, of course they are because they are couple goals, but also, when did we get old enough to be in weddings and watch our friends pledge their lives to each other?"

"For real." He paused. "There's a part of me that always thought it would be us first, though."

"Oh?"

"You didn't?"

I didn't know what to say. Obviously, I'd thought of us being married, but in the time that had passed since we broke up, I'd also worked really hard to get over my heartbreak from him. And there he was trying to pull the Band-Aid off a wound not fully healed yet. "Of course I did, Jake, but—"

"Yeah. I know. Always a *but*," he said, interrupting me and clearly wanting to avoid where our conversation was going. "Hold that thought. I think we need another shot."

I watched him as he ran off to the bar and began telling the bartender exactly what he wanted. Standing somewhat with a nervous energy, I saw him practically instruct her on which drinks to mix, all the while glancing back at me ever so slightly. It wasn't long before he was back before me with four shot glasses in his hands.

"*A* shot, huh?" I laughed nervously.

"Eh, I figured we probably really needed two to take

the edge off a bit. Just don't die like you almost did earlier trying to hold in your cough."

"Oh, my God, don't do me like that!"

"Just saying, I thought I was going to have to perform the Heimlich on you or something."

"Whatever. Bring on those shots, jokester." I grabbed my two glasses from him and quickly noticed why he'd been instructing the bartender so much. "You had her make mine Washington Apples?"

"It's still your favorite type of shot, right?"

"It is," I responded with a smile.

"Good. I figured these wouldn't make you cough up a lung and ruin my chances of spending more time with you tonight."

"Oh, boy, somehow I must have forgotten how charming you can be," I said, holding in my giggle. "Let's hurry up and take these shots before I—"

"What, jump on me?" he asked, stepping closer into my space.

"No! Get out of here. In your dreams." I playfully pushed him back a few steps, and we both cracked up laughing.

"All right, all right, you ready?"

"Let's do it."

We'd barely finished our drinks when I looked around and noticed the crowd had dwindled down even more around us, and we were quickly becoming the center of attention. Even Robin and Jennifer were eyeing me with such intensity it felt like the brightest spotlight shining on us, showcasing all my vulnerabilities to everyone still left at the reception.

"Come with me," Jake said, offering his right hand to me and jolting me out of my thoughts.

"I'm sorry, what? Come with you where?"

"Anywhere but here. Just somewhere we can talk and get away from everyone else."

"I don't know if that's a good idea, Jake."

"I know." A smile started to form on his face again. "But come with me anyway."

I titled my head, trying to determine how sincere he was, and then finally gave in and put my hand in his. Without saying another word, he started walking us out of the reception and onto the nearest elevator.

"So that was awkward for you, too, right?" I asked once we were alone.

"Are you kidding me? Our friends are brutal. I thought someone was going to erect a billboard about us while we stood there."

"Yes! Okay, I'm glad I wasn't alone."

"You're never alone when you're with me."

"Stop with the lover-boy moves, please," I said, rolling my eyes and chuckling at the same time.

He laughed. "You know I'm right."

I couldn't help but laugh as well. It was obvious that we were falling right back into the groove we'd had when we were dating, when we could just talk and laugh with each other for hours. In fact, the whole night with him reminded me of our time in college, when we effortlessly just worked, and before he threw it all away.

"That laugh... Damn, I missed that, too," he said as we stepped off the elevator and onto his floor. Still holding my hand, Jake turned to me once more before taking another step in the direction of his room. "I *can* drop you off at your room if that's what you'd rather do. I really was just hoping to spend more time with you, but this has to be your decision."

"No. I'm where I want to be." With my heels off and in my hands, it forced me to look up at him when I talked to him, creating a dynamic that gave him most of the power. The tricky part was I was all too ready to give in to him, the feminist in me be damned.

"Good."

With the answer he'd been waiting for, we walked down the hallway until we reached his hotel room, pausing just long enough to give me a chance to view it from his opened door. Like mine, it featured crisp white curtains flanking the widest windows I'd seen in a hotel before, and modern black-and-red furniture that provided a sleek getaway from the glitz and glam happening downstairs. But he also had a view of Philadelphia that was way more impressive than mine. It was striking just how beautiful it was, and I found myself staring out the window for a beat.

As if he could read my mind, Jake came up behind me and whispered, "You're even more beautiful, you know."

"I'm sure you say that to all the girls."

"Nah, just to you."

"Jake."

"I'm serious! Well, okay, obviously, I've said it to other girls before, but Rae, I meant it when I said I haven't been able to stop thinking about you lately. And then seeing you tonight, it all makes sense. We make sense."

My back facing him, his whispers conveniently hit right behind my ear, sending shivers down my spine. I was almost certain my knees buckled, giving me away, so I turned to face him and give myself a chance to stand straight again.

"I get that," I said, staring into the same eyes that had pulled the truth out of me on so many occasions in the past. "I always thought we were a perfect fit."

"We still can be, you know."

He leaned down and kissed me, our lips intertwining and breaths syncing up as we pulled each other closer. Instantly, I was swept into the moment and released a sigh of pleasure as I gave in to him and to my own desires. Putting up zero resistance, I melted into Jake's embrace as he dragged his hand from the nape of my neck to my back and slowly released the zipper from my gown. Then he swung me back around toward the window and began kissing my neck and spine and lower back as he made his way down, the dress falling with him. By the time he was done, I was standing only in my bra and panties and ballet flats, the dress gathered at my ankles.

"Wow," he whispered, his eyes following the length of my body. "Touching is allowed now, yes?"

I chuckled and stepped out of the dress to fully reveal myself—pink panties, pink bra, pink flats and brown skin. "Uh-huh. Very much so."

Without another word, he picked me up, laid me down on his bed and slid my underwear off in what felt like one fell swoop.

"You belong to me for the next few hours. Is that all right?"

He focused his eyes on mine again, waiting for my response, alternating sliding one hand down the side of my body and the other tracing the lips on my face.

"Mmm-hmm."

"Say yes or I'll stop."

"Yes." Slowly, I saw him stand up and begin to take

his suit off, piece by piece—first his tie, then his jacket, shirt, pants and finally his boxer briefs. This time I got to marvel at him; the way his shoulders rose up and down with his breathing, the vee-cut at his hips that led your eyes to his penis, the way it jumped when he caught me admiring him.

And with that same smirk and dimple peeking out again, he walked back to the bed, draping his body on mine, and took my lips into his.

Four hours later I awoke in Jake's bed, the light from his phone flickering on and off from texts he was getting throughout the night. I turned my head, trying to drown out the light and focus on the fact that he had his arms wound tightly around me. Our breaths were still in sync, too; our chests rising and falling on beat with each other. What did this all mean? I wondered as I felt him pull me tighter to him even as he slept. Was this the start of us getting back together? Had I misjudged him before? Was this his way of saying he was ready to fight for us now?

His phone light shone again from the nightstand. *Who could this be?* I thought, finally unable to resist checking. I leaned over, slightly releasing myself from his grip, and pressed the phone screen to drag the notifications down and see what the messages said. In an instant I found myself in the middle of a group chat with some of his best friends.

Hey, you still with Reagan?

Come on Fred, u know he is.

Guess he couldn't pass that old thing up, huh?

Wonder what Shannon would think about that.

Ohhh snap! She definitely wouldn't like that.

Man, don't listen to these fools. Hit us up when you done.

What? Horrified, I read on as each message threw me a new gut punch. Not only were his friends talking about me as just some "old thing" to have sex with, Jake maybe also had a girlfriend named Shannon? At the very least, she was someone they all knew who had the right to be upset about Jake and me together. It was too much to take in. I closed my eyes, trying to drown out what I'd just read, hoping it would somehow make it not real. After a few seconds I opened them again and checked. *Nope. Still there. I should have known.*

My head began to spin as reality came crushing down. He had only asked if I could be his for the next few hours, I remembered. And he'd never once said anything about us getting back together. Just that he missed me, and clearly wanted to have sex. But he had to have known that I would want more, right? *Ugh. How could I have been such an idiot? He's a man; why did I just assume this was anything more than sex?*

I slid out of bed so as not to wake him and caught the tears as they were just about to start coming down my face. No. He wouldn't get the pleasure of me crying again. Not this time. And I certainly didn't want to look him in his face again and have him break my heart once more. I grabbed my things from the floor—

my bra, underwear, purse, flats, dress and finally my heels—and began putting my bra and then dress on.

I had to get out of there as soon as I could. With my dress halfway zipped up, I walked out of his room, vowing to never be that stupid for him or anyone else, ever again.

Chapter 1

October 28, 2019

It was barely 7:00 a.m. when I heard my alarm blasting the sounds of Nicki Minaj's "Pound the Alarm."

"Not yet, Alexa." Groggy and yearning for at least five more minutes of sleep, I stretched my arm over the length of my bed and pressed down on the snooze button with my eyes still closed. It wasn't that I didn't want to get up, necessarily; it was just that the cocoon of my comforter in my queen-size bed felt so much better than whatever could have been waiting for me outside it. I pulled the cover over my head as an extra protection against the sun.

"Pound the alarm!"

"Agh!" I screamed out as it went off once more. "Fine, fine. I'm up now."

The music still blaring, I finally acquiesced and

rolled myself out of bed, one leg coming free from my cover cocoon, then the next, and made my way to my closet for what had become my daily routine: pick out shoes for the day, figure out the outfit that goes best with them, take a shower and then, of course, post my #shoeoftheday photo to Instagram before heading to work. Conveniently, I passed right over the red pumps that spelled disaster for me the night before.

"Hmm, now what do I feel like wearing today?" I questioned, dancing to my closet and scanning all the shoes I own with my eyes, from my flats to my heels, boots to sneakers, in every color one can imagine. They were all intricately displayed on the shelves—heels facing out to show the length and style of the pump, flats facing forward to make it easier for me to see if it was a peep toe, curved toe, pointed toe or square.

"Oooh, these!" Something about my deep red, almost maroon peep-toe heels from BCBG caught my eyes, and I knew they were the ones for the day. The shoes were adorned with a silver buckle on the side of each peep toe and would go perfectly with my red-and-pink floral blouse, black pencil skirt and peplum blazer to match. It was amazing how the rest of an outfit could come together for me once I picked out the shoes, and today was no exception. These might even be the ones to help me finally convince my boss to let me do the article I'd been pitching to him for months. Excited about my choices, I laid them out on my bed and hopped in the shower, continuing my best rap impressions as my playlist toggled through my favorite female rappers.

It was 9:00 a.m. when I walked into work at Washington, DC's premier political news online magazine, my heels clacking on the linoleum floors they must have purchased just to make it that much easier for women to alert everyone of their comings and goings in the office. Seated at her desk already was my always-early, no-holds-barred freckle twin, and the best IT specialist in the office, Rebecca, her reddish-blond hair pulled up into a loose bun and a smile on her face the size of a kid in a candy store.

"So…" she said, dragging out her first word. "Tell me about last night."

"Oh, my God, let me sit down first before I embarrass myself, please." Adding on the extra drama, I slid my hand across my face like a diva in an old Hollywood movie.

Rebecca blinked, curious of what could have happened in the ten hours since she'd seen me. "Wait, what? When we talked at happy hour last night, you had a whole plan to seduce 'ol' boy.'" She was careful to use the moniker we'd long ago decided to call any of the guys I dated since they usually didn't last long enough for my friends to remember their names.

"Oh, I'm aware," I said, finally sitting in my chair at my desk, conveniently located next to hers. "But let's just say things didn't go as planned."

"Okay, now you really have to tell me what happened. Is the man not seducible?"

"Ha! No, that's not it." I stopped myself. "I'm sure he's very seducible. I, however, may not be the one to try it again."

I paused for a second to turn on my computer and see if any emails were in my inbox, especially from either Peter, my boss, or any of the leads I'd been working on for the story I wanted to pitch to him. *Damn, not one. Just more of the same junk as always.* As my main act of defiance, work-life balance, or both, in the four years I'd worked there, I'd yet to put my emails on my phone, so my mornings usually consisted of me catching up on details in my inbox and gabbing with Becs.

I rolled my chair closer to her desk after I'd finished my quick scan so I could give her all the juicy details somewhat privately. "All right, he comes over last night looking so sexy," I recounted, beginning my story and halfway reminding myself how well the evening had started. "He's wearing gray sweatpants, so you know he knows what's up, smelling like YSL cologne, standing tall with his broad shoulders that make you just want to jump into his arms, those stunningly beautiful green eyes and of course, his man bun sitting perfectly on top of his head."

Rebecca pushed her chair even closer to mine, fully captivated and ready to hear the rest. "Mmm-hmm."

I spanned the office once more to see who all was around yet. Thankfully for us, it was still fairly empty. Most of the people in our office casually strolled in on a good day around 10:00/10:30 a.m., but Rebecca was an early bird, and I couldn't live down the reminder my parents always gave me as a kid: "You have to be twice as good to get half as far, Rae." That meant neither of us ever arrived later than 9:00 a.m. It was part of what had bonded us four years ago when I started.

I continued, "I answer the door, trying to be all Jessica Rabbit-like, letting him take in my lingerie. And you can tell he's into it. I catch his eyes roaming all up and down my body, so I'm just standing there letting him do it, like yeah."

Rebecca laughed.

"It doesn't take long before we're in my room. We're kissing, he's grabbing my hair, I'm holding on to his back, everything is going just how I wanted. Until he almost trips on my red pumps by the bed," I said, hanging my head in shame.

"Wait, why were they by the bed? I thought you were going to wear them when you opened the door?"

"I was, but then last minute I realized, I'm not fully that girl, so I tossed them off by my bed," I said, laughing. "Anyway, he's like, 'What are these doing here?' picking them up and mocking me with them. 'I know Reagan doesn't keep her shoes anywhere but her sacred shoe closet,' he says. 'What, were you planning to seduce me or something?'"

"Well, he's not wrong."

"Whatever." I rolled my eyes before continuing on with the story. "Can you imagine how embarrassing this was, Becs? Not only did I change my mind on doing that, now he's calling me out on it? Ugh! If only it didn't get worse."

"Oh, damn, girl. Worse?" Rebecca's face has already turned red from the thought of what could have gone wrong.

"Exactly. So now I'm trying to save face, and I'm all, 'How about you put those down, lie down and just let me take over.'"

"My girl. I see you!"

"Ha ha, don't be too impressed yet," I reminded her, using my hand to calmly bring down her energy from a ten to a two. "He lies down on the bed, and I start doing my thing—swaying my hips from side to side, winding my body down to almost a squat just to bring it back up. I drag my hands down my body, lingering on my breasts before making their way to my stomach and then my thighs. Like, I'm in *control*, okay?"

"Okay!" Rebecca chimed in again, still waiting for the embarrassing part.

"And he is just lying there, paralyzed into submission on the bed, watching me turn myself on. Wanting to move so badly, but not wanting the show to end, right? I do this for about ten minutes, and before he can get up, I drop down to my knees once more, turn back around and crawl my way up his body. I'm sliding my breasts up his legs, making sure they touch him just enough to tease him but not enough for him to fully feel their impact. And finally, I decide I'm going to do one more move. I wink at him, get up and wind my body around one more time, finally unhooking the back of my bra, letting the strap of one side down and then the other, and watching him watch me as gravity drops the bra out of sight and leaves my breasts in full view."

"Rae, I think we need to have a talk about the definition of *embarrassing*."

"Wait for it," I reminded her again. "Now, he's still lying there, and I can feel his desire oozing off of him. I swing my right leg out to kick the bra off the bed. And then, wham!"

"Oh, no!"

"Oh, yes," I confirmed, nodding to show it really did happen. "I fell. Lost my footing, tripped on the bra and went flailing over the side of the bed. Falling in the least sexy way possible. In slow motion. Backward. And onto those damn red heels."

Mimicking my fall, I slid down in my chair, but caught myself before I actually fell onto the floor. Pencil skirts weren't made for getting up off the ground, I chided myself.

"Ohhhhh nooooo."

"Yep."

"Oh, my God, Rae. What did he do?"

"Oh, that's the worst part! He laughed! He legit sat up and cracked up laughing at me on the floor."

"You've got to be kidding me."

"Nope. Unfortunately, I am not."

"What did you do?"

"I stood up eventually and kicked him out. Like, what? Okay, it was probably really funny, but make sure I'm okay first before you just start howling with laughter," I said, half laughing and half shaking my head. Rebecca joined in as the image of me falling off the bed hit her again. "Needless to say, that one is over."

"Yeah, I sort of figured by the end of the story he was."

"That's what, the fourth guy this year now that's made it past the first date and still ended up being a bust? Becs, seriously. There's got to be more than *this* out there, right?"

"Of course, honey, this was just one for the books," she replied. "But there's so many fish in the sea. This is just a blip and a funny story in your basically perfect life."

"Bleh, it's definitely not perfect," I groaned. "And I know, he's just a blip, but damn, I date all the time, and like, nothing. It always ends in some foolishness."

"I get that, but are we going to be honest here? Because it's not like you really invest in these guys anyway. Yeah, you date *a lot*." Rebecca emphasized her last words by punctuating them with air quotation marks.

"But you already know going in they are either not trying to do anything serious or they want to marry you tomorrow, which makes you feel instantly smothered."

"But don't you think that's crazy that's the pattern? What's a girl gotta do to get something in the middle?"

"Hmm. Maybe risk opening up to one of these guys and seeing if it can actually be something more?"

"Bleh." Even coupled with Becs's best older sister look, I was completely not interested in that idea. "Just call me 'five-month Betty,' I guess. I keep 'em for five months, and then I'd rather just focus on my shoe-of-the-day posts online and work on convincing Peter to let me write about the ways women are shaping the world of politics instead of having to write yet again about how the Republicans and Democrats aren't getting along in Congress."

"One, five-month Betty is hilarious and might be your new nickname now," Rebecca laughed. "Two, Peter loves you and everything you do, so I'm sure it won't take that much convincing."

"You say that, and all y'all think that and yet, every week I'm stuck still writing the same thing. Don't get me wrong, I get paid a lot, so I'm not *really* complaining, but like how many times can you write the same thing over and over? We get it. They don't like each other!"

"Three," Rebecca continued, undeterred from my interruption, "you are definitely doing your thing with those shoe-of-the-day posts. What do you have, like fifteen thousand followers now?"

"It's actually seventeen," I corrected her, jokingly patting the bottom of my hair in response. "And yet, I'm also the same girl who was ghosted by the last guy the day after we'd talked about me helping him prepare for his open mic and then had the next one not understand the rules of laughing at someone."

Rebecca raised her arms to pretend as if she was playing a tiny violin. "Oh, poor Rae," she said, winking to let me know she was at least somewhat messing with me. "Sounds to me like you need to listen to some more Megan Thee Stallion today or something. Get your energy back up."

In the distance we heard another pair of heels on the linoleum floor, prompting Rebecca to scooch a little back to her desk but stop in her tracks when she heard the shoes turn off to the right, away from us. At almost 9:30 a.m., we knew it was likely the Black woman in the general counsel office, her routine similar to ours.

The coast clear, Rebecca added, "Then, we can continue this conversation."

"You may be correct."

"Oh, I am. You can't let 'ol boy' and those red pumps get you down this much. You did enough of that last night," she muttered under her breath, chuckling at her joke.

"Oh, God, I'm never living this down, am I?"

"Yeah, probably not any time soon."

Defeated in getting her to join me in my attempt at having a woe-is-me moment, I rolled my chair back to my desk and scrolled through the emails in my inbox again.

Mueller report, congresswoman resigns after sex scandal, impeachment inquiry…

Damn, it was a depressing morning.

"I see Peter coming down the hallway, so now might be as good a time as any to catch him," Rebecca said, interrupting my thoughts. She was the perfect spy at our job, especially for Peter. Somehow, her desk was positioned just so that she could see him when he was anywhere near his office, and yet, he could not see her. I checked my watch and noticed the time: 10:00 a.m. Just like clockwork.

"Good looking out, Becs." I stood up from my chair and smoothed out my skirt, checking out the floor to see where he was in relation to his office. If I left then, I could meet him at his office door as he walked up to it and command his attention before the day got too busy.

"Good luck!" Rebecca whisper-screamed out as I *click-clacked* past her. Peter's office was only a few feet away, which meant it took me only a minute to catch up to him. He was, as was typical, preoccupied in his phone, likely checking to see what news he'd have to manage for the day.

"Peter!" I practically screamed as he walked up, realizing only too late that my enthusiasm was probably a bit too much. For better or for worse, he barely recognized it.

"Oh, hi, Reagan, just the person I wanted to see. Have a seat," he said, pointing to one of the chairs in his office as we walked in. He barely let me sit down before he started talking. "Now, as I'm sure you've seen, Representative Linda Frasier announced her resignation yesterday. I put something on the front page over the weekend that just covered the breaking news aspect, but I know you've been wanting to do more articles about women and politics, and this might be the place to try it."

I could hardly stop myself from rolling my eyes. *Wow, what a concept*, I thought. Finally talking about the challenges that women face in politics only after the Democratic congresswoman who is accused of having improper relationships with staffers resigns, but not when I initially wanted to discuss the ugliness of her intimate photos being released to the public. *Why was I here again?*

"I know, I know," Peter continued, completely oblivious to the ways I was biting my tongue as he spoke. "This isn't exactly what you were hoping for, but I'd still love to see what you can do with it."

"Oh," I blurted out before I could stop myself. "What exactly were you looking for?"

"I don't know yet, Reagan. I'm hoping you can tell me. There's a part of me that feels like we've beat this drum to death. Everyone's done stories about representatives having illicit affairs for decades now. But you told me you could do something different with it, right?"

"Yes, I did." It was moments like this with Peter when I appreciated being at a job with a boss who liked my work. He didn't always get it right; he had tons of blind spots as an early 40s white man from Maine who thought he was super liberal, but well...wasn't, but this was the kind of opportunity he dangled in front of me like a carrot, and I was all too ready to jump for it.

"I mean, you're right, it's not *exactly* what I've been pitching, but if it gets me closer to that, I'll take it."

"Okay, great." Peter smiled, feeling his own sense of satisfaction from the conversation. "Now, was there something you wanted to talk about?"

"Uhhh, no. Just, when do you want the pitch?"

"Sooner the better. If I like it, I'd like to run it by the end of the week."

"Done." I stood up to leave his office but stopped

before walking out. "Thanks again, Peter. You won't regret it."

"I know," he said. "Just don't make it about race, okay? Linda Frasier is a white woman who resigned because she was having affairs with white staffers. I know you're interested in this intersectionality thing, but let's see how this one goes first." He didn't even raise his head when he said it. Of course, if I just kept the story strictly about Rep. Frasier, focusing on the intersectionality of different forms of oppression wouldn't play an important role, but it hadn't been my intention to do so.

Putting on my brave face, I practically skipped back to my desk to mask the disappointment Rebecca was bound to notice if I didn't. It wasn't that she wouldn't be compassionate if I told her what happened; it's just that the last thing I wanted to do was talk to someone about it at that moment. Instead, I acted like I'd gotten everything I wanted.

"Be careful. We don't know if there are any red pumps lying around," Rebecca laughed as she saw me bouncing back to our desks.

"I'm so done with you right now," I laughed, plopping down in my chair and taking it for a spin. I was really putting on a show; one would never have known the thing I wanted to do the most was lay my head on my desk and break out into an ugly cry.

"I told you Peter loved you and everything you do," Rebecca said, turning back to her desk. "I can't wait to see this new article at the top of the site."

"Okay, okay, you may be right about that one thing," I joked.

"I've got eight years on you, dear Rae. I'm right about a whole lot more than one thing."

* * *

Sometimes you can tell how a day will end by the way that it begins. If the birds are practically singing with you down the street on your way to the Metro like you're freakin' Snow White, chances are pretty good that the day will be roses and sunshine throughout. But what about when you've been holding back tears since the alarm blared and you walked past the bright red symbols of your loneliness? That day probably won't end well.

It was 3:43 p.m. when I saw Robin's number on my office phone, not normally the number she would call if she just had a funny story to tell midday. Hesitant to pick it up, I let it ring a few times before I pulled my headphones out of my ears and grabbed the receiver.

"Hey, Robin, what's up?"

"Do you have a moment?" I heard her words but more importantly, her tone, and knew something was wrong.

"Sure."

"It's about Christine. She's been admitted to the hospital again."

"Oh, no." I felt my head get light but tried to concentrate on what she was saying.

"And this time her organs are starting to fail, so her mom asked me to call everyone and let them know what is going on."

"What do you mean her organs are starting to fail?" I could feel the dread growing inside me with every word Robin said. Christine and I had been friends since high school in New Orleans and both decided to go to college in DC, so she'd been with me through every significant moment for the past eleven years. It was her wild and crazy self that helped bring our quartet together—Christine, the raspy, speak-her-mind-at-all-times Afro-Latina who randomly, and often unconsciously, tossed in Spanish words as she spoke; Robin, the snarky but actually sort of sweet-at-heart girl from the Midwest; Jennifer, the compassionate one from sunny California who wore her heart and everyone else's on her sleeves; and me, the shoe fanatic who loved laughing, hated crying and always wanted to be the strong friend for everyone. Even as we'd all grown up and started our own careers, we stayed close, making sure to see each other at least once a week to catch up on the details of our lives. And now Christine's organs were failing? *In what universe was that okay?* I thought.

"You know she's been having these complications since her gallbladder surgery," Robin said, bringing me back into the phone conversation.

"Yeah, I know, but even after all her hospital visits, her organs never started failing." With tears threatening to pour down my face, I bit my tongue again, even as I tried to get as much information out of Robin as I could. "I mean, what does that even mean?"

"It's her lungs," she relented. "Her mom says they're not functioning properly."

I was silent. Numb even. A million thoughts raced through my head and then all stopped at one: Christine was going to die. Her lungs. That was all I could hear Robin say, *People definitely needed lungs to live.*

"The doctors are doing what they can to get them back working again, but I mean, you know when the organs start failing—"

I interrupted her, not wanting to hear the actual words. "I know, I know." My head began pounding, because it wasn't enough that I felt light-headed and had the deepest desire to slink down under my desk and never be seen again. I also apparently needed a headache on top of everything. On top of my best friend dying.

"I'm probably going to leave work in a few to go see her," Robin continued over the phone. "I don't think I'm going to be able to concentrate until I do."

"Yeah," I replied, not really knowing what other words to say and holding my forehead with one hand while I gripped the phone with the other. "I'll call you back in a little bit. Let me check with Peter to see if I can leave, too. This is the last place I want to be right now."

"No problem." Robin paused. "Hey, Reagan?"

"Yeah."

"I just want you to know that I love you." Her voice was filled with worry and concern, and you could tell she'd been crying.

"I love you, too, Robin," I said. "I love you, too."

I hung up the phone and stared at the ceiling for a brief moment before my feet had a mind of their own and my *click-clacks* ran through the hallway to the bathroom. Locking the door behind me, I stood facing myself in the mirror, holding back the tears so desperate to come out.

"It can't be her time yet," I said aloud. "It just can't be." I slumped down onto the counter, my legs no longer able to hold my weight up, and felt my thighs hit the cold, hard floor. It was no use in worrying about my pencil skirt when my world was falling apart. I vaguely heard Rebecca outside the door, asking if I was okay, but my mouth couldn't move to answer her.

Chapter 2

Bright and early on a Saturday morning, I found myself in a swanky gym locker room, less than a fifteen-minute walk from my apartment. Robin, Jenn and I had spent the past week sitting beside Christine's bed more than anywhere else, but in desperate need of a distraction, I'd agreed to join Rebecca at a morning spin class at our local gym. And while I'd jumped at the chance to do something, anything really, other than think about Christine's drip-drop slow recovery, it dawned on me not too soon after I met up with her that there was one small problem with me agreeing to the class: I hated spin.

Like, literally hated everything about it. It wasn't that I didn't think it could help; I knew a lot of people who swore by its health benefits, and certainly knew I'd be guaranteed to have an hour off from worrying. But over the years, spinning had become almost cult-like with its many variations, such as Soul Cycle, Trap Cycle and how could I forget the one that claimed it felt more like working out in a nightclub? Beyond even that, the thing I disliked most about spin was the way my butt felt during the class. Everyone always said that eventually your butt gets used to the feeling of the bike, but when I'd tried it before... Nah.

Regardless, there I was, putting on my spin sneakers on the wood-grain floors, marveling at the rotation of women coming in and out of the doors, looking like the exact models you might expect to see in spin class ads: blond hair tied in either a loose high ponytail or twirled in an up-do that took thirty minutes to do, but seemed effortless; Lululemon workout gear, S'well water bottles and enough sweat that they glistened, but not so much where they were actually drenched. I glanced up to see if Rebecca looked as nervous as I felt.

"Are you sure we're ready for this?" I asked, trying to give us one last shot at running away.

"Ha, yes, I'm sure." She paused. "I mean, kind of sure."

I could sense her hesitation. Maybe she, too, was worried that we weren't really the duo that fit in with the rest of the spin-bots before us? Even if we did have some things in common with them.

"You know our butts are going to be on fire afterward, right?" I asked, anxiously making sure the pink Velcro on my turquoise-and-white sneakers was fully snapped closed so that the shoes didn't become a death trap for me on the bike pedals.

"Yeah, I know." Rebecca's once assured voice had been replaced with a nervous chuckle, and I remembered exactly why we were friends. Neither of us felt entirely comfortable where we were, but we were going to try it together. "But we've tried other things before, and it worked out. I'm sure this will be fine. Remember when we did Zumba this summer for a couple months? That was fun!"

"Zumba was fun—wait, why did we stop going there again?"

"Umm, great question," she said, walking over to the water fountain to fill her own S'well water bottle. "Honestly, I think it's because we just didn't make the time for it. Who wants to go to Zumba when there's happy hours, right?"

"That's facts," I joked. "But this is different. Spin is…" I rubbed a butt cheek just thinking of how it felt previously and lost track of my sentence. "I just quickly found out last time I tried that I didn't have as much cushion in my tushion as I thought back then."

"Your tushion?"

"Yeah, my tushion! That's how much I thought I was packing behind me, but it wasn't enough."

The thought caused us both to laugh, one of those good, loud, from-your-stomach kind of laughs. It was the first one I'd had since getting Robin's call, and it felt good to have that feeling come through me again, even it meant enduring an hour of physical pain.

"First of all, that was like five or six years ago, so I'm guessing some things have improved since then. Second, you know you have more cushion in front of you than behind you," she added, making reference to the double-D breasts I'd acquired while gaining a few pounds over the years. I loved when Rebecca started making her points with numbers. It meant she was really invested in you listening to what she had to say. Unfortunately for her, it usually just caused me to chuckle inside, which was kind of the exact opposite reaction I'm guessing she wanted. "But," she continued, "even if neither of those things were true, we'd still push through. That's what we do."

I admired her tenacity, especially since I knew inside, she was just as concerned as I was, but was likely trying her best to be a good friend to me. Guess that meant it was my turn to stop complaining and join her in carrying the load of us having fun that morning.

"I sure hope so," I replied with a wink and then remembered one important fact I needed to correct her on. "But hey, don't hate, you know my butt is surprisingly very firm."

Rebecca rolled her eyes and shook her head at me. "All right, bootylicious. Yes, how could I forget? Now, let's get out of here before we're late."

We gathered up our items and slid them into our lockers, double-checking that we remembered our combination codes on the locks before clicking the doors closed. I turned to her once more, as we scooped up our water bottles and towels and began walking to our spin class like we were pros. It was clear she wanted to probe but wasn't sure if she should.

"How is Christine doing, by the way?" she finally blurted out. "Any better?"

"Not really." I fidgeted, not knowing how much I could talk about it without breaking down, but also wanting to be sensitive to her needs as a friend as well. I moved the water bottle to under my arm as we walked up to the classroom, needing something to do with my hands. "She's sort of touch and go, but still fighting to get out of the hospital."

"Okay," she said. "I know you don't want to talk about it, but I had to ask at least once."

"I get it."

The instructor was standing at the front of the classroom when we walked in, her enthusiasm leaping off her.

"Hi there," she nearly squealed out. "I'm Kelly, and we're so excited to see some new people join us today. I hope you enjoy yourself, and let me know if you need any help getting yourself set up."

"Thanks, Kelly!" we both said in unison, walking past her. "We hope so, too."

"And what about you? How are you handling everything?" Rebecca turned to watch me as she spoke, briefly halting our pursuit of a set of bikes next to each other.

"Becs, honestly..." I paused to get my thoughts together. "I'm mostly focused on being there for her. Obviously, you naturally start wondering if you're doing everything you should be doing while you have time on this earth. But I really haven't had the time to go there. As you know, this is the first thing I've done outside of going to the hospital and work in a week."

"Maybe you should be thinking about that, too, though," she suggested. "That's not you being selfish. It's just remembering to take care of yourself."

"Yeah, maybe," I said, pausing again. "I guess I have been sort of wondering, like, if I died tomorrow, could I say I was really happy before then?"

She blinked a few times at my honesty, but also

wanted to make sure she understood me correctly. "You mean, do you do enough?"

"No, I mean do I spend too much time trying to do everything I *think* I should?"

"Oh, now that's a great question, Rae."

Rebecca placed her hand on my shoulder and gave me a knowing nod that spoke volumes to what she believed my answer to the question would be. She wanted to dig in more, but she also knew I'd agreed to spin that morning to get away from having to think about death and the consequences of spending your life focused on other people's standards. After a few silent seconds she turned back around to restart our bike pursuit, noticing that more people were walking into the class and picking out their own bikes.

We spent the next couple minutes scoping out our perfect location: next to the window, not quite in front, but definitely not all the way in the back. This way we could see the instructor and be seen, but not find ourselves in front of the entire class. Then we began the grueling process of making sure the bikes we picked were perfectly adjusted for us, something that comes much more easily the longer one takes a spin class. Since we were new-ish, however, it took us a bit of time. We struggled raising the seat, felt out of place trying to measure how our legs felt on the pedals, and tried out the handles standing and sitting. Even after we finally felt like we had everything adjusted, we checked again. The last thing either of us wanted was to realize halfway through the class that we were too far away from the handles, and we'd made the hills even harder for us to climb.

With one last check and an extra look from Kelly, we

were both finally ready. Well, as ready as we could be. I felt my butt one more time and apologized to it again for the torture that I was about to inflict on it, hopped back onto my bike and slid my new sneakers into the straps, getting myself into position.

As soon as we were locked and ready, waiting for Kelly to begin, Rebecca leaned toward me, hoping she could put a nice pin on the tail end of our conversation.

"So," she said, "you think this means you're ready to put down your life to-do checklist and just figure out what makes you happy?"

A little caught off guard, I turned my head to her and squinted my eyes. *I thought we were done with this*, I thought. *But I guess not.* Seeing no way to avoid her question, I responded, "Don't act like there's not something extremely gratifying about checking off items on a to-do checklist. Don't hate," I halfway joked. "But maybe something like that. I don't know. Christine is always saying how I live a 'cautious life,' so maybe it's just doing more things outside my comfort zone."

Kelly cleared her throat, her passive-aggressive way of letting us know that class was about to begin, and waited for everyone to go silent and look in her direction before she turned on her first piece of music.

"Are you guys ready for a great class?" she called out to the room full of bikers, effectively, at least briefly, interrupting our conversation. "We'll be doing a combination of cardio and strength today, so I hope you're ready to work."

She scanned her attention around the class and waited for each person to nod before moving on to the next. When she stopped in my direction, it fully felt as if she was asking me the question personally. So I nodded just like the others. It was time to get the bike party started.

As we began climbing our fake hills, I couldn't stop thinking of the idea of a "cautious life." As much as Christine had chided me on it over the years, I'd always been able to come back at her with the truth of how we were both brought up: you follow the straight and narrow path, you get the results you want. You go to college and work hard, you come out and get the high-paying job you want. That motto then turned into: you date enough people, you'll eventually meet the person you're going to spend the rest of your life with. Spend time with your friends, and you'll have the perfect *Sex and the City*–like life with brunches and happy hours and all the shoes you could ever desire. Check, check and check. By the time we'd be done talking, she was on my side.

So why does it feel like all my accomplishments are holding on by a thread? My best friend who traipsed with me to every happy hour under the sun is in the hospital. I've dated more men than I can count and still haven't found "the one" and I am in a job that people wished for but sometimes made me want to pull my eyelashes out one at a time.

As if Rebecca could read my thoughts, she turned her head to me again. We were just beginning to pick up the pace on our bikes, and the burn in our calves was ever so slightly coming in.

"What do you think about doing a different kind of list?" she asked.

"Huh?" I was equal parts lost in my own thoughts and vividly realizing how long it had been since I worked out, so I'd barely processed her question.

"Like a list to help you break out of your comfort zone."

"Tell me more," I said, jumping back into my skin and hoping the conversation would distract from the pain jutting into my legs and butt cheeks.

"What if you made a list of things that you only consider in those quiet moments at home in your shoe closet, and then went about actually doing them?"

"Like a risk list?" I asked, my breath getting heavier as the hill became harder to climb.

"Yes!" she screamed out before realizing how loud she was. "Yessss," she whispered this time around, giving Kelly the my-bad look kids give when they do something like break a glass or accidentally pull down everything on your dresser. "Exactly that."

We eased up on our bikes a bit as we began going downhill. This was normally the time in the spin class when you had a moment to catch your breath, but Kelly wasn't letting up. I couldn't tell if she was always that evil or just adding a little extra because of the two chatty Cathys on the side of her classroom.

"Let's add some speed now that we're back on a flat road!" Sweat began pouring down my face as if it had been waiting for her to give it permission. *I was certainly not glistening like the ladies we saw in the locker room earlier.* I focused my attention back on my pedaling, the fast pace ensuring me that whatever else Rebecca wanted to talk about would have to wait. She was undeterred, however. Huffing and puffing, she leaned in once more.

"And while you're thinking about adding things to the list," she said then hesitated again. "I wonder if you might want to finally reach out to Jake to talk about what happened at the wedding."

Stunned and barely able to breathe, I spun my head around to showcase my displeasure.

"Wait, what? How did we go from Christine and a risk list to Jake?" I was completely confused but somehow able to pant out my response.

"I don't know. I've just been thinking," Rebecca said, shrugging. "You were talking about how awful dating has been lately and it might be because you never resolved that situation."

"That has nothing to do with Jake, Becs."

"Doesn't it have everything to do with him?"

In the background I heard "Over It" by Katharine McPhee begin playing on Kelly's speaker. *How apropos.*

"I mean, I still can't get that image of you running from his room out of my head," she continued while trying to whisper. "You tripped and everything, trying so desperately to get away from that man!"

"You know how hurt I was in that moment," I said, no longer even wanting to look at her for bringing up Jake. *This was supposed to be my time away from everything.*

"I know. But don't you think you've been taking the safe route ever since that relationship blew up in your face?"

"Twice," I reminded her. I may have been unable to breathe, but I knew all too well how much that relationship had hurt me.

"Yes, it blew up twice," Rebecca replied, her big-sister voice attempting to lull me further into a discussion I had no desire to be in. "So I get it. All you can remember now are the hurtful times between y'all. But if you really want to make a change, it starts with having a real talk with Jake. It's time."

Huge globs of sweat poured down both our faces as we attempted to one up each other in the conversation. It was a foolish plan, but we'd both entered that part of a girl-talk moment where neither of us was willing to back down.

"Listen, I can't be focused on Jake now. I need to concentrate on getting back in top shape, getting these thighs to come down from this size ten back to an eight. On being there for Christine, her family and our friends. Hell, even doing this risk list we were *just* talking about. There's no time for me to add him in the midst of all that."

I exhaled as we entered into an even higher-speed portion of the spin class, drawing breaths from some place magical inside me.

"Okay, Reagan, I hear you, but it just sounds like you're still running scared out of that room, except that it's in your head now. And with Christine in the hospital, I just don't want—"

I could tell the class was beginning to get hard for Rebecca, too, because her last sentence included an intake of breath after almost every word. It gave me the perfect opportunity to jump in before she could finish.

"No, I'm being smart," I whispered back defiantly. "Can we just focus on spin for now, please? We're getting dirty looks as it is."

"Sure. For now." Rebecca shrugged again and gave Kelly another "sorry" expression as her once polite and perky face had turned to that of a stern instructor clearly upset at us for talking through the length of her class. "I won't push it more."

"Thank you. Plus, there are a million reasons why we could never work," I said, attempting to get the last word.

"I said okay, Rae." Rebecca half threw her arms up in defeat but caught herself before it threw off her balance on the bike. We spent the rest of the class in silence, but her comment about me taking the safe route lingered in my head for a while, biting the air with its harsh commentary.

It wasn't long before class ended—a little more than twenty minutes later, in fact—but it gave me enough time to start thinking about what I'd want to include on my list of risks to finally try. None of them included anything about Jake, but I was sure they'd be impressive and also require a lot of work on my part.

As soon as Kelly announced we were done and it was time to go into stretches, I hopped off my bike like it was on fire. It had as much to do with my glee of making it through the whole class as it did with me severely needing the relief in my legs.

"It should be against the law to do the things we did to our butts and legs on a Saturday morning," I said, turning to Rebecca for the first time since my attempt at shutting down the Jake talk. I pulled a leg behind me, catching my foot with my hand, and felt the muscles in my body open up.

"Oh, my God, I know." Rebecca tried to catch her breath while she grabbed her right leg and crossed it in front of her left leg to mimic a seated position. "What the hell did we sign up for?" We both laughed again, any tension from earlier easily leaving us.

"Don't you kind of feel a little like Wonder Woman, too, though?" I asked, even surprising myself a bit. "It's amazing how a workout can be really hard, but as soon as you complete it, you feel like you can conquer the world."

"Maybe. Mostly, I feel like I can go home and take a nice long bath."

"Oooh," I exhaled. "Now, that sounds good, too."

We finished our stretches and began walking back to the front of the class, nervous about what Kelly might say to us as we passed her by.

"Bye, Kelly," we said in unison again.

"Bye!" It was clear she'd put on her best fake tone to get us out of her class as soon as possible.

"She probably hates us for how much we talked in her class," Rebecca giggled.

"Oh, yeah, I'm sure she couldn't wait for us to leave."

"Whatever, she'll be okay. More importantly, did you think any more about the list while we were in there?"

"I did, actually," I said as we entered back into the locker room. "I came up with four potential risks so far."

"Oh, tell me! I'm waiting on pins and needles."

"All right," I said, using my fingers to mark the numbers as I went through them. "First is be more vulnerable when dating and risk falling in love again. Then, allow people to be there for me, you know, and not always feel like I'm the only one who has to be the strong friend or family member. Third, ironically, do fewer lists." I paused so we could both chuckle at that part and to give us a chance to key in our codes to get back into the lockers.

"Oh, yes, I can see this is going very well so far," Rebecca joked.

"I know," I said, nodding my head at how funny I sounded. "But I don't think I'll ever give up lists entirely. That's me. It's just giving myself more opportunities to be spontaneous and not as planned out with all my decisions."

"I like that. And the fourth?"

I let out a big sigh before listing the fourth item, nervous about even saying it aloud, but especially to Rebecca.

"Leave our comfy job for one where I have more control of what I say and where I can champion women who look like me more often."

"Rae…" Rebecca stopped herself and thought about the best way she wanted to respond. I could almost see her pondering the different ideas in her head. Finally resolute, she continued, "I think that's one of the bravest things you could do. Honestly, they all are. But that one? I'm in awe!"

"You don't think I'm crazy? I mean, who thinks about leaving a job where her boss loves her and she's the author of the top article on the website at least once a week?"

"Someone who's not happy." Rebecca's matter-of-fact tone was not lost on me. "I don't think you're crazy at all. I love everything about this—oh! What if you rewarded yourself with a pair of shoes every time you finished something on the list?"

"Oh!" I was taken aback by the idea, but also kind of loved it. What could be more of a reward for someone like me than a brand-new pair of shoes as the ultimate checkmark? I wiped down my face and neck once more before grabbing my jacket from my locker. "I like that idea, Becs! It's sort of genius."

"And it won't just be the pleasure of buying new shoes," she interjected, agreeing. "They will also signify an investment, some intention behind your action. These are hard items, Rae. You're going to need some incentive to keep going with them."

"You're absolutely right," I said. This *was* going to be hard, but nothing spelled reward better than s-h-o-e-s. And I was essentially forcing myself to get four new pairs.

"Agh! Now that that's settled, what are you doing after this?"

"Umm, I don't know really. Probably get a salad down the street and then walk home. We're meeting up later to go see Christine this evening, but it's nice out today, and I could use the stroll. Wanna join?"

"Thanks, but no, thanks. Unlike you, who seems to enjoy being alone, I have a husband waiting on me to get back home."

I sighed. "You just won't let it die, huh?"

"Whaaat?" Rebecca smirked, knowing she'd accomplished her goal of putting the Jake idea back in my head. "You know it's all out of love, Rae. But you just remember. If you weren't so very single and wasting your time on all these stupid boys out here, you might have someone willing to rub that pained *tushion* of yours today." She emphasized her point by lightly smacking me on the butt right as she said *tushion*.

"Hey!" I screamed out. I was just about to remind her that doing a better job of being vulnerable was *on* the risk list, just not with people named Jake Saunders, when I realized she'd run out before I could turn around, effectively getting the last word that time.

Rude.

Alone again with my thoughts, I finished putting my jacket on—a slightly lined charcoal-and-turquoise windbreaker that was perfect for the unseasonably warm October weather—and walked toward the door. It was fifty degrees and sunny, and I wasn't going to let Rebecca, her grabby hands and her meddling push my buttons so much that I missed the beauty of the day.

Chapter 3

Once outside, I immediately breathed in the crisp, cool fall air, and then let out a sigh of relief. I'd made it through my first activity post "The Call," and it felt like a huge milestone had occurred.

Wow, DC can really be pretty when it wants to be, I thought, taking a look at the scenery around me. The brick sidewalks lined the streets of colorful row houses, tied together, but unique in their own ways, sometimes sporting two very contrasting hues, sometimes slightly blending into each other. A fountain to my left seemed to long for the days of summer when the children in the neighborhood would splash around in the water. Silent now, but still pretty, it made me yearn for springtime in the city when the trees that were losing their leaves would stand bright and green and towering in the sky, your ears filling with the sounds of laughter, and your nose delighting in the smells of empanadas and pastelitos on the street. To my right, towering over the other buildings in the neighborhood, also stood the expansive shopping mall, with my gym inside, to remind everyone of the sprawling growth that had happened in Columbia Heights within the past twenty years.

Yep, this was DC. Still packed with all the flavor and culture and traditions of the people who built it if you watched close enough, but also crawling with ambitious people ready to place more gyms and shopping malls on every corner they could.

I'd told Becs I would get a salad after I left the gym, but the truth was I didn't have much of an appetite. After a few steps in that direction, I changed my mind and decided to simply walk back home. Her statement about me not remembering the good times with Jake rang loudly in my ear and made me want time alone with my thoughts—just me and the city—more than food. I could remember the first time he broke my heart like it was yesterday, a fact that some of my friends didn't want to acknowledge. That pain still hurt and years later, was very fresh. He'd come running into my dorm room to tell me the great news: he was offered the investment banking job in New York, so come June, he was moving there. I was so excited for him. I'd been trying on my cap and gown when he barged in, but I ran into his arms right then and told him how proud I was of him and how I couldn't wait to see him take the world by storm. Jake had other plans, though. He kissed me and stepped back.

"I don't want a long-distance relationship, though, Rae."

"Oh." I was stunned and stumbled back a few paces as well.

"I'm sorry, I just don't think we could survive that. Not at twenty-one."

I could feel my heart crushing inside. Why had he come running to tell me this like it was good news?

"Then, what? Do you want me to move there, too?"

"No," Jake interrupted. "I… I think that would put too much pressure on us. Plus, you have a job offer here. I don't want you to give that up for me."

"Well, I wasn't saying…" I stopped myself once I realized what he was trying to say. "You don't want me anymore."

"Reagan, no, that's not what I mean." Jake put his hand on his forehead as he tried to find the words. "I—I don't know what I want, to be honest."

"I think it's pretty clear, actually."

I could play that conversation over and over in my head, word for word, each expression that we made, the way he walked out calmly before I crumbled into a ball of tears, the resolve I found within to never be that woman again, and the way I let myself get duped once more at Lance and Candice's wedding. Those memories were never too far away. But despite all that, was Rebecca right? *Was I so focused on those two memories that I'd skewed everything under whatever is the opposite of rose-colored glasses? Do I owe him anything different?*

All these thoughts ran through my head as I continued walking home, the sun beaming from the sky and onto my skin. If you were looking from a window inside, you would have thought it was eighty or ninety degrees outside. Instead, the brisk air was getting chillier as I walked, almost acting like an opposite attraction force to the sun's rays. Or maybe it was like my relationship with Jake. You could almost lull yourself into believing it was perfect until you stepped outside and the wind reminded you of the truth. I zipped my jacket all the way up to my chin to help block out the cold. At least that had an easy enough fix.

"Watch out!"

It's April in DC, the weather is a perfect seventy with the sun shining bright, and we are lying out, basking in the sun on our college campus's yard. We are in our own world, despite the fact that everyone else obviously had the same idea to come outside and enjoy the day.

And while some are chillin' like us, many aren't lying around and laughing with their friends. They are practicing step routines, running from water gun fights, dancing to mixes of '90s R&B and hip-hop and playing some college version of hide-and-seek. Some are even working on what seems to be the beginnings of a protest, one thing you could always count on at Howard University. And of course, some are playing football.

Which makes the football that has crashed into our makeshift picnic, tossing the strawberries, cheese and grapes onto our blankets and the ground, unsurprising, but no less annoying.

"What the…" Robin screamed out. Jennifer has grabbed the fried chicken in time to save a few pieces of it, and Christine and I jumped out of the way before the ball hit one of us in the head, but we are none too happy about the disruption. Gradually, we began picking up our items and trying to put our arrangement back together. But we were so caught up, we barely saw the cute, five-foot-eleven guy with the body of a safety standing over us until he cleared his throat.

"I'm so sorry, ladies," Jake said, extending out his arm to help one of us up.

"What?" I asked, finally noticing him.

"I said I'm sorry," he repeated. "We didn't mean for the ball to come this way. It's just that my boy over there is the world's worst non-quarterback ever. I keep telling him that thing is dangerous in his hands."

Jake smiled, showing off the cutest dimple I'd ever seen and pointed to his five friends, including one who was shrugging in the background. I assumed he was the culprit.

"Yeah, he shouldn't be allowed anywhere near a football or women." Robin, who'd finally noticed Jake as well, stared daggers back at him. She had no intentions of letting this guy think he could come and charm *the ladies*, as he'd called us. No, she wanted him to feel as uncomfortable as we did seeing a football come flying at our heads.

I, on the other hand, was already hooked and reached my hand toward his still outstretched arm, letting him help me stand up.

"Thank you," I mouthed to him, a smile starting to form on my face.

Jake held my hand in his and winked at me before returning to his back-and-forth with Robin. "Sounds like you could teach him a thing or two."

"I would destroy him and all your lil' homies, and then make you buy us new food to replace what you ruined."

Jake laughed. "For some reason, I believe you."

"You should," Christine chimed in. "My girl here is

a football fanatic." She placed her arm around Robin's shoulder. *"Y tal vez un poco loca también,"* she joked.

"Whatever," Robin said, playfully removing her arm as if she was upset about Christine's crazy comment. "He at least owes us food."

"Fair, fair," Jake interjected. "We are happy to make up for this incident." I could feel his thumb tracing circles in my palm as he continued holding my hand, sending tidal waves of nerves throughout my body, all while he carried on a conversation with my girls as if he was doing nothing at all. Meanwhile, I was starting to have trouble standing. I had to do something quick before I collapsed in front of everyone.

"Umm, what's your name?" I asked, turning my body toward his.

"Jake."

"Okay, Jake, well, I'm Reagan, and this is Christine, Jennifer and Robin." I pointed to each of the girls as I introduced them, casually using my other hand to do so.

"Nice to meet you, ladies," Jake said to the group and then winked at me again. I think he could tell I was trying to defuse the situation and also maybe distract myself from the feels he was giving me as we stood there.

"What if…" I said, then paused. "What if we all went to lunch down the street at Oohs and Ahhs. On you guys."

"Done," he said without missing a beat. "I mean, if that's what the rest of you want?" He looked to the other girls with his best puppy-dog eyes, one by one, even wearing down Robin until she agreed.

"Great. Let me just tell my boys, and I'll be right back." He turned to me before leaving and leaned down so he could whisper in the corner of my ear. "To be clear, I don't want to let your hand go, but if I don't right now, I might never do it again." He took his other hand and slid it slowly across the line of my jaw until I slightly closed my eyes and let out an audible sigh. *Damn*, I thought as he went running back to his crew.

"What the hell was that?" Robin asked as soon as he was far enough away, bringing me back down to this world.

"I don't know!"

"Oh, *lo sé*," Christine joked. "I've seen this before. Reagan just creamed herself." She laughed uncontrollably.

"Oh, my God, Christine, that's disgusting. I did not."

"Mmm-hmm, well, something just happened," Robin said. "Because you basically just asked that man out on a date and used us all as bait."

"I just thought it would be a good way to make up for messing up our food. And you know Oohs and Ahhs has some of the best fried chicken in the city."

"Okay, she's not wrong about that," said Jennifer. "But just be careful, Rae. Dude seems like a charmer to the nth degree. He even had Robin eating out of his hands at the end."

We all laughed as we began picking up the blankets to fold them. Jennifer had already packed up whatever food hadn't been thrown in our plastic trash bag because it hit the ground. So we stood there waiting and watching as Jake explained the situation to his boys.

"Not a bad-looking specimen to be used by, though," Christine said, tilting her head to the side so she could get a full view of him from afar. "Mmm, mmm, mmm."

"Please," I said. "It won't even be like that. It's the

end of our junior year. No one has time to be falling for someone or anything beyond just a little fun."

"Mmm-hmm," they replied in unison, with so much unbelief, it was almost hurtful.

Less than a few minutes later, we saw Jake walking back over to us, his friends in tow and his hand reaching for mine again.

"Y'all ready?" asked the quarterback.

"Nah, bruh, you owe us an apology first," Robin said. "I know y'all sent this one over here for a reason, but you're the one that needs to say the words." She folded her arms as she waited.

"You're right. I am very, very sorry," he said, bowing down in jest. "I promise it won't happen again."

"Uh-huh."

Jake laughed, and as he turned to me, I could finally understand part of why his smile was so perfect: he had the most beautiful, straight white teeth. The kind that made you think about licking them when you kissed. *He must have had braces as a kid.*

"Your girl's a bit of a hard-ass, huh?"

"She doesn't really believe in taking crap from anyone," I said, allowing his fingers to intertwine with mine.

"I can appreciate that. And what about you?"

"Me? I just tend to observe people for a while, see if I can trust them. That helps me avoid being around a lot of people who might want to mistreat me."

"And do you think you can trust me?"

"I don't know yet. You seem hot like the sun, but that can be deceiving sometimes."

"How about this? I promise to always be honest with you, and you can observe me as long as you need to.

I'll be here, because I want to know you." He raised our hands up to his lips, softly kissing mine without letting it go.

"Okay," I said, fully entranced by his brown eyes, and for the first time hoping my instincts were correct about someone thirty minutes into meeting them. "But first, let's get some soul food."

We looked up and noticed we were several paces behind the rest of the group who'd long ago left us to finish our conversation alone. Laughing, we ran to catch up with them, our hands still attached like it would hurt to break them apart.

The fifteen-minute walk back home felt like it took at least thirty-five minutes because my brain was on extreme overload. I could remember all the happy moments I wanted to, I realized, but that had been almost a decade ago. *What benefit did it serve me to remember the fond times when the most recent ones were hurtful?*

As I entered my place, I kicked off my sneakers and inhaled a long, deep, hard breath to try to release all the thoughts in my head. This was not the Saturday I had in my mind when I woke up earlier that morning. But there I was, exhausted and needing a nap before we went back to see Christine later. I placed my keys on the hallway table, slipped off my jacket and hung it in the closet before taking another step. Maybe what I really needed to do was write, I wondered. That seemed to always clear my mind when I couldn't get out of my own head. Plus, I had a risk list to write down before I forgot what it included. Sighing once more, I made my way through my living room and into my bedroom. I flicked on the light, walked past my white bed and tan end tables and straight to my shoe closet to find my shoe diary. Next to it was a set of six different color pens meant to symbolize how I felt at the time I wrote. Today was a blue pen day, for sure, for sadness, confusion, exhaustion and maybe a little bit of hope.

Chapter 4

It was a month and a half later before the doctors let Christine leave the hospital. In that time, she'd spent most of her days hooked up to machines checking her every breath, movement, heartbeat…for all I knew, maybe even her thoughts. The girls and I were there, not every day, but almost every day, reading to her and recounting funny stories. We'd made a pact that whatever we did, we wouldn't go in there and burden her with any of our current problems, especially as the weeks went by and it seemed like she'd never make it out of there.

We'd all started to really worry when she was still in there at Thanksgiving, but somewhere around the beginning of December, it felt like all her fighting spirit was beginning to pay off. I didn't know if it was her determination to not spend another holiday in the hospital or what, but by mid-December, they'd finally said the magical words: you can go home now, Ms. Vasquez.

You would have thought we'd each won an Olympic medal at the news, we were so excited to get our friend out of the cold prickliness of a hospital. Anyone who's ever spent any amount of time in one knows it is a place that doesn't allow for a lot of peace and quiet and tranquility, and Christine needed that more than ever. Her mom and boyfriend, Dominic, packed up her personal belongings so quickly it almost seemed like they were worried the doctors would come in and change their minds, but we understood why. As hard as being in a hospital was for the patient, it was just as difficult for the family, too.

A couple days had gone by since they released her when I walked up to Christine's familiar door, knocking on it to be let in. I'd wanted to give her some time with her family before the girls and I came by and started taking over, but it had taken everything in me to wait around for those two days to pass.

"Buenos días," her mom said, dropping the "s" on both words and hugging me extra tight as I walked through the door. Mama Vasquez, like her daughter, was quite the lively character. She'd been born in the Dominican Republic, moved to the United States as a child and later to New Orleans when she decided to follow her dreams to become a chef. This all meant she spoke and understood English perfectly, but when she was home or simply upset, she would automatically begin speaking in either her native Dominican dialect—which typically drops the "s" at the end of words—or a version that mixed Spanish and English, often toggling back and forth in the same sentence. It was how Chris-

tine developed her knack for dipping in and out of both languages and also how I learned just enough Spanish to understand them both when I needed to.

"Buenos días, Mama Vasquez." I stepped inside, removing my tan pea coat and slipping out of my ivory pointed-toe loafers as soon as I walked in. The familiarity hit me instantly. Her vintage lamp on the end table. Her collage of carnival masks flanking her sofa. The fireplace we'd all sat beside for so many years just having girl talk.

I couldn't believe it had been two months since I'd been in her apartment. I bit my tongue to stop the tears from welling up in my eyes.

"You can go straight to the back...*ella está esperando.*"

"Gracias." I tiptoed my way to the back in case she'd fallen asleep before I got there and peeked in once I came upon her bedroom door. There she was, halfway perched up so the top of her body seemed like she was seated in a recliner, but the bottom half was relaxed in the bed.

"Mi amor? Hello." Christine's voice was tiny, but still raspy, as I stepped into her room. I could even hear a hint of her boisterous tone trying to come out, peppered with the bit of Spanglish I'd heard many times over the years.

"Christine," I said, walking up to her and placing my hand on her right cheek. She was home, yes, but clearly still not out of the woods, mostly relegated to staying in her bed as her boyfriend and mom took turns bringing her food and water and to the bathroom when she needed.

"You look like you've been crying. *Cómo tú ta?*"

"Now you know I never cry," I replied, forcing a smile on my face. "I'm just happy to see you and hear your voice again." I sat down on the chair strategically placed next to her bed. I assumed it was the same chair her mom and boyfriend had taken turns sitting in for the past couple days. "Tell me, what are they saying in terms of recovery? How long do you now have to be in *this* bed?"

"They are still figuring everything out," Christine sighed. "I feel better for now, and my lungs are working again, so I'll probably be able to walk around for real in about another week. But I think I'm always going to have the complications that come with gastroparesis—the nausea, the feeding tubes, the constant worries I'll get another blood infection. It's exhausting, but it means I'm alive for now."

"Right," I said, suddenly at a loss for words. "That's... I mean, I didn't think I would ever hear your voice again without you sounding strained from all those machines." I leaned toward her, wanting to be as close as I could to my friend without suffocating her with my concern.

"Girl, I didn't think I would be able to do a lot of things. But I'm definitely blessed."

"You're a miracle, Chrissy," I blurted out.

"That's a lot of pressure, Rae." She could barely lift her head and there I was calling her a miracle. *What was I thinking*? I thought.

"No pressure! I'm just saying."

"One thing I've learned from this whole situation is that life is far too short. I knew it before, but this last bout in the hospital really brought it home for me."

"I think for me, too, honestly. I just kept replaying

all the things we've ever done in my head, all the she-
nanigans we've been part of since high school, and I
couldn't imagine…" I bit my tongue again, not wanting to cry and make her feel like she needed to comfort
me. "I don't know. It just had me thinking a lot. I even
started a risk list," I said, laughing. "I hadn't told you
about it when you were in the hospital because I didn't
want to bother you with it, but I think it's going to be
good. You have said for a while that I've been living
a—what was it you called it?"

"Vida cauteloso."

"Right. A cautious life."

"I like this," Christine said, straining to raise herself a little higher in the bed so she could talk easier.
I jumped up to help, moving one of the pillows to her
lower back to take off some of the pressure. "Yes, this
is very good." She paused. "Can I be honest? *Sabes que
te quiero, pero* it hasn't been just a cautious life, *chica.*"

"What do you mean?"

"This…fear of yours," she continued, "has also led
you to even worse, *an amor cauteloso*—a cautious
love."

"That's… Christine," I sighed, hesitating, and not
finding the words to counter.

"It's not just you, though, *chica.* I was, too. It's how
I can see it so clearly now. Something happened to you
when things ended with you and Jake in college. It was
like somewhere inside you decided you were better off,
safer, if you stopped taking risks in everything. And
don't get me wrong. That worked for a while. You have
all the things every little girl grows up wanting, except love."

And happiness, too, I thought.

I sat back in my chair. For someone who could barely speak a month ago, Christine had just read me for filth. But I hadn't brought up the risk list so she could spend all our time trying to fix me; I wanted her to know how she was inspiring me. And also give her a chance to say whatever she needed about what she was going through without doctors and boyfriends and moms hovering in the background.

"So what are you going to do about your *vida cauteloso*?" I asked, changing the subject back to her. "Once you recover a bit, of course."

"You're not slick, but I'll give it to you this time." She shifted in her bed again, trying to see if putting her weight on a different area of her body would help her regain some more comfort. "First thing's first, I'm going to focus my energy more on my singing and craft making. I'm realizing you can have all the money in the world, but you can't take it with you when you die. I'd just rather spend my time getting in all the experiences I can. And I'm going to work on spending more time with the people who positively impact my life."

"Wow."

"*Sí.* And it won't be easy. Especially because the doctors told me I will still have plenty of bad days, *pero mira*, I don't have the luxury of easy now. I need fulfilling. I need big rewards. I need to live the life I have as fully as possible."

"Who knew almost dying would make you such a guru," I joked. We both finally laughed, breaking the tension from all the sadness that had been in the air up to then.

"*Por favor*, you know I've been your Afro-Dominicana guru since we were fifteen. Remember that time you were making out with that guy—oh, what was his name?—when I drove you to his mom's salon and then had to scream out from the car for you to come up for air?"

"His name was Bobby. And how could I ever forget that? I was so embarrassed! All I heard was 'If you don't get your tail in this car, *mana*, we're going to leave you!'"

Christine couldn't stop laughing. "Yes, his name *was* Bobby! Oh, my God, that was hilarious. You two were just going to town like his mom couldn't come out of her salon at any moment and kick your curly-haired butt to kingdom come."

"I know," I laughed. "But he didn't care! And it made me not care." I put my head in my hands. Just saying it out loud helped me realize how foolish I sounded and probably looked back then, too.

"Exactamente. Y por eso me necesitas."

"Ha, that's true. I will always need you. Good thing you didn't leave me, huh?" I grabbed her hand and held on tight.

"You can't get rid of me that easily, *mana*. Plus, I would just haunt you anyway. You've got a risk list to finish."

A few hours later I checked my phone and noticed it was almost 8:00 p.m. We'd been laughing all day, but Christine's voice was starting to grow weaker and weaker as we continued.

"All right, lady," I said. "As much as I hate to leave you, I need to go to work in the morning, and you need your rest."

She didn't even put up a fight, but slightly closed

her eyes and nodded. "You're right. I am starting to get pretty tired."

"I sort of figured as much, but just didn't want this to end," I replied, glancing up from my phone where I was inputting the address to my favorite salad place in my Uber app. My appetite was finally starting to come back to me, and I was craving one of their popular "donut salads"—a name Christine often used to describe the unhealthy salads on their menu.

"I'm not going anywhere, Rae. Don't worry."

"I think those are supposed to be my words to you," I said, getting up and kissing her on her forehead. I'd just received an alert that my ride was three minutes away, and I wanted to have time to say goodbye to her mom and boyfriend, put my loafers and coat back on and still get outside before I received the dreaded "your car will be leaving in two minutes" message. "Be good, okay?"

"Nunca," she joked, winking at me.

I walked back into Christine's living room, gathering my coat and kissing Mama Vasquez and Dominic goodbye in one swoop. "Thank you all for letting me come see her."

"Reagan, you are welcome here anytime," her mom replied. "Honestly, if it were up to her, you girls would probably be here every day."

"It won't be every day, but I promise you might get tired of us as much as we are here."

"No, the smile you put on my baby's face will be worth it every single time."

"Thanks, Ma," I said, giving her one more kiss.

"Gracias, querida."

I stepped out into the cold air just as a silver Honda with flashing lights pulled up. "You're Reagan?"

"Yes, I am," I said, climbing into the backseat on the right side.

"You're going to Chopt, right?"

"Yes, definitely," I sighed and picked up my phone again. There was only one voice I wanted to hear after being with Christine all day, and it wasn't the Uber driver's. I scrolled to "Mom" in my phone and waited for her to answer.

"Hey, baby." Her voice sounded like that of an angel.

"Hey, Mom, got a minute?"

Chapter 5

"*Cher*, you know I always have time for my firstborn. What's up, Rae?"

I chuckled to myself; if it was one thing my mom loved calling me, it was her firstborn. There were times I thought it was a dig at my grandparents because she'd grown up as their first kid and had to bear the brunt of helping them take care of the other six children that came after her. Other times, I thought she was trying to be relatable in my mom's own way, which for her always sort of seemed to come off a little passive-aggressive.

In fact, Maria Chevalier Doucet, pronounced Mahree-ahh, was known for the kind of advice that started with "Well, if I were you, *cher*, I would…" It was endearing at times, because she was the kind of person who walked into a room and forced you to adore her since she stole your attention at "hi"; but also often annoying because it usually preceded advice she wanted to give especially if she knew you didn't want to hear it. And that was the paradox of my mom—she was a force to be reckoned with, a sixty-year-old Louisiana Creole diva mother of four who knew how to make you love her even if she annoyed you. I was willing to risk all that for the comfort of her voice.

"I'm leaving Christine's now," I said, leaning back into my seat.

"Oh, yes, how is she?"

"You know Christine. Always worried about everyone else when she's the one who just got out of the hospital and still has at least two more weeks before she can move around freely."

"Wow, you mean you're best friends with someone who acts just like you and thinks about others more than herself? That's just so odd." Her sarcasm sliced through the phone, and I could almost hear her giggling to herself for how perfectly she played that part of our conversation.

"I called because I needed you to help me relax after a whole day of being strong for Chrissy, Mom, not for a lecture."

"What? I would never give you a lecture, Rae." It was utterly amazing how she could put on such a shocked expression over the phone, especially when she was literally doing the thing that I'd called her out on. "I just… you know, if I were you, I'd think about how I feel the need to be strong all the time. I know you've been hurt more than any of us even know, baby, but you hold it all in. I bet right now, you're in a car, and your shoulders are higher than the Empire State Building."

I took a deep breath while listening to her and noticed my shoulders were tight and scrunched up toward my ears. She may have been correct about that part, I guessed. But still, this wasn't the calming talk I'd been hoping for. Even though I'd had a great time laughing with Christine, it was mentally exhausting pretending I wasn't scared for her life every second of every day. Rolling them down, I tried to restart the conversation. "Mom, thank you for your concern. Truly. But I really just wanted to hear you say everything is going to be okay."

"Ohhhh, of course everything is going to be okay, *cher*," she said, quickly reminding me of my mom's frustrating duality. "But I'm your mom. I want you to be *more* than okay."

"I know, Mom," I sighed. "I'm trying."

As we drove through the neighborhoods, I saw a few snowbanks left over from the last storm, still lingering on the edge of the sidewalk, the white now darkened by the steps of those walking on it daily. I'd have to be careful stepping back out of my ride to make sure I didn't go sliding down the street. Loafers were cute for wearing to someone's house, but not exactly sensible once I decided to make the detour to Chopt before heading home. Regardless, I was just looking forward to my favorite salad at this point—romaine lettuce, panko chicken, pecorino cheese, tomatoes, cucumbers and eggs, with Caesar dressing. Especially since my mom hadn't exactly provided the comfort that I was seeking.

We pulled up to the restaurant, and I carefully lifted my feet out of the car, one loafer at a time. "Mom, I'm going to have to call you back," I said. "I'm going in now, and you know I don't like to be on the phone when I'm ordering."

"I know, baby. Call me back later."

"Will do. Love you."

"I love you, too."

I knew she meant it, but boy, that call had gone the exact opposite of how I'd wanted. No less anxious, now I was just really hungry on top of everything. I hung up the phone and took my place in line, dutifully staring at the menu on the wall like a bad habit since I already knew what I wanted. There were three other people in front of me, so I guess I didn't exactly have to rush my mom off the phone. But better to be safe than sorry with Maria; who knows where that call could have gone if it had been five minutes longer?

While waiting, I noticed the door open and saw a young guy come in, dreadlocks down his back, with a hoodie peeking out of his winter coat. With him was a little bouncing baby girl in her stroller, filling the quiet space with her baby coos. *What a nice image*, I thought. A present father out taking a stroll with his daughter at night. It was only after I stared closer that complete dread came over my whole body. This was no regular young guy with a kid; it was my college ex-boyfriend who I broke up with two months before meeting Jake. If Jake was the one who set fire to my heart and ripped it apart, Matthew had been the one to light the first flame. He'd convinced me we were the best of friends for two years, then that us dating was the only natural progression, and then finally, that you couldn't even trust your best friend not to cheat on you.

Maybe he wouldn't see me, I hoped. Or at least have the courtesy to pretend like he didn't. I placed my order and tried positioning myself away from him while the guy behind the counter mixed all my ingredients together. It didn't take long before I heard his voice, loud and clear, calling my name. *So much for that.*

"Reagan, wow. Is it really you?" Matthew was still only feet away from the entrance, so to get my attention, he practically screamed my name across the whole restaurant. To say I was embarrassed was an understatement.

"Hi, Matthew," I said, turning toward him and trying to plaster a smile on my face.

"How are you?" He didn't bother to wait until he was next to me to start talking, but instead walked and pushed that damn stroller, even as he began asking me questions.

"I'm good. Just picking up a salad to go." I reached behind me to get my bowl from the server and tapped my phone on the scanner to pay for the meal, hoping that he would take the "to go" hint and leave me alone.

"Well, obviously, Reagan. I'm not blind," he responded as he finally stood directly in front of me. At five foot eight, Matthew wasn't especially tall, but he still managed to position himself where it seemed like he was towering over me.

"Still sarcastic as ever, huh, Matthew?"

"I'm still me," he said, grinning smugly.

Right. How did I ever fall for this guy again?

"But other than getting a salad, what's going on with you?"

"Matthew, I—"

"Listen, I know we didn't end well, Rae. I'm just hoping everything's all right with you these days," he said, interrupting me before I could go on my spiel about how I wasn't sure why he thought it was necessary for us to have this conversation.

So much for me finishing that thought, I guess.

"I heard about Christine being really sick, and I know how close you two were. I'm assuming you still are?"

"We still are, yes," I said, slightly calming myself down, but still ready to get out of this impromptu meeting as fast as I could. "She's doing better now. Out of the hospital. And I'm good." I kept my responses short and sweet. It wasn't like I wanted to sit down and catch up with him over donut salads, after all.

"Not married yet, though, right?"

"What?" I hadn't expected that question or that turn in the conversation.

"I just noticed you're not wearing a ring."

"Oh." I looked down at my bare left ring finger like it had betrayed me. "No, I'm not married. I see you are, though. And with a kid!" I gestured to the little girl who'd since fallen asleep in the stroller next to us.

"Yeah, I am. And two kids actually."

"Oh, wow. Okay," I said, suddenly stunned. This day had surely been a roller coaster of emotions for me, and it was apparently only getting worse. "Congratulations then, Matthew. I'm happy for you." I clenched my jaw, trying to get the last part of that statement out with a hint of bitterness sliding out of my mouth.

"Thanks," he continued. "I'm kind of surprised you're not married, though. Just knew you would beat me to the altar."

"Ha," I chuckled nervously. "As luck would have it, I did not." *Yep, it was definitely time for me to get out of there before I ended up saying something I would regret.*

"That's right. I forgot I heard you took the career woman route. You're this big-shot writer now, yes? I've heard a lot of people say you're doing some great stuff around politics."

"You could maybe say that," I replied, my plastered smile turning to a cringe. Was he trying to torture me for doing the smart thing and breaking up with his funky self when I found out he cheated on me? It sure seemed like it. "I mean, yeah, I am…just also thinking of making some changes lately."

"Oh, okay." His pause was deafening. "I'm sure you'll turn things around soon, then."

I wanted to punch him in his face right in front of his child and in front of everyone in the restaurant. What was that? Pity? No one had said anything about needing to turn my life around.

I steadied my breathing before responding. "There's no need to turn things around. As I said before, I'm doing all right. Things are good." I paused once more for dramatic effect. "But if you don't mind, I do have somewhere to be, so I must get going."

He didn't have to know that my somewhere was my living room couch in front of my TV while I plowed my salad into my mouth. I turned away from him and began walking toward the door in my best attempt possible to stop from screaming: "Are you kidding me? You were probably the first person to ruin my idea of men and relationships! *You* put me on this path that you now think needs to be turned around. And now you want to pity me? Ugh!"

But Matthew wasn't interested in ending the conversation. He kicked the lock off the stroller and followed behind me.

"No problem, Rae. I get it, and I hope I didn't offend

you. It's just… I really have heard great things. Figured you were living the perfect life by now."

"There's no such thing as a perfect life, Matthew. It's just what you make of the one you've got. Christine has taught me that." In the glass doors of the restaurant, I caught my reflection and noticed my loafers again, standing out among the mostly tan-and-green interior. It gave me the sense of confidence I'd lacked throughout most of our conversation. I straightened and turned back toward him. "One other thing. I'd prefer you not call me Rae anymore, okay? That's what my friends call me. And we're not friends."

"Reagan!" Now it was his chance to be stunned. "How can you say that? There was a time when we were best friends."

"There was a time when I *thought* you were my best friend," I said, my voice rising with anger, so high that I could see people stopping to pay attention to us out of the corner of my eye. "And then one of the hardest days happened to me, and my actual best friends came to my dorm and helped put me back together. How ironic you asked about Christine when she, Robin and Jennifer were literally the ones who came racing to my dorm room when that girl called me to say she'd been seeing you for months."

"Reagan, I don't think we need to go down this road again."

"Oh, we don't?" I asked, flabbergasted. "You don't get to decide that, Matthew. You don't get to decide how I remember you." I stood even taller and placed my salad on a tabletop next to me so I could fully express myself without worrying that I would drop it on the floor. I knew with how loudly I was speaking to

him that I was making a scene at this point and just
didn't care. "What I remember, and what I will always
remember, is that one month after losing my virginity
with you, my friends stood over me and watched the
tears pour from my eyes and blanket the brown suede
material of my Birkenstocks. It was Robin, of all people, who stopped Christine from coming after you that
night. She wanted to bang on your door and unleash
holy hell for hurting me like you did. And it was Jennifer who held me until my shoulders stopped shaking.
So I will go down that road as much as I want to, and I
will tell you what you can and can't call me!"

I made a point to look him in the eyes so he knew
I was serious and then turned around on the heels of
my loafers, grabbed my salad and trotted out of there
as fast as I could.

In my head, he was standing there, mouth agape,
trying to figure out what had just happened. And that
made me happy. Petty. But happy nonetheless.

I climbed into my next Uber ride—which thankfully
came only one minute after I called it—and settled into
my seat. Ten more minutes and I'd be back in the comfort of my apartment, away from ex-boyfriends who
cluelessly brought out the worst in me, reminders from
my mom about how great the outside world thought my
job was and the pressure of being the perfect friend
for Chrissy when all I really wanted to do was scream
and shout about how unfair it was that *my* best friend
was the one suffering from a chronic illness. I leaned
back farther into my seat and thought more about why
I despised crying so much. It had almost sickened my
stomach admitting to Matthew how much I'd cried the

night I found out about his affair. *But wasn't that natural? Didn't he probably assume I'd cried?*

He never saw it, though. I didn't flinch a bit when we argued during our breakup, no matter the numerous hurtful things he said to me, like how I was good enough as a girlfriend until he'd pledged and become the man on campus or how he was open to me being *one* of his girls if I wanted. I'd learned early on that crying was a form of weakness, so he may not have known it at the time, but he was never going to get that out of me again.

In fact, if I really thought about it, I couldn't remember a time when tears weren't shameful or meant to be hidden. And my examples of this fact were plenty: my dad struggling to withhold his tears when his mom died; my grandfather sneaking away from the family to cry when my uncle died; my mom trying to hold her head up and remain strong when my dad left. Even the refrains from family members when the children would act up signified that crying was inherently wrong. "Don't make me give you something to cry about," they'd say, as if that was the worst thing in the world, even if it was an empty threat. And inevitably the children would quickly straighten up and stop whimpering. They'd stop expressing their pain.

As far as I was concerned, the strongest people I knew in this world were made weak through their tears flowing, and that wouldn't be me. Not in front of Matthew or Jake, and after that night, not even my friends. That was the last time any of them saw me break down crying beyond a tiny tear or two for a *Grey's Anatomy* episode or Mufasa dying in *The Lion King*.

It wasn't that I didn't cry; it was that I didn't let others see it. But maybe it was time to change that a little bit. Stepping out of my Uber, I walked up to my apartment building and gingerly took the steps to the front door, making sure not to slip on the wet ground. It was too late tonight, but I vowed to call Robin and Jennifer for a long-overdue girls' night in just as soon as I had some time to myself to process it all.

Chapter 6

"You mean to tell me you ran into Matthew, of all people, and you didn't send out the bat signal for backup immediately?"

Sitting in my living room three days later, Robin and Jennifer listened intently as I recounted with a mouth full of nachos how crazy Sunday had been. And most of it was perfectly normal and familiar until I got to the part about running into Matthew while picking up dinner; that was when they each perked up in their respective places—Robin sitting up straight while on my couch and Jennifer moving from a seated position on the floor to one on her knees. Robin was also none too pleased about hearing of the meeting for the first time days later.

"It wasn't like I wanted to stay there any longer than I needed to, Rob! C'mon." I picked up another nacho

filled with black beans, shredded cheese, steak, pico
de gallo and jalapeños. There was a time when we had
Nacho Thursdays once a week, but that had petered out
with an influx of happy hours, dates and unexpected
long hours at work—from us all. Sunday's events were
the perfect excuse for me to ask the girls if we could
reinstate our tradition.

"I know, but I just can't believe that fool tried you
like he did. The nerve!"

"Don't worry. I told him that even fun-loving Christine wanted to kill him that night in college."

"I did, too," interjected Jennifer. "But you were so
devastated. I had to focus on that first."

"I know, honey… Never again, though, right?" I
raised my margarita glass in the air for Robin and Jennifer to join me for an impromptu toast.

"Tuh, ain't that the truth," Robin agreed, her "lob"
flipping on its own with her excitement.

We clanked our glasses together and took sips of our
drinks before continuing.

"Oh, my God," Robin said as she put down her glass.
"I can remember that night like it was yesterday. All
I heard was you crying and Christine muttering, 'I'll
kill him' under her breath and racing to the door, her
long, thick black hair giving her some sort of magic-
like speedy powers. I really thought she was going to
do it, too. It was nuts!"

"I remember jumping up when it didn't seem like
you could hold her back, and my Birkenstocks flying
off my feet and into the air," I laughed.

"Yes, that's right! They flew off your feet, didn't
they?" Jennifer asked rhetorically.

"Yes, yes, they did."

"Serves you good for still wearing those old-ass shoes from high school. Why did you still have those?" asked Robin.

"Okay, that's rude. They were my comfort shoes."

"Comfort shoes," Jennifer scoffed, trying desperately to hold in her giggles. "I mean, what Black girl even wears Birkenstocks?"

"Don't do me like that! You know I didn't go to a majority Black school in high school."

"That's true, all right. I won't joke on you too bad. I don't think they did a very good job, though."

"No, they definitely did not." I took another sip of my margarita and glanced down at the tan, fluffy hamster slippers I was wearing, hoping they wouldn't get joked on, too. To help, I turned the conversation back to Robin. "But to be fair, I hadn't planned on trying to stop a fight from happening that night."

"To be fair, I was all of a hundred and thirty-five pounds soaking wet in college, so I don't know why I thought I could stop anyone from leaving that room," Robin said. "We were all a little smaller then, but my grown woman thighs didn't come in until about two years after we graduated. Now, thankfully…" She slapped her legs and sang the rest of her statement to the tune of City High's "Caramel": "I'm five-nine with thick thiiiiighs."

"Lord, help us." Jennifer rolled her eyes and grabbed a nacho, stuffing it into her mouth so she wouldn't say anything else about Robin's singing or her thick thighs. "Can we talk about something serious now?"

Robin and I both groaned. "Sure," we said in unison.

"I've been so excited about having a serious conversation over nachos and margs all day, Jenn. You didn't know?" I winked at her and slumped down in my chaise a bit, hoping my sarcasm hadn't gone too far. I hadn't quite mastered my mom's endearing way of using it yet.

"Well, whether you were looking forward to it or not, we're having it. This is what friends do."

I slumped farther down into my chair, feeling like a kid who'd just been chastised by her sweet-as-pie big sister.

"Okay, okay. Just please spit out whatever it is you want to say. The suspense is making it worse!"

"I agree," Robin said in the distance as she poured herself another margarita from the pitcher. She had the right idea. I probably should get another drink before hearing whatever Jenn wanted to say but was hesitating to. I leaned back up and motioned to Robin to pass me the pitcher as well. Pouring my glass, I finally heard Robin say the magic words: "I want to talk about your list."

"*My* list?" I asked.

"No one else has one, Rae," Robin added. I was pretty sure she was just finding out while I was that this was what Jenn wanted to discuss and wanted to make sure the heat stayed on me and didn't come her way. She wasn't slick.

"Okay. What about it?"

"Have you done anything with it yet?"

"What's your definition of *done*?" I gulped down my latest glass of margarita, hoping to give myself a little more time to answer my newfound interrogation.

"This isn't Never Have I Ever. We're not giving definitions to try to find loopholes here. *You know* what I mean… Robin, help me out here."

"It has been two months since you told us about it,

Rae." Robin knew she was being such a traitor in that moment, so she poured herself another glass, too. This was the problem with Jenn's super-sweet demeanor and her "wear your heart on your sleeves" personality; it meant when she wanted to assert herself, no one felt like they could tell her no.

I peered at her sheepishly as she casually fixed her pixie cut despite not having a mirror, all while waiting for me to respond. Instinctively, I also put my hands to my hair and began twirling around one of my loose curls. "I wrote it down," I finally offered.

"Mmm-hmm." Jennifer didn't even look up and I could tell that wasn't enough. And Robin was still stuffing her face with nachos, so she was not going to be any help bailing me out of this one.

"Here's the thing. No, not really. But it's not like I've had a ton of time to do so since then. Peter has been up my ass about more stories since that last one was a big hit. We're all focused on Christine. I had the Matthew sighting. I've started spinning…you know, it's a lot."

I was hoping my attempt to tug at Jennifer's heartstrings would help me a bit. It wasn't like she was mad at me, after all; this was just her trying to show tough love—something she did maybe once a year, and it was clearly my turn this year. Last year Robin was the one caught in the fire because she'd mentioned wanting to try therapy to Jennifer and hadn't seen anyone six months later. *That was absolutely why she was staying as far as she could from the conversation.*

"I get that. And those would be legit reasons if only some of them couldn't be solved by actually, you know, doing. Something. On. The. List." She spaced out her words for dramatic effect and it was almost like those memes where you see the Black woman clapping emojis in between each word, except it was in real life. She was "Black woman-clapping emoji-ing" me with her words.

"You're right. I know."

"Thing is, Rae," Robin interjected. "Jennifer is probably being unnecessarily a hard-ass right now, but she's not wrong. If you say you want to take more risks because you're not happy, you're emotionally drained, you feel like you've been checking off all the boxes of what you should do instead of finding out who you are…that's not something life is going to just miraculously help you make time for. You've got to just do it."

Fine time for her to stop stuffing her face with nachos now, I thought. But I heard them both loud and clear; it was time for me to stop saying I was going to do something with the list and actually set about trying one of them. Especially since I'd also told Christine over the weekend. It was only a matter of time before she was joining in with them to gang up on me, and I did not want that.

"You're both right," I relented. "So what now?"

"Now you tell us which of the four has been on your heart the most. Which one do you want to try to tackle first?" Jennifer asked.

I sat there silent for a second, and even closed my eyes, trying to figure out which one made the most sense to work on first. None of them would be easy so it wasn't like I could pick the lowest-hanging fruit and start there, and each of them was going to require a ton of work before I felt comfortable checking off that I'd completed it. It's not like I could just go on one date and say, yes, I checked off that whole "being vulnerable and open to falling in love again" thing. Next!

There was one that was the most tangible, however. And it was the same one that was probably going to shake up the perception of my perfect life the most from the people who didn't really know me. I opened my eyes and saw Robin and Jennifer both sitting down and waiting for me, the support they always were, and it gave me the courage to finally say it.

"The job," I half whispered. Clearing my throat, I tried again. "The job," I repeated. "As scary as it's going to be, I can't keep doing stories that don't reflect me and what I'm passionate about."

"Rae, I'm proud of you," said Jennifer, rising up from the floor to come closer to me. She put her arms around me and whispered, "You got this. I know you do."

"Yeah," I responded. She let her arms down and sat next to me on the chaise. "I don't even know where to start with it, though. I haven't looked for a new job in years."

"Oh, that's the easy part," Robin said, reaching for the pitcher to pour us all a fresh round of margaritas. "The hard part, besides this conversation, is going to be letting your old job go when you find the new one. Just because, you know, comfort."

"That's true," I said. "As much as Peter frustrates me sometimes, at least it's the devil I know. And plus, I have Becs there, too."

"But Rebecca is one of us now. She's not going anywhere," Jennifer said. "And Peter will be okay. *This* is about Reagan now, and I'm so excited for what you end up taking on."

"And, we'll both be here to help you job search, too."

"Are y'all also going to help me search for the shoes that I buy when I complete the risk?"

"Uhhhh, that's a given," Robin replied. "In fact, that's really what we should be doing now instead of all this mushy crap. Go get your laptop, so we can pull up some of the sites you go on to get your sample sale designer shoes."

"Oooh, yes, I'm going to enjoy this part so much more than having to be the stern friend."

"Literally, no one told you that you needed to go all hard-ass Jennifer, so you get no sympathy, friend." I swished back to my bedroom in my comfy slippers and picked up my laptop to bring it back to the living room. In the distance, I spied them high-fiving each other on a job well-done. *Nothing like having persistent best friends, that was for sure.*

"I actually have a pair I've kind of had my eye on," I shouted as I made my way back to the living room.

"Of course you do. That would be the part of the list you've been working on instead of the risk part. 'What else can I add to my shoe closet?'" Jennifer replied, snickering.

"Okay, do you want to see the shoes or keep playing my life tonight?"

"You *know* we want to see the shoes. Stop making us wait."

"Okay," I replied with glee, plopping back down in my chaise. I opened up the laptop and went to my bookmarks, landing on the page I'd saved just a couple weeks before. "Feast your eyes on these beauties, ladies. Aren't they just to die for?"

Part 2: Trying on All the Wrong Shoes

"…it's not so much about the shoes, but the person wearing them."

—Adriana Trigiani, *Viola in Reel Life*

Chapter 7

This isn't going to be so bad, I thought, listening to the familiar sound of my heels *click-clacking* on the linoleum floor as I stepped off the elevator at my job. It's not like I was leaving my job today; just telling Becs it was coming. I'd finally started job searching. So why was I so nervous?

I glanced down at my shoes and wiped my sweaty hands down the sides of my thighs, along the seams of my mustard-yellow tapered pants that cut off just above my ankles. Paired with my ankle-strapped, pointed-toe silver stilettos and my cream blazer, it probably appeared as if I was dressed more appropriately for the spring than a few days before Christmas. But I needed to wear something light on what could very well be the first of my last days in the office.

Walking down the long and deserted hallway that

led to my and Rebecca's desks, I was once again grateful that we'd likely have the next hour to ourselves.
It would give me just enough time to catch her up on
Nacho Thursday and see if we were going to do anything over the weekend. I was steps away from her desk
before I realized she wasn't there.

*Oh, that's odd. She was always there or would have
texted me to say she wasn't coming.* I checked my phone
to see if maybe I'd missed a message, but no. It wasn't
until I fully walked up to her desk that I saw her trench
coat was casually draped over her chair and her laptop
open. *Oh, okay, so she was in the office somewhere.*

Selfishly, I wondered where she was at a time when
I needed to give her such big news but sat down at my
desk anyway, opened my laptop and began checking
my emails. Oooh, responses from Brittney Cooper and
Kimberlé Crenshaw. Maybe today was going to be better than I even expected. If I could get either of them to
speak to me about the topic of intersectionality, maybe
I could finally get Peter to okay my pitch.

"Hey, Rae." I heard Becs calling my name as she
walked up. She sounded groggy, but also a little excited.

"Hey, where were you? And why do you sound
tired?"

"I had to be here even earlier than normal this morning. You didn't see the email from Peter? They needed
IT to come in to do some backups to the site. Sounds
like we got another investor and they're asking to see
more traffic. The higher-ups wanted to make sure our
site could handle it."

"Oh. Okay." I scrolled through my emails again and
saw the one she was referring to. *I guess I missed it with
my excitement over the other two.*

"Plus, I got a promotion this morning."

"What? OMG, Becs, congratulations!" I jumped up from my desk to hug her and held on tight for about ten seconds. "I'm so happy for you—wait, does that mean Peter is here at nine in the morning?" I glanced at my watch to make sure I wasn't delusional about the time.

"You really did not read that email," she said, chuckling.

"I did not. But it sounds like I should have." I scrunched up my face as I bounced back to my desk. Who knew I'd miss so much since leaving yesterday evening?

I quickly clicked on Peter's name and saw his message:

Team, I'll be in early tomorrow morning. We have some B.I.G. developments happening with some B.I.G. investors. Rebecca and Tatum, we're going to need all IT folks on hand tomorrow, so I'm hoping you'll be available to pitch in as needed.

Leave it to Peter to say so little in something that was supposed to be a heads-up to his employees. I turned back to Rebecca, incredulous. "This email? This is the one you've been harping on me to read? The one that said absolutely nothing?"

"Well, you would have known he was here early."

"Which for Peter could mean ten-thirty. I can't believe you. Is this 'promotion Becs' speaking?"

"Oh, please." She threw her scarf in my direction in protest, but I caught it midair. "You know, I will forever be your big sister and call you out on your crap. It doesn't take a promotion for me to do that."

"This I know." I rolled my eyes, leaned back toward her and lowered my voice to a whisper. "And good thing because I also have news for you. I finally started job searching last night." With Peter already in, I made sure to keep my statement short and sweet. There was no use in getting fired before I'd found a new job.

"Rae, that's great news! I've been wondering but didn't want to push."

"Don't worry. Jenn and Robin did that for you. They pulled good cop-bad cop on me last night."

"Good for them!"

"Only problem was when we actually started checking out some of the job listings, they were a mess. One was for a technical writer, but they wanted you to have at least six years' experience in reporting and in simplifying technical/legal language, a law degree and were only offering fifty-six thousand dollars."

"A year?"

"Mmm-hmm. Amazingly, that wasn't the worst one. No, that honor goes to the listing for cat writers for a pets' blog that specified you must love cats over dogs, be willing to write various topics on cats four times a week and edit the writing of other cat writers. Serious inquiries only, of course."

"That can't be real."

"Oh, but it was," I snorted. "Thank God it was just the first night, but I'm definitely going to make sure I narrow my choices down a little better next time. And probably not drink tequila while searching."

Rebecca could barely contain her giggles. "That sounds like a good plan."

"What sounds like a good plan?" The two of us were

so in our own world, we hadn't noticed when Peter snuck up on us, catching the tail end of Rebecca's joke.

"Oh, nothing," I said, rolling my chair back to my desk. "Just girl talk, Peter. Nothing to concern yourself with."

"Is this what you all do this early in the morning? Just tell jokes at your desks?"

"One may never know. Unless—" Rebecca gasped "—you plan on showing up before 10:00 a.m. regularly now."

"No, I hate being here this early. You never have to worry about this being something I do very often."

Rebecca and I giggled quietly at our desks. We knew Peter was serious about his hatred for what he called "being at work early," but only in entertainment industries was 9:00 a.m. considered early. Peter had no idea how lucky he was. Rebecca and I had both endured the 7:00 a.m. expectations of the corporate world for short periods of time when we were younger, so this was a luxury. But he was the boss; it wasn't like we were going to be the ones to bust his bubble.

Peter barely registered our giggles at his expense. "Reagan, can you join me in my office? There's something I wanted to talk to you about."

"Sure," I replied, looking to Rebecca for some clue on what he wanted. She shrugged her shoulders, just as confused as I was.

Click-clacking back down the hallway to Peter's office felt a little like being walked to the principal's office. Sure, it didn't necessarily mean you were in trouble, but it felt like it did. And just my luck, other supervisors must have warned their employees they would be in the office early, too, because I saw more faces

watching me than ever at this time of the morning.
Great, everyone will be here just in case I get fired.
Suddenly, my silver stilettos didn't seem like the right
pick for the day, after all.

"I really just wanted to take a moment to tell you
how much your work has improved lately," Peter said,
easing my nerves as we stepped into his office. "I'm
really excited about where you're going with your articles these days. It's no longer just the same rigmarole
about Beltway politics and speculations." He closed
the door behind me and gestured to me to sit down in
one of his chairs.

"Oh! Thank you, Peter."

"That said, I want you to commit to even more. And
to do that, I want to offer you that promotion you've
been angling for. We know you've got *it*, Reagan, so
no more holding back."

"Really?" I was stunned. Peter was saying everything I'd wanted to hear him say for the past two years,
but of course, it was coming the day after I'd decided to
start searching for another job. Now what would I do?
I needed more information, that was for sure. "Does
this mean I can do more stories championing women,
dig into our complex needs and really tackle some of
the issues beyond what happens because of the White
House?"

"It means you won't even have to ask. I'm offering
you an editor position where you'll run your own vertical. I'll still have some say-so in your content, but this
will be your baby."

"Oh, my God." I had no idea what to say in that moment. My legs went numb under me, my fingers felt tin-
gly and my mouth could barely move. I'm sure I seemed

like I was out of my mind sitting across from him, but I was using all of my energy to formulate words, so I didn't have it in me to also change the look on my face.

"I'm guessing that's a yes, you accept."

"I… Well, I need to think about it," I blurted out. "Is that okay? Can I think about it?"

"Of course."

"Okay, that's what I'm going to do, then." I gathered myself well enough to stand up out of Peter's chair and began walking to his door. My hand on the knob, I turned back around to see if I could tell what he was thinking. I was usually pretty good at observing people, especially Peter, but this one caught me off guard. I wasn't sure if it was because I'd come in so resolute that I'd be leaving in the New Year, or what. But I'd missed all the signs—and there were plenty. Big investor. Supervisors in early. Becs getting a promotion, too. Why hadn't I realized this was where this was going? Maybe it was because I wasn't sure how I'd be able to turn it down. "Thanks for the offer, Peter. I appreciate it."

"You earned it, Reagan. Now, go keep proving me right that you deserve it."

I walked out of his office, completely unsure of my path going forward, but knowing I needed to find the leg movement to get back to my desk before people started asking me questions. Less than thirty minutes earlier, I'd been so confident, so certain I was doing the best thing by taking the risk of leaving my job of four years that no longer made me happy, but this was a different job, too, just at the same company. *Was the promotion a sign I should stay?*

If anyone could help me talk through something this monumental, it was Christine. But I wanted her focus to be solely on her recovery right now, not me. Rebecca, Robin and Jennifer were normally great listeners, too, but on this topic, they were already invested in wanting me to leave. I worried about their impartiality. But who else? Certainly not my mom.

And then it hit me. The person I would have wanted to talk to the most was Jake. There was a time when he could help me calm down all the thoughts swirling in my head and figure out which one to listen to; which thought wasn't being driven by fear or expectations, but was just the thing I wanted. A very big part of me craved that kind of reassurance, but another part just as equally big hated that I thought of him in that moment. That flood of emotions came pouring to the surface—the hurt of missing someone, the shame of missing that particular someone and the frustration of having not controlled those feelings better—as I made it back to Rebecca's desk.

"So what did he want?"

"To offer me my own vertical on the website."

"Whoa. That's big, Rae."

"I know." I ran my fingers through my hair and plopped down into my chair. "I asked him to give me time to think about it."

"Okay, that's good. No need to say yes or no at this very second."

"Exactly. But now I have too many things running through my head…do you have plans tonight?"

"Not really. Oliver wants to celebrate my promotion this weekend but he's working late tonight, so we can save that for tomorrow. Why, what were you thinking?"

"I'm thinking we need to get out—all of us. You, me, Robin and Jenn. We'll celebrate your promotion and my offer and most importantly, drink away all the cares of the world," I said, grabbing Rebecca's hands to pull her out of her seat and give her a quick twirl.

"Done, silly bird. Count me in. Just let me text my husband and let him know I'll be home late."

"Good. And I'll text the girls. It's about time we put our creaky knees to the test again."

Later that night the four of us strutted up to the entrance of one of DC's premier nightclubs, looking and feeling like a cross between your favorite girls' group from the 1990s and four of the "Big Six" supermodels of the same period. Jennifer, choosing to show off her best assets—her legs—had chosen a silver slinky number that hid most of her goods at the top but barely covered her butt. She paired that with a bright red pump to accent her outfit. Robin opted for a slightly more classic get-up, wearing a royal blue pant jumpsuit that hung loose on her five-foot-nine body but dipped low in the front like the infamous JLo dress from the Grammys. With that, she wore silver strappy sandals that took her fifteen minutes to buckle. Rebecca, standing five foot six like Jennifer, wore a black-and-white strapless mini dress that pushed up her B-cup breasts and platform black Mary Janes, making her legs appear extra-long, especially next to me.

I'd decided to really test the waters and do something I hadn't in a while—rock a short pink spaghetti-strapped dress that showed off both my legs and my cleavage. It was a break against my cardinal rule of only showcasing one body asset at a time, but I'd lost a few pounds since going to spin class with Rebecca twice a week for the past couple months and was feeling myself.

Plus, the dress wasn't *so* tight, so I figured that would take away some of the skank factor. In fact, it fit me like a corset at the top but flared out at the torso for a nice twirling effect at the hem, but the denouement was the way it complemented one of my favorite pairs of shoes: my nude platform sling-backs from Aldo. These shoes were perfect: sexy but simple, comfortable enough to wear for hours and they made me feel like a sassy diva ready to strut her stuff at the club.

Once in, I knew our first destination. The bar. But as we made our way through the crowd, I was quickly reminded of how packed clubs in DC could be on Friday nights and noticed the scores of people standing at the bar waiting for their drinks. There wouldn't be enough room for us all to head there together.

"Maybe I should go to the bar and get the drinks, and the rest of you find a spot for us somewhere?"

"That's not a bad idea," Robin replied, looking around to see how hard it might be to wrangle some space for us to gather. Everywhere she turned, in every corner of the club, people were standing tightly together. I could see her eyes get big as she scanned the area, but I also knew she had no desire to deal with the crowd at the bar and was all too happy to let me handle that part.

"You won't be able to carry four drinks on your own, though. I can come with," Rebecca offered.

"Okay, works for me," I said. "Tequila soda for you, Jenn, and rum and Coke for you, Rob?"

They both nodded their heads and walked away, determined to find us the perfect space—not too far from the rest of the clubgoers, but also not directly in the middle of the dance floor. It was certainly an art to doing so.

Rebecca and I were standing at the back of the

crowd, waiting to get to the counter, when I faintly heard someone say something that sounded like it was directed to me. I thought I'd heard "What would you like to drink?" but that didn't seem quite right because we were nowhere near close enough for one of the bartenders to be asking us for our orders, and I hadn't perfected my "hey, come and flirt with me" face by that point of the night to illicit someone else offering to buy our drinks. Instead of responding, I turned back to Rebecca to confirm what she would want in case I got to the counter before she did. I also began slightly shifting my weight on my four-inch heels to see what pose felt the most comfortable; the shoes may have been made for dancing all night, but not standing still, lock-kneed for long periods of time.

"What would you like to drink?" came the question again, this time with a bit of a chuckle, and with a much clearer indication that it was, in fact, directed to me.

"I'm so sorry," I said, finally looking up and noticing the man who'd apparently noticed me a few moments earlier. "I didn't realize you were talking to me."

"It's cool." He smiled. "Hi."

Damn my addiction to men with straight white teeth. And great shoulders. And legs. *Oh, God, I'm staring*, I thought. But it was hard not to; this guy seemed like the kind of man who'd happily scoop you up as you melted in his arms.

"Hi," I said, trying to gain my composure. I was not going to let this man see me sweat, and I surely wouldn't let him know that in a matter of fifteen seconds I'd gone from distracted girl who didn't notice him to a girl who might ask him what *he* wanted to drink.

"Now that you know who I'm talking to, can I get you that drink?"

He spoke slowly and deliberately, not at all like what you would expect for someone to talk in a club. He didn't scream or try to outtalk the noise in the background. No, he spoke with the confidence and smoothness of a man who knew his whisper could be heard above anything, including the sounds of the beats stemming from the DJ's booth.

"Sure," I said, attempting to look the six-foot-plus chocolate drop of a man deep in his eyes. Even with my four-inch stilettos on, he beat me by a good four to five inches. "How about a whiskey ginger?"

He leaned closer to me, maybe to hear me better, maybe because the crowd was still building around us, or maybe just to torture me further. Either way, whatever his reason, I didn't want him to actually walk away to get the drink.

"Really? No Moscato? No champagne? A glass of Amaretto sour?" His smile grew bigger as he teased me, shining bright like he could have been a Colgate model at one point in his life.

"Nope, whiskey ginger is perfect."

"Wow, a beautiful woman who wants a whiskey ginger, huh? That's not a little girl's drink."

"I'm not a little girl," I said, trying to tease him back but swallowing the gulp in my throat.

"Hmm, well, then that means you might be able to hang with me. I like that."

"I guess that makes you a lucky guy," I said with a smile, trying my best not to jump him right then, but every time he grinned at me, it made it harder and harder. I stood on my tippy toes to try and get closer to his face. As the music grew around us, I peeked at my watch and noticed it was 11:00 p.m., just about the time DJs in DC thought the music should get louder and faster. It just so happened that this time around, the 808s were in lock step with my heartbeats.

"I guess it does," he said, inching in closer to me, and bringing his voice to an even softer whisper. "A very, very lucky guy."

He stared at me. And smiled that big Colgate smile again. It was then that I knew I needed to pull myself together. I was all for the risk list and working to be vulnerable again, but that did not require me to be wide open with some stranger whose name I didn't even know yet.

But after only, maybe, five sentences, my legs were so weak, I couldn't stand on my toes any longer. Was it the heels or the man? Thinking it was the heels was easier to handle, so I slowly let my feet back down. This only caused him to lean in even closer to me.

"I'll be right back," he said. "Don't move."

He was just turning away from me when I suddenly remembered a very crucial detail: I wasn't meant to just be getting a drink for myself.

"Wait!" I called out and grabbed ahold of his nearest hand.

"Yes?"

"I just remembered I can't only get a drink for myself. I'm actually in line for my friends, too. So maybe you can just stand here with me while we wait?"

"Okay, I think I can do that." This time he was so close I could smell the hint of cologne on his neck. I didn't care that we'd just met; I wanted to know everything about this man, and possibly bury my head in his neck.

"Is that Pi cologne I smell?"

"Okay, you keep this up and I'm going to take you home and marry you tonight."

"What?" I asked jokingly. "I take it that means I'm right."

"Yes, you are indeed right." He watched me quizzically as if trying to study my face.

"How would you know that? You know what, never mind. Since you know something about me, how about you tell me something about you."

"Well, for starters, my name is Reagan," I said, placing my hand out to shake his. When we connected, I was pleasantly surprised by his firm grasp. Most guys tried to be too gentle with women, but he seemed to know just the right balance.

"I'm Luke."

"Nice to meet you, Luke."

"Same with you, Reagan," he said, finally dropping my hand. "So wait, as in Ronald Reagan?"

"Ugh, as in noble. Definitely not the former president."

"Don't pretend that's not a valid question."

"It's about as valid as me asking you if Luke is for Luke Perry."

"The 90210 guy?"

"Yeah."

"It's not, but now I wish it was. He was kind of a badass."

I blurted out laughing. "You're right, he was. But it's still not a valid question."

Inch by inch, we made our way closer to the counter

to place our drink orders. I noticed that Rebecca was still off to the side of me a little, so I could potentially slide her the rest of the drinks if I wanted to spend a bit more time with Luke before meeting back up with the rest of the girls. Luke had obviously realized we were near as well, and that his time to close the deal was getting shorter and shorter. His charm offensive suddenly became much more apparent.

"So when we get these drinks, what do you say you give me just a little more time to get to know you before you meet back up with your friends?"

"I like the sound of that."

"Yeah?"

"Mmm-hmm." I bit my lower lip and looked him in his eyes. He seemed kind, even with his cockiness. Like he had a good story underneath the cool and confident demeanor he showed overtly.

We finally made it to the bar and placed our orders. As promised, I gave the other three drinks to Rebecca and told her I'd be over to her and the others in a little bit. She was all too happy to oblige, giving me the most obvious wink that I'd seen in ages.

"Now, this is a way to jump-start your risk list," she whispered in my ear before leaving me.

Oh, God, I hope Luke hadn't heard that.

I slowly turned back to him, and all I could see was his grin and his outstretched hand.

"Come with me."

I took a huge gulp of my drink and placed my hand in his. We walked hand in hand until we reached a really crowded part of the club. At that point Luke positioned me in front of him so he could direct me from behind, his hand that once held mine slightly cupping my butt cheek and sending waves of pleasure down my spine.

Within minutes we'd found an empty place on a wall—just big enough for me to stand near it and for Luke to stand before me, enveloping me with his presence and height. I didn't know if it was the liquid courage, my desire to remove all thoughts of Jake from earlier, or just the way I was craving Luke all on his own, but I was suddenly pretty ramped up and feeling quite sexual.

"Reagan," he said, staring deep into my eyes. He leaned over me, put one hand on the wall behind me and used the other to cup his drink. Even with my heels, he still towered over me, which meant he had to lean closer in for us to talk, and it meant our lips were barely inches apart as he called my name.

"Yes," I answered breathlessly.

"A gender-neutral name for a pretty girl who likes manly drinks. There's so many things about you that make me want to know more."

I couldn't help the smile forming on my face. It had been quite some time since I'd felt this kind of chemistry with someone from the start. Probably since Jake. And back then I was way more willing to just throw myself out there, heart be damned. The guys since were all sexy and interesting enough to last a few months, but they never really wanted to know me. Maybe that was what instantly drew me to Luke. He had playboy charmer written all over him, but his words were different. *Maybe there was something to being open and the universe sending you what you wanted?*

"Tell me one thing you want to know besides why I like whiskey gingers and how I knew your cologne."

"I want to know what makes you happy."

He said the words so quickly, it caught me off guard. It was almost like he truly meant it, or really awful feeling alert: he was just *that* good. "I can't begin to tell you all of that in a club," I responded, trying to distract myself from the red flag rearing its ugly head inside.

"That's true, but you asked me what I wanted to know. Not what I wanted to know that you could tell me right now."

"Touché." I leaned my head down to mask my laughter. He was just as clever as he was attractive, obviously. "So what do you want to know that I can actually tell you here in the next five minutes?"

"Five minutes? That's all the time I get?"

"Afraid so. Anything more than that and you'll have to deal with the wrath of my friends. We came here to have a girls' night out tonight, and I've spent more time with you than them at this point."

"Fair. Okay, I want to know—" he stopped to let the suspense linger for a bit, knowing that made it sexier. Made him sexier "—how your lips taste. Can I know that?"

I nodded and closed my eyes as our lips connected and melted into each other. With his hands simultaneously roaming my body, Luke kissed me for what felt like hours of time floating in a cloud.

My gosh! My resolve was definitely wearing down. Thankfully, Luke took pity on me and stepped back to view his work on me, effectively ending the kiss and giving me just enough time to regain my composure.

"I think it's fair to say you know that now, yes?" I asked, clearing my throat.

"A little bit." He winked at me, and I could see he

was truly enjoying himself and the effects he had on me. And that, something about him being able to have that much control over me, snapped me out of whatever desirable feelings I'd had previously and sent those red flags bouncing up again.

"You know, I think I know your type, Luke."

"And what type is that, Mr. President?"

"Playboy charmer, curious about the woman before him for a time, but that curiosity will eventually burn out. And you'll be gone as if you were never there."

"Wow, interesting theory of yours. What happens if you're wrong?"

"I haven't been yet," I replied, lightly biting my bottom lip and stretching my legs up so I could get myself in position to leave.

"You hadn't met me yet, either." There was a defiance in his voice but also compassion, like he knew why I was scared to let him in. But as much as I wanted to, I just couldn't do it. There was a reason all my senses were screaming loudly at me to run as fast and far away as I could. Sure, it could be fear. But it could just as easily be the result of learning my lessons, and I wasn't ready to risk which one it was that night.

"What do you say, pretty girl? Can I get your phone number? We can figure the rest of this out later."

"How about we make a deal," I countered, not wanting to say no to him, but not quite ready to say yes. "You find me again before you leave and it's all yours."

"Okay. Bet," he said, leaning into me once more. "I'm going to hold you to that, you know."

"We'll see." I scooched myself away from the wall, sliding past him, and began walking through the crowd to find my friends. But as he faded farther away from my sight, Rebecca's words rang loudly in my ear: I always run away when it gets scary, she'd said. Well, she was wrong. Apparently, I walked away, too.

It was 3:15 a.m. by the time I was back home and in the shower, attempting to wash the club off my body. Despite the hiccup with Luke, the rest of the night had actually been exactly what I needed: me and my girls dancing the night away, twerking and laughing for hours. The only thing left that I wanted was to get a great night's rest.

I stepped out of the shower and noticed I'd missed a text while I was in the bathroom. It was a message from Luke.

Hey Reagan, it's Luke. I ran into your homegirl who was with you at the bar, and she gave me your digits. I hope these are actually yours now that I think about it lol. HMB. I'd love to take you out for dinner. Give me a chance to prove you wrong.

I stared at my phone in shock. Of course, Rebecca would give him my number. I couldn't believe she wouldn't also give me a heads-up, but maybe that was the result of tequila brain. But now the question lingered about what I would do in response.

To give myself time to think, I finished drying off and getting ready for bed. Because I'd worn my natural curls tonight, I didn't bother wrapping my hair to make sure it would be straight in the morning. Instead, I pulled my hair into a ponytail and picked up my silk bonnet to put over my head for the night. With that in place, I put on a pair of gym shorts from college and a tank top, and then climbed into bed, staring at that message over and over, trying to assess the best way to control the situation.

Finally clear, I took a deep breath and responded:

Hi Luke, it's Reagan. Dinner sounds good.

I quickly pressed Send before I could chicken out, put my ringer on silent and placed my phone on the far end of my nightstand…as far away from my bed as I could get it. If I was ever going to get some rest, I needed to forget I sent that message and anything that might come from it.

Chapter 8

When I woke up the next morning, I rolled over and reached for my phone, immediately freaking out about whether I should have replied to Luke last night. Maybe I should have waited until today when it was a more appropriate time to text? What if he took that to mean I wanted to see him last night on some booty call stuff? Or worse, what if I looked at my phone and there was nothing from him yet?

I turned the phone over and saw one missed text. From Luke. One minute after my reply last night. And all it read was: Yes!

It was a simple word, but that level of excitement from a guy this early on was refreshing. He used an exclamation point in a text, for goodness' sake. Most of the men I'd met were still trying to play it very cool to the chest in our first conversations, and there was

Luke, unabashedly showing his excitement. It was admirable and really sexy. And it most certainly deserved a reply back.

I sat up in my bed and texted him back:

lol good morning. Sorry I missed your text last night; I crashed after my shower.

I leaned back onto my headrest and waited to see if he would respond back immediately. I was fully prepared to have to crawl back under my covers if minutes passed by while I waited, but thankfully, I didn't have to. It took less than a minute before I saw his number appear on my phone again.

All good.

I kind of figured.

What are you doing tonight?

In three separate texts, in less than fifteen words, Luke managed to not only calm down my nerves, but also ask me out again. The man *was* good.

Nothing in stone yet. Are you trying to get dinner already? I replied.

Not dinner, yet. But I was thinking you, me, a bunch of lights and some animals lol.

I sat up again in my bed, excited at the possibility he was referring to one of my favorite Christmas things to do in DC.

As in Zoo Lights? I asked.

Ha ha, yeah. You probably think that's corny, right?

No. I love it actually!

Now I'm the one responding with exclamation points, I thought. Was this contagious?

See? I knew there were things I liked about you, Reagan. Text me your address, and I'll pick you up at 6.

I dutifully did as I was told and slid back down into my bed. Something felt different about this guy, like maybe he wouldn't just be another notch in five-month-Betty's belt. Or maybe it was me who was different? I didn't know for sure; I just knew I was going on a date with him less than twenty-four hours after I'd made up my mind to never see him again. That was impressive. I pulled my comforter over my head to block out the sun that was beginning to invade my bedroom and screamed into my pillow. I was going on a date and could hardly contain my enthusiasm.

The neon, multicolored lights flanking the trees at the entrance to the Smithsonian's National Zoo were perfect in the evening, lighting up the sky and inciting joy for all the children and adults walking up to them. And Luke and I were no different. In fact, we might have been as excited as the kids who ran past us while we marveled at the glittery passageway lighting our way into the park with red, green, blue, yellow and orange lights above and around us. It was one of those sights where, if you stood there for a moment, you could get lost in the wonderment of it all…watching the lights twinkle under the moonlight and then catching them as they bounced off the skin of the man next to you.

I peeked over at Luke with a smile plastered on my face and saw that he was staring in awe just as much as I was. "When's the last time you came here?" I asked, tapping his hand to get his attention.

"Man, it's been a while. Maybe three, four years. I don't remember it being like this."

"You've been in DC that long?"

"Yeah. I came here fresh out of college five years ago, wanting to make a difference in the nation's capital."

"Ahhh, so that's why you became a teacher. Altruistic goals."

"What can I say? I've got a heart of gold." He grinned at me to show he was joking, at least a little bit. "What about you? What drew you to writing about politics?"

"DC did, actually," I replied as we began walking through the rest of the zoo. "I always knew I wanted to be a writer. It was the thing that remained a constant for me as a little girl, even as my parents divorced and everything changed about our family dynamic. All of a sudden, I had three little siblings looking to me to be an example for them on what to do at all times. And I never knew anything, except that I could write. It took living here to help me figure out what I wanted to say, though."

"Wow. That was probably a lot to handle. I'm sorry you felt so much pressure as a young girl."

"It doesn't go away, honestly. I still feel it all the time, even now with my brother at twenty-six and my sisters at twenty-two and seventeen. I feel like I have to constantly be perfect for them. It's part of why I like living so far away. I get to make mistakes without them knowing about it."

"Well, I'm glad you're here, too. And you can make all the mistakes you want with me," he said with a wink. "Plus, this place just has an effect on people, you know? Once you're here, like you said, you realize how much politics is in every single fiber of our lives, whether we realize it or not."

"Exactly. I usually have to try to explain that to people. It's nice to hear someone say it to me, instead."

"Told you, girl. I'm going to prove you wrong if it's the last thing I do."

"I see."

Luke grabbed my hand, and we continued strolling until we came upon one of the new glowing animal lanterns: a lion family perched regally next to an LED-powered tree. The power that exuded from these lanterns was astounding. It was almost as if we were watching the real thing, with the way they stood and the attention to detail that was given to everything from the dad lion's hair to the expressions on their faces.

"So beautiful, right?" I turned back to Luke to see if I would catch him in awe again. I'd loved seeing the look on his face when we first walked in; it was like a kid who first tastes chocolate cake. They are all at once in awe, but also trying to figure out where this amazingness has been all their lives. But this time he wasn't watching the attractions in the zoo. His eyes were squarely on me.

"Yes, you are," he said.

"Luuuuke!" I playfully slapped him on his shoulder.

"Turn down the cool factor for me. We're still getting to know each other." I immediately regretted my last statement when I saw his shoulders slump down a little before he could catch himself and hide his expression of disappointment. It didn't last long, however; within seconds he'd recovered and was back to charmer Luke. But I'd seen a glimpse of what a dent in his armor looked like, and felt horrible to have caused it, even if just for a moment.

"Never mind," he said. "You know what? Let's play a game of Truth or Dare."

"Okay," I said hesitantly, but after my last hiccup I didn't want to seem like I was scolding him again.

"All right, you go first. Truth or dare?"

"Definitely truth."

"Do you like me, Reagan?"

"Wow, no start-up questions, huh?"

"Nah," he chuckled. "I think you know by now I don't do things at Level One."

"That I do. From you kissing me in the club to texting me out of the blue to our first date in less than twenty-four hours. I'd say that's definitely not Level One."

"Exactly. So stop stalling and answer the question."

"Yeah, I… I think so. As much as I can like someone in such a short period of time."

"Mmm-hmm," he said, scrunching his face at me.

"I wouldn't be here if I didn't like something about you, Luke. You are intriguing, for sure. And very sexy, but you already know that."

He bent down so his face could be next to mine, and I could see the smirk on his face from my periphery as I tried to avoid his eyes. "That's a really long answer to avoid saying yes, Mr. President."

"I said yes at the beginning. I just explained it a little, that's all."

"Whatever you say."

"What about you? Do you like me, Luke Perry?" Since he'd apparently deemed *Mr. President* his nickname for me, I figured it was only right I also sometimes called him by his not-namesake as well. Plus, I needed something to get some leverage back into this conversation that was equally jokey but also kind of intense.

"Nope. You have to ask truth or dare first."

"Ugh, fine. Truth or dare?"

"Dare," he answered with a smirk, purposely choosing the opposite of what he knew I wanted from him.

"I dare you to do the Zootube slide," I said, pointing to the slides that spanned the length of the lion exhibit, mimicking snow tube slides found in ski resorts across the country.

"On one condition."

"You can't have conditions on Truth or Dare!"

"Sure, you can. My condition is that you slide on the one next to me."

I glanced at him for a beat and contemplated how hard I wanted to press that you could not, in fact, create conditions around Truth or Dare. Problem was I did want to get on the slide, too, so he'd put me in a position where I both wanted to disagree with him and wanted to say yes. Placing my hand on his shoulder, I looked him dead in his eyes and said the only thing I could say: "Deal."

He grinned with satisfaction.

"But if I beat you, I get to skip my next turn and you have to answer truth next time around."

"I'm not afraid of you, Reagan. Let's do it." He removed my hand from his shoulder and shook it with that same firm grip from the night before. And then the race was on. We both took off running to the slides. I was thankful I'd chosen to wear my midnight black, flat, thigh-high boots instead of heels. Not only were they the perfect touch for turning jeans and a blouse into a sexy outfit, there was also no way I could have run anywhere with any of the three-inch-plus stilettos in my closet.

"On your mark," I said as we both climbed into our tubes and prepared to be pushed by the zoo employees.

"Get set," he screamed back at me.

"Go!"

Off we both went down the slide, screaming like we were on the world's largest roller coaster and not the little kid slides that had been erected to introduce some interactive fun at the zoo. I hopped out of my tube as fast as I could and ran to him.

"I won! I won!"

"That you did," he said, laughing and trying to climb out of his own tube. With his long legs, he was having a hard time getting out on his own, so I reached out my hand to help him up. As soon as he grabbed me, we both went soaring feet away from the slides. I was amazed neither of us fell onto the ground, but I think just when we were about to, he caught me midair and steadied us both.

"Okay, so a deal is a deal. Truth. Do you like me?"

"I can't believe you wasted your truth on something you already know."

"Maybe a girl needs to hear it sometimes."

"Reagan Doucet, I will tell you all day long how

much I like you," he said, bending down again so he could stare directly into my eyes. "But you have to believe me when I do. No more of that 'c'mon, Luke' stuff. You either believe me or you don't."

"Deal," I said, grabbing ahold of the loops on the waist of his pants to bring him even closer to me. "You got it."

"Mmm, no. I've got you," he whispered, bringing his lips centimeters away from mine but refusing to kiss me. Instead, he stood there, making me wait, and then flicked out his tongue with a grin, barely scraping the skin on my lips. It was clear Luke wanted me to want him. Better yet, crave him. And while I could also tell this was him putting on his charm armor again, I didn't care. I was in shoe, Christmas lights and sexy guy heaven, and for once I was determined to enjoy it. Not much could top that.

"Now, let's go find these pandas."

I reached out my hand, and he took it as we went skipping to the next exhibit.

Chapter 9

"You should try some of this salad."

"The salad made of seaweed?" I asked, scrunching my face.

"Yes, that one," Luke laughed. "C'mon, it'll be great. I promise."

"Okay, sure. Why not," I said, first hesitating and then relenting to his persistence. In a weird way, that was sort of indicative of me and Luke anyway. His persistence in getting my number from Rebecca after I snubbed him caused me to give him another look and rethink my position on his charmer, playboy ways. And in just six weeks, even with the Christmas holiday interrupting us, he was already doing a pretty good job of convincing me that my first impression may have been off. Maybe that would be the case with this seaweed salad, too.

He dipped his fork into his bowl and twirled around a tiny portion of the seaweed before lifting his eyes back up and bringing the fork to my mouth. "What do you think?" he asked as I chewed on the dish.

I think it's hilarious you just fed me, I thought to myself, *especially considering how intimate that is.* But since I'd learned that Luke was the kind of guy who enjoyed being open and vulnerable, including wanting to do intimate, if slightly uncomfortable things, like feeding me in the middle of a crowded Thai restaurant, I did not say what I was really thinking.

"It's actually not bad," I replied.

"Not bad?"

"Yes, not bad." I burst out laughing at how upset he was that I didn't fall out for his seaweed. If only he knew what my original reply was going to be.

"And by *not bad*, you obviously mean best salad you've ever had, right?"

"Not quite, Luke Perry," I said, laughing. "But if it makes you feel better, it's a lot tastier than some of the food you've cooked for me so far."

"Wow, that stings, Mr. President. For real?" Like a little kid, he held another piece of seaweed salad on his fork, and I could almost see his desire to flick it at me oozing off him. If we were at either of our homes, I'd be toast by now, seaweed flying through the air in my direction. "You know you like my cooking. C'mon, you can admit it," he added, taunting me with that fork across the table.

"Me? Like your cooking?"

"Yes," he laughed. "You."

"I think… I liked maybe *one* of the meals you made, but I'm not sure I can speak to your cooking as a whole just yet." I looked back at him with a smug smile. *Two could play his taunting game.*

"It didn't seem like that when you were in the clean-plate club for the last three."

"Oh, right," I replied, pausing to pretend as if I was considering his counterargument. "You do make a good point. So maybe I enjoy your cooking just a little bit. Like this much." I used my right hand to show a tiny space between my pointer finger and thumb.

"Oh, just that much, huh?"

"Wellll, okay. Maybe this much." I opened the space between my fingers to about the size of a ballpoint pen.

"I don't know if you know this, but—" he sucked his teeth before continuing "—that's still not all that great, babe."

"Oh? It's not? Hmm, maybe I meant this much?" This time I used both hands to show the space between them, giving about a ruler's length in between as my description.

Luke leaned across the table, drawing himself closer to me so that his hand could almost touch me if he wanted to.

"I'm still not completely sold on this appreciation yet."

"No? Darn. Well, what do you say about this much?" I winked and spread my arms, open wide, just in time for him to sneak over and begin tickling me, causing me to have a laughing fit in the middle of the restaurant.

"Wait, wait, wait," I said in between uncontrollable giggles.

He paused briefly, allowing me to pant out a paltry "No fair!" right before tickling me some more.

"Sorry, sweetheart. All's fair in love and war," he said, winking at me like a man who'd just won the night.

"This isn't over."

"Yeah, yeah, we'll see. Maybe you'll have a better chance when you come visit me in New Orleans."

"Ugh, don't remind me." I sat back into my chair, my mood completely changing from the jovial joking one to one of sadness. It took three dates and a Christmas break for Luke to tell me that, of all the times for us to meet, we met just as he was getting ready to move away from DC. At the time he told me, I was ready to call it quits, but then he said the one thing I'd wanted Jake to say all those years before: "Reagan, the moment I saw you standing at that bar, I knew I had to meet you, potential long distance be damned."

How could I resist him when he was willing to fight for me after only a few weeks? That was not to say the revelation had been easy, but we both hoped that his moving to my hometown would make things slightly better to manage.

"Don't pout, pretty girl. This is our last dinner together before I move. I don't want it to be sad."

"I don't, either. And I'm trying not to make it that way, I promise. I just…can't stop thinking about how hard it's going to be."

"You don't think it's damn near fate-like that I'm moving to where you're from, of all places?" He reached over the table again to hold my hand as he spoke.

"That is pretty freaky," I replied with a grin starting to grow back on my face.

"Exactly."

"But," I reminded him, "that doesn't change the fact that I live in DC now, and New Orleans is thousands of miles away from here. I may be from there, but I get to go home maybe three or four times a year, max. That doesn't sound like the makings of a great relationship."

"It can be. I can come up here three or four times a year, too. And then before you know it, it's only a little over a month in between the times we get to see each other in person."

"And that sounds ideal to you?"

"No, of course not. But you're worth it."

There he went again, saying words I wasn't quite sure I believed, even though I desperately wanted to.

"And you're already coming home for Mardi Gras in a couple weeks."

"Yes, I am," I said with a sigh, already sensing that once again his persistence was wearing me down. "And you're going to meet my family. Are you ready for that?"

"Nothing can be more intense than meeting Robin and Jennifer, so I think I'm good."

"That's true. They did put you through the wringer."

"Yeah, but they also said something to me about a list you're working on?"

I almost spit my food out of my mouth. Had they told him that he was potentially a check on it when I hadn't said anything to him yet?

"List? What list did they tell you about?" I asked.

"I don't know. Just something about how they thought you might be buying a new pair of shoes soon to check off a thing on it."

"Ahhhh, well. It's not, like, literal. Just something where I'm keeping track of stuff that I want to do more," I said, trying to find the best words so I didn't offend him and have him thinking he was just part of some game.

"And I'm one of those things you want to do more?" He licked his lips and raised his eyebrow toward me. "Maybe more of what we did the other night?"

"Not like that, silly. Just in terms of me being more open with someone like you."

"Okay. I like the sound of that. And the shoes? Why are you buying a new pair of shoes?"

"The shoes are just for the ball, babe," I said, lying. I wasn't ready to get into the intricacies of how the shoes were my reward for the list I'd just told him wasn't real.

"Now, that makes sense and sounds like the Reagan I know." He moved his hand closer to me and began lightly tickling me again.

"Whatever," I said, playfully slapping his hand away.

"But for real, we're going to make it, okay?"

"Okay. I trust you." And maybe in some small way, I actually was beginning to.

My visit home for the last week of Mardi Gras started off no differently than it did whenever I went down there with the addition of a few parades. I'd been home for a few days, spending most of my time either with Luke or my family, when before I knew it, my last night was upon us. And while I didn't want to leave, I woke up that morning with an air of expectancy all around me. It had been years since I'd made it home during Mardi Gras, and that night I would be attending one of the famed carnival balls along with my mom and some of my other family members.

I rose out of bed with an extra pep in my step, made sure to lay out the dress I was wearing that night—a floor-length royal purple gown that cinched at my mid-section and flowed downward with ease—and pulled out the heels that would accent my outfit. Sure, I had my mask and jewelry as well, but c'mon, this was always going to be all about the shoes. The girls had almost let the cat slip out of the bag, but the truth was I had been thinking about buying a new pair of shoes, not for the ball, but to symbolize me finally being open to love again. Luke had gone from a cute and sexy guy in the club one night to meeting my friends and making me reconsider all the notions I'd had previously about men, trusting them and putting my heart on the line. We'd even talked about him meeting my family when he picked me up from the ball. This was insanely fast for my normal timeline, but if I was going to take the plunge into trusting love again, letting him meet them as we left seemed like the perfect compromise. We could spend about ten minutes laughing with everyone and then have the rest of the night to ourselves.

When it came time to get ready, I carefully put my dress on, took my pin curls down to let my hair fall past my shoulders, meticulously applied my makeup and then stepped into quite possibly my new favorite shoes—a pair of gold lamé heels that made just the right statement. You could see the sparkle of the lamé from the front and the shine of the gold-plated heel from the back. They were, to put it in one word, heavenly.

Unfortunately, they were not the best-feeling shoes with their five-inch stiletto heel and barely a platform style, but at that moment it didn't matter. I hadn't been to a Mardi Gras ball since I was seventeen, and on this night I wanted to be sure that I would sparkle and shine. Plus, I also knew that at midnight, Luke would be coming to pick me up from the ball so that we could spend the rest of my last night together.

This night was like my own little version of Cinderella coming true! The biggest difference? I didn't have the ugly stepsisters and stepmother trying to make my ball experience a downer, and midnight would be when I got to spend time with my prince, instead of the other way around. So I guess it was like the opposite of Cinderella, but with those shoes I felt like the belle of the ball.

Before we left the house, I looked around to check out how good my family looked in their outfits. My mom stood five foot nine, with her black-and-gold gown flowing to the floor, slightly tickling the kitten heels she had on underneath. Her olive skin tone perfectly matched the gold accents and accessories she wore that night, giving her a flawless glow. But she wasn't the only one who would be stopping cars in the street; the rest of my family looked just as good and debonair with their suits and gowns, too. My youngest sister, Charlie, wowed in my old red mermaid gown from college, and her best friend sparkled in a yellow dress that had hints of gold in it, too. I even caught some of the guys straightening their bow ties on their immaculately tailored tuxedos and making sure their shoes were buffed to perfection. We looked good! Right before we walked out the door, I slid on my grandmother's faux mink coat that had been passed down through the Chevaliers to my mom and then to me, picked up my mask, and we made our way to the New Orleans Convention Center.

At the ball, the place was filled with beads and masks, confetti and doubloons, massive spreads of food and liquor overflowing. I saw plenty of happy faces talking as they waited for the parade to enter in. Everyone seemed to be enjoying the debauchery of just being alive. We were in New Orleans during Carnival after all, so there was nothing to do but to live it up. There was dancing and drunk singing, loud laughter and complete disregard for everything outside those four walls. And once the parade floats poured in with beads flying everywhere, you could see gala patrons drunkenly swinging the beads around after they caught them. Music from the brass band blared through the ballroom, enticing everyone to keep the party going and let the music take control of their limbs. It was a sight to see. At least for everyone but me.

Sure, I was having a great time—more than a blast, really—but I'd also silently begun my countdown to midnight. While for most people, the ball wouldn't be over until about 4:00 a.m., I was looking forward to my shortened experience, because that meant more time with my man. I kept thinking of the moment he would see me when he walked through those doors, and his breath would be caught somewhere deep in his throat. Truthfully, I also couldn't wait to be in his arms again and feel his hands all over me, especially when it would be another month or two before we'd see each other.

My mom could sense my excitement as well. "He's going to be blown away when he sees you tonight," she said. "You are absolutely stunning." *Nothing like a confidence boost from your mom, right?*

"But you know, that's not for another few hours." Maria ended her statement by slightly raising her eyebrows and giving me a very knowing look.

Leave it to my mom to make her point without saying too much. Her words helped snap me out of my Luke trance, though, and I realized that I still had another two hours before I would see him. I finally lost myself in the fun that was surrounding me, drinking champagne and becoming one of the people making loud sounds of laughter. No longer an onlooker, I danced and tipsily sang songs like "Another One Bites the Dust" and "Low Places," while simultaneously calling out to the float riders to "Throw me something, mister!"

"I'm so glad you're here tonight, Rae," my mom said as she handed an enormous set of beads to me. "I only wish I could see my babies more often. Charlie and I miss you, your brother and sister...just leaving us and spreading out to cities all over the country."

"I am, too, Mommy," I said, ignoring her patented passive-aggression again. "And I'm glad you reminded me that I should be enjoying myself while I'm here."

"Did I do that?" she asked, knowing full well she did.

"Uhhhh, yeah," I laughed.

"If I said anything at all, it was only out of love, *cher*." She winked at me in the way she always did when she knew her ways had worked.

We continued on, reveling in the joyous occasion, jumping around and dancing and maybe even spilling the champagne we were drinking, but definitely laughing with our whole bodies for the next two hours. At 11:50 p.m., everything stopped for me, and I began to prepare myself for midnight. Luke and I had already talked about how he would meet me in front at that time, so there was no need to check in. Still, I took my phone out of my purse anyway—you know, just in case. I kissed my family goodbye, slid my coat back on and made my way to the front door.

I walked out to the lobby of the convention center

and impatiently waited, tapping my shoes on the floor and looking around for my beau. I also practiced my poses and daydreamed about what he would say when he saw me. I thought about how he would react. Would he scoop me up in his arms and twirl me around or just stand there in awe? Would he kiss me as soon as he saw me or wait until we walked back to his car? We'd been dating for a couple months at this point, but he'd never seen me dressed up like this, and I just knew he was going to be in for a good surprise.

After twenty minutes of still no prince, I began to worry. He hadn't called or picked up the phone when I called. He hadn't shown up when he said he would. He hadn't even texted to let me know if something had changed. But I knew how much Luke liked me, so I tried not to panic that something had happened to him on his way to come get me.

It wasn't easy, however. And my brain kept coming up with the worst possible scenarios. What if he'd gotten into a car accident on his way to get me, and he was somewhere lying in a ditch, calling out for help but no one could hear him? What if he'd been kidnapped and thrown into the river because someone mistook him for some other smooth, dark-skinned guy who just so happened to be in the mob? What if a friend of his had gotten really sick and he'd had to rush him to the hospital and there was no time to call me to let me know he'd have to cancel?

· All kinds of scenarios ran through my head. And as each minute passed, they progressively got worse. I mean, what could be so wrong that he couldn't pick up the phone?

I looked at my phone again and saw it read

12:30 a.m. Thirty minutes and no call. I dialed his number again. *Ring. Ring. Ring.* A gazillion rings and still no answer.

I dialed again.

And again.

And again.

And again.

There was no denying I was in full panic mode at this point. Sweat was beginning to drip down the sides of my head. My heart was racing. My palms were so sweaty, my fingers could barely make the contact to press his name on my phone.

And then a sudden, heartbreaking feeling hit me deep in the pit of my stomach. What if he'd just decided not to come?

With that last question, I stopped calling and slid my phone back into my purse. I didn't have the energy to walk back into the ballroom, however; instead, I decided to just stand on the wall for a little longer.

Finally, at 12:45 a.m., I felt my phone vibrating through my purse. I caught my breath, reached inside and answered before even looking at the screen. Something inside me already knew it was him. And it was. He was calling to tell me that he wasn't coming. That he'd gone by a friend's house to hang out instead. That he'd been thinking about it, and maybe it was best that we just ended it that night instead of dragging out the long distance further. That maybe we'd moved too fast too soon, and he wasn't ready to come to an event with my family attending. That he was sorry he didn't say something earlier. That… Honestly, the rest of what he said really didn't matter anymore. I hung up the phone, shell-shocked, not quite sure what had just happened and dejected that I would have to walk back into the ball and admit to everyone that I'd never left. Disappointed in the knowledge that this was surely the end for us. That my last thought had come true; he'd really just simply chosen not to come. I couldn't believe he'd chosen this moment to make a fool of me.

I walked back into the hall to everyone's surprise, making the statement entrance I'd intended for earlier in the evening, my shoes sparkling even while the light in my eyes dimmed. There I was. Cinderella. Stood up at midnight. It was surely a sight to see.

"*Cher*, is everything okay?" my mom asked as she came running up to me, her hair flying behind her like a superwoman cape.

"Yeah, I don't really want to talk about it."

"Are you sure?"

"Yep, I'm sure." I walked past her, my head down, attempting desperately to hold my tears in. *This isn't anything new*, I reminded myself. One thing I could always count on was the other shoe dropping as soon as things seemed to be going too well, especially with the men in my life. Time and time again it happened, and Luke had been no different.

When I arrived back at our table, I quietly slid off the heels that had now become constricting to my feet and exchanged them for my comfy ballet slippers. There was no need to keep playing the part. The ball was over. I'd been stood up by the man who was supposed to be my Prince Charming. Those damned shoes seemed more cursed than favorites.

Chapter 10

"Alexa, play Ariana Grande's *Thank U, Next* album on shuffle."

I took one huge gulp from my wineglass and breathed in deeply, preparing myself as I waited for the music to begin. To say it had been an excruciating past eighteen hours would be putting it lightly. After being embarrassed in front of my family, I then had to endure the next several hours of questions and attempts of people being comforting that just fell flat every time. There was nothing they could say to me that would make me feel better, because it was my fault for thinking that things would be different with Luke than with any other man in my life. Jake left me. Matthew cheated on me. Countless other guys either ghosted, bread crumbed, or laughed at me falling off a damn bed.

All I really wanted was to get back here, back to

my apartment, so I could kick off the combat boots I wore on the plane, blast my music, sing and dance and scream around my place until I was worn out and then go to sleep.

As the intro to "In My Head" began playing, I took another swig of wine before helping Ariana belt out the tragic tale of a woman who fell in love with someone who was only amazing in her dreams. Instinctively, my arms began to sway and feet started to move on beat. It wasn't long before I'd danced my way into my closet, my safe haven when things got really hard to handle. Everyone always teased me about how much I loved my shoe closet, but nothing in there had ever disappointed me. I could put on a pair of any of the shoes surrounding me, and they would instantly make me feel better, help me stand taller, remind me who I was and to never let the pain sit too long before I sucked it up and moved on.

The only problem was in my closet was also my shoe diary, and inside my diary was that damn risk list. The song changed, and I twirled around in my closet for the first verse, letting the music speak to my soul, closing my eyes and taking it all in. I was done, I thought to myself. Done with the risks, done with the men, done with it all, because each time it didn't work out, it was too painful, too heartbreaking and too devastating. And I was tired of encouraging myself to get back up just to get hurt again.

I picked up my diary and stared at the list I'd written four months before in my blue pen because I'd had some sense of hope that day, even despite the doubts I had. There was no hope anymore. Just frustration and finally, resolve. I tore the page out of the diary, crumpled it up and leaned out of my closet so I could throw it into the trash can in my room. If I'd learned anything from the past couple days, it was a reminder that safe might be boring, and it might not get the kudos from your friends, but it felt a whole lot better than this.

Turning back around to my shoes, I breathed in deeply again and began looking for what shoes I'd wear to work tomorrow. I'd need something to give me an extra pep in my step when I told Peter I was finally accepting his promotion offer.

At work the next day I sat at my desk and furiously typed on my laptop, earphones in to try to avoid any questions from Rebecca about how things had gone on my trip home. In my peripheral I saw her repeatedly turn to me and think about interrupting me, slightly leaning in but each time, ultimately changing her mind. I knew she was curious, but we also had a long-standing pact that when either of us had earphones in, it meant we were head down in a project and should be disturbed for emergency purposes only. We'd always respected that pact, but I could tell she must have been torn on whether my trip constituted an emergency or not. After all, I'd walked in and barely said a word to her before sitting down and immediately burying my nose into my computer.

She finally decided to message me on our company instant messenger.

I know what earphones mean, but just making sure you're all right.

Yeah, I'm good. Just busy, I replied. The truth was I didn't want to answer questions or have to tell her I was waiting on Peter to come in so that I could accept the promotion offer. I knew she'd try to talk me out of it if I did, and I'd already made up my mind. But I was far too chicken to handle any probing from her in the meantime. Can you let me know if you see Peter come in, though? Need to talk to him.

Sure.

Thanks.

I went back to pretending like I had the biggest breaking story on the way when really I was just going over in my mind some of the topics that I thought might be good for my vertical and what stories and content I would want to roll it out with. *I'd love to get some really great quotes from various women in politics, media and pop culture and have them to pepper throughout the week as new content*, I thought. One thing I knew from working to raise my profile on Instagram around my shoes was that the more content you released, if it was compelling and people could count on it consistently, the more viewers and followers you got. And it didn't need to always be long, drawn-out content. A quote here, an image there, even the right video could keep my readers coming back while I worked on features to deliver to them every week.

He's here.

A little after 10:00 a.m. I saw Rebecca's message come across my screen. *Peter is nothing, if not consistent*, I said to myself.

Thanks, Becs! Really appreciate it.

No problem.

I saved my work, took my earphones out and stood up from my seat, sliding my silver-studded, black "smoking loafers" back on. At some point they'd slipped off the heels of my feet while I was typing, and I hadn't stopped to fix them at the time. Out of the corner of my eye, I saw Rebecca studying me to figure out what was going on, an act she continued even as I walked past her. She seemed even more confused when I winked at her as I awkwardly tried to comfort her clear concerns without actually using my voice.

"Hey, Peter, you have a second?" I was maybe a minute behind him when he'd walked into his office, so I initially peeked in to at least give the impression like I wasn't stalking him.

"I already know Rebecca alerts you when I come in," he said as he placed his briefcase down on the floor and sat down in his seat.

"What? I don't know what you're talking about."

"Sure, sure, Reagan. What's up? How can I help you?"

"Well," I said, stepping fully into his office and cracking the door behind me. "I wanted to officially see if your offer was still on the table for my own vertical."

"Yes, absolutely," he said, sitting up in his seat. "I've been waiting for you to get back to me on this, rather patiently might I add, but I'm glad you finally decided to say yes."

"I'm sorry about the delay. It's just between Christine and then the break for the holidays and..." I stopped myself before I added any more details like being stood up in front of my entire family.

"I understand completely. That's why I hadn't pushed you. Plus, you've still been delivering on your normal content. Your opinion piece on the ways Senators Warren and Klobuchar were pitted against each other in the Democratic primary was gold the other day. This promotion really is because I believe you've earned the opportunity to be our leading voice on women and politics."

"Thank you, Peter. Truly."

"Don't mention it." He leaned back in his chair and reached into his desk to pull out a stack of papers before handing them to me. "Now's the fun part. You have to fill out all this paperwork for HR for it to go into effect. You do that today, and I'll make sure it all goes through pretty quickly. You could be up and running beginning of April if we're lucky."

"That would be amazing," I said, that much happier I'd taken the time this morning to work on the beginnings of an internal production schedule. "I'll be sure to fill these out today and let you know when I'm done."

I stepped farther into Peter's office and took the stack of papers from him, then turned on my feet and began walking back out to get to my desk. *See?* I thought. *The risk list might not have gotten me this at another job.* Sometimes it took staying where you were to get where you wanted to be.

Halfway down the hallway, I turned around again when I heard Peter calling my name.

"Yes?" I asked, looking at him quizzically.

"Sorry," he said, attempting to catch his breath. I imagined he'd run out of his office to try to catch me, thinking I was farther away than I actually was. "In all the excitement, I forgot to mention a couple parameters around the vertical, since you know, this is your first one and all."

"Sure, that's understandable." I stood facing him, my hands clutching the papers he'd just given me and wishing he'd either remembered these parameters in his office or waited to talk to me at my desk. In the middle of the hallway was kind of weird, but I'd go along with it. As if he could sense my apprehension to the location, he started walking with me to my desk, his breath now back to normal.

"The first thing is I'll need to see an initial list of the topics you're thinking of covering so I can be sure we're on the same page about what the vertical is intended to do."

"Of course. I was actually working on that this morning. I think I have some ideas that will really help increase our audience, especially among young women who aren't largely targeted by political online magazines."

"Great, that sounds great. I'm also going to want you to finally add our email app to your phone and also to send me a list of the potential people you're thinking of interviewing or including in your first posts."

With each step we took closer to my desk, the *parameters* as he'd called them grew more and more restricting. I'd assumed the first two were probably part of the deal. But the last one felt like it meant more was coming with it. I turned to Peter to stop our progress and look at him face-to-face, no longer caring where we were in the building. "Is there something you're not telling me, Peter? Just a minute ago you were telling me that I earned this opportunity, so I thought that meant you trusted my judgment as a valuable staff writer over the past four years. Why does it seem like you're hesitant now?"

"I wouldn't say hesitant, Reagan. I just know that you are really excited, and I applaud that, but I also want to make sure that even as we're thinking of expanding our audience, we're true to this site's current audience," he said. "It doesn't help us to get younger, more diverse readers if we lose the people who built our readership in the first place."

"Honestly, Peter. I think that's a misunderstanding of who reads my articles on our site," I countered. "But I get it. Don't go too radical too fast is what you're saying."

"Your words, not mine, Reagan," he said. "But yes."

I watched him as he walked back to his office, steadying my breathing once again, but this time to calm my frustration. *So much for the ideas I was working on earlier*, I thought. When I opened my eyes and turned back around, I suddenly realized just how close we'd gotten to my desk before I'd stopped him. And there was Rebecca, sitting in her chair, staring at me with disgust. It was clear she'd not only overheard the conversation, but she also thought it was a load of crap.

She was not wrong.

I spent the next few hours continuing to avoid Rebecca, filling out my paperwork and desperately trying to tweak my earlier ideas into what I thought might be more palatable for Peter. Gone were the plans for developing hashtags, posting memes and using things like music lyrics over the decades to show the progression, and sometimes regression, of women in American society. Instead, I replaced those ideas with more prototypical ones, such as exploring maternal mortality rates in light of health care discussions being such a point of contention in the Democratic primary. I kept in my desire for interviewing influential women and using pop quotes as intermediate content, but I replaced potential interviewees like Austin Channing Brown, the amazing author of *I'm Still Here*, with women more conventionally viewed as being in politics.

By the time I was done, Rebecca had gone home, as had many of the other employees at our job. She'd messaged me after observing the fiasco with Peter and simply said we could talk later, because she knew I probably didn't want to at that moment. I appreciated her grace, because I wasn't sure I would have been able to keep my composure if I'd actually started expressing myself out loud. I felt the anger tears trying to surface when I'd sat back down, and the one good thing about having to rework all of my ideas was that it gave me enough incentive and distraction to stuff all those feelings and do what I needed to do. After all, I'd chosen this promotion, and I was going to do my damnedest to try to make the best of it.

I reread my plans once more to check for spelling errors or any potential hiccups that might give Peter heartburn and then sent him my email. After closing my laptop, I took a brief moment for myself and enjoyed the quiet in the office. No *click-clacks* of heels or friends to avoid, just peace and silence. I could have probably stayed there for longer if not for the vibration I heard stemming from my phone.

Oh, goodie, I thought, picking it up and noticing

it was my first official email alert on my phone from work. From Peter.

Reagan, great ideas so far. I like the direction you're heading in. Let's talk some more tomorrow.

"Of course you do, Peter," I said underneath my breath. I'd built it to be the perfect amount of me, but with slightly less soul. That could work for now, but I was going to have to figure out how to slyly bring back in some of my *radical* ideas or I'd drive myself crazy.

Chapter 11

The next morning I awoke reinspired. I'd spent most of the evening pouting, and then needing a respite, so I went scrolling through my Instagram and Twitter feeds. That was when it hit me. Peter and I didn't have to be on opposing sides. The reality was that I wanted to write the stories that were more conventionally around women and politics. There wasn't anything on the ideas list I shared with him that made me cringe or feel like I was being asked to compromise my beliefs. It was just that Peter and I had slightly different opinions on what constituted politics. I wanted to bring in more sociopolitical issues, appeal to a younger audience, bring them all to the table.

And I finally figured out how to merge the two so we could both be happy.

I stood outside his office at 9:50 a.m., going over

my pitch once more in my head. He wasn't there yet, of course, but I wanted to be ready and waiting for him when he walked in. It was that important. I tapped my leopard print, sling-back kitten heels on the floor while I bided my time and contemplated all the different ways the conversation could go. Peter was a reasonable man, but he was also very stuck in his ways, something I'd have to be sure to combat strategically in our discussion. I shifted in my heels to distract myself and continued waiting.

By the time Peter walked up, I was on pins and needles, and practically jumped him upon his arrival.

"Hey, Reagan, ready for the day, I see?" he asked, glancing down at his watch.

I chuckled awkwardly. "I guess so. I just realized I had some more ideas I wanted to talk through with you if you have time."

"Sure, come on in," he said, stepping inside and proceeding with his morning routine. I'd ambushed Peter so many times at this point, I could recount his steps play by play with my eyes closed: he places his coffee cup on the edge of his desk, shimmies out of his coat, puts it on the coat hanger, walks around to the back side of his desk, sits his briefcase on the floor just off to the right corner of the office, reaches around to get his coffee again and finally, takes a seat in his chair. He does all of this without saying a word, and I oblige, too, not wanting to interrupt him but also to observe. He never looked bored with his routine, I realized. It was who he was and what he liked. And all of a sudden, I had a better understanding of why he was so resistant to my changes.

To Peter, change was opposite from him, and it

made sense until now because I was also a creature of habit. My attempts to shake up our content the past few months probably felt like an attack on him, and not what it actually was—an attack on my previous belief in the status quo.

I knew then that I needed to frame my first idea perfectly or he would flip.

"Okay, Reagan. Talk to me. What did you have in mind?" he asked after taking a sip of his coffee.

"So last night I'm home, scrolling through social media, and I had a genius idea I think you'll love." I walked over to the seats in front of his desk and sat down as well.

"I'm intrigued."

"What if I reached out to some female politicians and got them to tell me who they have their eye on in pop culture at the moment? And then did the same with a few women who are making a name for themselves outside Capitol Hill? Then give them a chance to conduct five-to-ten-minute interviews with the women they mentioned, covering the important topics happening each month we do it. I'm talking everyone from Representatives Maxine Waters and Alexandria Ocasio-Cortez to Senator Kirsten Gillibrand and Representative Rashida Tlaib. This way we're staying true to the people who want their Beltway politics, while appealing to a younger online magazine audience." I sat up on the edge of the chair, trying to both contain my excitement but also convey just enough of it that Peter understood I wasn't presenting him with a fly-by-night idea.

I continued, "Can you imagine how dope it would be to read an interview by Elizabeth Warren with Megan Thee Stallion on the cost of college and student loan

debt? Now, I have no idea if Senator Warren even knows
Megan exists, but if she did, that would be perfect! The
no-nonsense rapper who is blowing up right now and
also happens to still be in college, obtaining her degree, sitting down with one of the more famous female
advocates for student loan relief and higher education.
You thought my last piece was gold? This kind of series would be groundbreaking, Peter."

After I'd finished my pitch, I looked at him and held
my breath while I tried to read his reaction and get a
sense of what he was thinking. He did not make it easy
for me, sitting stoically in front of me an entire minute
before speaking. And when he finally did, he hemmed
and hawed so much at first, I had a nagging feeling I
wouldn't like what he wanted to say.

"Reagan, I appreciate your enthusiasm. Really, I do.
But this still sounds too kitschy for me. Elizabeth Warren and a gangster rapper? What makes you think a
middle-aged white woman in northern Virginia wants
to read that?"

"First, she's not a gangster rapper. Jesus, Peter, seriously? And second, I think the beauty of the idea is
that the middle-aged white woman in Virginia will want
to read it. You know why? Because her daughters will
read it and comment about it and post it on their social
media, and that mom wants to know everything her
daughter does. But so will the hip-hop blogs and the
students currently in college dreading the debt ahead
of them six months after they graduate and the women
in their thirties poised right between both of these gen-
erations—too young to have gone to college for fifty
dollars like Warren did, too old to benefit from the information most people know now about predatory lend-

ing, but still young enough to listen to Megan in their earphones while they are out conducting grown woman business. This is a win/win. No one could say we're being too light, but it also gets those new investors the increase in eyes and clicks they want."

"I understand, Reagan, but I just don't think this is the proper venue for it. Three fourths of the people you named are not our core audience, and I think we risk alienating them by going this rogue so quickly."

"Okay," I said, leaning back into the chair. "Do you want to hear any of the other ideas I had?"

"Please. Yes." He rubbed his forehead and watched me as I gathered myself again in the chair, feeling defeated, but hoping I could take one more crack at finding a good balance in what we both wanted for the new vertical.

"Black female mayors," I started. "Latoya Cantrell in New Orleans. Keisha Lance Bottoms in Atlanta. Lori Lightfoot in Chicago. And DC's very own, Muriel Bowser. Are they the new Black quarterbacks? And what are the challenges both face to being viewed as quarterback/mayor first before their identities?"

"No," he replied, not even allowing me the chance to finish. "What is the disconnect we're having here, Reagan?"

"I'm wondering the same thing, to be honest," I said, stunned at his candor. "You told me you trusted me and that this was my opportunity to have my voice heard."

"I did—" He stopped himself before continuing. "I do. But that trust was based on the kind of stories you've produced for us the past four years. These are… different, to say the least. I don't understand what's wrong with the ideas you sent me yesterday. Those were great!"

"They were good, but they were also stories that I knew fit your vision. Not mine. They don't challenge me or push me beyond anything I've done since I got here."

"That's not true. You were just praising me for giving you the chance to do more stories focused on women because that wasn't always the case. How easily you forget having to go to those White House briefings and simply regurgitate whatever news they wanted to give us that day. I'm not the bad guy here."

"Peter, I would never say you're a bad guy. Ever. I just think we are not on the same page about what this vertical can be and the impact it can have. I'm not saying everything I think of will be perfect, but you're not even giving the ideas that aren't the same cookie-cutter ones we are known for a chance."

"You're right, I'm not. But it's because I know what works here."

"Your vision, yes?"

"Let's not forget the success you've had executing my vision." He was definitely growing annoyed with me the longer we kept discussing the issue, but he was not alone.

"Then why offer it to me? Why say the vertical was mine?" I asked on the verge of tears but holding them back.

"Because I thought you got it. I thought you understood what we're doing here. Maybe I was wrong." He spoke with a low voice as he stared me down, very clear on who held the power in our relationship and not needing to raise his voice to get his point across.

"I do get it, Peter," I replied. "But maybe it's not

enough for me anymore." I looked across the desk at the man who'd given me my biggest breaks in journalism thus far, the man who'd put my articles on the homepage when he didn't have to, who'd been generous enough to offer me a promotion and wait two months for my response, but he was also the man holding me back, and I couldn't let him or my fears do it anymore.

"I quit," I said quietly. "I'll pack my things up and be out this afternoon."

"Reagan, you don't have to do that. You presented me a great proposal yesterday. Let's just take some time and focus on that, and maybe these other ideas can come about later."

"I appreciate you, Peter. I really do. But I can't wait anymore. I didn't know that until this conversation, but I just can't."

Seven hours later Rebecca, Robin, Jennifer and Christine were all at my front door, knocking on it incessantly while I walked from my bedroom, through the living room, into the foyer, and until I actually, physically, opened the door.

"Oh, my God, y'all. I was in bed. You didn't have to knock the whole time."

"Please. Be happy we didn't start doing the Total 'No One Else' beat on your door. We're not playing with you," Robin said as she walked past me.

"Ten more seconds and we would have," added Christine.

"Well, I am glad you did not. The unrhythmic knocks were more than enough. Trust."

"What song are we talking about again?" asked

Rebecca, prompting Robin and Christine to burst out laughing as they slid their shoes off in the hallway.

"Oh, Becs," said Jennifer, throwing an arm around her shoulder. "We'll have to school you on '90s R&B another day."

She turned to me before continuing. "Today we're here to celebrate Rae finally quitting her job and checking off the second risk on her list."

"I love you guys for being here, but I wouldn't necessarily call this a celebration," I said, walking behind them as we all moved to the living room. "In fact, I'm pretty sure I might have just made the dumbest decision of my life." I plopped down dramatically onto my chaise as the other girls stared at me with equal parts concern and amusement.

"We thought you might be feeling this way, which is why we all came by to remind you how brave you were today."

"I don't feel brave. I think if I learned anything from Luke—"

"Ew, please do not bring his name up," Jennifer interrupted.

"Seriously, he may have been ridiculously sexy, but he was also obviously an idiot. So let's not talk about what you think you learned from him, okay?" Robin added.

"I just mean that there are consequences to these risks," I said with a sigh. "Sure, in that moment it was exhilarating and exciting standing up for myself. But now I'm like, 'Uhhh you don't have a backup job, Rae!' Who quits a job without a job?"

"You!" they all shouted in unison.

I couldn't help but laugh. "Yeah, I guess me. *Ay dios mio!*"

"No, no, no. Don't bring my people into this. *Hablas inglés mientras dudas,*" Christine said, chastising me.

"Bleh." I wanted to throw a tantrum, but I knew they weren't about to let me do so, at least not while they were there. "Okay, fine. You're all here now, so what's the plan?"

"Oh, I'm glad you finally asked," Rebecca said with a smile. She bent down and picked up the big bag she'd brought with her while Jennifer leaped to her feet and headed toward my kitchen. "You can't celebrate without champagne!" she exclaimed, pulling out four bottles of bubbly from what had initially looked like a shopping bag.

"And…" Jennifer added as she strutted back into the living room with five of my champagne glasses in her hand.

"You definitely can't celebrate without shoes." Robin winked at me as she pulled out a box from the other shopping bag that they brought with them. I looked back at her curiously as she handed me the box. As I gingerly opened it, I heard Rebecca popping open one of the bottles and begin pouring champagne into the glasses. In my lap was a pair of Sophia Webster chocolate satin sandals with brown, tan and crystal floral appliques adorning the straps that crossed your toes.

The very shoes I'd shown Robin and Jennifer months ago when they pressed me about the risk list.

"Oh. My. God," I said in shock. "What did you all do?"

"We got you some shoes, silly," Christine replied.

"Well, yeah. I see that, but—"

"No buts," Robin interjected. "You deserve these. And it helps that we got them the week after you showed them to us."

"Wait, what?" I was blown away. *What did I ever do to deserve these girls?* I thought. In fact, I didn't deserve them, these shoes, or the first pair I bought as a reward on the risk list. But if they thought I did—with all the ways they showed up as dynamic, awesome, boss-ass friends—then maybe I could start to believe them.

"We knew you would get to this point, eventually," Robin continued. "To be honest, we thought you'd quit *and* have a new job, so we wanted to be ready. When you showed us those heels, Jennifer and I instantly decided they were going to come from us. And then we couldn't leave Christine and Rebecca out."

"I thought I'd have a new job before quitting, too," I laughed.

"But that's okay. Because, honestly, this took so much more courage. And I, for one, am in awe of what you did today." Robin raised her glass and pointed to the rest of the girls to get them to do the same.

"Absolutely," Jennifer shouted.

"Sabes cómo me siento," said Christine.

"I'm going to miss seeing you at work every day, but I couldn't be prouder," Rebecca said.

It took everything in me to stop from crying. Instead, I raised my glass to meet theirs and cleared my throat before speaking. "I love you girls, for real."

"We know," they replied in unison, laughing, as we all took big gulps of our drinks.

"Now can we talk about how this one spent all day yesterday avoiding me because she knew accepting that promotion was wrong to begin with?" Rebecca asked, pointing toward me.

"Wow, this is what we're doing?"

"Oh, yes, this is definitely what we're doing." She nudged me in my side and took another sip of her drink.

"If I'm being fully honest, I wasn't just avoiding you because of the promotion. I also didn't want to talk about Luke."

"Right. I learned that, too, after meeting up with the girls," she said with a little bit of annoyance in her voice that turned back to folly quickly. "But you all should have seen her. Just typing away like a mad woman. No, better yet, like that gif of the cat on the laptop."

"OMG, the one where the cat's going crazy and just beating the keyboard with his hands all fast?" Jennifer asked.

"That exact one."

"You are wild for that," Robin said, chiming in.

I shrugged and laughed off their jokes. "It was an act of preservation," I admitted. "You see how she's being now. Just think about how it would have been in the office."

"Mmm, she does make a good point," said Christine.

As they were talking and debating the merits of my avoiding Rebecca's glares at work, I heard my phone begin vibrating. I pressed the screen to see who it might be and saw a familiar name: Jake Saunders. *Damn.*

I looked up to see if anyone else noticed his name and saw Robin giving me a knowing look. "Please don't say anything," I mouthed.

"I won't," she responded, picking up her phone as she kept her eyes on me.

Is that a thing again? she asked over text. I reached

for my phone once more so I could reply without anyone discovering this conversation, too.

Absolutely not.

Then why is he calling you?

That's a great question. I have no clue.

Hmm. I think I know.

Do you?

Yeah, he got the bat signal. You know how guys are. Somehow they are immediately aware as soon as you either start dating someone or you break up.

I need him to lose my signal and my number.

I tried to stop myself from laughing but was having a hard time as Robin and I continued texting in the middle of the living room with everyone else unaware. I knew I wouldn't be able to keep going much longer without alerting the rest of the group, especially with Robin—of all people—texting about bat signals. I placed my phone back on the coffee table and turned it upside down.

"Anyone need any more champagne?" I asked while popping another bottle.

"Ohh! Someone's finally ready to celebrate?" Rebecca asked.

"Might as well," I replied and poured myself another glass.

Chapter 12

Alone at home a few days later, I found myself staring at those Sophia Webster heels again. They were so beautiful, and I loved the way the chocolate satin complemented my skin tone. It was as if we were made to be together, with the way the colors and jewels popped when on my feet. But as much as the girls tried to convince me that I deserved them, I couldn't shake the feeling it was simply a really pretty pity gift. After all, just two days before then, I was doing the exact opposite of the risk list: accepting the promotion because it felt like a safer bet.

Had I really been that brave or just so fed up that quitting became the only option?

I honestly didn't know the answer. But one thing I did know was that even if I didn't truly earn those heels now, I could make damn sure I deserved them soon enough. And the best way I knew how to do that was to type out what I wanted in my next job and commit to myself that no matter what, I wouldn't settle for less. I grabbed my laptop from my desk and began typing:

- *Must be a job that allows me to champion women across age groups, race, ethnicities, sexuality and cultures.*
- *Must come with a level of autonomy, not a promise of it to come.*
- *Must allow for a broader definition of politics that speaks to the sociopolitical ways we are affected in our daily lives by the policies enacted throughout the country.*
- *Supportive, non-micromanaging supervisor.*
- *At least $10K more than what I was making at my last job.*

I looked over my notes again. Now, this was a list I could truly get behind. I sat for a beat to consider if I was forgetting anything before beginning my job search again. I wanted to go into it this time with more intention than when Robin, Jennifer and I were looking. Maybe I could avoid the cat blog and technical writer job descriptions.

After adding three more items to the list, I felt satisfied. It wasn't going to be an easy task, but it was one I was willing to take on, for the love of those chocolate sandals. Just then, I heard my phone vibrating.

"Hello?" I answered, always sort of stunned when someone picked up the phone and actually called me.

"Buenos días, querida."

"Hi, Mama Vasquez, what's wrong?" I could hear in her voice she'd been crying.

"Christine was rushed to the hospital again."

"Oh, no. Same one as before?"

"*Si, mija.* Dominic is there now, *pero* I can't get a flight until this evening."

"I'm leaving now. I should get there in fifteen-twenty minutes. Don't worry, we got her."

"*Gracias, mija. No puedo tomar un vuelo hasta noche.*"

I hurriedly threw on some jeans to go with my T-shirt, pulled out my slide-on mules to make putting my shoes on at the door go faster, grabbed my coat from my closet and began calling my rideshare car before even stepping out my front door. Time was of the essence, and I wanted to be outside as soon as it arrived so I could jump in and get to the hospital as soon as possible.

Three minutes later I was in the backseat of the car as we drove through the streets of DC. Christine had only been out of the hospital two and a half months this time around, which was certainly not a good sign for her health. Scared and anxious to get to her, I tried closing my eyes for the rest of the ride to steady myself. I knew I'd have to be strong when I got there, but right now everything just hurt.

It took us twenty minutes in traffic to arrive and another five for me to race through the hospital to get to the intensive care unit, explain that I was basically family and then get to her room door. Dominic was seated next to her as she lay still trying to breathe through a hundred million tubes and wires. I walked in and put on my best brave face.

"Christine Vasquez, what are we doing back here?" I asked with a forced small smile. "I believe we made a pact of no hospital visits this year. Do you know what a pact is, *mana*?"

"Chica," she said with a weak voice. "It doesn't look like it, but I did try."

"Hmph. Seems to me like March isn't much of a try."

She laughed as much as she could before beginning to cough and then starting to cry.

"No, no, no, I'm sorry," I said, rushing to her side. "It was too much. I shouldn't have gone that far."

"It was perfect. I just hate being back here again."

"I know, honey. I know." I took her hand in mine and held it. "But you are in the best place to feel better. What happened, by the way?"

I turned back to Dominic, looking to him to help explain since I could see she was straining to talk.

"We were at her place, and she started coughing up blood. We thought maybe it was just a side effect of one of the medicines or she had overdone things, but as I was walking her to her room so she could lie down, she almost passed out in my arms. I knew then I had to call 911."

"Oh, my God, friend." I looked back at Christine and saw the fear in her eyes. She was worried about this one, which made me that much more concerned. "So what are the doctors saying?"

"They need to run a bunch of tests and see what's going on," Dominic replied. He sounded so exhausted and defeated as he explained the details to me. "Honestly, Rae, it feels like dèjá vu all over again."

"I can understand that, Dominic. Do you feel that way, too, Chrissy?"

"I do, Reagan. I really do." Tears streamed down her face as she held my hand tightly.

"Then it's a good thing I'm here to remind you both that things have looked bleak before, and you made it through, because you are a warrior. You may not feel that way at this very moment, but the fight you have inside you has kept you alive all this time, and that's not stopping. And the people who love you, both of you, will be here to pick up that fight if you don't feel you have the strength to do it right now." It was all I could do to keep it together, but I looked at her and then him to make sure they understood me clearly.

Squeezing Christine's hand, I turned back to her and invoked a *Game of Thrones* expression that we'd taken on as our own over the years. "What do we say to the god of Death?" I asked.

"Not today."

"Exactly. Not today."

"Thank you, Reagan," Dominic said.

"Don't mention it… I should step out for a second to make sure your mom called the girls. I know she was planning to, but she was really flustered when she called me, so who knows."

"Oh, please check, Reagan. I would hate—"

"Ah, not another word. I'll be back," I said, finally letting her hand go. I definitely did want to check to see if the girls were on their way, but it was also the perfect excuse to leave the room before I started crying in front of her. The last thing she needed to see was me losing it, but I was struggling to hold back my tears each time she squeezed my hand or broke down herself.

I opened her room door and stepped out into the cold, sterile hallway. It was something about the crisp whiteness of hospital hallways and the stillness in the atmosphere that always did me in. They just felt so impersonal and isolating for a place meant to be a spot where people went for healing. I was two steps down the hallway when I looked up and saw Jake turn the corner, recognize me and come running to my aid.

He was inches away from me when I fell into his arms and began crying. All the anger I'd felt toward him, the hurt he caused me, the stupid ways he'd played me…they all meant nothing in this moment. He was here when I needed him the most. And I could no longer hold my tears back as he stood without a word and let me soak his shirt with sobs for minutes, only occasionally rubbing my hair to bring me comfort.

"Maybe we should go for a walk," he finally said.

"A walk sounds good."

"Wait, what are you doing here?" I asked once I had a moment to calm down. We'd walked to Jake's car to get some privacy while I tried drying up my tears, but the peace and quiet away from the hospital walls also brought me back to reality. It certainly didn't help that Jake had the kind of car a man gets when he has no intention of having obligations any time soon: a two-seater, silver Jaguar F-TYPE. It was gorgeous on the outside, intimate inside and was also a stark reminder of the reason we broke up in the first place.

"Christine's mom called me. I assume she was just going through the numbers she had of her friends, and I was still on the list."

"Oh."

I guess I'd forgotten that Mama Vasquez had Jake's number from when we were in college. And that we hadn't exactly updated her to let her know he shouldn't still be on the call list of people to inform if something went wrong.

"And so you came all the way from New York?"

"Actually, no. I was in town already for work. It's why I called you the other night as well. Was hoping we could talk after all these years. But then when Chrissy's mom called, I just figured it was fate I was here, and so I should come."

"You definitely came around that corner just as I needed you to," I admitted with a sigh. "I'm sorry about that, by the way. I just… I couldn't cry in there and then I saw you and—"

"Hey, you don't have to apologize for that. I'm—I don't want to say glad but—grateful I was there when you needed someone."

"Thank you. I don't want to make this about me, though. She's the one in there fighting for her life. I was simply trying to encourage her to keep doing so because… I'm… I'm just not ready to lose my friend." I held back more tears that were aching to flow down my cheeks.

"And it's okay to feel that," he said, lifting my head so we were eye to eye. "It's okay to not be everyone's strength all the time. That's all I'm saying."

"Yeah, I hear you."

"I don't think you do, but that's okay, too. Just know you don't have to be strong with me. I can take your tears and your questions."

And there it was: Jake's habit of saying the perfect thing at the right time. It had always been a hallmark of his, but since we hadn't spoken in so long, I'd somehow forgotten how comforting he could be. Which meant

I was all at once calm and also fighting not to run out of his car as fast as I could to get away from him and his charm.

"Um, so back to why you called me the other day," I said, trying to move on to a different conversation. "I feel like a jerk now for not answering, but I was sort of in the middle of something."

"You must have been in the middle of something for four years," he said with a slight chuckle.

"Okay, don't act like you've been calling me nonstop and I just haven't answered."

"I've called you a few times and you never answered. Maybe not nonstop but enough for me to get the hint you didn't want to hear from me."

"What changed this time? Why call now, just because you were in town?"

"No, I'm in DC a lot lately actually. I don't know, I think maybe I wanted to try my luck again. See if you believed me this time when I told you that I was sorry for not choosing you before and that I miss you."

I fought back tears again while I listened to him, my heart swelling from the words I'd so desperately wanted to hear years before.

"The truth is I miss my best friend, Reagan, and my partner, the woman I always hoped I'd spend the rest of my life with. And, I don't know, I just thought I'd try calling you again."

The silence between us was still and felt like it would never end, but I had nothing to say to break it. My brain was too full replaying Jake's words to formulate my own as we sat there staring at each other. A tear I couldn't catch trickled down my cheek as I thought about this being the first time that he apologized for how he'd hurt me senior year and how badly I'd needed to hear that from him. Coupling his apology with also calling me the woman he'd hoped to spend the rest of his life with in the very same breath was almost too much for me to handle.

Jake leaned closer to me and wiped the tear off my face. "I told you I can handle your tears, remember? You don't have to hold anything back from me."

And with that, he kissed my forehead, his lips lightly pressing against my skin as I cried softly underneath him. Within seconds I angled my face upward and his lips moved down to mine, kissing me deeply and with urgency like his life depended on it. A moan escaped from my mouth as pleasure shot down my spine, and his right hand grabbed a handful of my hair, pulling me closer to him.

"I missed this, too," he said breathlessly. "I could have kissed you all night after Lance and Candice's wedding."

Ugh. The wedding.

Hearing those words sent shivers through my body, and I pulled back from him, suddenly wishing his car allowed for more room between us. How could I have forgotten the last time we were kissing had led to me realizing I still loved him when all he was looking for was a wedding fling with an ex?

"Damn, I shouldn't have said that." Jake leaned back against his window after seeing the hurt in my face, putting even more space in between us.

"I don't look at that time between us fondly," I admitted.

"I know you don't. I do, though," he said with a sigh. "At least part of it. I thought we had a really great night,

Rae, and then I woke up the next morning and you were gone. No note, no explanation."

"You don't think I had a reason to leave?"

"I think you probably saw some texts on my phone and jumped to conclusions."

"Oh, I saw them, yes. And it didn't take much of a jump, trust me."

"Are you kidding me? We're adults. You could have asked me about it. Or, here's an idea, not been snooping in my phone in the first place."

"I wasn't!" I could feel myself getting heated. No way was he going to try to turn this argument on to me. "Your boys were blowing you up the whole time we were in bed, and I ignored it until I couldn't take it anymore. What started as me trying to silence your phone turned into me seeing just how you felt about me, learning about your *girlfriend* and realizing how much I'd been played."

"For the record, Shannon was not my girlfriend at the time. If you'd talked to me, I could have told you that she and I broke up because I realized I was still in love with you. But you didn't give me that chance. The fact is the only person who got played that night was me." Jake sat up straight and folded his arms as he sought to get his point across. He'd clearly lost his lovey-dovey feelings from moments ago as well. "Because it was once again you deciding on a story about us and allowing every little thing to fuel that belief."

"Every little thing?" I was incensed. "I don't call those texts some little thing, even *if* the Shannon part wasn't true. The rest of the texts were proof enough I was right not to trust you, that all you'd wanted from me—"

"Was what? Sex?" he asked, interrupting me.

"C'mon, Reagan, you think I'm that hard up for sex I'd trick a woman I loved for a one-night stand? What the hell?"

"I don't know, Jake. I just know what I saw."

"Exactly. You let one thing you saw negate everything I'd been telling you all night. Just like you let one moment between us, when I was young and dumb and not knowing what to do with a relationship at twenty-one, define everything about us. But I shouldn't be surprised. That's what you do. You've never fully trusted that I loved you. You've never trusted…me."

"I did trust you at one point. And you broke my heart." My eyes swelled up with tears again as my voice cracked. I wasn't sure if they were angry tears, sad ones, or some combination of both, but I knew I had to fight them at all costs. "You were my best friend. You knew it all, how scared I was to be played again after Matthew, how my parents' divorce messed me up, and still—"

"So I couldn't be scared, too? Is that what you're saying?"

"No, I'm saying you could have been scared and still decided we were better off figuring it out together. You could have still chosen me, and you didn't."

"I'm trying to now." His voice lowered as he calmed himself and slumped down in his seat, exhausted.

"It's too late, Jake. I can't take the chance of being disappointed again right now, especially not by you. It would hurt too much, and I can't handle that between everything with Christine and…" I stopped myself before continuing, realizing I hadn't told him about quitting my job just four days earlier or my breakup with Luke. He wouldn't understand the pressure I was feeling from the work decision alone, and I didn't want to get into either of them with him while he was basically telling me I was the reason we never worked out. *Hadn't this all started as an apology from him?* That seemed long gone.

"And what, Reagan? Please, tell me what's the excuse now," he said, the frustration spewing from his mouth.

"And nothing," I lied. "I just want to be off this merry-go-round. You should probably go back home where you don't have to worry about people disregarding your feelings, as you said, and creating stories that paint you in a bad light."

"And I guess you'll go back to that guy you've been seeing."

"Wow, so is that what all this was about? You heard I was seeing someone and that's the real reason you called."

"Here we go with the stories again. I just sat here and told you why I called and what I wanted, but you still don't believe me." He threw up his hands in defeat. "I can't do anything about that."

"You're right. I don't believe you. And I wish you'd never come today." I opened my passenger door and began climbing out of the car. "Please don't call me again."

"Bet."

I heard his last word before slamming the door shut and turning to go back to the hospital. This was definitely goodbye. That much was clear. Looking down at my shoes, I realized just how much I'd still been subconsciously hoping for something that brought us back together, that made me believe in him again, because for some reason I still loved him. But just like the mules I had on, I couldn't count on him when things got rough.

They were easy to put on when needed, but ever try running in shoes with no back to them? That was how I felt every time I thought about being with Jake again; like whatever benefits might come, the danger was too much to risk it. The more I looked at the shoes, the more I felt the tears start to well up inside me once again.

I was barely feet away from his car before I heard him speed off. *Typical. And Rebecca always chided me for being the one to run away.* Now furious on top of my hurt, I walked back into the hospital and texted Robin and Jennifer to see if they'd heard from Mama Vasquez. In all the chaos, I realized I hadn't reached out to them or Rebecca yet, but in that moment I desperately needed a distraction from what I'd just gone through. Still, the last thing I could stomach was three individual phone calls then so text would have to suffice.

Hey girls, did you hear from Mama Vasquez? I typed.

Yeah, I'm on my way now, Jennifer wrote back.

Two minutes later Robin chimed in. Same.

Okay, good. I'm here now. See you soon.

Next, I texted Rebecca:

Hey Becs, Chrissy was rushed to the hospital today. She's stable and I'm here with her now, but they are running a bunch of tests. Just wanted to let you know.

Thanks, Rae. I'm so sorry to hear that. Please give her my love and let me know when it'll be appropriate to come visit.

Will do. Thanks, Becs.

* * *

Back in Christine's room, I sat down next to Dominic as we both quietly watched her sleep. Even with all the tubes connected to her, she looked peaceful and without pain. I only wished she could feel that peace when she was awake and not tied to a hospital bed by machines both monitoring her and working to keep her alive.

"Everything okay?" he asked.

"Yeah, I just needed a breather earlier, but I'm good now. Found out Robin and Jennifer will be here soon, too."

"She may not even know they are here, you know. She's pretty worn out."

"Doesn't matter, Dominic. They'll know," I said, reaching for his hand. "And you'll know, too. We are here for you as much as we are for her."

"I appreciate it," he said. I could tell he really meant it, but also saw that he was just as exhausted as Christine.

"How about I go wait in the visitors' lounge until they get here? That way I can update them on everything before they come in the room, and you can get some rest while she sleeps."

"You sure you're okay with that?"

"Yeah, very. I am happy to do it."

"Thanks, Reagan. That would be great. I can't wait until Mama Vasquez gets here to help, but I think I *could* use a few minutes of resting my eyes. It was a really hard day."

"I bet. Just text me if you need anything, okay?"

"Will do."

I walked back out of Christine's room and put my earphones in to drown out my thoughts and the white noise hum of the hospital. Music was what I needed in that moment, and I knew just the song. I'd be on my fifth replay of Jhené Aiko's "None of Your Concern" by the time Robin and Jennifer came into the visitors' lounge and caught me lip synching the most important lyric, my head to the sky, feeling every single word to the core.

Like Jhené, I was completely over the idea that some guy could question me when he was the one who left.

Chapter 13

"Dammit!"

I dropped my charcoal-gray work bag in my hallway in complete frustration of how my latest interview had gone, walked into my living room, kicked off my shoes and sank into my couch like a woman with the weight of the world on her shoulders. I was supposed to be coming home and changing really quickly so I could go see Christine in the hospital again, but first I needed a chance to sit and take a deep breath. I looked down at my cobalt blue Jessica Simpson pumps adorned with a sky blue bow at the tip of the shoe and contemplated pitching them straight out my window. Sure, it wasn't their fault I'd just been on yet another disappointing interview, but in that moment they were the symbol of everything that had gone wrong in the month that passed since quitting my job.

Christine was still in the hospital. After seven interviews, I was no closer to finding a new job, and my savings was steadily dwindling down. And oh, I couldn't stop replaying that horrible fight between me and Jake, so my dating life had basically dried up, too. April was turning out to be a really big bust.

Having breathed long enough on my couch, I stood up to pour myself a glass of wine and then walked to my bedroom to change clothes. Pulling out a pair of jeans and a T-shirt, I went over in my head the course of the interview, just to see what I could have possibly done differently. It was a practice I'd started after the first interview to make sure I did my part to be better at each one, but this one felt different the more I thought about it. It started out fine enough. That is until the two men interviewing me started speaking about the real duties of the job, which were quite different than what I read in the job description and compared to my list of what I wanted in my next job.

One guy sat behind a chrome desk, his left leg casually placed over his right and lightly grazing the desk while he leaned back with his hands behind his head. The other, possibly meant to be the formal bad cop of the two, sat in a chair next to me with a checkered blue-and-white shirt, tie to match and sleeves that were rolled up perfectly halfway up his arms.

As I sat there stunned, sitting across from them in an office decorated in what could only be described as medical office chic, I quickly learned that my impressions of what they were offering—a chance to write about complex women's issues for a popular national website—were very off. In fact, what they were really looking for was a woman to write features that were all about men. This triggered a very visceral and un-professional reaction from me, but one that made me proud of myself just as much as I was upset with the circumstances.

"You see, Reagan, we've noticed that our webpage hits grow exponentially when the column focuses on content centered around relationships and dating—"

"Right," interjected the other editor, his matching checkered tie all of a sudden commanding my attention. "Kind of like *Cosmopolitan* magazine meets Carrie from *Sex and the City*. You girls like that kind of stuff, yes?"

"Uhhh, yeah, I enjoy both *Cosmo* and *Sex and the City*," I started, trying not to focus too much on his usage of girls vs. women. "But I was under the impression this column would focus on a range of *women's* issues, and that I'd have the opportunity to cover everything from relationship concerns to healthcare to sports, reproductive rights, politics and everything in between?"

"Well, it *was* that, but we just don't think it's in the website's best interest to continue that sort of column. That's not what girls want to read. They want to read things like *Fifty ways to please my man*—"

"Oh, and *How to tell if he really likes me*," interjected the second editor again.

"Wow." I was practically speechless and couldn't believe these two men were trying to tell me, a woman, what women wanted to read.

"Do you not agree?" the first editor asked, looking at me with his forehead beginning to crease.

I sat there for a beat, trying to decide just how honest I should be in that moment. The composed, young and

Black professional in me wanted to be the bigger person, put on my best fake smile and politely leave when the time was right. But the longer I sat there, the more I realized I wouldn't be able to hold much of my contempt in, and I didn't leave my comfy job with Peter to put up with this crap from two tone-deaf men who had reduced a groundbreaking women's magazine and TV series to simply being about what men wanted from women. Then to insist on calling us *girls* after I corrected them and imply that we wouldn't want to read compelling content that spoke to us as more than just objects for men to ogle? My blood was literally boiling.

"Hmm. I guess it depends on your target audience," I said, hedging my words at first. "I see your target audience as independent, fiery, yet intelligent women between twenty-five and forty-four, who, sure, may want to discuss fun things like dating and marriage, but also want to delve into the serious issues that concern them. Especially in this time, I think women are looking for more. I know I am."

The second editor sat back in his seat and made awkward eye contact with the one behind the desk. I guess it was their time to be speechless.

"And frankly," I continued, emboldened. "I don't think any woman reading *my* work would like to be put into one neat little box that focuses only on what men want from women. That's too simple and far too one-dimensional. You'll notice that even *Cosmo*, to use your example, not only has a bustling money and career section, but also ones on politics, health and fitness and college in addition to their famed sex and relationships posts. That's because they understand women want to read about more than just men, and it's worked out really well for them. *Teen Vogue*'s profile rose specifically because of the ways they've connected with their audience on sociopolitical issues they care about in addition to fashion. This just seems like really outdated thinking to me."

"Well," said the first editor, "we're not looking for some 'Me Too' writer here, so—"

The second editor interrupted. "I guess it's safe to say this probably isn't the job for you, missy."

Damn. And he hit me with the universal blow-off missy *moniker. Oh, well.* I knew as soon as I said my last statement that I wouldn't be getting the job, but I also knew I'd regret it if I hadn't. I wanted to protest further that it was a lazy and poor characterization to just lump anything not about relationships as a part of the "Me Too" movement, but that also it was ironic they were disparaging it and highlighting the reasons for it at the same time. But sadly, it just felt like it would be a waste of my time. Instead, I opted to make a gracious exit before I said anything else that might get me thrown out of the building.

"Thank you for your time, gentlemen," I said while placing my résumé into my portfolio. "I really appreciate the opportunity I've had to speak with you."

I stood up and shook both of their hands, looking them straight in their eyes to show I held no regrets for standing up for what I believed in during the interview. Even if my insides were screaming, "Retreat! Take it back! Hurry!"

"Have a wonderful afternoon," I said before turning on my heels to walk out of the office.

"Same to you, Ms. Doucet," said the first editor.

"I'm really sorry we couldn't make this work," the second one offered as well.

And to be honest, I was, too. Before they switched it up on me, I'd gone into that interview really excited about the opportunity and hopeful that this was the one that made quitting my job worth it. So while I was proud of myself for not settling, this was yet another blow to the armor I'd been carrying to shield me from the thing I was desperately trying not to feel: that I was a failure.

I pulled a pair of white-and-gold sandals out of my closet, buckled them around my ankles and grabbed my bag back from the hallway on my way out to the Metro train station. I'd been home less than twenty minutes, but I knew if I stayed any longer, I'd just want to sink into my couch and will everything to disappear. Better to at least go spend some time with Christine; she needed the company, and I needed to hear her raucous laugh.

"Hey, boo," I said, walking into Christine's new room in the step-down unit. In the past week she'd been transferred there as her doctors felt she needed less intensive care. While that was an improvement, we were still very worried that they didn't think she was healthy enough to go home or even just a general medical ward. When I walked in this time, however, she had a different glow about her.

"Hola, mana. Cómo tú ta?"

"I'm all right," I said with a sigh. "Just happy to see you sitting up. You look a little livelier today."

"You know, when the good days come, I try to enjoy them as much as I can. And today has been a good one so far. I even started catching up on some podcasts earlier today."

"That's great, Chrissy. I'm so happy to hear that." I took my seat and moved it closer to her bed like always before sitting. I understood why the chairs were positioned away from the beds so they didn't block any of the doctors or nurses when they needed to come in to see a patient, but I hated how far away from her I felt when I kept the chair where it was supposed to be. I was there to visit her, after all, not look at her from behind a glass window.

"Are you, *mana*? You seem not really happy at all, actually."

Leave it to Chrissy. Somehow, she always knew.

"You have a lot going on, Chrissy. You definitely don't need to hear about my little guitar woes."

"Girl, please. Trying not to die does not constitute a lot going on."

"Christine!"

"Lo siento. Pero es verdad," she said, chuckling, giving way to that laugh I'd been missing. It boomed louder than her frail body would ever look like it could make, but it filled the room so gloriously. *This was what I needed.* "Plus, I need someone to talk to me about anything other than my recovery or lack thereof. So go, tell me."

"You make me want to slap you sometimes," I said, laughing back with her. "Anyway, I had another interview today, and it went, in one word, horribly."

"Ay, dios mio. What happened?"

"Basically, I thought I was going in there, ready to become this generation's mixture of Christiane Amanpour, Soledad O'Brien and Danyelle Smith, and they shut that right on *down*," I said, telling her the story of what happened. By the time I'd finished replaying the whole scene, props and all, Christine was barely able to breathe from laughing so hard. Thinking back on it and hearing her get so much joy out of it, I guess it was kind of funny. But I'd still felt so discouraged by it, I explained.

"Oh, pobresita," Christine said, still trying to catch her breath. "You stood up for what you believed in. You can't fault yourself for that."

"I know. But look where it got me. Still jobless. Still waiting for the perfect opportunity to prove I was right turning down Peter's offer. Stuck in the same place I was a month ago."

"You want to talk about being stuck in the same place for a month?" she asked, pointing around the room and raising her right eyebrow at me.

"Ugh, okay, fair."

"I'm just saying. You're not stuck. You're in transition, and that is not an easy place to be. But you and I both know there's no point in jumping from the pot to the frying pan."

"Oh emmm geee, sometimes I don't know if you're really Latina or secretly country as hell!" I screamed out in laughter.

"What?"

"That's definitely something my mom would say. Or my grandpa. And you know they both have that good old-school Creole country in them."

"Hey, those are smart people! And you know what I mean. There's no point in you leaving someplace you didn't like just to wind up in another place that you like even less."

"No, I get it. Don't move just to move. I just didn't think I'd still be job searching at this point," I said with a sigh. "To be honest, even though I threw out my risk list, I still thought the universe was using it somehow. That I'd get rewarded, and things would fall into place because I—"

"Because you leaped?" she asked, interrupting me.

"*Yes*. Isn't that supposed to mean something?"

"It does. It means you have an even greater chance for falling." Christine repositioned herself in the bed so she could face me more directly. "That's not a bad thing, though, *mana*. It's actually what's beautiful about stepping out of your comfort zone, because without that, you don't ever get the greater chance for soaring, either. I'm learning that in here. Not something I thought I'd learn within these four walls, but I get it now. I used to feel like such a failure every time I ended up in the hospital again—and tomorrow I might go back to feeling like that—but after four years of this, I realize each time is another chance for me to get back up and live out loud again while I still can."

"I don't know, *chica*. I'm just not sure it's worth it for me anymore. You? Yes. And I love that you've found that spark, especially in here," I said, moving my hands to indicate the space in her room as well. "But I'm so tired. I took on this risk list because I thought it would make my life better, and it's only made things worse. Everything I've tried has failed. Maybe safe wasn't so bad after all." I slumped down in my chair and hung my head, afraid to even look at her with my last words.

"Safe was really bad, Rae. It was," she said, leaning closer to me and taking my hand. "And you can't tell me it felt good faking happiness all those years. Doesn't

matter if other people looked at you like this super-suc-
cessful woman living the life if you were so busy playing a role, you don't even know yourself, much less like
what you see. But the risk list and this thing that you
want to do—write about all the ways women are impacted by what surrounds them and the ways we then
impact our surroundings? Those are *absolutely* worth
the struggles and the ups and downs. You just can't
buy into the myth that it will be easy to strike out and
do the scary things, because that's—*una mentira*. If it
was easy, everyone would do it, *mana*."

"Yeah," I sighed, still refusing to look at her,
ashamed for complaining to her about job searching
for a month and being dumped when she'd been fighting for her life at the same time.

"*Mirame*. You've come too far to turn back now,
mana. I want to see you get this right, and not to make
things too depressing, but I don't think I have that much
longer to see it." She squeezed my hand as I finally
looked back at her, tears welling in my eyes.

"What do you mean?"

"I don't know. I just feel it. The doctors say I'm getting better, but I can tell. I'm dying. And I know that's
sad, and it sucks royally, because I'm not ready. But it
also kicks my butt into full gear. I can't waste any more
time. The last hospital visit made me want to sing more,
but now I simply want to *feel* more, touch everything
around me, smell the amazing food people cook that I
can't eat. I want it all!" Her voice cracked as she spoke,
and I could hear her swallow back her tears, which only
made me want to grab her and tell her she was wrong,
and we could beat this thing once again. Something told

me it wasn't what she needed in that moment, though, so I quietly just listened.

"I'm not saying this to guilt trip you," she continued, her voice getting quieter. "*Pero*, I want you to live, *mana*. And not perfectly. *No cautelosa*. Just happy, *bueno*."

I laid my head on top of her hand and let a single tear finally drop from my eyes. If I could, I would bottle her up and never let her leave my side. Since I couldn't, I tried to take in her scent and her touch as much as I could. "I'm sorry, *mana*," I said, once I finally lifted my head to look at her. "I should be talking about this with anyone else but you. But thank you anyway. *Te quiero mucho*."

"Because I don't take your mess," she said, flashing a smile again.

"Something like that."

"And I love you, too. The ways you've been there for me over the years, but especially these past four... I can't begin to tell you how much that means to me." Her voice cracked again, and I knew it was officially time to change the subject.

"Okay, so what does living out loud mean this week for you?" I asked.

"First, I have to go on a QVC cleanse this week."

"Wait, what?"

"*Lo sé!* Hear me out. When you're home all day for weeks and weeks, it can really catch up with you. I was on there buying stuff that I seriously have no need for. I thought y'all were going to have to do an intervention or something."

"You know what? I can't with you."

"It was getting ugly, *mana*. The other day I bought

some baking contraption. I can't even eat like that. What the hell am I going to do with a baking contraption?"

"I have no idea," I said, bursting out laughing. "But I'm glad you caught yourself before QVC sent you into deep debt."

"Seriously. And I can't explain that to my mom or Dominic. Like, can you lend me some money, Mom? No, not for my medical expenses, for my QVC expenses."

"Bwahahahahaha that would not go over well."

"Not at all."

"All right, *after* the QVC cleanse, then what?" It was her turn to be on the hot seat now.

She thought for a second before answering, and then sat up straight as the idea popped into her head. "Do more of this, I think. I've belly laughed more today than I have in weeks."

"I like that. That's a good one."

"What about you? What is my little Reagan Doucet going to do when she leaves me this evening?"

"Hmm. You know what I was thinking of? I left my cobalt blue heels in the middle of my living room floor when I came here—"

"Oh, my God, Reagan, no one cares you didn't put your shoes back into the closet!"

"No, that's not what I meant. Now *you* hear me out."

"Okay, okay," she said, throwing her hands up.

"I left them in the middle of the floor because I was upset and feeling like they were just another reminder of my failures. But I want to change that. They are actually the shoes I wore when I didn't settle for less than I deserved. And that's something I know about myself now—when pushed, I can and will push back. For me.

I like knowing that. So I want to commemorate them when I get home with a shoe of the day post. Let the people know what they witnessed today. And then, yes, I need to put them where they belong." I winked at her and cracked up at my own joke.

"What am I going to do with you, *chile*?" she asked with an eye roll.

"Love me, of course. And stay on me about stepping out of my comfort zone."

"Lo tienes."

Part 3: There's No Point in Owning Perfect Shoes that Never Leave the Closet

"I like Cinderella; I really do. She has a good work ethic. I appreciate a good, hardworking gal. And she likes shoes. The fairy tale is all about the shoe at the end, and I'm a shoe girl."

—Amy Adams

Chapter 14

"Okay. You can do this. Be confident. Be assured. Be yourself."

I looked at myself in the mirror one last time, straightened out my black pencil dress and slid on my nude semirounded-toe, three-inch pumps from Aldo. It had been a week since my conversation where Christine ran me over the rails and kicked my butt good enough that I went home, found this posting and applied immediately. *SELENE* was a national publication that was only a few years old but seeking to rebrand itself to the modern woman, and the deputy editor was looking for someone with the drive and direction to help them do just that. We'd already spoken on the phone and talked salary, so all that was left was to actually go and meet her for the interview.

Picking up my work bag before I walked out the

door, I double-checked to ensure I had my résumé and
a formal notebook and pen, took in a deep breath and
then finally made my way to the Metro station near
my apartment. It was another thirty minutes before I
stepped into the building for my interview, and when
I did, I felt an energy with me I hadn't had in months.
While the glass exterior of the building felt odd in a city
not really known for that aesthetic, the marble floors
and the mile-high ceiling in the lobby made me feel like
you had to have your big-girl panties on to work here.
And I wanted something just like that.

I silently shifted my weight on each heel while I
waited for Alexandra, the deputy editor, to meet me. I
had only found a few photos of her online, but when a
tall, brown-skinned woman stepped off the elevator a
few minutes later and practically glided toward me, I
knew it was her. She reached her hand out to mine and
introduced herself.

"You must be Reagan," she said with a smile that
seemed completely genuine.

"Yes, I am. And it's so great to meet you."

"Same here. I'm looking forward to our conversation." She motioned toward the conference door to the
right of us and walked in ahead of me. Inside was a glass
conference table that looked like it easily fit forty or
fifty chairs around it. She chose two seats on the corner, so we could sit facing each other without it being
uncomfortable. Before I knew it, what I'd thought would
be an interview had turned into a discussion between
two women about the viability of women's magazines
and the content women wanted to read at the start of
a new decade.

"I understand many people feel that printed magazines are a dying business," I said. "But I don't think that's the case. I think if you give people good content, they'll read it in any way that they can. And I also think that we underestimate how much some people love to still turn the pages of their materials. I do. I have a Kindle and a tablet, but I still believe there's nothing like having good content in your hands."

"I agree with you, Reagan. But how would you convince the digital age of women to go out and buy our magazines or subscribe?"

"We've seen certain models work better than others when you talk about incorporating digital media into your world. But one that seems to work best is using the website and social media accounts as opportunities to discuss sidebars of the original content that's given in the magazine. You can even tease the audience with great excerpts online and then make it so that the rest of the content needs to be viewed in the actual magazine. It's all about letting both work together instead of competing with each other for content and audience."

"Basically, it's not about reinventing the wheel—"

"But about understanding your audience and making the wheel work best for you," I said.

"Mmm. Okay. And what kind of content do you think women are clamoring to read?"

"Everything," I blurted out. "I know that sounds generic, but I think far too often we've attempted to box women in when I know my friends and I like to read about a whole host of topics. Unfortunately, we usually have to go to different forms of media to get bits and pieces. I think *SELENE* could change that."

"I think you're right. And it's why we're looking to do a restart. We've had moderate success over these past few years, but I'm hoping to revamp our social media outputs, our website and even some of the sections in the magazine. This position would be working with me and would most likely be twofold—serving as a vertical editor for the website, but also contributing a small section to the magazine around current events and their effects on women."

"Honestly, that's one of the main draws for me. I have so many ideas for ways to integrate content, and I'm passionate about the fact that politics encompasses a mixture of impacts on people. One month we could talk about the fight for women's reproductive rights and look into the ideas on both sides of the table. The next month could be about domestic violence and the fact that while it's so prevalent, it's still not really discussed among women. And the very next month we could discuss the viability of women's sports or intersectional feminism and the different ways women experience the consequences of say, environmental sexism or dating."

"Wow, from environmental sexism to dating, all around sociopolitics. That's quite the range. But I like it. When people think of dating in a women's magazine, it's usually stuff that's fun and light and playful. And we'll obviously still have that section for our magazine and that vertical on the site. But I really enjoy the spin that even our dating lives are affected by the political environment of today. I see that you've really thought about what you could do in this position," she said, flashing that same smile I saw when I first met her.

"To be honest, this position is a dream come true, Alexandra. I know it's not perfect, and it will be hard work. But that's part of what I love about it, too—having the opportunity to help build on the foundation that's already there and create magic together."

"Reagan, I like what I'm hearing from you," she said. "I think the only thing left is for me to say that we'd love to have you here with us."

"Wow, really?" I asked in shock. I'd literally never been offered a position within an interview, so even though I could tell we'd clicked, I imagined she'd need to wait another couple weeks before getting back to me.

"Absolutely."

"I…am thankful. Is it okay if I get back to you by the end of the week?"

"Yes, of course. And you can always contact me if you have any questions before you decide," she said, standing up and walking us back to the conference room door. I was fairly certain I was going to accept the position, but since I'd never been offered a job on the spot before, I needed to get home, think through my options and the opportunity and make sure this was the one.

Back in the lobby, we shook hands again as Alexandra reiterated her excitement and her hope that she'd hear from me soon to let her know I'd accepted the position. We'd had a great chemistry and connection from the first time I spoke to her on the phone, and today's interview had only solidified that for her.

"What size shoe do you wear, though?" she asked, a twinkle in her eye revealing her intrigue.

"An eight," I giggled. It was totally a question I would have asked as well.

"Be glad it's not a nine or I might have to take those from you the next time we see each other."

"Depending on the shoe, I have to wear a nine sometimes, so I'll be sure to watch my back from now on anyway." *From now on.* Just then, I caught myself. As Alexandra chuckled to herself, I realized I didn't need to go home and fill out a list of pros and cons about whether I wanted this job. I knew it already. I just needed to get out of my head and go for it. Before she could turn back around and head into those glass elevators, I stopped her.

"Actually, Alexandra...what if I accepted the position now?"

"Really?" she asked.

"Yeah, I just realized I don't need to overthink this. I said it was a dream come true, so why wait?"

"That's great, Reagan. Oh, I'm very excited. I'll need to inform my HR department, but if you can come by in the next couple days, we can formalize this pretty quickly, have you sign your paperwork and figure out a start date. How does that sound for you?"

"Wonderful," I said, the smile on my face growing with every second. This had been the moment I was waiting for, where the sacrifice paid off. And like Christine said, when it happened, it felt glorious. "I can come back Friday, if that works for you."

"That's perfect. Welcome aboard, Reagan. I hope you're ready for the ride."

I watched as Alexandra walked back onto the elevator, following her stride again. It was as if she'd been a model in a former life and every floor was her runway. And she was going to be *my* new boss. I couldn't wait. Finally, I turned around and made my way out of the building, desperately trying to keep my composure, but wanting to jump into the air or dance around in circles, call my friends and squeal—something!

Holding it together as best I could, I hopped back into

the Metro station and waited until I was on the train before I let out a silent squeal and stomped my shoes like a praise dancer in my seat. Things were finally starting to come together. It was just the job, yes, but it was the first thing that had gone right since working on my risk list, and I knew it had to be the start of more. I also knew there was one person I needed to see—Christine. She had to hear the good news in person.

On my way to the hospital, I shot off a few texts to the other girls and to my mom, letting them know I'd said yes to my dream job. Then an email to Alexandra, thanking her once again for meeting me and that I'd see her on Friday. All that was left was to break the news to Chrissy. My heart couldn't stop pounding with anticipation.

Back at the hospital, I fast walked in my heels to get to Christine's floor as fast as I could. She'd been right all along, and I needed her to hear from me that as much as she had inspired me to keep fighting for my happiness, she had to keep fighting for herself as well. No more talks like she was giving in. We were warriors. We fight.

I stepped off the elevator and saw Dominic walking out of her room, his head hung low. *Oh, no*, I thought. She must be having another bad day. I picked up my pace that much more and raced down the hallway, catching my breath as I neared him.

As soon as he saw me, he broke down crying and fell into my arms.

"She's gone, Rae," he cried, holding on to me tightly. "She's just…gone."

Speechless, I wrapped my arms around him and let

the tears fall down my face. No way this was happening. Not right now. Not when I was on my way to remind her of all she still had left to live for.

"Where's Mama Vasquez?" I asked once my mouth could move again.

"In the room with her. They said we could stay in there while we waited for the people from the funeral home to come get her so that she could be transported to New Orleans, but I couldn't look at her any longer like that. I can't believe—"

"I know, I know. Me, either." I stood there in shock as all the years that Christine and I spent together flashed before me. It wasn't like we didn't think this day was coming, but she'd beaten her sickness so many times, I'd almost thought she was invincible. And yet, here we were, facing down the reality of life without her. *How in the world was I going to do that?*

I felt my phone vibrating in my purse and thanked it for the distraction. Looking down at it, I saw Jennifer's name as a notification on my screen along with a missed call from my mom.

Yesss girlfriend! I knew it was coming! Drinks on me this week, Jennifer had texted.

Damn. The job. I didn't have the heart to tell her or the others what had just happened, but I knew I'd have to find the strength somewhere. For now I had to go in that room and see my friend and take care of her mom. I'd figure everything else out later.

After six hours of comforting Dominic and Mama Vasquez, making sure Christine's body was transported correctly and calling our closest friends to deliver the news, I was finally home alone with no one else to take care of but me. I walked to my shoe closet, hoping that writing in my diary would help me sort out my thoughts, but once in, I dropped to the floor and cried, the pain hitting me intensely all at once.

The person who spent so much time reminding me to live was gone. *In what world was that fair?* Tears poured down as I scanned all the shoes I owned. There were easily 200 pairs of shoes in my closet, but how many of them could tell stories of me living out loud? Maybe one or two, I guessed. Certainly, my cobalt heels from last week, but that was only after Christine had helped me realize how big of a moment that had been for me. Truthfully, most were like the life I'd been living— beautiful on the outside, perfectly pristine, full of fun, sometimes embarrassing, sometimes sexy stories they could share to keep a party interesting but unfulfilled. This was what Christine had been teaching me, even trapped in the hospital for the past month: life was too short to not take it by the throat, get your shoes dirty and live with no regrets.

Before standing, my eyes caught a pair I realized I'd never worn outside my apartment. My hot pink suede, four-inch pumps from Victoria's Secret. With angel wings as pendants on the heels, they stood out as not my most expensive pair, but the lone ones without any sort of story. In fact, they'd been sitting there since I purchased them four years earlier, when I deemed them the perfect date shoes at the time. But years had passed by with no perfect date prospects and so no reason to wear them. Plus, who wanted to risk ruining the suede material on something that could turn out to be a complete bust? *What if it rained or I stepped in a puddle and it was all for naught?* I'd often thought.

"For Christine, I'm going to wear you guys very soon," I said aloud. "And it won't be on a perfect date. I'm just going to wear you." It was a promise I knew I'd have to keep.

It was time for a change; a real one this time with less complaining, less pouting about things not always going my way and less worrying about perfection. Christine had all but told me this as her last wish, and I was damn sure going to honor it. For her. And for me.

I stood up with tears still in my eyes and walked into my bedroom, opened my laptop and began retyping the risks from my list. I wouldn't be able to rip it out of my journal this time and toss it away if something went wrong. No, this time I was making a commitment to get them done and make sure the shoes I bought as my rewards lived as incautiously as Christine had been begging me to do for at least the past couple years.

Chapter 15

Walking into Christine's home church in New Orleans was quite possibly one of the hardest things I've ever had to do. And it was probably why, even though we were running late for the funeral, I hesitated before entering. I stood still, trying to face what was to come, staring at those wooden doors for what seemed like hours but was only probably a few seconds. In that span of time it felt like I would never be able to move from that spot again. And I certainly didn't think I'd be able to face the fact that the woman who'd been my best friend for over a decade would be lying in a casket when I made my way in.

Standing there, in quiet frustration, I wanted so desperately to move and be strong for everyone else like normal, but I was frozen in my tracks. Finally, after some careful nudging by Jennifer and my mom, both flanking me to the left and right, I began inching my way closer to those big wooden doors of that itty-bitty church. An itty-bitty church hosting the funeral of a larger-than-life woman. To say it took that nudge, me talking myself through it and God for me to move, is probably still an understatement.

"Just put one foot in front of the other," I quietly reminded myself. "You can do this. One foot in front of the other. Repeatedly."

I looked down at the shoes that were carrying me on my journey: a pair of black sandals with a three-and-a-half-inch heel and leopard-print fabric that laced around your ankles to create a bow. As soon as I saw them in the store, I knew they were the shoes for Christine's funeral. She loved leopard print, for one, and two—she would have appreciated that the first thing I wore them to wasn't a cute and funny outing, but something dark and hurtful. Christine didn't believe in living a life that avoided pain, and I was trying to learn from her.

Besides, we had the whole tribe with us today to help us get through all of our feelings. Along with my mom and Jennifer were also Jenn's boyfriend, Robin, Rebecca and her husband, all three of my siblings and even miraculously, my dad. Together we walked to the front of the church, tiptoeing into the congregation hall that was already packed with people dressed in what I presumed were their Sunday bests: pressed blue, black and gray suits from the men, knee-length A-line skirts and dresses from some of the women, pencil skirts with suit blazers from the others. When we reached the bronze casket Mama Vasquez had insisted on for her baby, I nearly lost it. There she was, twenty-nine, full of so much life just a week ago, and now lying in a casket. Never getting the chance to marry her guy, to grow old with some kids, to become Tia Chrissy to mine. *How was any of this okay?*

The only thing that stopped me from falling apart was Mama Vasquez. Sitting in her pew to the right, she was the picture of strength as person after person flooded her and Dominic with condolences. If she could make it through today, then so could I. I straightened up my back, took in a deep breath, ran my hands down my black pencil skirt, finding courage from somewhere unknown to approach her as well.

"Querida," she cried out as I grabbed her and held on.

"I'm so, so sorry, Mama Vasquez."

"No lo sientas, mija. I hurt so much, *pero sé que ella está en paz.* You must remember that, *bueno."* She grabbed my face with both hands and stared into my eyes until I nodded. Clearly, mom and daughter were one and the same.

I hugged her tightly once more and walked to a pew a few rows behind them, watching as she had similar exchanges with Jennifer, Robin and Rebecca. *What kind of strength does it take for a mother to bury her only child and be there for others as they grieve?* I was in awe but wished she could simply be there and mourn her baby instead. As we sat, I felt my mom take my hand in hers, and it was a feeling I didn't realize I needed. Maria's comfort couldn't have come at a better time because instantly, the tears began to fall down my cheeks. With her sincere touch, I could no longer hold them in, and it seemed like the waterworks would never stop.

"I love you," I whispered, facing her, my eyes soaked.

"You could feed the whole world with the amount

of love I have for you, my firstborn." She squeezed my hand and smiled. "You got that?"

"Yeah, I got that."

By the time our whole crew sat down in the pew I'd chosen and the one behind me, the opening prayer and first reading were just about to begin.

"We gather here today to say farewell to our dear Christine Vasquez, and to commit her into the hands of God," the priest said, looking into the crowd and then compassionately at Mama Vasquez. "I've known Christine since she was a little girl, so this won't be easy for me, either. But God is with us, and we are with each other." He cleared his throat before continuing, "The grace and peace of God our Father, who raised Jesus from the dead, be always with you."

"And also with you," the crowd responded.

"We'll now have our first reading from the Book of Ecclesiastes by Dominic Ríchard."

As Dominic walked slowly up to the podium, I felt my dad's strong, firm hand grip my shoulder from the pew behind me. Between him and my mom, whose hand I was still holding, maybe I could get through this funeral mass after all.

Later that evening I lay in my mom's bed, my heels kicked off and placed on the floor near her nightstand. We'd had a full day, and although I could hear my brother, sisters and my dad joking around and reminiscing about Christine as they ate crawfish at our dining room table, I needed time to simply lie down for a bit and take it all in. Sitting next to me, my mom calmly placed her hand on my head, enticing me to crawl closer and lay my head in her lap. She ran her fingers through my hair and softly sang a few verses of her favorite calming songs while my breathing steadied and my tears soaked her pants leg.

"Everything's going to be okay, Rae," she said. "But you feel as much of it as you need to right now, *cher*. I'm here, and I can take it."

I closed my eyes and listened to her as she continued on. "I just miss her so much already, Mom. What am I going to do without her?"

"You'll do what she asked you to do. You'll live and you'll honor her every time you are scared and still do something. And it'll hurt for a long time. And time won't heal that pain. I don't care what people say. But what will happen is you'll have some good days and some bad, and at some point the good days will outweigh. I won't lie to you. You will have moments when that pain is just as hard as it is today. And when that happens, you do what you're doing right now all over again—feel it, Rae. Let yourself grieve. And then it'll get good again."

"And what if it never gets good?"

"Oh, baby, it will. I can't tell you when, but it will. I just don't want this to stop the really good progress you've been making this past year. You don't think I noticed, but I have seen a different woman in front of me."

"I've been scared ninety percent of the time, Mom."

"That's okay, because it means you've already been doing it scared. I know you think you have to be perfect for everyone, Rae. But this year where I've seen you make mistakes and get hurt and get back up, it's the proudest I've ever been of my firstborn. It couldn't have been easy quitting your job and handling whatever it was that happened with you and Luke, much less watching as your best friend slowly deteriorated before your eyes. I know you've been hurt more than we could ever see down here—but you got up every time. Every single time. And you'll do it again and keep doing it."

"Because it's worth it…that's what Christine said two weeks ago while we sat and laughed in her hospital room. That it was all worth it." I turned my head to face my mom, still lying in her lap, but suddenly needing to see her eyes as we talked.

"She was right," she said, still running her fingers through my hair. "And I'm going to try to be more understanding and less demanding when you call me for help. I know you don't always like when I offer my advice, even if it is usually very good." She couldn't help herself adding in the last part with a chuckle.

"Never change, Mom. I need you just like you are. Just like this."

I turned my head back to face the TV as my mom continued singing, and my eyes caught my shoes again, standing up tall near her nightstand. It was then that I realized one more important thing: these were my third pair of shoes from the list. I could finally officially mark off "allow people to be there for me." Christine would be oh so proud.

Chapter 16

"What do you girls want to drink?" Robin asked from her kitchen. "Because we definitely need drinks!"

"You have some bourbon?" I asked. "I could definitely go for a whiskey ginger about now."

"Do you even have to ask me that?" She poked her head out the door to the living room where Jennifer and I were sitting around the gray tufted ottoman she used as her coffee table. "Of course I have bourbon. And I have ginger ale. Is that good with you, Jenn?"

"Absolutely. But don't judge me, because I'm probably going to need several tonight."

"No judgment," I said. "Trust."

Robin walked into her living room in the most Robin-est way, carrying a round silver serving tray with handles. On top of it stood three whiskey glasses, a bottle of Maker's Mark bourbon and a two-liter of ginger ale.

"Never," she said, putting the tray on top of the otto-man. Carefully lifting each glass off the tray, she gave us our first pours. We heard the crackle from the bour-bon hitting the coldness of the frozen whiskey stones she'd placed in the glasses while in the kitchen. And then the calming fizzle from the soda joining in. It was amazing how the simplest sounds made so much noise two days after burying your best friend.

"To Christine," I said, lifting my glass up for a toast.

"To Christine," Robin and Jennifer said, joining in.

"May you continue to rest in peace. We sure do miss you, *mana.*"

"And we'll drink one extra of these since you can't," Robin added.

We clanked our glasses together and took huge gulps of our drinks, almost finishing what we had in one swallow. I closed my eyes and sat back as some of the memories between us flashed through me, breathing in deeply and remembering what my mom had said about allowing myself to feel everything that came with grief when it did. Robin lay fully down on her couch, stretching her body the length of it, and watched me and Jennifer as Jenn curled her arms around her legs and soothingly rocked herself back and forth. The three of us sat just like that, in silence for about five minutes, until Robin broke the ice.

"Anyone need another pour?"

"Yes, please," I said, jumping out of my position. "You know, I remember that Memorial Day party we went to some years back and how much whiskey we had that night. Oh, it was crazy, and Christine was, of course, the life of the party—what was the name of it again?"

"The Pumps and a Bump party?" Robin asked as she made us more drinks.

"Yes! That was the one. What an awful name."

"It was kind of an awful party, too," Jennifer said.

"No, it wasn't." I took a sip of my drink while disagreeing. "We had a blast. I can still hear Christine's booming voice piercing through the noise at that party. '*Manas!* Come, sit, drink.' She was in her element that night. That was, what, a couple years after college?"

"Yeah, I think so," said Robin. "I remember the horrible outfits everyone had on that night. You had on, like, a multicolored, plunging one-piece bathing suit, and I wore a silver metallic two-piece that barely covered my butt. Oh, God, those were so awful!"

"They really were! And Chrissy had on some booty shorts with a fire-red bikini top. What were we thinking?" I laughed, taking another sip and sitting back again.

"We weren't. That's the point," Jennifer said. "That party was like the Black version of *Eyes Wide Shut*. You only liked it because you got laid that night."

"One, I didn't get laid *thank you very much*. And you only hated it because you didn't! There were so many fine men that night. You could have had your pick, but that's not what you were on."

"It certainly wasn't."

"Okay," I said, rolling my eyes. "My point was just that's one of the times I recall Chrissy having fun before she ever got sick and had that damn procedure in the first place."

"That was a fun night, Rae. I agree," Robin said. "Especially the part where we had to help your drunk ass try to find the shoe you lost after rolling around in the hay with some rando."

"All right, no need to bring that part up."

"Christine couldn't stop laughing at you. She was like, 'Oh, I know Reagan is dying about her precious shoe.' Can't believe we never found it, too."

"Ugh, I know. RIP to that heel," I said, imitating as if I would pour some of my drink on the floor "for my homie." "I learned a valuable lesson that night."

"What was that?" Jennifer asked.

"No man, not even one who just wants to eat you out for hours with no reciprocation, is worth the cost of a lost shoe."

"Girl, bye! I can't cosign that," Robin screamed out.

"No, I'm serious!"

"I know you are, but I am, too. Screw those shoes. I'll take the hours-long eating fest."

Robin and Jennifer high-fived each other and cracked up laughing.

"Oh, you agree with that, but was just ragging on me about the actual party?" I asked, looking at Jennifer.

"Hey, what can I say? I'm a complicated woman."

"Indeed," I said, shaking my head.

"The memory I keep coming back to was meeting you and Christine for the first time in college. I thought you two were inseparable, and I'd never be able to live up to that friendship for either of you."

"Oh, Jennifer, I didn't know you felt that way."

"I mean, you two had those wallet-size photos you took together in high school and would use them to give out your phone numbers to guys. Photos with both of you in the picture! How was anyone supposed to compete with that?"

"Well, that was a foolish idea of ours anyway, and it only worked like maybe once or twice. Most of the time the guys didn't remember which one he'd met the night before and wasn't sure which girl he was calling when he did…all that to say, it was just us not knowing what we were doing in college. Not some impenetrable bond."

"No, I know that…now. But initially, when we met in the dorms, I didn't think there was any space for anyone else. It wasn't until Christine pulled me aside one day and told me I was one of the few people she felt comfortable being herself around outside home that I knew we were all really starting to become friends. That was maybe end of sophomore year?"

"You spent almost two years thinking we weren't actually friends?"

"More like just not believing the extent of the friendship. Like I said, complicated."

"Oh, friend." I leaned over and grabbed Jennifer's hand. She had always been the sensitive one of our group, but I hadn't realized how far that sensitivity went until then. To think she ever thought she meant less than everything to me and Christine was just too much to take.

"I know, I know. I'm crazy. This is why I say everyone needs therapy."

"It's worked for me so far," Robin chimed in. "Matter of fact, I need to make sure I still have my appointment this week. I am definitely going to need to talk some stuff out, okay?"

"I know that's right," I replied. "We're going to all need to keep talking, too, honestly. Especially as May nears and what would have been Christine's thirtieth birthday comes around."

"Ugh, that reminds me. We were talking about her joining me for another of my work trips to London one of the last times I visited her in the hospital," Robin said. "She knew I had a trip coming up, and you know she was on her live-out-loud kick, so I told her she should come. She was so excited to get out of that hospital and join me."

"You think she really thought she was going to be able to go?" I asked, vividly recalling our conversation where she'd admitted to me that she felt like she was dying. I hadn't told anyone about that belief at the time because it felt too personal, but I wasn't sure if she'd relayed the same sentiment to any of the other girls.

"She was trying to. I know she didn't think she had a lot of time left, and she wanted to make sure if she saw thirty, she saw it in style."

"That sounds about right," Jennifer said.

"You know, now that I think about it, you guys are more than welcome to come, too, you know."

"Come to London?" Jennifer asked.

"Yeah. Why not? I'll have to work, obviously, but if we time it just right, you all could come to London for my last few days and then we could hop over to Paris for another few. Just live it up in honor of Chrissy."

"I like that idea a lot," I said.

"And you're there at least three times a year, so you could be our tour guide," Jennifer added as she started calculating the possibility in her head.

"Exactly. I have to leave next week, but we could look up what flights look like in May, and if they are reasonable, you guys should really come. I would love it."

"Let's do it," I said, jumping up again.

"Really?"

"Yeah, like you said, why not?"

"Okay!"

"All right, I'm down, too," Jennifer said. "No way I'm letting you two go on this trip without me."

"Yes!" Robin leaped up from her couch and began dancing. "I think this is going to be so good. We're going to have tons of fun. I'm a little surprised you didn't need to make a pros and cons list about it before deciding, but I'm going to take it. No backing out now," she said, pointing to me.

"No more pros and cons lists!" I said, laughing. "I've got a spontaneous checkmark to fill out."

"Ooooh, someone's back on the risk list?" Jennifer asked.

"Indeed I am."

"Good, I'm glad to hear that."

"I'll have to figure out how it works with the new job, but that should be easy enough. I'll just tell Alexandra I had a trip already planned before accepting the job. She feels like the kind of person who would understand."

"Ohhhh, yes, the new job!" Robin yelled out again. "In all the death and funeral madness, we never properly celebrated your big win. I'm so sorry."

"Please, it's not like we could have done that before now. And seems to me London and Paris are a great place to celebrate."

"Ha! Very true," Jennifer said.

"Okay, then it's settled. You two look up flights and let me know as soon as you can when you want to come. I'll be free after the first week of May."

"Perfect."

"And in the meantime, we need another drink. This

time to Chrissy and to Reagan. I see big things coming for you, *chica*," Robin said, pouring whiskey into each of our glasses once more.

"To Chrissy and Rae," Jennifer said, raising her glass. "And big things coming."

"For us all," I added with a wink.

Chapter 17

Stepping out of the airport in London, I immediately felt the cool, crisp air and was all too happy to be wearing my new navy blue Joules knee-high flat boots. While the temperature had begun warming up back in DC, London was still firmly in the fifties, especially at the break of dawn. It didn't hurt that I was also simply in love with these shoes: with the cute little red bow in the back of them tied around a gold buckle on the outside portion of your calf, jazzing up what could have been just a plain blue boot.

By the time I saw Robin and Jennifer outside waiting for me, I was in full happy travels mode. Initially wanting to do something silly like throw my hat in the sky à la Mary Tyler Moore, I ultimately decided to take in a deep breath and release the biggest twirl I could imagine while shouting out "I am here!" It didn't even matter that people were watching. This was *my* way of releasing all the pressures I'd been mounting on myself for the past several months, maybe even years.

"Reagan, you are so crazy," I heard Robin scream out to my left just as I was rounding my third twirl.

"Aggggh. Hey, girls!" I ran toward them and hugged them both tightly.

"What in the world were you doing?" Jennifer asked.

"Dancing! You want to join?"

"Uh, no, thanks," they said in unison, unable to hold in their laughter.

"How about we just get you and your stuff to the car, and we can dance later tonight," Jennifer added through her fit of chuckles.

"Wait, we have a car? Ooh, y'all are fancy."

"Nah, don't say *y'all*. Robin is fancy, but then she always has been. No surprise there."

"That's true."

"Uh, no, Robin has been in London for the past two weeks and she needed a car for things like grocery shopping," Robin chimed in, speaking in third person as if it would help her case.

"Grocery shopping and picking folks up from the airport, you mean," Jennifer clarified.

"Right. I feel like I've used the car more for that than anything else, honestly."

"Who else have you had to pick up?"

"Who haven't I come to get is probably an easier question to answer. I didn't realize how many people I invited to London this time around, and nearly everyone took me up on my offer. My parents stopped in for two days on their way to Amsterdam and Belgium, Rebecca and her husband came through on their way to see his people in Scotland, Lance and Candice came for a day before heading to Paris and even my hairdresser stayed for an extended layover."

"And you picked them all up?"

"I'm a glutton for punishment," she said, jokingly hanging her head in shame.

"Good thing, then, that you can turn this car in forever in about three days, since we'll be off to Paris!" I made sure to say Paris where it sounds like Par-eeh, because I'm *cultured*, and was maybe a little tipsy from the whiskey gingers I had on the plane.

"Yes," Robin screamed out excitedly. "Now, that's something I can dance about."

"Oh, yeah." My ears perked up.

"No, no, no, that still doesn't mean here. Let's get your bags and go," Jennifer said, interrupting my would-be triumph to get them, or at least Robin, to join me.

"Fine, we can do that, too," I responded defiantly.

"If it makes you feel any better, I think your boots are super cute."

"Thanks, girl, they are another reward from the list." I twirled around once more for effect.

"Okay, see? Come on, now. I just told you later," Jennifer said, bursting out laughing. "Got these people looking at us like we're crazy."

"Whatever. Let them look. I'm tired of caring what other people think about what makes me happy," I countered, grabbing my bag and turning my twirl into a skip.

As we approached the car, I noticed the sun was finally starting to come out. While the weather had been slightly overcast when I deplaned, it had dramatically changed in the hours since then, and the sun was shining brightly through the clouds.

"Where to first, girls?" I asked as we packed the car with my luggage.

"We need to bring your things back to my flat, and then we can go wherever you want."

"Oh, that's a no-brainer, then. We have to start at Buckingham Palace," Jennifer responded.

"Agreed. Definitely the palace," I added with a high five to Jennifer.

"All right, then, first stop on the Robin Johnson London Tour—my flat. Second stop—Buckingham Palace! Prince Harry, we're coming for you, boo." Robin started up her car and pointed her hand in the direction of what we guessed was her flat or at least something close to it. But Jennifer was stuck on the Prince Harry part, and couldn't let it go.

"First of all, isn't he married?" she asked.

"Don't hate! I can still look and dream about having a royal wedding, damn it."

"And, also not here! He and Meghan moved to the US, remember?"

"Oh, damn, that's right."

We all fell out laughing. If this was what the whole trip would be like, I was going to need stitches for my stomach when we returned to the States just from giggling so much. I only wished Christine could have been there with us.

The next ten hours went by like a blur. We walked what seemed like every street in London, stopping to take silly photos at everything from Buckingham Palace to Big Ben, Westminster Abbey and more. We saw the grandeur of the old buildings in Europe and marveled at the seamless mixture of old Victorian architecture with pointed arches and steep roofs and modern skyscrapers slowly but surely changing the landscape of the city. And with each place we went to, I made sure to feature my boots prominently in every picture for the Gram.

The day before, I'd decided that I would take my shoe-of-the-day posts to the next level for this trip and chronicle every part of it, not just once a day, showing the ups and downs and funny and ugly parts about traveling. Not leaving out the ugly bits, like Christine would say. Sometimes I jumped up high and kicked my boots in the air. Other times I posed as if I was kicking down a building. But I started the day by taking an introspective photo of my shoes walking down the pathway to Buckingham Palace that was dedicated to Princess Diana and showing how I'd accidentally stepped in some gum. *Talk about apropos.*

"Wow, dahling," Robin mocked in her very bad, very fake, British accent. "The uni-verse certainly wanted to welcome our dear Reagan to this city of luxury in the oddest of ways." She spread out her arms to emphasize her point about the grandeur surrounding us.

"Is this the same universe that is supposedly matching you up with a very married, very not here, Prince Harry?" I asked. "Because if so—"

"Don't be such a jerk," Robin interrupted, pretending to be upset.

"What?" I asked. "I'm just saying that it might possibly be a long shot."

"Whatever. You never know," Robin responded, but I could see that her attention had been distracted by a horse-drawn carriage riding past us on the street. *Now, this was some real deal London extravagance.* The three of us watched, enthralled as the carriage came to an alarming stop right outside the palace gates, almost like what happens when someone realizes in the middle of walking out of their apartment that they forgot something. This was what it looked like we were watching take place in front of our very eyes. But what prince or princess forgot something just as they were entering the gates?

We slowly tried to inch ourselves closer in an attempt to see if someone was getting out; none of us saying a word but moving in sync with each other. We noticed the man on the horse get down, reach into the carriage and slowly but assuredly begin walking toward us. Frozen, we watched as that same man walked straight up to Robin.

"Good afternoon, miss," he said, slightly bowing his head.

"Good afternoon," Robin replied and then curtsied.

The man smiled politely, but you could tell he wanted to laugh at the American curtseying in such a nonformal situation.

"Prince Eric has asked me to give you this note."

"Oh?"

"Yes, madam."

Robin reached for the note, opened it and let out a very big grin. "Please tell Mr. Eric thank you, and that I will be sure to do so."

"Thank you, ma'am."

The gentleman turned back around as quickly as he walked up to us and headed back to his horse. In awe, we watched as he mounted the horse again and drove the carriage through the palace gates. It wasn't until it was completely out of sight that Jennifer and I turned our attention to Robin.

"Ummmm, what the hell just happened?" Jennifer asked, being the first one to break the silence.

"I think Robin's ass just got asked out by a damn prince," I shouted with glee.

"It would appear so. Is that what just happened, Robin?"

"No comment," Robin replied, smiling harder than I'd seen from her since I arrived in London. She folded the paper up and put it into her purse without saying another word.

"Seriously? No comment?" I asked.

"Nope. So maybe we should change the subject. Are you guys ready to go to the London Eye?"

"Yeah, sure, whatever," Jennifer said drily. "Let's do the London Eye and not talk about the craziness that just went down in front of us. Because that makes sense."

"But don't think this is the end of this conversation," I interjected.

"And don't think you can say I told you so, either," Jennifer corrected. "It's still not Prince Harry."

We all busted out laughing again and walked to our next destination.

After about thirty minutes of walking and trying to get more information out of Robin, we finally reached the London Eye. Seeing the huge observation wheel in front of us, it seemed to jut into the clouds, making it a magical sight to see even from below. It was also somehow in the perfect placement for viewing, being just to the side on the River Thames, across from Big Ben.

"Well, ladies, let's do this," I said, walking up to the line to board the wheel.

As we waited, the conversation turned to me since

Robin had only given up that "it was a nice note" from all our prying on the walk over.

"Rae, are you liking the new job?" Robin asked.

"You know what? I really am," I said. "I'm not going to lie, I have been super nervous about making a good impression and not falling flat on my face, but I'm also pretty excited to see if I have what it takes."

"I get that. Totally. First time my job sent me here as the ambassador for our European sales team, I damn near threw up in my flat every morning before I went to work. But at the same time, I couldn't have been more excited to be doing what I always said I wanted to do."

"That's exactly it! And the fact that I've wanted it for so long makes it that much scarier. It's like, okay I can't mess up the thing I've been asking for forever."

"Ha ha, right," Robin agreed. "But you got this. You know this stuff in and out. I have no doubt you're going to soar."

"And at the very least, we don't have to worry about job searching on Friday nights anymore," Jennifer added. "At least not for a while."

"Hell, yeah. I hate job searching. But more than that, I just hated how I'd let so many things get in my head this year. Making that change from playing it safe to jumping out there on everything threw me for a bit of a loop at first. I think I'm starting to get the hang of it now, though."

We walked farther through the line, inching our way closer to the actual wheel.

"Does this mean you've let go of those nasty things Matthew said to you earlier this year, too…and the disappointment of Luke?" Robin asked.

"You know what? I hope so. I realized after that he

was just Matthew being Matthew. And with Luke, I think I'd put so much pressure on that situation to work because I wanted him to be the perfect foil to Jake. And the moment he didn't live up to that, it crushed me. Truth is, he was simply another guy who didn't live up to expectations, not the referendum on dating and love that it felt like in the moment. I don't know why I'd expected more from either of them, to be honest."

"Because we all make the mistake of expecting more," Robin replied. "And then find ourselves extremely disappointed when they don't live up to it."

"So true," Jennifer added.

"Mmm-hmm," Robin agreed again.

"What do *you* mean, *mmm-hmm*?" I asked, turning to Robin.

"*Whaaaaaat?* I get a secret letter from a prince and all of a sudden I can't agree about men being trash sometimes?" She put her hand to her chest as if she was really offended.

"Yes. That's pretty much exactly what it means," I replied. "You have nothing to say in this conversation from here through the rest of the trip."

"Hmph, Jennifer's got a whole boyfriend and she gets to cosign."

"But mine isn't a secret prince."

Robin fake stomped her feet onto one of the passenger capsules and finally gave in to the peer pressure. "Whatever. You know I'll tell you guys the deal later." She turned around to face us after she entered. "Just know that Eric is someone who has reminded me that none of my success means anything without someone to share it with."

"Aww," Jennifer said with a sigh. "We surely can't wait to finally get these details then, girl."

"And y'all will…just later. In the privacy of my home. Promise."

"All right," we responded in unison.

Jennifer and I walked into the capsule behind her, one by one, and prepared our minds as it began to lift into the sky. It was one of the most gorgeous and breathtaking sights we'd ever seen. Up, up and up we went, first glancing at places like St. Paul's Cathedral and the business district, then the Tower of London and the Palace of Westminster as we continued traveling in a circle overlooking the city. We also saw the top of Big Ben and could just make out what looked to be Trafalgar Square, but it was the beauty of the river and the chain of parks stretching from the Palace Gardens to Kensington Palace that caught all our breaths.

I couldn't stop thinking about Robin and her prince, though. It was funny how the woman I considered to be the most career focused of us all was the one who seemed to secretly have been following her heart while in London, maybe every time she came here. I glanced over at her and suddenly saw my friend in a totally different light. Sure, she was still take-no-mess-from-anyone Robin, but what if she had also been becoming live-your-life-with-no-regrets Robin and I'd just not noticed because I'd been in my head the whole time? More important, she made it very clear she wasn't looking for our approval or our feedback. It was refreshing, and just like Christine used to do, challenged me a bit. *What prince had I been missing out on all this time?*

"Wow," I said, leaning on Jennifer's shoulder and

refocusing on the sights in front of us. "This might be one of the most beautiful things I've ever seen."

"Completely agreed."

"And I couldn't be happier that I'm seeing it with you girls."

"Completely agreed," Robin mimicked. "Now, let's get a picture of the three of us on here before it's time to get off."

"Oh, yes," I said, pulling out my phone so it could go on the Gram as well. I approached the nearest couple and asked them to take our photo.

"Say cheese," exclaimed the woman behind her beau as he positioned my phone to get the best angle of us.

"Cheese!"

Three days later I had on my favorite low-top Chuck Taylors as we traipsed down the Champs-élysées. Surprisingly, it was even more beautiful than our view on the London Eye with its mixture of high-fashion stores and history. If you looked straight down the avenue, you could see the Arc de Triomphe standing massively in its own existence, waiting for you to visit it. But in between that and the Place de la Concorde stood cinemas and cafés by the dozens, luxury shops and the grandest greenery you could see bordering the sidewalk.

We'd just left the Louis Vuitton store when we noticed a young couple that looked as if they'd just been married. He was dressed in a black tuxedo; she in a mermaid-cut ivory gown with crystals on the bodice. Their photographer, bless his heart, was attempting to guide them into different poses, but the two of them just keep staring at each other and smiling.

"Okay, now release each other's hands, and you caress her face," the photographer yelled out to no avail as the two lovebirds remained in their own world no matter how hard he tried to get their attention.

"Excusez-moi," he said in a very thick French accent, all the while still getting ignored. It was as if the couple had completely forgotten they were supposed to be taking pictures.

"Ahem, *pardon*." He cleared his throat and tried speaking louder. "We're going to miss this sunset if you two don't work with me here."

"Oh, no, we're so sorry, sir," the woman cried out with a slight Texas accent. "I simply can't get over the fact that I married the love of my life. In Paris!"

She squealed, and her husband grabbed her up in a familiar embrace, prompting the photographer to finally relent and begin taking candid photos of them.

"We'll do better, I promise," she said, giving him her best attempt at puppy eyes.

"That's okay. That's okay. These will do just fine. *Mais oui*?"

Watching from afar, I guessed the sad eyes must have worked or the photographer was simply tired of being ignored and decided to give in to what was in front of him. Either way, it looked like all parties were finally getting what they wanted out of the photo shoot. The photographer, his shots in the sunset. The couple, more chances to play around with each other on the streets of Paris. It reminded me of how I'd seen Candice and Lance holding on to each other at their wedding. And the undeniable chemistry of a couple who's in love.

Just like then, I felt a certain sadness grow inside me that hit like a ton of bricks even as I stood there happy for the couple in front of me. But unlike then,

I was determined to not let love pass me by anymore. Rebecca and Christine's words flooded my consciousness as I remembered them both persuading me to take a chance on giving my heart to someone again. Things with Luke had admittedly stalled that progress, made me believe that living my life cautiously, afraid of the other shoe dropping at any moment, was better than feeling the knife to my heart when he left me at that ball. But I had been wrong. Playing it safe all these years hadn't stopped the pain from coming or made it hurt less; it just either made me numb or far too excited about a prospect before really getting to know him, and ultimately caused me to miss out on the kind of happiness this couple was allowing themselves to experience.

"Reagan?" I heard Robin call my name in the background, jolting me out of my thoughts. "Looked like you were in your own world there for a second."

"Yeah, I guess I was. But I'm good now."

"You sure?"

"I'm sure. I was just having a moment, watching that couple and thinking about redoing my try at being vulnerable with a guy again. Not just to check it off on a list, though. But to give someone a real chance this time and also not rush it into being something perfect before we really get to know each other."

"I'm really glad to hear you say that, Rae. In fact, maybe you should know that I've been talking to Jake nonstop since your blow up at the hospital. He called me later that night when he calmed down and realized he never actually saw Christine that day, but still wanted to know how she was doing. He's been a wreck since then, trying to figure out what he can do to apologize and win your trust again. He even came to the funeral, but decided at the last minute he didn't want to make things worse by letting you know."

"What?" I was floored once again by Robin in a matter of three days.

"I know. I didn't say anything because I wasn't sure you were ready. Plus, once Christine passed, it just didn't feel like the right time. But that man loves you. He hasn't always expressed that like he should, and he needs to do better with that—which I've told him over and over again. But he does love you. And I know you still love him. That's why that fight hurt so much."

"I don't know, Robin," I said with a sigh. "No man has ever hurt me as much as he has. Am I really going to put myself in the position to be destroyed by him again?"

"If you think the risk is worth it, yeah."

Those words stuck with me as we raced to catch up to Jennifer, who'd flagged down a taxi cab so we could get to the Eiffel Tower before it lit up at night.

"Pouvez-vous nous prendre à la Tour Eiffel, s'il vous plaît," Jennifer said to the driver as we hopped in the backseat of the car.

"What did you say to him?" Robin asked.

"Can you take us to the Eiffel Tower, please."

"Ohhhhh, fancy, *oui oui*."

"Mock all you want. But when we get there on time to see those lights, I don't want to hear a word. The sun's already setting and you two were, what, gazing lovingly at some strange couple?"

"Maybe a little more than that, but you're right, we need to stay on track," I said, nodding to Robin on the side about our little inside conversation. "I also want to get some crepes across the street while we watch."

"Oh, and some mulled wine," Robin added.

"Any other requests you all want to add as we're crunched for time?" Jennifer asked jokingly.

"Nope, that pretty much covers it. I'm just ready to see and experience it all," I said, staring blankly out the window as we passed by some of Paris's historical landmarks and saw more couples strolling the streets, hand in hand. *So this is why they call Paris the City of Love*, I thought. It had certainly made me reconsider the biggest risk of all and ask myself that age-old question: Was it worth it?

Chapter 18

*D*ing. *Ding.*

I raced to the buzzer near my front door, looked in the camera and saw Jake standing outside. It was 7:15 p.m. on the dot, and he was on time for our date. *One notch in his book*, I thought.

"Hello?" I asked, speaking into the intercom system.

"Hey, it's Jake."

"I know," I said with a laugh. "Just wanted to hear you say it. Okay, hold on just a sec."

I pressed the button to open the door to my lobby entrance and then quickly attempted to compose myself one last time before he reached my door. This obviously wasn't our first date, but it was the first time we were seeing each other since our fight, and more importantly, since I called him when I returned from Paris. Still, even though we'd aired out our dirty laundry and spent the majority of that call apologizing and admitting that our fears had stopped us throughout the years, it had taken everything in me to say yes when he asked me for this date. Only acquiescing after we both agreed it would be a real first date and not a quick speed bump to an immediate relationship.

We had to learn each other again, despite years of history behind us. I was nervous beyond belief as he came up my steps and desperately trying not to sweat through my blouse before he got a good look at me. I steadied my breathing, forced myself to stop pacing the length of my living room and took in three deep breaths before I heard him knocking on my door.

"Jake?" I asked through the door, giving myself some time to simultaneously remember that I was the catch, and he was here to see me, so I could enjoy tonight and stop wasting time on all the what-ifs that had been swirling in my head since I'd agreed to see him.

"That's me. The man of your dreams."

"Now that is a lofty title for someone who sped off and left me the last time that we saw each other."

"Oh, too soon, Rae." I swung the door open with a smile on my face and saw him posted up, pretending as if he'd been jabbed in the gut with a knife. I knew the feeling, but I figured I'd let his joke slide. That had been a bit of a low blow. Besides, it would have been hard for me to say anything in retort without the ability to breathe. There he stood before me, the epitome of handsome, five foot eleven in a striped crewneck sweater and pants that made him look like he could be a J. Crew model, and his dimple radiating off his cheek. It was fair to say I was mesmerized by his presence and the night hadn't even begun.

"Hey there," he said, after giving me a very obvious and long once-over as well. "You look…absolutely beautiful."

The pause in between his words were for emphasis, but they were also absolutely working. I steadied my breathing again and stared into his eyes for a good twenty seconds before responding. Long enough to let him swoon, watching me stand at my door with my cream button-down blouse, black matte liquid leggings and those hot pink suede pointed-toe pumps I'd been holding in my closet for years. I forced him to gaze at me while neither of us spoke a word, knowing he enjoyed the view, and that I liked having him enjoy it.

"Thank you," I finally said and allowed him to walk in.

"So how much time do we have before we need to leave for the concert?" he asked, casually grazing my left leg with his hand as he took his shoes off at my door.

"Probably no more than about twenty minutes."

"Oh, good, that works perfectly."

"Perfectly for what?"

"For us to enjoy a little wine and some snacks," he replied, showing off the items that were in the bag he was holding when he came in.

"Really? Wine and strawberries?" I asked mockingly.

"What?" he asked, feigning innocence. "It's just something to drink and eat."

"Mmm-hmm, if you say so."

He winked at me and smiled. "I do. You still have a wine opener, right?"

"Oh, hi, I'm sorry, do we have to introduce ourselves because you don't know me? Of course I have a wine opener."

"I never know what could have changed in four years."

"Please. You follow me on Instagram. I know you see my posts. Don't act like because we haven't talked you don't know what's going in my life."

"You're right. I do know."

As we walked to my kitchen to open the wine, Jake wrapped his big arms around me and placed his head in the nook of my neck. It didn't make for the most elegant walk, but the smell of his cologne, with its subtle intoxication, made up for any awkwardness and almost served to put me in a trance.

"I'm so glad we're going to see Snoh Aalegra in concert together," he whispered from behind me into my right ear, the hairs on his goatee slightly grazing my neck.

"Me, too," I said breathlessly, trying to keep my composure enough to release actual words from my mouth. "I'm really looking forward to it."

"As much as these strawberries?" he asked while releasing me from his embrace as we entered the kitchen.

"Surprisingly, yes, even more than the strawberries."

"Now, that's saying something. Because *these* strawberries, I have to tell you. They are top-notch."

"It's crazy, right? Imagine me anticipating a concert more than some fruit. I mean, how could I?"

We both cracked up laughing at my sarcasm. I was mostly just happy to regain control over my wits again. There was no way I could make a decision about if it was worth it to try again if I couldn't think straight. And on top of that, I wanted tonight to be fun, not some tired version of a soap opera story where the lead character is so overcome by passion she jumps into bed with the guy and everyone watching the show wants to scream out *"Nooooooo, don't do it!"* I needed tonight to not just be about sex with him, especially after what went down at the wedding. But he surely made it hard by oozing sex with every word he spoke.

I picked up the wine opener and attempted to play keep-away from him to keep the jovial atmosphere going; standing on my tippy toes, running to the back of the kitchen and tucking the wine opener under my arm. Each time he came near me, he was very close to getting it from me, but never did.

"You know, there's only so much of this you're going to be able to do in those shoes of yours," he remarked from the other side of the kitchen with a devilish look in his eyes.

"Ha! That's where you're wrong," I said through heavy breaths from running. "I can do a lot in these heels."

"Oh, really?" he asked with a raised eyebrow.

"I didn't mean it like that, nasty."

"What? I just—" He stopped himself and started laughing again.

"You just nothing, exactly," I replied. "But since you're wondering, yes, I can do those things in these heels as well. Just not tonight."

With a sly smirk, I casually let him know that maybe there had been some things he didn't know about me in the four years since the wedding, but also that anything like that would have to be saved for his imagination.

"That's fine. Tonight is all about Snoh anyway. I wouldn't want you to sully her night."

"Sully *her* night?" I asked, incredulous at the thought, but soon realized my surprise response was exactly what he'd planned on. He'd distracted me long enough for him to take the wine opener from me and also grab me toward him.

"Just so we're clear," he said, looking at me with a sudden very intense stare. "If we continue talking about what you can do in those pink shoes, we won't make it to the concert."

"No?" I asked.

"No."

"Then we should open the wine and talk about other things, huh?"

"Yeah, I think so," he said, releasing me from his grip, but not before allowing his right hand to slide down the side of my body, and his lips to graze the side of my neck. My knees almost buckled under me, and my body betrayed me by instinctively allowing him full access.

"That won't help things, either, I'm sure," I stammered, slowly taking a few steps back from him.

"Sorry, I couldn't help myself."

His smile was so big now I could see his teeth glistening in the kitchen light, but he wasn't the only one losing control. Biting my lower lip slightly, I tried to stand back up straight, shaking that familiar chill out of my spine.

Fifteen minutes later we were still standing in my kitchen, feeding each other strawberries and drinking wine. Luckily, he'd set an alarm on his iPhone so at minute eighteen, it went off with a loud blare.

"You ready?"

"Yep. More than you know."

"Woman."

"Yes?"

"You want to go to this concert, right?"

"Yes!"

"Okay, because I'm this close to snatching you up and ravaging the hell out of you. So you better stop playing with me."

I busted out laughing, but I could tell he was serious.

"Okay, okay. Let's go. We can't leave Snoh waiting, and if we stay here any longer, I might end up doing something I don't want to do."

"Trust me, neither of us wants that," he said. As we gathered our things to leave, he looked down at my shoes and noticed they were suede. "You know they're saying it may rain tonight."

"Yeah, I know. But it's high time these shoes get out of the closet, rain be damned."

We stepped into DC's Constitution Hall, a popular midsize concert venue, holding hands as we maneuvered through the crowd.

"Now, where are these seats?" I asked.

"Section B, F 7 and 8," he replied, looking down at our tickets once more.

"Oh, okay, cool."

We continued walking and looking for our section, until we'd walked almost the entire circle of the hall. Clearly, we had gone the wrong way when we entered, but I was too distracted by the handholding to have noticed or cared.

We finally got to our seats just as Snoh came onto the stage and began singing her hit song, "I Want You Around."

As the beat dropped on the song, we danced at our seats with Jake's hand sliding across the small of my back.

"I love this song," he exclaimed in between notes.

"Me, too!"

We both looked at each other knowingly, but simply continued dancing and singing.

Song after song, we joined her on her love journey. We danced in each other's arms on "Find Someone Like You." We prodded each other on "Love Like That." We let our eyes and hands roam on "Here Now." But as the concert wrapped up, I rested my head on his chest as Snoh sang what had become our theme song in my head in the days since I said yes to Jake's invite: "I Didn't Mean to Fall in Love." In my ear, Jake sang along with her, and it was like she was providing the words he'd wanted to say to me all along.

I closed my eyes and listened to them both, letting the feelings I'd been struggling to hold back for so long invade my everything. There I was, finally allowing myself to believe in the possibility of love again, believe in me and Jake of all people. And it was scary and unfamiliar, but also damn good. Unfortunately, immediately after the song ended, all my fears came rushing back into my head. *You know better than this*, I said to myself. *He's shown you that you can't trust him. Just as soon as things go too well, he's shown you—he'll bail. Why should now be any different?*

I could feel my body tense up and my chest get tight as one part of me tried to fight back the fears and the other acknowledged they were there for a reason. I slowly peeled myself from him, first my hands dropping from his chest and then lifting my head up and taking a few steps back.

"Reagan," he said with a look of concern washing over his face. "I love you. I know we have a lot to work on, and it will take time for the both of us to trust each other again. But I need you to know that it starts with me loving you—and I'm hoping the rest can fall in place. I'm ready for things to be different this time, but are you?"

I looked back at him, still unsure of what path to take and what to believe. I wanted to trust him; I wanted to be the person everyone had been pushing me to be lately, the one who was more open and willing to really take this kind of risk, but I was also so frightened of being hurt again. Especially by him. *How could I trust that he wouldn't say he loves me and then walk away again, that the long distance wouldn't get in between us, that somehow if we put in the work, these two highly imperfect people would soar instead of falling?*

A million questions ran through my head in the seconds it took for me to respond, but one voice instantly calmed them all. Christine's. "Stop living cautiously," she'd warned me. "Take some risks and be willing to fall, and when you do, just get up and try again. And it will always be worth it." This wasn't just about Jake, I realized. All of the risks had been about me learning to trust myself again, as well as my ability to get back up if things didn't work out how I'd planned. This thing with Jake was no different, but going through the rest of them helped me better know the strength I had within me and the bravery it took for me to be with him in this moment. And I didn't want that feeling to end any time soon.

Taking in one more deep breath, I paused briefly and spoke what was on my heart. "Jake. I love you, too. And things *absolutely* will be different this time, because we've both done a lot of growing, and we're not going to hold back anything from each other anymore. Which means I have to tell you I am scared to death to be with you, but it's worth it to me to acknowledge that fear and then do it anyway."

"Good," he said, taking me in his arms. "Then we can face those fears together."

* * * * *

Acknowledgments

I started writing some version of *The Shoe Diaries* more than a decade ago, so to say that I have a lot of people to thank for keeping me going along the way would be an absolute understatement.

But first, I *have* to thank God. I often talk about hearing God's whispers any time I doubted if I could do this or if I was holding onto a pipe dream, but I'm thankful for so much more than just how God has kept me. God literally saved my life and put this dream on my heart. And so, without God, none of this matters.

Now, to the village that God put around me. I am so incredibly grateful to the countless people who helped me realize a dream that I've had since I was a second grade student creating her first book for class. I am especially thankful for my amazing agent, Latoya C. Smith. Without your belief in me and my vision, I wouldn't be here. You helped me take a very rough draft with a lot of promise and turn it into something that exceeded even my expectations. But you didn't stop there. You've pushed me, guided me with important decisions, had my back at every turn, and taken me under your wing in a way that I can't express fully in words. Perhaps most importantly, you led me to Harlequin and to Gail.

Gail Chasan, your enthusiasm for this book and for my work is contagious, even to me! You have been the celebratory rock in my corner from the moment Latoya connected us, and I couldn't be happier to be on the Latoya/Gail dream team with such fantastic thought partners and ship steerers. From the moment we first virtually met, you got the story I was trying to tell. That's every writer's dream come true. Megan Broderick, you've answered every single question I've had (and there were many) with such ease and have been the biggest help as I've navigated new and exciting things like art sheets and rounds of edits and book prelims. You have taken such good care of my book baby at every step, and I'm truly thankful. Each of y'all are legit my sheroes, as are the rest of the Harlequin family—from the art team (yess first book cover!) to copy editors to marketing to author communications and everyone in between, I've continued to be in awe of your support and excitement for this project. You make it easy to want to shout that I'm a Harlequin author!

My family is also out of this world. The support you all have given me can't be quantified, but whether it was messaging me from Japan just to ask how my writing was going, showing up to every virtual event I've participated in, or simply reminding me that I was called to do this over and over again, I've needed y'all more than I've said. And yet, somehow, I never had to say it. To Mom, Dad, Mawmaw, Brittany, Marley, Amber, Tayler, Glen, Lana, Jason, Aunt Leslie, Uncle Curt, and so so many others, thank you for believing in me and showing up for me always. You all are my innermost circle, and I'm thankful you've let me lean on you like I do.

To Enjoli, Cora, Nyanquoi, Candice, Erika, Katy, Anna, Maranda, Amanda, Ashleigh, Talia, Carla, Aria, Xayna, Anika, Lakelle, Lloyd, Ebony, Barbara, Aghogho, Selena, Tim, Amie, Keila, Keith, Michael A., Brittney C., Shaton, Amir, Kimberly, Canisha, Soraya, Erlie, Brenda, Michael L., Charreah, Alison B., Jackie, Jenna, Ruschelle, Renee, Nicole J., Floyd, and so many others, thank you for being my guide posts. Thank you for your various counsels over the years, for the times I brainstormed ideas with you, or maybe even told you that something that happened in your life inspired a piece of my book and you didn't recoil lol. Thank you for your constant encouragement, for talking me down from bouts of overthinking, stepping in to remind me of the promise God made to me long ago, and checking me when I was editing the same chapter over and again. You all have even been editors and thought partners before I had professional editors and thought partners— and still are! I'm not here without you.

Lastly, thank you to the other authors I've met in real life, or just in my head, who to this day continue to inspire me. Whether it was a chance meeting in Union Station in DC, or we spoke on a panel together (and you've been in my corner ever since), your storytelling and the way you approach life pushes me to be better, kinder, more vulnerable, more giving, and of course, a better writer. That kind of motivation is not something I could ever repay.

I've named a lot of people in these acknowledgments, and in truth, there's probably so many more I could have added to these lists. For there has never been a time that I can remember when I wasn't dreaming to be a published author and having the opportunity to tell the extraordinary stories of ordinary people around the world, but there's also no world in which this dream is just mine. I am the luckiest girl on planet Earth to be able to share it with all y'all.

The best is yet to come! (#Nkiruka)

HARLEQUIN

Save $1.00

on the purchase of ANY Harlequin book
from the imprints below.

*Heartfelt or thrilling, passionate or
uplifting—our romances have it all.*

PRESENTS   INTRIGUE

DESIRE   ROMANTIC SUSPENSE   SPECIAL EDITION

LOVE INSPIRED

Save $1.00

on the purchase of ANY Harlequin Presents, Intrigue, Desire,
Romantic Suspense, Special Edition or Love Inspired book.

Valid from June 1, 2023 to May 31, 2024.

52617414

5 65373 00076 2   (8100)0 12532

Canadian Retailers: Harlequin Enterprises ULC will pay the face value of this coupon plus 10.25¢ if submitted by customer for this product only. Any other use constitutes fraud. Coupon is nonassignable. Void if taxed, prohibited or restricted by law. Consumer must pay any government taxes. Void if copied. Inmar Promotional Services ("IPS") customers submit coupons and proof of sales to Harlequin Enterprises ULC, P.O. Box 31000, Scarborough, ON M1R 0E7, Canada. Non-IPS retailer—for reimbursement submit coupons and proof of sales directly to Harlequin Enterprises ULC, Retail Marketing Department, Bay Adelaide Centre, East Tower, 22 Adelaide Street West, 41st Floor, Toronto, Ontario M5H 4E3, Canada.

U.S. Retailers: Harlequin Enterprises ULC will pay the face value of this coupon plus 8¢ if submitted by customer for this product only. Any other use constitutes fraud. Coupon is nonassignable. Void if taxed, prohibited or restricted by law. Consumer must pay any government taxes. Void if copied. For reimbursement submit coupons and proof of sales directly to Harlequin Enterprises ULC 482, NCH Marketing Services, P.O. Box 880001, El Paso, TX 88588-0001, U.S.A. Cash value 1/100 cents.

© 2023 Harlequin Enterprises ULC

HSERIESCOUP0623

Get 4 FREE REWARDS!

We'll send you 2 FREE Books plus 2 FREE Mystery Gifts.

FREE Value Over **$20**

Both the **Romance** and **Suspense** collections feature compelling novels written by many of today's bestselling authors.

YES! Please send me 2 FREE novels from the Essential Romance or Essential Suspense Collection and my 2 FREE gifts (gifts are worth about $10 retail). After receiving them, if I don't wish to receive any more books, I can return the shipping statement marked "cancel." If I don't cancel, I will receive 4 brand-new novels every month and be billed just $7.49 each in the U.S. or $7.74 each in Canada. That's a savings of at least 17% off the cover price. It's quite a bargain! Shipping and handling is just 50¢ per book in the U.S. and $1.25 per book in Canada.* I understand that accepting the 2 free books and gifts places me under no obligation to buy anything. I can always return a shipment and cancel at any time by calling the number below. The free books and gifts are mine to keep no matter what I decide.

Choose one: ☐ **Essential Romance**
(194/394 MDN GRHV)

☐ **Essential Suspense**
(191/391 MDN GRHV)

Name (please print)

Address   Apt. #

City   State/Province   Zip/Postal Code

Email: Please check this box ☐ if you would like to receive newsletters and promotional emails from Harlequin Enterprises ULC and its affiliates. You can unsubscribe anytime.

Mail to the **Harlequin Reader Service:**
IN U.S.A.: P.O. Box 1341, Buffalo, NY 14240-8531
IN CANADA: P.O. Box 603, Fort Erie, Ontario L2A 5X3

Want to try 2 free books from another series? Call 1-800-873-8635 or visit www.ReaderService.com.

---

*Terms and prices subject to change without notice. Prices do not include sales taxes, which will be charged (if applicable) based on your state or country of residence. Canadian residents will be charged applicable taxes. Offer not valid in Quebec. This offer is limited to one order per household. Books received may not be as shown. Not valid for current subscribers to the Essential Romance or Essential Suspense Collection. All orders subject to approval. Credit or debit balances in a customer's account(s) may be offset by any other outstanding balance owed by or to the customer. Please allow 4 to 6 weeks for delivery. Offer available while quantities last.

Your Privacy—Your information is being collected by Harlequin Enterprises ULC, operating as Harlequin Reader Service. For a complete summary of the information we collect, how we use this information and to whom it is disclosed, please visit our privacy notice located at corporate.harlequin.com/privacy-notice. From time to time we may also exchange your personal information with reputable third parties. If you wish to opt out of this sharing of your personal information, please visit readerservice.com/consumerschoice or call 1-800-873-8635. **Notice to California Residents**—Under California law, you have specific rights to control and access your data. For more information on these rights and how to exercise them, visit corporate.harlequin.com/california-privacy.

STRS22R3

HARLEQUIN
PLUS

Try the best multimedia subscription service for romance readers like you!

Read, Watch and Play.

Experience the easiest way to get the romance content you crave.

Start your **FREE TRIAL** at
www.harlequinplus.com/freetrial.

HARPLUS0123